MYTHMATCHEDLETS

E.J. RUSSELL

MYTHMATCHED COMPANION STORIES

Cover art: L.C. Chase, http://lcchase.com
Edited by Meg DesCamp

ISBN: 978-1-947033-95-5

First edition
July 2024

Contact information:
ejr@ejrussell.com

MYTHMATCHEDLETS

E.J. RUSSELL

MYTHMATCHED
COMPANION STORIES

Contents

For my wonderful readers

second
First Date

About second First Date

Spoilers!

Second First Date is what I call a "sidecar" or companion stories: It's not intended to stand alone. In this case, it's essentially a seven-chapter epilogue to *Vampire With Benefits*, its first scene overlapping the last scene of *VWB*. So if you haven't read the Supernatural Selection series (specifically *VWB*) yet, you'll probably want to do that before diving into this tale.

Go ahead. I'll wait...

I wrote this little adventure for all my readers who wanted to know how Rusty wins Cas back again. It's a peek at a previously hidden period in the lives of two of my personal favorite characters. I hope you enjoy spending more time with Cas and Rusty as much as I did!

Cheers!
—E

Chapter One

When Casimir Moreau walked into the Supernatural Selection lobby, it was empty except for one man, a bearded mountain of a guy reading a magazine in the corner. He looked up when Cas entered, and the smile that bloomed on his face was bright enough to make Cas's skin sizzle. Figuratively, of course.

He studied the guy, eyes narrowed, trying to scope out his nature. In this place, he had to be a supe. But what? *And why do I want to thread my fingers through that beard? Why do I remember threading my fingers through that beard?*

Bearded Guy's smile didn't dim. "May I help you?"

"You can't be a shifter. You don't—"

"Stink?"

"Uh…"

"Beaver shifter, as it happens. Inactive status."

Cas cocked an eyebrow. "Thanks for that." He was hit with an odd wave of déjà vu, but shook it off. After ninety-two years as a vampire, there wasn't a lot that he hadn't experienced at least once. "But perhaps TMI?"

"I don't know. You *were* wondering, weren't you?"

"I suppose."

Bearded Guy chuckled and nodded in the direction of the unoccupied reception desk. "They'll be back in a few minutes." He held out his hand. "Rusty Johnson."

"Rusty?" Cas hesitated. *Why does that seem wrong?* Nevertheless, he shook hands, Rusty's grip strong and firm, yet somehow intimate.

He held on to Cas's hand for a moment too long, and oddly, Cas didn't want him to let go. "What's the matter?"

"I don't know. I'm sure it's nothing, but for some reason, I was suddenly certain your name was something entirely different." Cas shook his head. "But it couldn't be. You don't look anything like— Never mind."

"Come on. Don't leave me hanging. Like what?"

"Like—and I know it's ludicrous, so don't get insulted—but, well, Elmer?" Cas inhaled. "And you smell... familiar." *Earth and spice. The sough of pines. Cool water and hot skin.* "Do I... know you?"

"Not yet. But you will." Rusty grinned—a groin-tighteningly attractive flash of teeth framed by his red-brown beard—and held up his phone, where the Supernatural Selection app displayed Cas's picture. "I'm your perfect match."

Cas snorted. "Oh, please. In that case, these so-vaunted spells can't be as superlative as they claim. A shifter and a vampire? Impossible." Although... He gave Rusty's big body an appreciative once-over. If the Supernatural Selection witches could have read Cas's mind and delivered the perfect *physical* specimen, they'd certainly hit the bulls-eye with this one. "Compared to this pairing, Romeo and Juliet were rank amateurs in the star-crossed department."

"Obviously. Since they died and we didn't."

Cas raised an eyebrow. "Didn't?"

Rusty's cheeks pinked above his beard. "I mean— Since you — We're both— And the—"

"*Elmer*, for pity's sake, use your words." For some reason, Rusty's smile bloomed brighter than before. Did the man have a snark kink? "What is that smile for?"

"You always say that."

"How do you—"

"Cas." Rusty stepped closer, derailing Cas's tart comment and emptying his mind of anything but the desire to plaster himself against that broad chest and *inhale*. Or… taste? His mouth watered and his fangs descended.

What am I doing? He's a shifter! *One taste and I'd be dead. Again.* He caught another whiff of that tantalizing scent. *But what a way to go.*

"I'm so sorry to keep you waiting!" A lean, bespectacled man with tousled dark curls hurried out of a hallway behind the reception desk, a pillar swirling with indigo-shot gold light at his heels. "I had to check on— Oh. Mr. Moreau. You're here."

Cas tore his attention from Rusty with difficulty and spread his hands, palms up. "As you see."

The man smiled tightly, clutching a manila folder against his spotless white shirt. "I'm Zeke Oz. Welcome to Supernatural Selection."

Cas inclined his head in what he hoped was a dignified manner, but given the way his cock was straining at his fly— and the furtive glance Zeke cast at his midsection—the effort undoubtedly fell short. "Charmed." He waved an airy hand at the light pillar. "And your companion?"

Zeke shot a decidedly irritated look over his shoulder. "That's the Angel interface."

"It doesn't deign to speak on its own behalf?"

Zeke turned back to Cas while the pillar pulsed green. "No."

Rusty leaned down to murmur in Cas's ear, eliciting a shiver. "Zeke's a demon on the Sheol work-release program. The AI is his assigned snitch."

Well, *that* provoked a response. Red and turquoise sparked inside the pillar and it surged forward, colliding with Zeke, who winced.

Gods above and below, but Cas hated bullies. He flicked his fingers at the AI. "Away with you. If you must lurk, do so from a respectable distance. Perhaps from the next county."

The AI's turquoise darkened to navy. Zeke bit his lip. "He, um, prefers to keep a close eye on... proceedings."

"That's hardly my concern." He fixed the AI with a glare at approximately where its eyes should be, assuming it was even humanoid inside its stupid light show. "I'm the client, am I not?" Red and gold fireworks ignited amid the blue. "Just so. Then please remove yourself. You're giving me a sunburn." Cas shot his cuffs. "And as you know, that's not an optimal situation for vampires, as the sun will *literally* burn us to a cinder. Now go. Shoo. Vamoose. *Vite, vite.*"

Its pillar seething with sullen ochre—a passive-aggressive color if ever Cas had seen one—the AI slunk away, although it apparently couldn't resist a last eye-watering flare when it got to the doorway, making Zeke wince again.

Cas stared at it until it vanished, then turned back to Zeke with a fang-edged smile. "That's better."

Rusty grinned down at him. "That was *awesome*, Cas."

The praise—not to mention Rusty's continued shortening of his name—kindled unexpected warmth in Cas's chest. Gods, was he really so starved for affection that a comment from a random shifter would make him want to roll over and beg for more?

He looked up into Rusty's deep brown eyes, at the warmth, the approval, the... lust? *Yes, apparently I am.* At least for affection from this particular shifter. He cleared his throat. "Now. Where were we?"

Rusty held up his phone again, displaying Cas's picture. "Perfect match." His grin widened. "Don't bother to deny it. Supernatural Selection spells say it, so it's gotta be true."

Cas frowned. "I find that very hard to believe."

"I know." Zeke shrugged apologetically. "But he's right. That is, about the spells allowing the match. I didn't believe it either, but no matter how often I reset and invoke it, the spells still return the same result." He lowered the folder to his desk. "Of course, the spells are constrained by our available client pool, so there may be another person somewhere—"

"There isn't," Rusty said, voice firm and—*shiver*—masterful. "A perfect match. Guaranteed."

"Yes," Zeke said, "but—"

"No buts." Rusty glanced down at Cas's picture with a fond smile. "They got it right."

Cas huffed an exasperated breath. "I don't mean to cast aspersions on your no doubt stellar intellect, *Elmer*, but have you forgotten the little matter of shifters being poisonous to my kind?"

Rusty ran a hand through his hair—medium brown, while his beard tended toward red, which was more attractive than Cas would have expected. "Look. You know Bryce MacLeod?"

Cas frowned. "The druid? Who doesn't?"

He jerked his chin at Zeke. "Call him, please? He'll vouch for me." He gazed down at Cas again with that soft expression, a smile curving his full lips. "He'll tell you if you give me—give us—a chance, you won't come to any harm."

Cas pretended annoyance, but he was seriously intrigued by Rusty's certainty and persistence. How long had it been since someone had made this much effort to be with Cas? Not since the beginning of his Second Life, certainly. He'd rarely bothered with a second hookup, let alone an association that could qualify as a relationship. If a human blood host—none of them qualified as lovers—got too needy, a flash of vampire *mesmer* would cloud their minds and send them on their merry way.

Rusty, though… He presented a promise and—quite possibly—a threat. The threat: Vampire *mesmer* didn't work on shifters, so if Rusty was a crazed, obsessed fang groupie, he'd be difficult to shake. On the other hand, no shifter was quick enough, especially in human form, to match vampire speed.

And the promise? The promise of all those muscles holding Cas down and fucking him into the mattress was deliciously enticing. No vampire in Cas's memory had ever attempted a liaison with a shifter, primarily because vampire noses, calibrated as they were for seeking out compatible blood hosts, couldn't be close to a shifter without retching. That whole sulfur-and-sewage stench—not to mention the stink of their animal nature, which they could *never* outrun—made it impossible.

But Rusty didn't stink. In fact, Cas wanted to get closer and revel in his seductive scent. Could it be the result of an especially effective smell-masking spell? Perhaps he should conduct an experiment, just to make sure.

Strictly for science and the good of the vampire species, of course.

Cas turned to Zeke. "If you would please make the call?"

Zeke nodded, wide-eyed. He seated himself at his desk and picked up the phone's handset, his fingers blurring as he dialed faster than Cas could do himself. "Hello? Dr. MacLeod? Please hold for Mr. Moreau." He passed the handset to Cas.

"Elder MacLeod? Casimir Moreau here."

Elder MacLeod snorted. "Please. No need for outdated honorifics. It's just Bryce."

"Bryce, then. I'm here at Supernatural Selection with—"

"Rusty Johnson."

Cas held the phone away and stared at it for a moment before placing it gingerly against his ear again. "Yes. How did you know?"

"That's irrelevant. However, I want to assure you that you may trust Rusty implicitly. He will go to extraordinary lengths —in fact, he has done—to ensure your safety and, more importantly, your happiness."

Cas frowned a little at that. Happiness more important than safety? He considered the long, arid decades of his second life, the endless search for connection, for belonging, for love. *Yes, maybe happiness* is *more important than safety.* "Very well. Thank you for your insights, Bryce."

"My pleasure. And Casimir?"

"Yes?"

"Have Zeke give you my number. If at any time, day or night, you feel uncertain or threatened in any way whatsoever, you can come to me."

"Th-thank you." *I think.*

Bryce chuckled, and if Casimir didn't know that druids *never* made jokes about their responsibilities, he'd have called that sound amused and slightly wicked. "You're welcome. Enjoy your evening."

Cas passed the handset back to Zeke, along with his own phone. "Bryce asked that you give me his number."

"I can do that," Rusty said, but then winced. "Sorry. It's best to have Zeke do it. Then you can be sure I'm not trying to pull something over on you."

"Oh, I already think you're trying to pull something. I'm just not certain *what.*" He smiled, exposing a hint of fang. "And to a vampire, new experiences are irresistible."

Zeke returned Cas's phone. "I've added my direct line as well. I'm always on call, so you can call Supernatural Selection at any time, too."

Cas glanced at the screen. The Supernatural Selection app was active, the message alert blinking in the corner. Just out of curiosity, he touched the alert icon and an explosion of animated hearts filled the screen. A message popped up:

Congratulations! Our spells have found your perfect match! Swipe up to see his photo!

Cas swiped up, and was unsurprised to see Rusty's broad, bearded face smiling at the camera almost shyly. Before he could forget his dignity entirely and simply moon at the picture, Cas tucked his phone into his pocket. "So. Are we going on a date or what?"

The crease between Rusty's brows smoothed out and he grinned. "Absolutely. Although…" He patted his jacket, frowning, then reached into the inside pocket and drew out a sealed envelope. He held it out to Cas. "Take this. Keep it safe, but don't open it until after dawn tomorrow."

Cas took the envelope, fingering it gently. It wasn't at all bulky, probably holding nothing but a single sheet of paper. "Now I'm intrigued. Perhaps I'll take a peek while you're not looking."

"Don't. Please." Rusty gazed down at him, expression somber and intent. "I know it's asking a lot right now, but do you think you could trust me on this?"

How long had it been since someone had sincerely *asked* Cas for something that wasn't related to sex, money, or power? Forget Second Life. His First Life had nothing vaguely resembling it either. In 1920s Hollywood, the power and money had all been in the hands of the studios. The sex too, if he wanted to get technical, although for him, it was mostly in the hiding of his preference for men. But despite his innate compulsion to buck authority, *any* authority, Cas found himself nodding. "Very well."

Rusty's brow cleared and he smiled, holding out his arm in a courtly manner. "Shall we?"

Cas slipped his hand through Rusty's elbow, noting with satisfaction some *very* impressive muscles. "Why not?"

"Thank you for using Supernatural Selection," Zeke called after them. "Enjoy your perfect mat— Ow!"

Rusty winced. "That stupid AI. If you ask me, the witches' collective should be doing a better job of taking care of Zeke."

"You'll get no argument from me," Cas said as they stepped out onto the sidewalk. The November breeze ruffled his hair, and although he couldn't feel the cold himself, the humans passing by were all huddled in coats, scarves, and in many cases, hats.

Hats. Cas snorted. Really, the beanies and knitted monstrosities common these days held not a candle against the boaters, fedoras, and toppers of his First Life. It was so difficult to keep up an acceptable level of style nowadays.

He glanced sidelong at Rusty, whose leather jacket was open over his flannel shirt. Hunh. Apparently, shifters weren't as affected by the cold, either. He wondered if any of the council vampires had ever inquired about shifter abilities or preferences. Probably not. If it didn't add to their wealth, increase their influence, or feed their undead bodies, vampires couldn't beat back their ennui long enough to care.

Rusty stopped next to an extended cab pickup. "Here we are."

Cas stared at the truck, nonplussed. "Seriously?"

Rusty tilted his head, gazing down at Cas, lips quirked. "Would you rather take your Jag?"

Cas's brows snapped together. "How do you know I have a Jag? That's not something in my Supernatural Selection profile."

He shrugged. "You look like a guy who'd drive a Jag." He opened the passenger door and gestured for Cas to climb in.

Cas rolled his eyes. The stupid thing had no running board. He could make the leap with no trouble if no humans were around to witness it, but otherwise he'd need a ladder to scale the heights. He grabbed the handle and sniffed. "For your information, I drive a MINI Cooper."

Rusty snorted a laugh. "Pull the other one, Cas. Come on. Hop in."

Cas did—it really wasn't that hard, despite his internal griping. When Rusty got behind the wheel and started the car, Cas asked, "Where are we going? The Bull Pen?"

Rusty shot him a nervous smile. "Not tonight."

Despite Cas needling him as they drove away from the Pearl District and into the West Hills, Rusty wouldn't say anything more.

Cas frowned when he eased the truck to a stop in front of very familiar gates. "This is my house."

"I know."

Maybe Cas should be more worried about that whole obsessed fang groupie thing. "The code is—"

But before Cas could blurt out the letters, Rusty had punched the keypad, and the gate swung open. "You know, you should really change that. *FANG* isn't that hard to guess."

Cas glared at him. "Yes, if you know I'm a *vampire*."

"I do."

"Yeah." Cas flung himself against the seat, arms crossed, as Rusty drove through the gates. "I've noticed."

Chapter Two

Rusty had to grip the steering wheel with both hands. When Cas got into one of those snarky vampire snits, he had a *really* hard time—like *literally* hard—not pouncing on him and kissing him stupid.

Down, boy. Take it easy. He needed to work up slowly to the whole *"I time-traveled to save us both from death and destruction and, by the way, my blood and spunk allow you to go out in the daytime"* scenario.

Rusty parked in the drive and leaped out, running around the truck to open Cas's door. He held out a hand to help him down, but Cas glared at him.

"I could have used the assistance when there were actually *people* around, but behind my own walls? No, thank you." He jumped gracefully to the ground in a flare of black cashmere duster. "Speaking of being behind walls, why are we here? Usually, it's for me to extend the invitation to *my own home.*"

"I know. Sorry about the presumption." Rusty reached behind the seat to snag a small case. "But I wanted you to be somewhere you felt comfortable for this next part."

Cas eyed the case. "The next part doesn't involve dismembering me and hiding my body parts all over Forest Park for unsuspecting hikers to discover, does it?"

"Nope." Rusty unzipped the case and displayed the contents —three small vials.

Cas squinted at the case and then up at Rusty. "Do I need to warn you that roofies don't work on vampires?"

"Nope. Besides, these aren't roofies." More like anti-roofies, when it came down to it. Rusty lifted one to display the seal with Bryce's druid glyph. "Potions."

Cas sniffed. "I'm not sure roofies wouldn't be preferable. Druid potions are dreadful."

Rusty chuckled. "Now you're just being contrary. You can't taste anything except blood."

He gave Rusty a disgusted glance. "Nobody likes a know-it-all." He huffed. "Well, if dismemberment isn't the next part, I can guess what you've got in mind. But I'll warn you—" He shook a finger under Rusty's nose. "—rumors about the fabulousness of vampire sex do not extend to shifters."

That's what you think. But Rusty shook his head. "Just go inside, Casimir."

"Fine." Cas opened the door and marched inside, heading immediately for the hallway that led to his bedroom.

"Hold up," Rusty called. "We're not going there."

Cas turned and did he actually look... disappointed? Well, he might. He'd told Rusty that he preferred to bottom and for some reason, vampire blood hosts turned submissive and the best he could usually manage was getting them to suck his cock. "Why not?"

"We've got some things to discuss first." Rusty gestured toward the dining room. "In here." He headed inside and sat at the table. "You know what I could never figure out?" he said conversationally as Cas approached cautiously and sat next to him at the head of the table. "Why do you even *have* a dining table? You don't eat."

"Tables can be used for things other than eating." Cas ran a finger along the walnut inlay that edged the maplewood table. "Besides, it's beautiful."

And so are you. It nearly gutted Rusty to see the sadness in Cas's gorgeous gray eyes, and he ached to thread his fingers through that silky caramel-colored hair. *Later*. First, he needed to get the preliminaries out of the way.

He pulled his phone out of his pocket, set it on the table, and extracted the three vials from the case. As he lined them up, his phone dinged with a text. He glanced at the notification and flinched. *Fletcher*.

Cas lifted an eyebrow and Rusty wanted to go down on him right then and there, because that little peak was just so fucking *cute*. "Important message?"

Rusty shook his head. "It's nothing. Just my ex."

"Ah. The fuckhead."

Rusty's chin jerked up and he stared at Cas, jaw slack. *He remembers?* If he remembered Fletcher, remembered what he'd always called him, maybe he'd recall more of their time together. Cas was clearly surprised by his response, because his brows were now bunched in confusion.

"Why'd you call him that?" Rusty asked gently.

Cas laughed hollowly, his gaze sliding past Rusty. "It's obvious, isn't it? All exes are de facto fuckheads."

Damn. Rusty picked up the phone and keyed in the direct number for St. Stupid's SMTs, but didn't connect the call. He nudged the phone over in front of Cas.

Cas peered down at it, scanned the little line of potions, and —*score!*—both eyebrows peaked. "What's this?"

"Insurance."

"For you?"

"No. For you." Rusty swallowed. This next bit would be tricky. He had to depend on what Cas had said that night, the first night he'd had a taste of Rusty's blood following that horrible vampire reception. "Remember what Bryce said? That I wouldn't let any harm come to you?"

"Yes," Cas said slowly.

"I need you to keep that firmly in mind." He drew out his pocket knife and flicked open the blade.

Cas reared back in his chair. "I realize druids are very skillful, but I've never heard of any who could actually piece somebody back together again. Frankenstein, yes. Druids, no."

"Don't be such a drama queen, Casimir. This blade is smaller than your little finger. I couldn't dismember a cockroach with it."

Cas sniffed. "So you say. But you shifters have secrets we vampires have never had the opportunity to delve."

"We're not that mysterious." *Other than the whole inactive shifters are the perfect food for vampires who want to evade their sun sensitivity thing.* But Rusty was the only one who knew that now. Well, Rusty and Bryce. "Anyway, this knife isn't for you. It's for me."

With a quick swipe, Rusty opened a gash across the ball of his thumb in the exact spot where the sign had cut him on that night.

Cas pushed himself away from the table, knocking his chair over as he struggled to his feet. "What are you doing? You promised no harm." He pointed a shaking finger at Rusty's thumb as a drop of blood plopped onto the table. "Yet you're trying to *poison* me."

Rusty stayed purposely still, not wanting to spook Cas any more than he already had. "I'm not. I promise I'm not."

"*You* promise? I don't even *know* you!" As the words left his mouth, though, his eyes lost focus and he bit his lip.

That's right, sweetheart. You do *know me, don't you?* "If you don't believe my promise, believe Bryce's." He pointed to the vials with the hand that wasn't bleeding. "Those are all antidotes to shifter blood." He nodded at his phone. "And if those don't work, the SMTs can be here in minutes."

"Is this some kind of snuff kink? You get off on bringing people to the edge of death and back again?"

"I could point out that you've already passed the edge of death."

"But that would be rude," they said simultaneously.

Rusty grinned as Cas narrowed his eyes. "I'm not sure whether it's disturbing or arousing that you seem to know me so well, but you are seriously the weirdest person I've ever met."

Rusty touched the edge of his phone and waggled his eyebrows. "Since I'm your perfect match, what does that say about you?"

"I can't believe those spells weren't compromised somehow because—" Cas's nostrils flared. "—gods above and below, your *scent*. Is poison supposed to smell so *good*?"

"Nope. That should be a clue that my blood's not poison to you, don't you think?"

"Not necessarily. Consider cyanide. Some people would think it was nothing worse than almond biscuits." He glared at Rusty. "And they'd be *wrong*."

"Not this time." Rusty squeezed the ball of his thumb, forcing out another drop of blood. "Come on." He dropped his voice into what Cas had called his bedroom register. "You know you want to."

Cas glowered at him, eyes hooded. "Giving in to wants instead of common sense is what got my sire staked in the sun, so that isn't a particularly cogent argument."

"What about Bryce's word?" He pointed to the vials. "Antidote overkill at your elbow."

"*Aha!*" Cas crowed. "Over*kill*. You *are* trying to murder me!"

Rusty sighed. "Casimir. I know you're feeling a little off-kilter right now—"

"You *think*?"

"But I promise you, I vow on Gaia's bones, that I want nothing but the best for you." *Of course, the best for you is to be with me, but we'll leave that tidbit for now.* Rusty extended his thumb. "You don't want me to bleed out, do you?"

Cas's nostrils flared again, his pupils enormous. "I could point out that you're unlikely to lose enough blood from that cut to put you in danger, but I'm sure you'd have an answer for that." He sighed. "Fine. Let's get this over with."

He grasped Rusty's wrist and lifted his hand toward his mouth.

Chapter Three

"Wait!"

Cas glared at the truly annoying—although seriously hot—man who'd just yanked his hand away. "You've been tempting me with your blood since we arrived and now you've changed your mind?" He let his fangs drop. "What's the matter, Elmer? Afraid of the scary vampire?"

The infuriating man had the gall to laugh. "Not of what you can do to me, no, but I've gotta ask. Have you ever been high?"

Cas lifted his eyebrows, which, for some reason, filled Rusty's eyes with decided lust. "I was a silent film actor. When *wasn't* I high? After floating through the early '20s on a perpetual cloud of bootleg liquor and studio-prescribed cocaine, imagine my dismay after my Turn when I could no longer achieve even a halfway decent buzz." Cas scowled. "My sire left more than a few pertinent details out of his sales pitch."

"There's a… distinct possibility that my, er, bodily fluids will have a mind-altering effect on you."

"Wait." Cas leaned forward, grin dawning. "Are you saying I'll get drunk on your blood?"

Above his beard, Rusty's lovely cheekbones pinked with a blush. "And other things."

Cas frowned, head tilted, translating Rusty's vaguespeak. "When you say *and other things*, do you mean that your blood will induce intoxication and other effects? Like, I don't know—" He widened his eyes. "—*death*, perhaps?"

"No." Rusty's blush deepened. "I mean, my blood isn't the only thing that will have that effect." He grimaced. "Maybe. I mean, I've been— There's research— Although not much, because— If you consider—"

"Elmer." Cas forced himself to keep his tone even. "Use your words."

"Spunk," he blurted. "Although not spit. Maybe."

"Hmmm. You don't say?" Cas grinned and propped his chin on his hand. "Where did you come by this data? Have you conducted experiments with other vampires?"

"No!" Rusty's tone was a nice blend of outrage and horror.

"Then how do you know so much about the side effects?"

"Please, Cas." His wide shoulders slumped. "I don't know what else to say to convince you." He fixed Cas with an earnest gaze. "But no matter what you believe right now, I am absolutely convinced the spells got it right. You're my perfect match. I hope that after tonight, you'll agree, but if it takes longer? I don't care. I'll wait. There's nobody else for me, and never will be. Only you."

Cas's throat burned, his eyes prickling. There was something about Rusty's heartfelt declaration that pierced his shell of hard-won cynicism and planted a seed of hope in a heart he'd been convinced hadn't survived his Turn.

He didn't believe for a moment that Rusty was his perfect match, because that was ludicrous. A vampire and a shifter? It had never happened, and it wasn't likely to start with Cas, the vampire community's most disappointing representative. But the look in Rusty's eyes, the conviction in his voice, the naked desire on his broad face… Well, Cas had never kicked a puppy, and he wasn't about to start now.

Besides, the man was seriously hot, built like a tank, and smelled *incredible*. If nothing else, Cas could finally get laid tonight.

He folded his hands on the table. "So after I have this little amuse-bouche, what happens then?"

Rusty straightened, his smile dawning. "You'll do it?"

Cas waved one lordly hand. "I'm taking it under advisement. Assuming I taste you and don't require immediate transportation to the vampire unit at St. Stupid's. Then what?" He leaned forward. "Are you going to fuck me?"

That blush was back again. Cas was rapidly becoming addicted to it. "Uh…"

"No?" Cas pouted. "And here I was hoping our date would have a happy ending. Unless you're not that kind of boy?"

Rusty's eyes kindled, his smile crooked and wicked enough to make Cas shiver. "Where you're concerned, I'm *definitely* that kind of boy."

"Excellent." Cas made gimme motions with both hands. "Then hand over your thumb, big guy, because it's been a very long, very dry spell for me."

Rusty lifted his hand out of the way. "Not here."

Cas huffed in exasperation. "You were waving that under my nose not ten minutes ago, and now you're playing hard to get?"

"That's not what I meant. Yeah, we're gonna start with a taste, but like I said, it'll have an effect. I want it to wear off before we go any further. I want you to *know*." Rusty put an odd emphasis on the word.

"What I *know* is that I'm as horny as a basket full of weasel shifters."

"Well, that's gonna get worse," Rusty muttered.

"What was that?"

"Nothing."

Cas threw up his hands. "For pity's sake, Elmer, *make up your mind*. Do you want me to suck your thumb or not?"

Rusty huffed a laugh. "You make it sound like we're a couple of codependent toddlers."

"What *I* am is extremely annoyed. So tell me. What's the plan?" Cas pointed one finger at Rusty's nose. "No more waffling or vaguespeak. Spill."

"Okay." Rusty rubbed the back of his neck with the hand he hadn't cut. "First, you'll taste my blood."

Cas waggled his fingers. "Yes, we've covered that, although since your thumb has stopped leaking, you'll have to wield your ridiculously tiny blade again."

Rusty waved that away, apparently unconcerned that he'd be re-ventilating himself. "After that, we'll get back in my truck and drive down to Eugene while the effects, er, wane."

Cas narrowed his eyes. "Eugene? Eugene doesn't have any medical facilities for vampires. I thought you were all about my safety and the consequences of an accidental poisoning."

"The taste will prove that it's okay. I mean, other than making you a little high and horny—"

"You mean horni*er*."

"Trust me, it'll escalate. But you'll have the chance to decide whether you want to continue our date. If you don't, I'll go and you can take the antidote or visit St. Stupid's and you'll be fine. If you do, though, we'll head down to a place I've got on Dawson's Lake for the next part."

Cas lifted an eyebrow and had the satisfaction of seeing Rusty's gaze darken. "Is *that* when you'll fuck me?"

"Not immediately."

"But fucking *is* on the agenda for this date?"

"Gaia, I hope so." Rusty exhaled gustily. "But that'll be up to you once we get to that point. Because I want you to—"

"To *know*. Yes, you said so. But trust me when I tell you that if I don't get some dick tonight, I will be an extremely unhappy vampire." He bared his fangs. "And unhappy vampires can cause some unfortunate *effects* of our own."

Rusty smiled softly, shaking his head. "You don't scare me, Cas." He took out his knife again. "If you're sure?"

"Oh, get on with it already. Knives as foreplay *never* did it for me."

Rusty's shoulders rose and fell with an enormous breath, as though he were steeling himself for something worse than a trifling slice across a finger. Then he opened that gash again, releasing a fresh swell of blood, and extended his hand.

Cas took a moment to inhale deeply, because he was absolutely certain that *nothing* had *ever* smelled this good. Grasping Rusty's wrist, he gazed into those warm brown eyes. Rusty didn't flinch, didn't look away, just gave a tiny nod and a crooked smile.

Cas sucked Rusty's thumb into his mouth and, *gods*, the *taste*. Like fire and air and lust. His eyes fluttered closed. He hadn't thought anything could be as delectable as the scent of Rusty's blood, but the flavor topped it by several orders of magnitude.

He hollowed his cheeks, sucking harder, fangs dropping. If he pricked the skin just a little, he could get *more*, and he wanted more, he wanted—

"That's enough for now."

Rusty withdrew his thumb and took his hand away. Cas climbed onto the table to chase it, growling low in his throat. "Give that back. I want another taste." A really *big* taste.

"Later. How do you feel?"

Cas blinked and had the oddest urge to giggle. "I'm on my table." He waggled his eyebrows—and for good measure, his ass. "I guess I'm serving up *something* in the dining room, after all."

"Focus, Cas. Do you want the antidote? Should I call the SMTs?"

"What?" Cas's own blood was singing as it did in the days before his Turn, after he'd downed his second glass of champagne in that speakeasy by the Santa Monica pier. He wanted to rub against Rusty like a cat.

"The SMTs. Do you want me to call them?"

"No. They're no fun." Cas flopped onto his back. The chandelier overhead sparkled and flared. *Wow. I don't remember it being this beautiful.* Of course, he'd never looked at it from this angle before. He spread his arms and legs as though he were making a snow angel on his table top, his trousers and jacket sleeves sliding effortlessly over the polished maple. No friction, damn it. Friction would be a good thing. He *liked* friction, especially in certain areas.

He turned his head to find Rusty watching him with a frown, his brows bunched together. *Bet he'd be good at friction.* "Rusty," he sang, "my dick is hard." Because it was. So hard it ached.

Rusty glanced at Cas's groin, blushing again. "I can see that."

"Well?" Cas pushed himself to his elbows. "Aren't you going to *do* something about it?"

Chapter Four

Rusty had known Cas would get… frisky. The same thing had happened the first time, so this behavior wasn't a surprise. Except then, they'd been outside, at least at the beginning, and Rusty hadn't known exactly what sex with Cas would be like. He'd had absolutely no inclination to do anything but get Cas someplace he could receive medical attention.

Now, though…

His mouth watered with the memory of Cas's cock in his mouth, Cas's taste on his tongue. *Cas's fangs in my throat*. But he couldn't give in. Not yet. This date was about recreating their journey, about *reminding* Cas of the timeline that had been overwritten by Rusty's time surfs.

Please, Gaia, please *let him remember*. Bryce had said that intense feelings or meaningful events from prior timelines would leave echoes, footprints in time that might spark memories under the right conditions. Unfortunately, he hadn't known what those conditions might be, so basically Rusty was just winging it.

"Well?" Cas's imperious tone was accompanied by a thrust of his hips. "I'm waiting."

"I told you." Rusty returned the antidotes to the case and zipped it up. "Next, we drive to Eugene."

Cas lay back on the table with a pout. "I've decided I don't want to go to Eugene. I want to stay here. My skin is *tingling,*

Rusty. I want you to touch me *everywhere*." He ran his hands down his chest, aiming his fingers at his belt.

"Nope, not doing that." Rusty stood and grabbed Cas's wandering hands. With an ease born of hauling sacks of concrete mix and stacks of lumber, he hefted Cas over his shoulder in a fireman's carry, just as he had after that other first taste. "Let's go."

"Rusty!" Cas protested. But then his hands roamed down Rusty's back to squeeze his ass. *Also just like that other first taste.* "Oooh. At least the view is good."

Rusty sighed and shook his head. He tucked the antidote case under his other elbow and managed to maneuver out the door and shut it behind them, trusting the lock to engage as he knew it could.

He strode toward his truck, Cas humming under his breath and copping a squeeze with every step. When they reached the passenger side, he set Cas on his feet. Cas wobbled a little, so Rusty slapped the case on the cab roof and gripped Cas's shoulders to steady him. "Easy there. Still doing okay?"

Cas peered up at him from under his lashes and walked his fingers up Rusty's chest. "I'm not sure. I'm not breathing. I think I might be in need of some"—he leaned forward, pressing against Rusty's hold—"mouth to mouth resuscitation."

Rusty's lips twitched. "Casimir. You don't have to breathe. Not to survive. I don't think you need CPR."

"Are you sure?" He grabbed one of Rusty's hands and drew it to the middle of his chest. "I'm sure chest compressions are in order." He drew Rusty's hand down further. "Or maybe compressions of a different nature."

"Casimir—"

"Please, Rusty? Just one kiss? Or if not—" He waggled his eyebrows. "—bend over so I can get another look at that spectacular ass?"

Rusty ground his teeth together. *Gaia give me strength.* "Casimir, *please.*"

"Oooh." His gaze locked onto Rusty's groin, and the obvious bulge that hadn't disappeared since Cas had sucked on his thumb. "Look here. Something even *more* spectacular."

He reached for Rusty's belt, but Rusty caught his hand. "Casimir. Nothing else is going to happen now. Not until we get to Eugene and you come down off this high. Unless..." He peered down into Cas's eyes. "Unless you'd rather bail. The antidote's right here, and we can still call St. Stupid's."

Cas frowned, his face scrunched like an angry preschooler's. "I told you no. I don't want the SMTs, those spoilsports, and if the antidote stops me from feeling like this, I don't want it either." His gaze morphed into something hotter, slyer. *Predatory.* "What I want is right there in those dad jeans of yours."

"They're not dad jeans." He gripped Cas's shoulders again and moved him farther away. "Why do you want me, Cas?"

Cas scoffed. "Have you *seen* you? Everybody wants you."

"Not so's you'd notice," Rusty muttered.

"Oh." Cas nodded sagely and poked Rusty in the chest with a forefinger. "*You're* thinking about the fuckhead, right? Felcher."

Rusty's belly somersaulted. *Does he remember? Surely he remembers. He nearly sent Fletcher out of his fucking mind, calling him that.* "What did you say?"

Cas frowned. "When?"

"Just now."

Cas leered. "You mean about your dick?"

"No, about—" Rusty sighed. "Never mind." He let go of Cas's shoulders and opened the door. "Just get in the truck, Casimir."

Cas glanced from Rusty to the seat and back again—twice. "Your truck is so *big*."

"I hope that's not a euphemism," Rusty said dryly.

He held out his arms. "Help me up?"

"Cas. You're a vampire. You could probably leap the whole truck in a single bound."

Cas's face shuttered. "Don't remind me."

Throat tightening, Rusty swallowed twice against a flash from the overwritten timeline: Cas huddled in the darkened bedroom of Rusty's Eugene house and shouting *"I hate being a vampire!"* as Rusty tried to vampire-proof the place.

He couldn't undo Cas's Turn, but if their second first date was successful? He could at least make his Second Life easier to bear.

Rusty settled his hands on Cas's ribs and lifted him onto the seat. "There you go. Fasten your seatbelt. And remember." He retrieved the case from the roof and chucked it in the well by Cas's feet. "If you change your mind, the antidote is right there. Say the word at any time and I'll bring you home. Never bother you again."

Cas was looking at him with what Rusty could only describe as heart-eyes, with the result that his dick throbbed. *Damn it.*

"You lifted me into the truck, Rusty. Why would I bail now? I feel like a princess." He nestled into the seat with a wiggle of his ass and lifted a hand in the royal wave. "Onward, Johnson. Our adventure awaits."

Rusty chuckled as he jogged around the truck and took his place behind the wheel. They had a two-hour drive ahead of them, and unfortunately, Rusty had no idea how long that little hit of his blood would keep Cas flying. The first time, Bryce had gotten the antidote down him within ten minutes, and then the SMTs had hauled him to the VER, so he had no benchmark.

The first half hour of the drive fulfilled most of his fears, because Cas abandoned his princess progression persona and turned amorous again.

At the Tualatin exit: "I heard that click, Casimir. Put your seatbelt back on."

"I'm a vampire. It's not like I can die again unless you keep me out past dawn."

At the Wilsonville turnoff: "Casimir, I'm trying to drive here. Stop trying to grab my dick."

"But Rusty, it's *right there*. You can't expect me to *ignore* something *so large*."

At the Woodburn outlets: "If you don't get your head out of my lap this instant—"

"But Rusty, what do you expect? I'm tired and you didn't provide me with a pillow."

By the time they passed Salem, though, Casimir had grown quiet, staring out the window into the dark. When Rusty left the highway north of Eugene and headed into the woods owned by the beaver clan, Cas turned in his seat, crossing his arms, and Rusty could almost feel the heat of his glare.

"Where are you taking me? I've heard about people disappearing in forests like these."

Rusty flicked on the turn signal and headed onto the gravel road that led to his lot. "Were those people abducted by vampires?"

Cas snorted. "Vampires have more sense than to venture into uncharted woodlands. We're civilized. We stick to modern urban architecture and Zen gardens."

"Uh huh."

"Vampires can be very Zen!"

"Oh yeah? Before or after you chow down on some guy's carotid?" The silence from the other side of the truck was as loud as if Cas had shouted. Rusty glanced at him to find Cas staring at him, narrow-eyed. "What?"

"You know," he said slowly, "most people go for the jugular."

"Excuse me?"

"When they talk about vampires. It's all, *Shall I open a vein for you?*"

Rusty winced internally. *Privileged information.* Something he only knew because Cas had told him, back when they'd been together. Before Rusty had wiped that existence away to save Cas from Second Death. "Arteries have more oxygen content. Right?"

"They do. But it's not a fact many people care about when contemplating deadly creatures of the night."

"I'm not most people." He cleared his throat. "Anyway, you weren't especially Zen back at your house just now."

"That was different." Cas's tone was sulky, and was it weird that it made Rusty want to kiss him? "You... you *beguiled* me somehow. And now..." He mumbled something that Rusty didn't catch.

He shot a sidelong glance at Cas after they passed the tree line and he'd parked the truck in the clearing next to the lake. "What was that?"

"Nothing," Cas said to the window.

"It was something, Cas. Come on."

He swiveled in his seat to glare at Rusty, although his expression held a hint of hope and desperation in the faint glow of the dashboard lights. "Fine. You want me to say it?" Rusty nodded. "I... I haven't felt that good since before I was Turned. Giddy. Bubbly."

"High?"

He shook his head. "Happy," he whispered.

"Oh, Cas." *You're breaking my heart.*

"And..." Cas's chest expanded, and since he didn't technically need to breathe, he must be gathering breath for *words*. "... I want more."

Rusty's heart jerked and heat pooled in his middle. "I can arrange that," he growled.

"Really?" Cas's grin held more than a hint of fang. He unbuckled his seatbelt.

"Yup." But when Cas reached for him, Rusty reared back out of the way. "*After.*"

Cas peered at him in the dimness. "After what?"

"After you join me for a swim in the lake."

Chapter Five

Cas's jaw sagged. "Are you delusional? I can't do that."

"Don't worry. I won't let you sink."

There it was again. Another hint that Rusty—an inactive shifter, by all the gods—knew more about vampires than three-quarters of the supernatural community. In fact, since shifters and vampires avoided each other on a species-wide level, the fact that he knew *anything* was remarkable. But the comment about arteries? That vampires would sink in water?

Well, he'd never find out if he didn't ask. "How do you know so much about vampires?"

Rusty shrugged, and if it hadn't been so dark in the truck's cab, surrounded as they were by towering trees with only the glint of moonlight on the lake and the fading dashboard lights, Cas suspected he'd have seen the blush. He certainly detected it —the way the heat shifted in Rusty's body, rushing up the column of his throat and—*interesting*—pooling in his groin.

"I hear things."

"I sincerely doubt that details about vampires would be popular topics of conversation at shifter barbecues. Unless you're all plotting ways to wipe our species off the planet."

Rusty met Cas's gaze and did his eyes flare gold? Was that a shifter thing, even for Inactives? Maybe *only* an Inactive thing? "Even if I were welcome at my clan's parties—which I'm not—I would never, *ever* hurt you. I would risk everything to keep others from hurting you, too."

Cas lifted an eyebrow, just to see whether the heat below Rusty's belt would spike—it did. *Something to keep in mind: This man has an eyebrow kink.* "And yet you want to toss me into a lake."

"Not toss you. Swim with you. Hold you up. Please, Cas? It's a beautiful night."

"It's *November.*"

"Yes, but I'm a shifter and you're a vampire. Neither one of us feels the cold the way humans do. I promise it will be all right." A sly smile curved his full lips. "And afterward you'll get another… taste."

At that, Cas's below-the-belt temperature rose too. "Promise?"

Rusty nodded. "Absolutely."

Cas bit his lip, something that was still a challenge after the, er, dental modifications following his Turn. "Since you planned this so thoroughly, did you bring a swimsuit for me?"

Rusty shook his head slowly. "We won't need those."

Cas gulped. That meant… *skin.* How long had it been since he'd felt another man's skin on his, head to toe? Too long. Although… He had a brief flash of a big, bearded man, gazing at him with total adoration as he breached Cas, warming him from the inside out.

That can't be right. He never got completely naked with blood hosts. And the men he'd slept with before the Turn had all been clean-shaven, as was the fashion at the time. He shook off the thought and concentrated on the heat in his own dick. Which, sadly, would be seriously cooled by a dip in a lake.

"All right, then. Lead on."

Rusty's grin put the moonlight to shame. He jumped out of the truck and raced around to open the passenger side door. Cas squeaked when Rusty scooped him right off the seat, cradling him in his arms in the time-honored bride-across-the-threshold position, and nudged the door closed with his hip.

"Not that I'm complaining," Cas said as Rusty strode across the wide clearing toward the lake, "but I believed I proved my ability to get out of the truck myself two hours ago."

"I'm proving a point." Rusty's boots crunched on gravel as they left the shadow of the trees.

"What's that? Other than you've clearly made this trip before, since you've prepared a path."

"Not just a path." Rusty set Cas on his feet, although he kept an arm around his waist, which was beyond satisfactory. Being tucked against Rusty's side was the most comfortable place imaginable. *Although being tucked under Rusty would be unimaginably spectacular.*

Cas looked around. A wooden dock extended about fifteen feet into the lake, and set back from where it joined the shore was a wood-framed building with windows facing south over the lake and east into the woods. It was larger than the average garden shed, but smaller than the cottage in the Carpathians where Cas spend his childhood. "Is this your den, Elmer?"

He chuckled, vibrating Cas's bones. "In a way."

"Rather a small home for someone of your size."

"It's not my home." He nodded back the way they'd come. "I'll build my house in the clearing. This is just to make things easier at the lake."

"Easier for whom?"

Rusty looked down at him, and for an instant, Cas was sure he was about to say *For you,* but that was ridiculous. They'd only met this evening. "You'll see."

He dropped his arm, but before Cas could protest its loss, he took Cas's hand and led him to the door of the little building. He opened it and flipped a switch, filling the single room with soft, amber light from a soffit that bordered the ceiling. Shelves lined one wall, stacked with what looked like fluffy white towels and high thread-count sheets. A row of hooks was mounted directly beneath them, a couple holding life vests. A canoe and two kayaks hung on the opposite wall, and a four-fold wooden screen decorated with delicate scrollwork masked one corner.

"What's behind the screen?"

Rusty smiled down at him. "Take a look."

Cas huffed, but it was only for show, because he truly was curious. As he trod across the wide-planked floor, he noted that the windows were fitted with high-end blackout shades, the same kind most vampires used in their own homes. He shot a suspicious glance at Rusty, who merely smiled benignly back at him. Cas peeked behind the screen.

A large… well, he couldn't call it a *cot* because it was too sturdy, and *bed* was a little too formal a term. But it was long enough for Rusty and wide enough for two. A narrow shelf above its pillows held what Cas recognized as premium lube.

Cas shot Rusty a sardonic glance. "Well-prepared, I see."

"Better to have it and not need it than need it and not have it."

"Are you referring to the bed or the lube?"

"Both." He pointed to the hooks. "Take off your clothes, Casimir. It's time for our swim."

Cas grimaced. "Are you sure I can't talk you into skipping the swim and cozying up in this nice little love shack?"

"It's not a shack. It's an outbuilding."

"Whatever."

"Clothes, Casimir." Rusty shed his own jacket and hung it on a hook. But as he began to unbutton his flannel shirt and Cas still hadn't moved, he stopped, uncertainty creasing his forehead. "Unless… Have you changed your mind? You still can, and I'll take you home."

Cas dropped his cashmere duster faster than Rusty could blink. Vampires could move fast when they wanted to, and Cas really wanted to feel Rusty's skin against his. *Heat.* He hadn't been truly warm since his Turn. He undressed so quickly that

Rusty had only shrugged out of his shirt and taken off his shoes by the time Cas was naked.

Rusty froze, his hands on his belt, gazing at Cas with unmistakable lust. "Gaia, Cas. You're so beautiful. Your skin is like silk. I'd forgotten."

Cas frowned. "How can you forget something you've never seen?"

Rusty's eyes popped wide. "Uh…"

"Never mind." Cas flicked his fingers. "Carry on. I'd like to get the water torture over with as soon as possible."

When Rusty dropped his jeans and kicked them aside, it was Cas's turn to goggle. The wide chest, the bulging arm muscles— yes, Cas had clocked them when Rusty had picked him up. He'd appreciated the shirtless view, too. He adored a furry man, and Rusty's defined pecs were liberally dusted with hair that glinted with copper highlights. But the rest… *Gods*.

Those horrible jeans had masked narrow hips, a defined Adonis belt, long, muscular legs. Not to mention a truly magnificent cock.

Oh my stars. To have that inside me.

Cas marched across the floor and grabbed Rusty's hand. "Come on. We've got things to do"—*namely me, I hope*—"and the night's not getting any younger."

Laughing, Rusty let Cas tow him to the end of the dock. But once there, Cas hesitated. Yes, the moon just above the treetops gilded the lake with silver, but the water was still really dark. What kinds of creatures lurked under there? How far down was the bottom? Could Rusty really keep him safe?

"Hey." Rusty circled Cas's waist with both arms, his skin like heated velvet against Cas's back. He lowered his chin to Cas's shoulder. "Second thoughts?"

"N-no. I think." Cas shivered, and Rusty's arms tightened.

"It'll be okay."

Cas twisted to look up into Rusty's face. "You promise?"

An odd expression flickered over his face. "Let's say I'm betting everything on it. I can promise *you'll* be okay. The jury's still out on me."

"All right." Cas straightened his shoulders. "Here goes." He bent his knees in preparation for jumping in, but Rusty hauled him back against his chest.

"Whoa there. Let me go first and I'll catch you."

Cas's belly tumbled, his cock flagging. "Right. Of course. What was I thinking?"

"You just forgot for a minute." Rusty let go of him and crouched down. He propped one hand on the dock and slipped into the water without even a splash.

"Forgot what?"

Rusty trod water—Cas could see the white blur of his legs scissoring under the surface—and held up his arms. "You forgot I'll always be here to catch you."

Chapter Six

Rusty's heart had dropped to his feet when Cas had nearly jumped in the lake without him. Given that vampire bone density meant they sank like stones, Rusty doubted he could have caught up to Cas in time in the dark water.

But now, Cas sat on the dock and, with a little wiggle, slipped into Rusty's arms. Hardly daring to breathe, Rusty turned Cas so his back was to Rusty's front and lay back on the water, kicking gently to propel them further onto the lake.

The stars spread out above them, a spangled canopy edged by spires of fir and pine.

"Oh," Cas breathed, and relaxed against Rusty's chest, his head nestled against Rusty's shoulder.

The sense memory was so strong it threw off Rusty's rhythm and he simply kept them floating, motionless, for a moment. Cas's reaction when he'd seen the sky—both sound and movement—was exactly the same as the first time Rusty had taken him for a swim.

Perhaps, even if he couldn't jog Cas's memory enough to penetrate the altered timeline, he could recreate enough of their experiences that the result would be the same: Cas in his life forever.

Just as before, Rusty's cock was nestled in the crease of Cas's ass. Just as before, the movement of his legs generated friction, constant small thrusts that kept Rusty's cock alert despite the water's chill. And just as before, Rusty let his hand drift across Cas's ribs to his chest to fondle one erect nipple. He was rewarded with the barely perceptible hitch of Cas's breath.

Just as before.

"D-do you do this a lot?" Cas asked. "Swim at night, I mean."

"Often enough. I always take a dip after I've finished a construction project. It's kind of a—"

"Tradition."

He's finishing my sentences now. "That's right. I like to come at night because the clan mostly den up at night and there's nobody in the water. During the day, they usually swim in shifted form. It's a little…"

"Uncomfortable?"

"Yeah."

"Does it bother you?" Cas's hand barely skimmed the hair on Rusty's arm, making it stand erect. He didn't protest when Rusty trailed his fingers to Cas's other nipple. "Being inactive, I mean?"

"Of course—" Rusty sucked in a breath, close enough to a squeak to be embarrassing, when Cas wriggled his hips, nestling Rusty's burgeoning cock tighter between his ass cheeks. He cleared his throat. "Of course it does. I've got a calon. I'm technically a supe. But the one thing that most shifters pride themselves on, the thing that sets us apart from other species—the magic that lets us change our shape—is beyond my ability and will always set me apart. I'm a member of a community to which I can never belong."

Cas hummed, setting up a resonance in Rusty's blood. "That's sort of the way vampires are, too. I mean, we're probably less social even than bear shifters. Glitzy cocktail parties—with no cocktails—aren't exactly a substitute for real friendships. Real relationships."

"Not even with each other?"

"Too much competition for the same resources. Vampires might form convenient alliances for power or money or influence, but we're never *friends*. More often than not, we're rivals at the least, and mortal enemies at worst."

Rusty rested his cheek against Cas's silky hair. "So you're lonely?"

"Considering we're always looking over our shoulders to make sure one of our erstwhile associates isn't sneaking up on us with a stake in their hands, lonely is actually the best we can hope for."

"Do you miss that? Friendships? Relationships?"

Cas sighed, tucking his head closer against Rusty's neck. "I can't really say my life as an actor was much different. Navigating studio politics. Fighting for the same roles. Hiding our desires, our true selves, from everyone who had the power to hurt us—who, more often than not, were the same people we'd been fucking the year, the month, hells, the *night* before."

"What do you miss then?"

"Honestly? I miss the taste of bourbon." His voice turned dreamy. "The fizz in my veins after a night drinking champagne and dancing at a speakeasy. The burn in my ass the day after a hookup." He sighed again. "I miss... I miss the sun."

Oh, Cas. Rusty pressed a kiss to the side of Cas's neck, directly over the carotid, the spot that always drove Cas wild in bed. "Let's go back. I want to make love to you."

Cas shivered, then heaved a theatrical sigh. "Finally. As lovely as the night is, that monster cock nudging at my backside is far more inspirational." He executed another royal wave. "Home, Johnson. And don't spare the horses."

Rusty kicked out, strong and steady, aiming for the dock and keeping Cas steady with his arms wrapped across his middle. With every thrust, his cock slid in the cleft of Cas's ass, pulling twin moans from both of of them. When they reached the dock, Rusty stopped kicking and let their feet drift down. "Can you lever yourself onto the dock?"

"Please. We vampires are like—"

"Ants. You can lift fifty times your own weight."

Cas paused with his hands gripping the edge of the dock. "How do you do that?"

"Do what?"

"Finish my sentences?"

Rusty ducked his head. "Sorry. Don't mean to interrupt." But whenever Cas said something that he'd said before, it sparked such a surge of hope and elation that Rusty couldn't help it.

"Don't apologize. It's just… You seem to know what I'm thinking."

To banish the puzzlement on Cas's face and cover his own desperate longing, Rusty fell back on snark. "What I'm thinking is that vampires might talk a good game, but they can't back it up with actions."

As he'd hoped, Cas's eyes glinted. "A challenge. Observe, oh ye of little faith." He braced his hands on the dock and practically flowed out of the water. "Voila."

Rusty followed, although he wasn't nearly as graceful. He took a moment to shake his wet hair—he'd managed to keep Cas's mostly dry except for the ends of a few locks that had trailed over Rusty's shoulders—and push it back. When he opened his eyes, Cas was staring at him with that same heat and intent Rusty remembered.

He moved closer, slowly, gaze never leaving Cas's, until they were chest to chest, nothing but droplets of lake water separating them.

Then he bent down and kissed Cas for the second first time.

Cas flung his arms around Rusty's neck, plastering himself against Rusty like a very enthusiastic limpet. He adjusted his head to the perfect angle, tongue meeting Rusty's in a sleek slide and stroke.

Rusty moaned into Cas's mouth, because *this* was perfect. Cas's mouth tasted like silk felt, like music sounded, his coolness countering Rusty's heat. With a quick flex of his knees, Cas leaped into Rusty's arms, wrapping his legs around Rusty's waist so their cocks slid together and Rusty could swear the last drops of lake water evaporated into steam at the touch.

Rusty strode up the dock, never taking his mouth off Cas's, and bumped the outbuilding's door open with his hip. *Good job, past me, for not latching it when we left.*

Once inside, he fumbled blindly on the shelves until his hand closed on terrycloth. He managed to shake out the towel and drape it over Cas's back as he tottered toward the cot.

When Rusty tore his mouth away from the kiss, Cas uttered a wordless protest. But when Rusty tossed the towel onto the bed and lowered Cas onto it, the grumble changed to a purr of contentment.

"Now this is more like it." He wriggled, making himself a nest in the terrycloth and bedclothes, and held up his arms. "Grab the lube and a condom and come here."

"Um…" Rusty screwed up his face. "About the condom…"

Cas frowned, dropping his arms and propping himself on his elbows. "What about it?"

"I wasn't planning to use one?" Rusty's smile probably looked like that teeth-bared emoji.

Scowling, Cas pushed himself all the way up and grabbed his knees. "So just because your blood didn't kill me—yet—you want to introduce other *fluids*?"

"Yeah. There's a good reason, I promise. Even if Inactives could contract human diseases—which we can't—it's not like you can catch anything at all. Your immune system—"

"Stop. Just stop." Cas flopped back on the bed. "Immune systems? Seriously? You're really killing the mood here, Elmer."

Rusty lay down beside Cas and stroked his hair. "I promised you that nothing I do would harm you." He gestured to the shelf above the bed. "I don't only have lube up there. I've got extra antidotes too, so if something goes wonky, we can dose you right away." He nuzzled Cas's neck, right over the carotid, and was rewarded with Cas's shiver and gasp. "I'll make you feel good. I promise."

"Oh, well. If you *promise.*" Cas's snarky tone was blunted by breathlessness.

"Mmmhmmm." Rusty drew his hand down Cas's chest, bypassing his burgeoning cock—which earned him a growl—and trailed a finger across his taint to tickle his hole. "But if you don't want to, if you don't feel safe, if you've changed your mind"—*please don't have changed your mind*—"we can stop right now."

Cas glared at Rusty, his gray eyes sparking with ruby glints, and jabbed a finger into Rusty's chest. "If you stop now, I will *murder* you, Elmer." He reached up, scrabbling on the shelf until his hand closed on the lube. "Here. I haven't been topped since 1926, and I refuse to go another fucking *minute*. Even if I expire from extreme shifter anaphylaxis, it will be worth it if you know how to use that monster between your legs."

Rusty took the bottle. "If you're sure…"

Cas narrowed his eyes. "Have I mentioned the part about murdering you? Get *in* me, Elmer. Right fucking now."

Chapter Seven

Fucking had never *been like this.*

If it had, Cas wouldn't have waited nearly a century to do it again. He was *flying*, every inch of his skin afire in the *best* way, colors not found in nature dancing before his eyes, and every time Rusty pegged his prostate, Cas nearly launched both of them into orbit.

"Gaia, Cas," Rusty panted between thrusts, "you feel so fucking good. I'd forgotten how *good* you feel."

There was something wrong with that statement. "What— *ungh*! So close. Do that again." But instead, Rusty reared up over him, the muscles in his arms bunching, and Cas bared his teeth. "Don't you dare stop."

"Bite me, Cas."

"Now is not the time to get passive-aggressive."

"I mean it." Rusty angled his head, baring his throat. "Bite me. Right there. Drink."

It was hard to think with Rusty so deep in his ass that Cas could feel him with every heartbeat. But that... That required brain cells. "Rusty. A taste is one thing, but—"

"I promised, remember?" Rusty's hips moved in a series of tiny prods, just enough to remind Cas how *full* he was. "Bite me. Please."

Despite his better judgment, Cas's fangs dropped. He'd never fed from someone who was fucking him, especially someone who was fucking him bare. His mouth watered. To be filled from both ends at once—what would that be like? Rusty's blood, even the tiny bit he'd ingested earlier, had been better than the finest vintage of real champagne. To have more, to drink his fill... "What if I can't stop?" he whispered.

Rusty smiled down at him, an expression so tender and full of affection that Cas had to remind his heart to beat again. "You won't hurt me. You're not that kind of man. I trust you."

Trust. Nobody trusted Cas, unless it was to trust him to do the opposite of what he was supposed to do. Even his clan chief had to force him to toe the line by confiscating his phone when he was... *What? Kristof never took my phone. Why do I—*

"Cas?" Rusty's eyebrows bunched, his forehead creasing. "If you don't want to"—his hips never stopped the micro-thrusts that were driving Cas wild—"you don't have to. But—"

Cas struck, burying his fangs in Rusty's throat, and with the first spill of that exquisite heat across his tongue, his eyes rolled back in his head. He couldn't have stopped if the sun rose at that moment and struck him full in the face because *gods*.

And Rusty... Rusty *roared*, pounding Cas hard and deep until he froze, back muscles clenching under Cas's hands, and Cas felt it—the gush of semen hotter than his own skin, and fireworks ignited in his spine until he was coming too, his cooler spend pooling between his belly and Rusty's.

If Cas's mouth hadn't been full, he would have laughed in delight and relief and wonder, because for the first time in nearly a century, he was satisfied. For the first time in a century, he was warm.

For the first time in a century, he was happy.

Was it strange to spend an hour when he could have gotten fucked again—for the fourth time—just watching someone sleep? Maybe. But the fierce euphoria that had followed the first time—and the second, if Cas were honest with himself—had...

well, *dimmed* wasn't the precise word. Diffused, perhaps? Because he felt as though he were glowing from the inside out, as though if he turned off the lights, he could illuminate Rusty's little love shack with nothing more than this settled, all-encompassing joy.

He gazed down at Rusty, his ridiculously long dark lashes a fan across his cheeks, his hair rumpled, but a smile curving his lips even in sleep. *He's exhausted, poor darling*. Athletic sex and the effects of two feedings—although Cas had been very careful the second time to take no more than a sip—had taken their toll.

Cas touched the two nearly vanished puncture wounds on Rusty's throat below his beard. He couldn't remember anyone ever tasting this wonderful, this *complete.*

He frowned, one finger still resting on Rusty's skin. *But I do remember. It's familiar.* The same way the glory of the stars was familiar as they'd drifted atop the lake water, the same way he'd recalled the feel of Rusty's beard against his skin, the same way he sometimes knew what Rusty would say next.

Déjà vu? Could it really strike quite so many times? Cas wasn't an oracle by any means, and he'd never been subject to prophetic visions. Maybe in a dream? Cas brushed a lock of hair off Rusty's forehead. *You're literally everything I ever dreamed of.* But after so many disappointments, stretching all the way back to his first life, Cas didn't believe in dreams coming true.

Rusty had been awfully cagey about explanations when Cas had pointed out things they both seemed to know that shouldn't be possible. He glanced at his duster, still crumpled on the floor where he'd dropped it in his haste to get naked.

The envelope.

Rusty had told him not to open it until after dawn. According to Cas's inner time sense, the one every vampire possessed, sunrise was at least half an hour away. *Close enough.*

He eased away from Rusty, who muttered something in his sleep and reached out. Cas captured his seeking hand and kissed its palm before laying it atop the blanket. He waited for a moment, but Rusty settled back into slumber.

Cas crept across the floor. It didn't creak once, a testament to the care and skill Rusty applied to things other than Cas's ass—although he'd been as careful and skillful with *that* as Cas could have wished. Rusty's spend trickling down the inside of his thighs made Cas twitch. As much as he liked the reminder, the love shack wasn't equipped with a shower, and things down below could get very sticky and uncomfortable. Maybe another dip in the lake was in order.

No. Can't risk it. Not with sunrise so close. *Gods, sometimes I hate being a vampire.*

He extracted the letter from the inside pocket and plopped down on the end of the bed near Rusty's feet.

My dear Cas.

Okay, now that I've written that, I'm not sure how to go on. I can hear your voice now, telling me as you've done so many times: "Elmer, use your words." So here goes.

Time surfing is a real thing. I know, because I've done it. I did it twice, actually, because it's not an exact science, and getting it right was more important to me than anything.

It was more important to you, too.

Cas let the paper drop to his lap and glanced over his shoulder at Rusty. He'd be tempted to write this off as a scam or a delusion, but Rusty had written this letter before they'd left on their date, when Cas had only known him for a matter of minutes.

He tore his gaze away from Rusty's face and kept reading.

There's a lot that supes don't know, or have forgotten, or intentionally suppressed about vampires and shifters. Well, probably about every other species too, because we can all be a bunch of pigheaded assholes at the best of times. I won't go into the details here, but you should talk to Bryce about it.

Cas glared at Rusty. "Like hells I will," he muttered. "I'll ask *you*, Elmer, and you'll tell me."

Anyway, I surfed for good reasons. Important reasons. To right a wrong. To save an innocent man. To prevent an unjust execution and make sure the truly guilty person paid for his crimes.

You stood behind me, encouraging me, even though it meant that we would never have met. Never fallen in love. Never gotten fake married.

Cas blinked. "Fake married? Seriously?"

I'm not sorry about my decision, because what I did means that you're still in the world. Even if you never remember. Even if you can't love me again.

There was a blot on the page, smearing the ink. *A tear.* He'd been crying when he wrote those words. Cas dashed a hand across his own eyes.

I don't have the words, Casimir. I don't have the words to tell you how much you mean to me. But know this:

I will always love you, even if you can't love me back. Even if you walk away and never speak to me again. That will never change.

What happens next is all to up you. You know the secret about Inactive blood. I trust you to keep it, because you're a good man. Never doubt that, just as you should never doubt that you have all my love forever.

Your Rusty

Cas laid the letter aside. "What secret about inactive blood?"

"You weren't supposed to read that yet." Cas twisted to find Rusty sitting up in bed, his elbows on his knees. "It's not dawn."

Cas bit his lip. *So many questions.* But one of them leaped to the front of the queue. "What unjust execution?"

Rusty winced. "Can we table that question for a bit?"

"Don't dodge, Elmer. What unjust execution?"

Rusty met Cas's gaze, his expression somber, and for a moment Cas thought he'd refuse to answer. Then his big chest rose and fell with a sigh. "Yours."

"Mine?" Cas croaked. "What— Why— Did they—"

"Casimir," Rusty said with a crooked smile, "use your words."

"Fuck words, Elmer. I want actions. I want results. I want you to show me what the hells is going on!" Rusty glanced away from Cas, his gaze landing on the window. "Look at me, Elmer, not the window. Time surfing? What the actual fuck?"

Rusty gave another big sigh. "Do you trust me?"

"What I'm going to do is murder you if I don't get some answers."

Rusty didn't respond. Instead, he rose and walked to the window, giving Cas a tantalizing view of how that spectacular ass looked in motion. He lifted one side of the blackout shade and peeked outside. He turned. "Cas. Get under the blanket."

"I will not! Not unless—"

"Casimir." Rusty's tone held a steel Cas could have never suspected. "Under the blanket. Now."

Cas huffed. "Oh fine." He flopped onto the mattress and flung the blanket over himself.

Rusty strode over and jerked it up to cover Cas's face. "Stay there."

"So now you're going to suffocate me?"

"You don't need to breathe, Casimir. Don't be dramatic." He twitched the blanket near Cas's feet. "Don't move."

Cas crossed his arms but stayed put. "I'll count to ten, but then I'll—

Rusty sucked in a breath. "Okay. You can come out now."

"Finally." Cas flung the blanket off his face and sat up.

And froze.

Because a ray of early sunlight was slanting through the window where Rusty had raised the blind a few inches—and it fell across Cas's bare foot.

"I'm... I'm not..."

"Bursting into flames? No." Rusty held out his hand. "Come with me."

Cas clutched the blanket to his chest. "But—"

"It will be all right, Cas. Trust me?"

Cas glanced at the letter. "Apparently I did once."

He laid his hand in Rusty's and let himself be pulled to his feet. Rusty enfolded him in his arms and murmured, "It'll be all right." His breath stirred Cas's hair. "I promise."

With his arm around Cas's waist, Rusty led him toward the door. Cas balked at the last minute. "You're sure?"

Rusty nodded. "Your foot's fine, isn't it? Not even a little toasty?"

"Yes. No. Whatever."

"I've got special druid burn ointment if anything goes wrong, but I don't think it will."

"Thinking is not the same as being certain, Elmer," Cas said crossly. "But let's get this over with. If I meet the sun today, at least I had a night of spectacular fucking as a send-off."

Rusty opened the door. Outside, the sky was tinged pink and orange, tender colors Cas hadn't seen for nearly a century. The sun was still below the trees—that sunbeam must have cut through the branches, and Cas wondered if Rusty had planned it that way. He seemed to have thought of everything else.

"Come on." Rusty took Cas's hand and led him outside.

Into the dawn.

"Rusty," he said, his voice broken.

"Let's go down on the dock and watch the sun rise."

Cas blinked up at Rusty, the first face he'd seen in the daylight since 1926. *And it's the one I'd have chosen above all others.* "I can do that?"

He nodded. "We haven't got the timing nailed down on how long the effects last—"

"Effects of what?"

"Effects of Inactive bodily fluids. My blood and my..." He blushed, and, yes, it was even more glorious in the natural light. "... you know. But it's good for at least two or three hours."

Cas inhaled sharply. "I can be outside in the light for *hours*? What..." He paused and sniffed, eyes widening. "Rusty, I can smell the *trees*." Cas let go of his hand and raced down the dock, flinging his arms wide and dancing in a circle. "The wood of the dock. The *water*."

Rusty joined him. "That's another effect. We're not sure about taste, but—"

"Can we go for a swim?"

Rusty blinked down at him. "You want to go back in the water?"

"I want to watch the sun rise from the lake. Can we do that?"

His smile was like a second sunrise. "We can absolutely do that."

"And it's all because you're inactive?"

Rusty nodded. "Yes. And Cas?" He glanced across the lake at where the boathouses of his clan dotted the shore, wreathed in morning mist. He turned away from them, those horrible people who'd always made him feel *less*, and faced Cas, cupping his cheeks in both big hands.

"If someone could wave a magic wand and make me active today, Cas, I'd refuse. If they find a therapy that could make me active tomorrow, I'd turn them down. I'll be inactive until the day I die and not regret it for an instant." He leaned down and kissed Cas softly. "Not if it means I can give you the sun."

RUSTY'S REALLY
Bad Day

About RUSTY'S REALLY Bad Day

More Spoilers!

Rusty's Really Bad Day is another "sidecar" or companion story: It's not intended to stand alone. Instead, it assumes the reader's familiarity with other books. In this case, if you haven't read *Vampire With Benefits*, the story will make little sense. It also includes references to other Mythmatched universe tales, notably the Fae Out of Water trilogy (*Cutie and the Beast, The Druid Next Door*, and *Bad Boy's Bard*), *Howling on Hold, Five Dead Herrings*, and *The Skinny on Djinni*.

In the Mythmatched story world chronology, *Rusty's Really Bad Day* happens during the second week in March—between the end of *Howling on Hold* (which takes place on Cas and Rusty's wedding day) and the last chapter of *Demon on the Down-Low* (which occurs on the vernal equinox, Mal and Bryce's handfasting day).

(For more on the the Mythmatched chronology, see the Mythmatched Timeline on my website at https://ejrussell.com/extras/mythmatched-timeline)

Cheers!
—E

Chapter One

When Rusty jerked awake, his bed was spinning.

No. Not the bed. But his head was definitely on a merry-go-round and his stomach was *very* unhappy about it.

"Cas?" he croaked, then clamped his lips shut to keep from hurling. He groped for his phone on the bedside table, but the dizziness must have messed with his spatial awareness too, because the bedside tabletop was in the wrong place, four inches shorter than it ought to be. He scrabbled the phone onto the bed, nearly dropping it from his trembling hand. The screen blinked on, a wan illumination in the dark bedroom. "Eleven-thirty? Shit." He hadn't even been asleep for an hour after… after… What had he been doing? Clearly eating something that had disagreed with him because his stomach heaved again and he curled into a fetal position, eyes shut, phone clutched to his chest.

I just need to get back to sleep. Everything will be better in the morning.

When he drifted into consciousness again, his stomach had settled and the dizziness had passed. *Thank Gaia.* He took a relieved breath and cracked his eyes open.

"Shit!" He flailed, his phone flying across the room as he struggled out from under the blankets and sat up, because sunlight was flooding into the room, and… and…

Wait.

Why was that a bad thing? He was starting a new job today and excavation was always easier when Oregon didn't decide to dump spring rain on his crew's heads. He scrubbed his hands through his hair as he glanced around the room, snorting at the partially sanded crown molding. What was it they said about the shoemaker's kids going barefoot? Well, apparently the contractor's house was the last on the agenda for renovation. He'd been intending to refinish the bedroom woodwork for months, but somehow focusing on fixing his own place just made it more obvious that it was empty and he was still alone.

He sighed as he swung his feet off the side of the bed. Someday he'd finally get around to building his house out by the lake, but there didn't seem to be much point with nobody to share it. Of course, he thought he'd already built his own house, his and Fletcher's, for them to move into after the wedding. Too bad Fletcher hadn't mentioned the tiny fact that Rusty wouldn't be standing on the other side of the altar when Fletcher said, "I do."

When he stood and turned to straighten the bedclothes, the morning sunlight splashing on the opposite side of the bed turned his belly to lead for some reason. He paused, the edge of the comforter in his hand, eyebrows bunched as he frowned at the undented pillow. *Somebody should be there. Somebody who... who...*

Scowling, he yanked the blankets straight. "Somebody who isn't Fletcher," he growled.

He stalked across the room and crouched on the worn pile carpet, something else he'd been meaning to replace. As he reached for his phone with his left hand, he froze, staring at his fingers.

Something's not right.

He lifted his hand slowly. Why did he think something was wrong? Same square palm. Same scar at the base of his thumb from his first bout with a ratchet screwdriver. Same calluses along the base of his fingers from wielding shovels and sledgehammers and—

His cheeks heated when he remembered using the sledgehammer on his—on *Fletcher's* house, when Fletcher had told him the news. Not Rusty's proudest moment, but damn it, Fletcher had never said a word the entire time Rusty had been building the house. Gaia, they'd had sex on the air mattress in the wine cellar the day before the announcement when Earl, Fletcher's father and the clan leader, had smiled fulsomely as he'd introduced Sylvie, Fletcher's fiancée, and told the oh-so-charming story of how Fletcher and Sylvie had met at the last clan muster—the one Fletcher had sympathetically told Rusty to skip. *"You don't like the way they look at you, Rusty, you being inactive, so you might as well stay home. And bonus—I won't have to listen to your complaints afterward."*

So yeah, Fletcher had been courting Sylvie for almost a year and hadn't mentioned her to Rusty once.

His phone pinged with an incoming message, and Rusty picked it up to peer at the screen. He nearly threw it across the room again, because it was another text from Fletcher. He choked on a laugh. He didn't remember changing Fletcher's screen name to *Fuckhead*, but it certainly fit.

Fuckhead: Problem with guest bathroom shower. U need to look. B here at 1.

"Not a chance, fuckhead," he muttered as he plugged his phone into the charger. The last time Fletcher had insisted Rusty fix something at the house, he'd tried to yank Rusty into a closet and grab his junk, with his wife in the kitchen, FFS. Fletcher couldn't seem to get it through his thick, entitled head that what they'd had was over. The idiot assumed that since Rusty attended the wedding without a date—and hadn't *that* been a picnic—that he was still pining. *That would be a no.*

Rusty rubbed his chest. Last night's upset must not have faded, because he still felt…off. Although *not* because he was pining for Fletcher. He didn't even have the urge to take the sledgehammer to another wall in Fletcher's house. *Fuckhead's not worth the effort.*

Rusty glanced at the bed again, still rubbing his chest, some faded memory tickling at the back of his brain about a person who *was* worth the effort. But since Fletcher had been his first and only boyfriend, there weren't a lot of possible candidates. Or any, when it came down to it, since his one attempt to use a matchmaking service had failed spectacularly.

Shaking his head, he headed into the bathroom and turned on the shower, letting the water warm up while he brushed his teeth. As he rinsed his mouth out, from the corner of his eye he caught movement in the steam beyond the glass shower wall—a glimpse of pale, smooth skin and caramel-colored hair. He spat the mouthful of water into the sink, toothpaste foam dribbling on his chin as he turned, heart jerking in his chest.

But the stall was empty except for the steam.

Whatever. He stepped under the spray, idly wondering why he'd decided to sleep naked last night. It wasn't exactly balmy in Eugene in March, especially at night, and Rusty usually opted for sleep pants and a T-shirt. The only time he slept naked was when Fletcher had stayed over, and that hadn't happened for months. *And would never happen again.*

He hurried through his shower, deciding not to bother with his beard. It could last another day before a trim—it wasn't as though he needed to impress his crew with his grooming. Construction workers as a generic class weren't known for their personal fastidiousness, especially on the job site. Besides, at least half his crew were supes, mostly shifters, so they tended to be a bit shaggy on any given day, anyway.

Once he was dressed in jeans, a thermal Henley, and thick woolen socks, he made his way to the kitchen, squinting a little at the sunlight pouring through the glass door. *I need to lower the blackout shades before I leave.*

The dizziness returned for a moment and he gripped the edge of the counter, clenching his eyes shut. *What blackout shades? I don't have blackout shades.* The spell passed as quickly as it arrived, and he took a shaky breath. He straightened slowly, cracking open his eyes, but his vision wasn't blurry and the room stayed put. *Must be left over from whatever was going on last night.* Maybe food poisoning? Supes as a rule didn't succumb to food-related illnesses, but as an Inactive, Rusty's DNA was wonky.

He pulled the coffee beans out of the cupboard, making a mental note to ask his doctor about it at his next mandated physical, and automatically reaching for the electric coffee grinder. Once it was in his hand, though, he frowned at it. *Didn't I take that to the lake house?*

The vertigo struck again, because the house that rose clear as day in his mind's eye wasn't Fletcher's house. It was across the lake, a lovely Craftsman set back among the trees. On the shore, a small, neat structure at the head of a short dock—clearly not a boathouse since it didn't extend over the water—made Rusty's blood heat and his cock stiffen.

What the actual fuck?

He dumped extra beans into the grinder. "Because I need coffee." He rubbed his chest, trying to ease the pain under his heart. "And maybe a nice cup of ibuprofen."

Chapter Two

While his coffee machine did its number, the scent of dark roast scenting the air, Rusty strode back to the bathroom and rifled through his medicine chest. *Shit.* He was out of painkillers. He rubbed his chest again. Maybe it was indigestion? He popped a couple of antacids just to be sure and retrieved his phone from the charger. Only half juiced. He'd finish it off in the truck. But a glance at the screen told him he'd have enough time to stop at a convenience store for some Advil and still make it to the job site on time.

He returned to the kitchen and jammed his feet into the boots waiting by the back door, then filled his travel mug and slopped the rest of the coffee into his favorite OSU mug. With the bootlaces *click*ing on the tile underfoot, he yanked open the refrigerator and reached for the creamer, but his hand closed on the ketchup instead. For a moment, he just stared at the bottle, because it was *wrong*. Wrong for more than one reason. For one thing, his creamer should be *right there*, but instead it was on the other side of the shelf. For another, while there ought to be *red* in the fridge, it shouldn't be ketchup.

He put the ketchup back but rethought the creamer and slammed the fridge door. If he was hallucinating not just houses and blackout shades but random kitchen contents, he needed his coffee black today.

He knocked back the extra from the OSU cup, wincing at the heat and the bitterness, then stowed the cup in the dishwasher. He laced up his boots, shrugged into his down vest, and left the house with his travel mug in hand. He checked his truck bed, but it seemed normal, the tool box securely locked. He wondered if he should risk driving. What if the dizziness hit again while he was on the road? The twinge in his chest had faded, though, so maybe the antacids were doing the job.

Not taking a chance. He backed out of the driveway and headed for the convenience store at the end of the road as he sucked down half his coffee, driving slowly, just in case. He blew out a breath after he parked, because he felt... okay? Maybe still a little off-kilter, but nothing that affected his balance or vision. He probably just needed to wake up properly. Without question, he'd need more coffee. He swished his half-full mug, grimacing. The idea of topping it up and polluting his druid-blessed beans with convenience store swill set his teeth on edge, but if it meant getting his head on straight, he'd do it.

Walking into the store, he nodded at the latest in a rotating cast of clerks on his way to the over-the-counter meds section. He grabbed the largest bottle of Advil on the shelf, then headed for the coffee station. He glanced at his travel mug. *Nope. Not gonna pollute it.* He used one of the store's extra-large insulated cups instead. *Backup caffeine. Break out only in emergencies.*

At the checkout counter, he took his place behind a glassy-eyed guy in a business suit who was buying a coffee as large as Rusty's, along with a Slim Jim and a giant brownie. Rusty chuckled under his breath. *Not exactly breakfast of champions, dude.*

While Rusty waited for the guy to wrestle his debit card out of his wallet, his gaze drifted to the wire newsstand next to a rack of candy bars and chewing gum. The headline screamed *Bigfoot Sighted in Coast Range!* Rusty snorted. *Bigfoot, my ass.* Any supe could tell the figure in the grainy photo was a bear shifter in partial shift. He idly scanned the sidebar headlines and—

"What the fuck?" He nearly fumbled both his coffees. He set them on the counter and snatched the top paper off the stack as the guy ahead of him staggered out the door with his giant cup and sketchy snacks. But even holding it closer to his face didn't change the words: *Search for Archie Ellis Called Off.* "Archie Ellis is missing again?"

The cashier raised his bushy eyebrows. "What do you mean again? He disappeared months ago and he's been gone ever since."

The cashier's scruffy face swam in Rusty's vision and the Advil dropped from his numb fingers. He swayed, the floor seeming to tilt under his feet.

"Hey, man. You okay? 'Cause if you're gonna hurl—" The clerk thrust a ladle, a key dangling from a chain attached to its handle, at Rusty. "Here. Use the restroom."

Rusty braced his hands on the counter and tried to corral his galloping breath. *This is wrong. Something's wrong.* Archie shouldn't be missing. He should be… Should be…

"Mister? You're not, like, drunk, are you? Because I gotta tell you, it's a little early. Not that I'm judging."

Although the floor hadn't returned to level yet, Rusty managed to glower at the cashier, whose name tag read *Jason.* "I'm not drunk, and I'm not going to vomit." *I hope.* "Are you sure about Archie Ellis?"

Jason scoffed and pointed at the paper. "It's in the news. It's gotta be true, right?"

Rusty refrained from rolling his eyes because it would make his dizziness worse. "The lead story was about Bigfoot."

Jason shrugged. "So?"

Rusty pushed himself off the counter, widening his stance to keep himself steady. Maybe Jason's somewhat laissez-faire attitude toward factual reporting wasn't completely off the mark. Maybe the search was called off because Archie was never missing. *But if that's the case, why would they have been looking for him in the first place?* He picked up the paper and rifled through the pages, looking for the story.

"Hey! This ain't a library. You want to read the news, you gotta buy the paper."

"Right. Right. Sorry." Rusty tossed the paper next to his coffee and retrieved the Advil from where it had rolled between an ice cream chest and the lottery machine. As soon as Jason rang him up, he paid and lurched for the door.

"Have a nice day," the cashier called as the door tinkled closed.

"Nice day," he muttered as he climbed into the truck. "Not likely."

As he settled the cardboard cup in the holder next to his travel mug, it happened again. Dizziness, the pain in his chest, labored breathing, roiling belly. Because the cup holder shouldn't be empty. It should already be full. For his passenger.

He glanced at the empty passenger seat, and just for an instant, a pale oval face glimmered there, lips spread in a smile with very prominent canines.

Then, in a blink, he was alone in the truck again.

Chapter Three

He dropped the cup in the holder and rested his head against the steering wheel. "Fuck. What is wrong with me?" But something in the back of his mind whispered that he was fine and the *world* was wrong.

"And if I'm starting to get paranoid as well as delusional, no way can I operate any heavy machinery today."

He grabbed his cell phone and speed-dialed his foreman. "Hey, Octavio. It's me."

"Hey, man. Ready for the Del Santo job? At least it's not raining, right?"

"Yeah, about that." Rusty took a deep breath. "I'm, um, not... That is, I... Well, the thing is..." Another whisper in his mind: *"Elmer, use your words."*

WTF? His mother was the only one who ever called him Elmer. She'd never said that to him and that was *not* her voice he heard in his mental ears. *I'm losing it.* Rusty cleared his throat. "I have to head into Hillsboro for a... a meeting. Could you run the job site for me today?"

"Sure thing, Rusty. Anytime."

"Great." He swallowed. "I'll check in with you later. Call if you need me."

Rusty disconnected the call and cut a glance at the newspaper lying on the passenger seat. He picked it up as though it were a live wire and stared at the Bigfoot photo. *Bear shifter.* That matchmaking agency had paired him with a bear shifter. In fact, the guy—what was his name? Ted?—was supposed to attend Fletcher's wedding with him, but something had happened and he'd canceled. Or rather, the agency had canceled on his behalf when they'd discontinued their services, which was why Rusty ended up going stag and feeding Fletcher's already inflated ego.

He peered more closely at the front page. A credit was printed under the photo in minuscule type: *Photo by Matt Steinitz.*

He frowned. If he contacted the paper, would they give him Steinitz's contact info? If he called Matt, maybe he could find out—

"I really am going off the deep end." He let his head fall back against the headrest. Steinitz was just the photographer. Of a fake Bigfoot sighting. Why would he know anything about Archie Ellis's disappearance? That story didn't even have a picture, so why was Rusty somehow certain that Steinitz had the answer?

He eyed his phone again. He shouldn't waste time calling the paper, even assuming they'd give out Steinitz's contact information. He knew exactly who he should call, because these feelings, these symptoms, were not normal for a supe.

But then, Rusty wasn't a normal supe. He was an Inactive. And whatever was going on with him right now was probably related to his condition. Two weeks ago, he'd had his mandated quarterly check-in with Dr. Alun Kendrick, the go-to psychologist for the supe community, but Dr. Kendrick had always stressed that Rusty could call him any time with any concerns.

Concerns? Yeah, you could say I've got a few of those. He picked up his phone and placed the call.

"Good morning." At the unfamiliar woman's voice, Rusty disconnected the call. How had he gotten the number wrong? The number was in the damn contact record, for the love of Gaia. But he'd been seeing Dr. Kendrick since he was a kit, once it became obvious he'd never shift, and he'd *never* heard that voice. In fact… He squinted through the windshield at a faded poster for Monster Energy® drinks. Shouldn't a man be answering the office phone?

Was that one more delusion? Shit, Rusty *really* needed to talk to the doctor. Then he smacked his forehead. It was just past seven. It was probably the answering service. He tried again.

"Good morning. Dr. Kendrick's office. This is Brina. How may I help you?"

"This is Rusty Johnson. I'm a longtime client of Dr. Kendrick's. I was wondering if he had time to see me today? It's kind of an emergency."

"Of course, Mr. Johnson. We're always happy to see you."

They were? She was? "Oh. I'm, um, in Eugene at the moment, so it'll take me a while to get up to the office." Especially since he'd be taking the drive *really* slow. For an instant, he was certain there was another way, a quicker way to make the trip, but the thought vanished as quickly as it arrived. Besides, what other method could there be?

"Will eleven o'clock suit you?"

That would give him about four hours to make a two-hour drive. Sounded about right. "Yes. That would be perfect."

"Excellent. We'll see you then."

He stared at the phone for a moment after the call ended. Why would the answering service see him? He shook his head. It was probably just a figure of speech. He tried not to think about it, in case it brought on another bout of dizziness. In fact… He stuffed the newspaper under the seat, well out of sight. He cracked open the Advil and downed three—his usual dose—dry. By the time he'd swallowed the rest of the coffee in his travel mug and half the nasty convenience store brew, he hadn't had another dizzy spell, although the dull pain in his chest persisted.

Still, his vision was clear and his head wasn't spinning. He'd take it. He pulled out of the parking spot and started the slow drive to Hillsboro.

Chapter Four

By the time he pulled into a spot in front of Dr. Kendrick's office, Rusty was feeling decidedly foolish. He'd had no trouble on the drive. Yeah, that little twinge under his heart hadn't vanished, but it was annoying rather than debilitating. After he spoke to Dr. Kendrick, he could always stop by St. Stupid's, the supe-only wing of United Memorial Hospital, and have them check him out. Of course, he could probably get that taken care of right here at Dr. Kendrick's office since—

The wash of disorientation that swept over him this time made Rusty gag. He grabbed the steering wheel and tucked his chin down, teeth gritted, as his stomach tried to crawl up his throat. *Breathe. Breathe. Think about subfloors. Joists. Stair treads.* Nice, flat, level things that didn't spin like a freaking vortex of doom.

The nausea gradually faded, and he relaxed his death grip. Thank Gaia he hadn't had an attack on the way up here, but this one clinched it: He was taking an Uber to St. Stupid's if Dr. Kendrick couldn't help, and if the medimagical staff couldn't fix him up, he was staying overnight at a hotel. No way was he getting on the road again until he knew what the hells was wrong with him.

He leaned back in the seat, eyes closed, counting his slow inhales and exhales, until he'd returned to a more or less even keel. *The office door is only ten feet away. I can do this.*

As he grabbed the door handle, his gaze caught the corner of the newspaper peeking out from under the seat. As much as he didn't want to look at it again, he retrieved it and stuffed it into the inner pocket of his vest. Dr. Kendrick kept abreast of news in both human and supe communities. He'd be a much more reliable source than the paper's help line.

Rusty climbed out of the truck, giving himself a mental high five when he remained steady on his feet, and entered the building. The office was only one flight up, but he took the elevator, just in case. Supes were sturdy, even inactive ones, but Rusty had no desire to take a header down the stairs if he had another dizzy spell halfway up.

The floor behaved itself in the elevator and when he stepped into the hallway. But when he opened Dr. Kendrick's office door and spotted the unfamiliar woman behind the desk, he literally fell on his ass. He clapped both hands over his face, but light and shadow continued to revolve behind his eyelids. *Subfloors. Joists. Stair treads. Subfloors. Joists. Stair treads.*

"Rusty?" Dr. Kendrick's usually soothing voice was edged with worry. "Are you all right?"

"Fine," he managed to croak through his spasming throat. *Subfloors. Joists. Stair treads.* He took a deep, shaky breath. "Well, not fine, since I just ass-planted on your carpet." Experimentally, he lifted one hand and blinked at his knees. Dots danced in his vision, but at least he had the usual number of legs and they weren't doing a metaphysical cha cha. But when he risked dropping both hands and peering up at Dr. Kendrick, his jaw sagged and—

The next thing he knew, he was flat on his back, staring up at the ceiling tiles. Dr. Kendrick was sitting on a chair at his side, gazing down at him. *With a monster's face.*

Rusty clamped his lips together before he blurted out anything rude or inappropriate, but this was *wrong*. Not because of the doctor's appearance per se—not all supes fit human standards of ordinary beauty—but because his face should be *different* now. And it wasn't.

Dr. Kendrick's eyes, shadowed under the craggy brow ridges, were kind. "Do you think you could make it into my office with a little help?"

"Yeah. Sorry about this."

"Nothing to be sorry about." He stood and glanced toward the receptionist's desk. "Brina, could you bring Mr. Johnson a glass of water, please?"

"Of course, Doctor."

Dr. Kendrick extended a hand to Rusty. "Up you get. Slowly, though. Lean on me."

Rusty allowed himself to be pulled to his feet—and yes, he did need to lean on Dr. Kendrick, who was about his height, with the musculature of a fae warrior, since that's what he'd been before he was cursed.

Brina emerged from the inner office. "Water is on the table, Doctor. Please let me know if you need anything more." She took her place behind the reception desk as Dr. Kendrick helped Rusty inside and settled him on the love seat.

Rusty glanced at her once more—another dizzy spell, but not as severe—as Dr. Kendrick closed the door. "I, um, expected somebody else out there."

Dr. Kendrick settled himself in the wingback chair across the low table from Rusty. "Vanessa's on maternity leave for another three months. Although between you and me, I suspect she may decide to stay home with Sasha for a while longer, at least as long as her husband is still deployed." He nodded toward the crystal tumbler on its marble coaster. "Please. Drink. You look as though you could use it."

Rusty obediently picked up the glass and took a swig, although he was still reeling. Vanessa wasn't who he'd expected to see, either. But who *had* he expected? He sighed as he set the glass down, movement once again hitching when his gaze snagged on his left hand. He forced himself to sit back and lace his fingers together in his lap.

Were Dr. Kendrick's hazel eyes worried? It was hard for Rusty to tell, because the doctor's face wasn't easy to read. *But it used to be.*

Didn't it?

He scrubbed his hands across his face and then just left them there, pressing tight from forehead to chin, because he couldn't trust his eyes anymore.

"Rusty, suppose you tell me what's brought you here today."

Sighing again, Rusty dropped his hands to his lap. He met Dr. Kendrick's gaze once again with that jolt of *wrongness*. But since both the doctor and Brina—whom Rusty was almost certain he'd never met before—acted as though it was a perfectly ordinary day, clearly the wrongness was with Rusty.

But then, it always had been.

"To tell you the truth, Doctor, I'm not really sure. I woke up in the night, feeling dizzy and nauseated."

"So it's a physical issue?"

Rusty spread his hands, palms up. "Yes and no? The dizziness has hit again periodically all morning."

Dr. Kendrick's gaze sharpened. "The nausea too?"

"Yes. And a pain." Rusty laid a finger on his chest, just under his heart. "Right here."

"Are you experiencing these symptoms at the moment?"

"Not the dizziness or nausea, but the pain is still there. Not sharp. More a dull ache."

Okay, this time he couldn't mistake the worry on Dr. Kendrick's face. "You realize that's where your *calon* is located."

Rusty blinked. He never thought much about his *calon*, the extra organ that every supe possessed, the seat of their supernatural nature. Mostly because his had betrayed him, something about it preventing him from shifting. "So you think it might have something to do with me being inactive?"

"Possibly. Any other symptoms?"

Rusty swallowed thickly. "I'm… seeing things."

Dr. Kendrick's brows bunched, which, given the size of the ridge they sat on, made a statement. "What kind of things?"

"Just…" Rusty grabbed the water and took another gulp. "Glimpses. Out of the corner of my eye. Like afterimages. Photo overlays. Those whatchamacallems—Pepper's ghost effects, like at Disney's Haunted Mansion."

Dr. Kendrick steepled his fingers. "Mmmphmmm."

"And something's wrong with my memory." He reached inside his vest, pulled out the crumpled newspaper, and laid it on the table with a futile attempt to smooth the creases. He tapped the sidebar headline. "Archie Ellis. It says they called off the search but—"

"When did you get this?"

The sharpness in Dr. Kendrick's voice brought Rusty's head up with a jerk. "At a convenience store in Eugene."

"*When?*"

"Today. Right before I called you."

Right in front of Rusty's eyes, Dr. Kendrick… deflated. "Damn."

"Is something the matter?" *Please say yes. Please say you know what it is.*

Dr. Kendrick's massive shoulders rose in a sigh. "Many things." He tapped the Bigfoot photo. "This is one of my clients, a bear shifter. He's already under sanction for his involvement in the death of a dynastic incubus. He'd promised that he'd stopped the Sasquatch impersonations last fall, but if he's at it again, the council has threatened to form-lock him."

"F-form-lock? As a human or a bear?"

Dr. Kendrick's full lips pressed together in a grim line. "Bear."

"Shit," Rusty muttered. He studied Dr. Kendrick's face. "Is there something else wrong, Doctor? I know you're the therapist, not me, but you've looked"—*wrong*—"worried since I walked in, and I don't think it's just on my account."

"You're very perceptive, Rusty. But then, I've always believed that your clan in general, and you in particular, underestimate your abilities." He rested his hands on the chair arms, but his fingers dented the brocade. "I may need to step back as your therapist, in fact."

"What? Why?"

"I may have to leave the area. Things are... unsettled in Faerie. The Queen's illness hasn't responded to treatment, and the Consort is assuming more authority. The Unseelie court is, well, living up to their tenets, particularly with regard to chaos."

"So it's politics that's got you upset?"

Dr. Kendrick's mouth twisted. "I've personal issues, too. My brother Gareth is determined to sever his link to the One Tree."

Rusty's eyes widened and he inhaled sharply. "But won't that make him..."

"Mortal? Yes. But his grief over his lost love has overtaken him. He doesn't want to face millennia with the same pain."

"Can't you talk him out of it?"

"Me?" Dr. Kendrick lifted one eyebrow. "My dear Rusty, Gareth would hardly take my advice. He hasn't spoken to me voluntarily in two hundred years."

Chapter Five

Spots danced in front of Rusty's eyes again. *No. That's wrong. The Kendrick brothers are... are...* What? He gritted his teeth, willing the spots to dissipate. Nobody knew better than Rusty that the definition of *family* could be problematical, but since when did he care about Dr. Kendrick's brothers personally? He didn't—

"Rusty? Rusty!"

The doctor's misshapen head swam back into focus. "Yeah. I'm..." *Not okay.* He grabbed his water again and gulped it down so he wouldn't have to finish that sentence.

Dr. Kendrick's lips flattened. "I'm quite concerned about your symptoms, Rusty. Taken as a whole, I don't believe they're anything I can adequately treat." He rose and walked to his desk. "I want you to speak with Dr. Mori, the head of the diagnostic department at United Memorial." He pulled open a drawer and withdrew a little square of thick, cream-colored paper. "In the meantime, this is a mild anti-anxiety spell."

He strode back to Rusty and handed him the piece of parchment. "Just press your finger against the rune and say *dawelu*. It's good for three uses, but not more than once every six hours. I'm sure Dr. Mori will have a more targeted medimagical option for you."

Rusty stood and took the paper numbly. "Thank you, Doctor."

Dr. Kendrick gripped Rusty's shoulder. "Try not to worry. Whether I'm forced to close my practice or not, be assured that I'll arrange for your continued treatment. It will be all right."

But will it? And will it be all right for you? "Thank you."

"Perhaps it would be best if you stayed in town for the time being. I don't want you behind the wheel until your dizzy spells are stabilized."

"Right. I'll take an Uber to St. Stupid's—I mean United Memorial—and check into a hotel if things don't get better."

"Good. Good." He ushered Rusty to the door. "I'll call Dr. Mori immediately. She's quite busy, but I'll stress the urgency of your case. You can expect to hear from me within the hour."

Rusty walked out into the lobby, Dr. Kendrick closing his office door softly at his back.

Brina smiled up at him from behind her desk. "Oh, Mr. Johnson. This came for you while you were with Dr. Kendrick." She held out a small manila envelope.

"For me? Here?" Rusty accepted it gingerly. "Nobody knew I'd be here. Hells, *I* didn't even know I'd be here until this morning."

She shrugged. "It arrived by special messenger. And it's clearly addressed to you."

Rusty peered at the return address. The sender's name was smudged, but he could make out the town. "I don't know anybody in Dewton. Who'd be sending me something from there?" And to his therapist's office, for Gaia's sake?

Brina shrugged again, rather helplessly. "I couldn't say. But since it's here and so are you, I guess that's serendipitous." She smiled, a little mischievously. "Then again, we're supes, Mr. Johnson. If somebody wanted to find you, they could always consult an oracle."

"I guess so." He lifted the envelope in a halfhearted goodbye salute. "Thank you."

"Of course. Have a lovely day."

He trudged out of the office and down the stairs. After he climbed into his truck, he simply stared out the windshield for a moment, at the humans strolling along the sidewalk, all of them completely unaware that supes lived among them.

He glanced down at the items in his hand. The spell beckoned, but since Rusty wasn't experiencing any severe symptoms at the moment, he set it aside on the passenger seat. Instead, he tore open the envelope and drew out a tri-folded paper, one edge ragged as though it had been torn out of a spiral notebook. When he unfolded it, a tiny wrapped packet about the size of his thumbnail dropped into his lap.

The letter—if you could call it that—only had three words on it:

You need this.

He flipped it over and looked at the back. Nothing. Just those three words: *You need this.*

What I need is to figure out what the fuck is wrong with me.

He picked up the tiny packet. It took him what seemed like forever to undo the wrapping, his fingers feeling huge and clumsy. When he undid the final fold, something fell between his legs and disappeared under his ass. Cursing, he lifted one cheek and dug around until he touched something small, round, and metal.

"Gotcha." He scrabbled it into his hand, thankful his truck's tinted windows prevented passersby from peering in, since he probably looked like he was trying to fist himself.

He uncurled his fingers. In his palm lay a ring. Not just any ring. A platinum wedding band. Rusty's lungs seized, his head swam, and his hand shook as he raised the ring closer to his eyes. But not even the dizziness and trembling kept him from reading the inscription:

Cas & Rusty. A perfect match.

Rusty doubled over, the ring clutched tight in his fist, drowning in heat and loss and longing.

Casimir.

Chapter Six

Gasping, tears leaking down his cheeks to wet his beard, Rusty slid the ring on. The instant it was seated at the base of his finger, it all came back, crashing over him, in him, through him: meeting Cas the first time, their fake marriage bargain, their first kiss, their first fuck. Despite the grief hollowing his chest, Rusty's cock thickened at the memory of Cas's fangs at his throat.

My lover. My husband. My perfect match. A match they'd fought for so desperately that they'd taken an extreme, risky step, a last-ditch effort to escape the disaster bearing down on them.

He pounded the steering wheel so hard the truck rocked, much to the alarm of a couple wheeling their baby past in a stroller. "That's it. That's what's happened. Someone's time-surfed."

Rusty had done it to save Casimir, to save Archie Ellis from being turned into a vampire fledgling by that asshole Henryk Skalding. Dr. Bryce MacLeod, the druid who was the only other person Rusty knew who'd time-surfed, had warned him that there could be side effects, including a sensitivity to what the professor had called footprints in time.

But who had done it this time? And more importantly, what had they changed, because it was obviously something fundamental? Bryce was clearly the person to consult, but before Rusty sought him out, he needed someone else.

He needed *Cas*.

So what if Cas didn't remember him at first? Rusty had wooed and won him a second time after Rusty had surfed time to prevent Archie from meeting Cas and starting the chain of events that led to them meeting at the matchmaking agency, Supernatural Selection.

He started the truck and threw it in gear. "If I did it twice, I can do it again."

He peeled out of his parking spot, his head perfectly clear, although his *calon* still ached. *No, not my* calon. *My heart.* He didn't have the time to get pulled over by the human cops, so on his way to Cas's house in the West Hills, he kept within the posted limits. Mostly.

When he reached Cas's neighborhood, he whimpered with relief, because there it was: the high wall, the wrought-iron gate, the security keypad. He pulled up to the entrance, laughing breathlessly as he keyed in the code, the one he'd given Cas grief about because it was so freaking obvious.

Three-two-six-four. FANG.

The indicator light stayed red and the gate didn't budge. Frowning, Rusty keyed it in again. Again, nothing happened. Okay, maybe Cas had changed the code after all.

He caught sight of the front door opening, so he climbed out of the truck and approached the gate, gripping the bars with both hands.

The person who emerged wasn't Casimir. It was a thirty-something woman in workout clothing. Rusty grimaced. It was the middle of the day. Of course it wouldn't be Cas. Without Rusty, without Rusty's *blood*, Cas couldn't be out in the sun. He was a vampire, for fuck's sake.

"Excuse me?" Rusty called. "Is Casimir awake?"

Her head jerked up from where she was locking the door. "Who are you?"

"I'm a... friend of Casimir's." *Or I will be.* "I really need to talk to him. Is he awake?"

Sympathy replaced the suspicion on her round face. "I'm so sorry. Do you mean Mr. Moreau?"

Rusty nodded, trying not to plaster himself against the gate. "Yes. Casimir. May I speak with him? Or if he's asleep, I don't mind waiting. I can wait out here. In my truck. I won't bother anybody."

She crossed the bridge spanning the Zen rock garden and walked toward him, although she kept well out of his reach. "Mr. Moreau was the previous owner. My wife and I purchased the house at the estate sale."

Rusty's hands were blocks of ice. "Estate?"

"I'm so very sorry. But Mr. Moreau is dead."

"No," Rusty croaked. "He can't be." *He's more alive than anyone I know. He makes* me *feel alive.*

"I'm really very sorry. Would you like the name of the lawyer who handled the estate? Maybe she might—"

"No. Thank you. But no." Somehow, on legs that seemed like they were at once too long and too short to reach the ground, Rusty stumbled back to his truck. He had to try three times before his numb fingers could grasp the door handle and he could drag himself behind the wheel.

Casimir. Gaia, Casimir. What happened?

Chapter Seven

His cell phone rang from the passenger seat. "Go away," Rusty said, his voice as broken as his heart. He caught Dr. Kendrick's name splashed on the screen, and though the doctor wasn't anyone who could help him, now that he knew what the real problem was, he couldn't very well ignore him. He answered the call.

"Yeah?" he said dully.

"Hello, Rusty. Dr. Kendrick here. Dr. Mori will see you at four this afternoon."

"Thanks."

"Rusty?" Dr. Kendrick's voice morphed from brisk and businesslike to concerned. "Are you all right? Have the symptoms gotten worse?"

Fuck the symptoms. The *world* was worse. "Dr. Kendrick. This might sound like an odd question, but you mentioned problems in Faerie earlier. Have there been issues in other parts of the supe community?"

"Interesting that you should ask that. There's been some upheaval with the werewolves. It seems the prospective alpha of the Wallowa pack has gone missing from his Howling Residence. The archdruid from this region passed on and the local circle is therefore hobbled by having only six members instead of seven. And the Sheol C-suite demons have decided to pull the plug on the work release program, despite my recommendations to the contrary."

"What about the… the vampires?"

Dr. Kendrick's heavy sigh was clearly audible. "Since their clan chief met the sun last summer—"

Rusty sucked in a breath. "Kristof Czardos was murdered?"

"Murdered? No, of course not. He was unable to feed, so he made the choice to greet the sun. Duly witnessed by representatives of the supe council, including me." He sighed again. "But his Second Death left a bit of a power vacuum in the vampire hierarchy, and by the time the dust settled, they'd lost several more of their number. Considering there are so few of them to begin with, I was sorry that they couldn't come to a less… final resolution."

"W-who did they lose?"

"Irina Dragelescu, the person Kristof had chosen for his successor. A fledgling who never recovered from a brief sun exposure shortly after his Turn. And Casimir Moreau, who was convicted of creating that fledgling illegally."

"He didn't," Rusty growled.

"I beg your pardon?"

"Nothing. Sorry. I've got to go."

"Very well. Be sure to keep that appointment. I'm very concerned about you."

"Yeah. Sure. Thanks." Rusty hung up before a buried sob could choke him. *Casimir. And Archie.* But with what Dr. Kendrick had just told him, Rusty's grief and denial were only part of the bigger picture. All the progress the supe community had made over the last months had been completely wiped out. What the fuck had *happened*?

Rusty only knew one person who might know, who might be able to help. He threw the truck in gear and burned rubber back to Hillsboro. When he reached Bryce MacLeod's house, he'd barely braked to a stop in the driveway before turning off the engine and leaping out of the cab.

He raced up the sidewalk and banged on the door. When nobody answered immediately, he pounded on it again. Was the professor teaching? If Rusty remembered his schedule correctly, his office hours were in the evening, as were many of his classes. If he—

The door cracked open and Bryce peered out at him, the lenses of his glasses glinting in the sun reflecting off Rusty's windshield. Bryce's dark hair was never precisely neat—he had that whole absent-minded professor thing going on—but today it looked as though he'd styled it with an eggbeater.

"Rusty? What are you doing here?" He ran a hand through his hair, making it stick up even more. "It's not my practice to see students—especially former students—at my home."

"I know, Bryce." When Bryce raised his eyebrows, Rusty backtracked. "I mean, Professor. But this is really important."

Bryce sighed. "I'm sorry. But this isn't a good time."

You're telling me. "I know, but—"

"If this has anything to do with your academic interests at the college, you'd be better off checking in with the dean. I've resigned my post for… medical reasons."

"Shit, are you sick?"

Bryce's glance cut to the side and he paled. "In a manner of speaking."

Rusty braced his hands on the door frame. "You're seeing things that aren't there, right? Maybe a dark-haired man with blue eyes and a snarky grin?"

Bryce's eyes widened. "How did you—" But then he shook his head. "I'm sorry, Rusty, but I'm really not up to conversation. If you wish to speak with me, make an appointment with the college and I'll fit you in before my last day."

"But—"

"Goodbye." He shut the door.

Rusty let his forehead thunk against the wood. "Fuck." Whatever had happened had prevented Bryce from discovering his druid nature. He wouldn't know about time-surfing. He wouldn't have the potion Rusty needed to ride another wave.

Even assuming I knew when to go.

He trudged back to the truck. *I need a drink.* Or maybe ten. Hells, twenty-three. And if he was going to get totally shit-faced, he ought to do it in the company of other supes, not humans, so he put the truck back in gear and pointed it toward the Bullpen.

Chapter Eight

The Bullpen wasn't too busy in the middle of a weekday, but it wasn't empty either. Rusty recognized one person right away. Mal Kendrick was hunched on a barstool, a glass of amber liquid cradled between his hands.

Rusty took the stool to Mal's left. "Is that mead or whiskey?"

Mal didn't bother to look up. "Not interested, mate."

"I'm not hitting on you, Mal. I'm looking for a drink recommendation. The stronger, the better."

At that, Mal cut a glance at him in exactly the same way Bryce had done. "They've got duergar holly ale."

"I want to get drunk, not comatose."

Mal flagged the bartender down and pointed to his drink and to Rusty. "What's your excuse for day drinking?"

"Lost someone."

Mal snorted as the bartender delivered Rusty's drink. "Join the club." He held up his glass, and Rusty clinked it with his own. "Although in my case, it's a future loss. One at my own hand." He took a gulp of his drink, which must have burned all the way down, considering his wince. "Bloody Consort."

Rusty sipped his own drink. Macallan. Yeah, this would do the trick. Eventually. "Your brother said there were some political issues in Faerie."

Mal's shoulders hunched. "Politics. That's one word for it. Complete and utter shite is what I'd call it."

"Want to talk about it?"

Mal glared at him. "Not likely. Not when I've got to arrest my own brother. *Execute* my own brother."

Rusty's jaw sagged. "You have to execute Gareth?"

"Not Gareth. Alun. On the Consort's orders, as an oath-breaker."

"But—"

"Not *interested*," Mal barked, glaring at someone on his other side, someone hidden from Rusty by Mal's massive shoulders. He tossed back the rest of his drink. "Sorry for your loss, mate, whatever it was, but I've got my own problems right now." He pushed off his stool and stalked across the bar, yanked the door open, and stepped outside.

Rusty gaped after him. Mal was supposed to *execute* Dr. Kendrick? Was *that* why the doctor had said he couldn't be Rusty's therapist anymore?

The guy who'd approached Mal before his sudden exit sighed brokenly. Apparently, everybody was having a bad day —a *really* bad day. Rusty studied the guy over the rim of his glass. He wasn't more than a kid, really, brown hair flopping over his forehead.

Wait. I know this kid.

"You're a little young for the Bullpen, Jordan," Rusty said before making a closer acquaintance with the bottom of his glass.

Jordan spun to face him with a gasp, nearly falling off his barstool. "Mr. Johnson! You recognize me?"

"Of course. You and your Howling pack crashed my..." Rusty couldn't bring himself to say *wedding*. Not when Casimir was dead.

"But Mal didn't. It was like he'd never even *seen* me before. He barely *looked* at me."

"There's a lot of that going around," Rusty said, signaling for another drink for himself and a soda for Jordan.

Jordan shot him a shaky smile when the bartender set a Coke in front of him. "Thanks, Mr. Johnson." He jostled the ice with his straw.

"What's your excuse for day soft-drinking?"

"I did something really stupid," Jordan muttered into his glass, "and now everything's *wrong*."

Rusty snorted. "Tell me about it."

"Okay." Jordan swiveled on his stool. "Well, it started the other day." He scrunched up his face. "Well, maybe before that."

Rusty sighed. Apparently Jordan was going to take his comment literally. He set his empty glass aside and started on his second drink. "Uh huh."

"Dakota and Gage, they were talking about this club they'd been to. Not Hector. He didn't go because that was one of his gaming nights, and Chase didn't because he's *Chase*, and he'd never do anything sketchy, and of course Tanner would never do anything Chase wouldn't like, but Dakota and Gage *definitely* would."

Rusty's vision was starting to blur from the alcohol rather than hallucinations. "Your friends went to a club? While they were underage?"

Jordan gave him an overly innocent look. "It was a *human* club. And you can go if you're eighteen, you just can't drink."

"So why didn't you go?"

"They went the week before I moved into the Doghouse. I mean, the Portland Howling Residence. But they talked and talked and *talked* about it, how cool it was in the club, and how great the band was, and how this near brawl had broken out between a couple of guys who wanted to dance with this same man, even though Dakota said the man was the worst dancer he'd *ever* seen. But anyway, I just wanted to see it for myself. You know?"

"So you went to the club last night?"

Jordan gazed at him, his brown eyes wide. "No. You don't get it. I went to the club *that* night."

Chapter Nine

Rusty dropped his glass, and it tipped over onto the bar, the dregs of his second whiskey spilling across the wood. He grabbed a handful of bar napkins to mop it up, but the bartender waved him away. "Don't worry, sir. I've got this."

Rusty gripped Jordan's wrist. "C'mere." He towed him off the barstool to a table in the corner. "Sit." Jordan plopped down, and Rusty pulled another chair next to him. "Are you saying you *time-surfed*?"

Jordan's eyes widened. "You *know* about that?"

"Yeah. I've done it myself." Rusty scrubbed his hands through his hair, wishing he hadn't downed that second drink. Or the first, for that matter. If he'd been less impaired, he'd have realized that he shouldn't have recognized Jordan. They hadn't met until the day of Rusty and Cas's wedding. Which, in this timeline, hadn't happened because Cas was fucking *dead*. He stared into Jordan's eyes. "This is really important, Jordan. *What did you do?*"

Jordan gulped. "Well, I was kind of whining about it one day at the Doghouse, and this guy, he and his brother had come in to upgrade our internet so Hector would have better bandwidth for his games."

Rusty took a deep breath to control his temper. "The Purls? Ferret shifters?"

Jordan blinked. "Yeah. How did you know?"

"They've worked for me before."

"Oh. So anyway, one of them—"

"I'm guessing Ronnie."

"Yes, that was his name. He said he had something that would let me go back and join the guys in the club, so of course I said yes." He peered at Rusty from under his floppy hair. "Pretty stupid, huh?"

"Never mind that. What happened then?"

"Well, he sold me this potion. It took my entire allowance, so I had to call my mom and ask for an advance so I could buy a new outfit. I didn't have any clubbing clothes, you know?"

Rusty pinched the bridge of his nose. "Jordan. You can't wear any clothes when you time-surf."

"Well, I know that *now*! But Ronnie didn't say so, only that it wouldn't last long, so I waited until I was in the alley next to the club before I took the potion." He sighed. "I was so excited. I could picture the whole thing in my mind—how I'd stroll out of the alley, all nonchalant, and surprise the guys in the queue so we could all go inside together. And it worked. Sort of. As soon as I drank it, there—I mean *then*—I was. Except..." He glanced around and lowered his voice. "*Naked*. And just then, there was a guy coming down the alley. When he saw me, he was so startled he flailed and tripped over a... well, over nothing. But he broke his ankle." Jordan bit his lip. "I wanted to help him, but I was, you know, *naked*, and before I could do anything, I was back to now. Or rather then. I mean last night. In the alley. Still naked, because my clothes were just *gone*, which was really awkward, you know? Although at least my phone was still there. It had fallen under a dumpster. So I called Hector to bring me something to wear because I knew *he* wouldn't laugh at me."

The hair lifted on Rusty's nape. "Jordan. Did you recognize the man?"

Jordan nodded. "It was David," he whispered. "David Evans. The *achubydd* who's married to Dr. Kendrick."

"Except now he's not." Rusty had heard the stories about how David and Dr. Kendrick had met. But if David had never temped for Dr. Kendrick, then...

Holy shit. Dr. Kendrick would still be cursed. The Consort's treasonous plot would still be in play. Mal wouldn't know Bryce, who'd still be ignorant of his druid nature. Gareth's lover, Niall, would still be imprisoned and his brother still cursed. The old Unseelie King would still be in power—hells, the list went on and on.

David was the linchpin, the catalyst, the first toppling domino in the cascade of recent changes. Somehow, they needed to undo what Jordan had done, because without David, their whole world had gone to fucking hell.

"Jordan." Rusty scooted his chair around to he could lean his elbows on his knees as he faced the young werewolf. "Listen very carefully. We've got to rewind. Know what I'm saying?"

Jordan nodded emphatically. "Go back and keep David from falling."

Rusty swore under his breath. "We can't go anywhere without more time-surfing potion, and the only person I know who could make it doesn't even know he's a druid anymore."

"You mean Professor MacLeod?"

Rusty nodded. "The very same. Although I can't see Bryce selling any black market potions to Ronnie Purl, of all people." He drummed his fingers on his knee.

"Mr. Johnson? If you don't mind my asking... How come you can remember how things ought to be, and so can I, but nobody else can?"

Rusty sighed. "From what Bryce told me before my first surf, the person who takes the potion, who effects the change, can remember both timelines, at least partially. And people who have surfed before have a... a sensitivity to any change, I guess." That's why both he and Bryce were being tormented by visions—they'd both surfed, so they had the sensitivity, but since they hadn't made *this* change, they didn't have the whole picture. Rusty glanced down at his left hand. *I didn't have the whole picture until I put my ring back on.* Whoever had sent it to him had gotten it right—he *needed* this ring, for more reasons than one. "Did Ronnie have more than one potion?"

Jordan shrugged. "I don't know. I could only afford one, so it's not like it mattered to me."

"Did he sell you the potion at the Doghouse?"

"No. He didn't have it with him. He told me to meet him here." He pointed to the floor. "Downstairs, in the storeroom on the way to the fight pens. He said he does most of his business here."

"I can believe that," Rusty muttered. He never could understand how a stand-up guy like Devin could end up with a squirrelly—or rather ferrety—brother like Ronnie, but the two of them were devoted to one another. "Since the Purls work for me, I can call Ronnie and ask him to meet us here."

"Don't bother." Jordan jerked his chin toward the door. "He just walked in."

Rusty glanced over his shoulder. Sure enough, Ronnie had just waltzed in, an oversized backpack dangling from one hand as he raked the bar with a narrow-eyed gaze. That gaze morphed into wide-eyed panic as Rusty surged out of his chair and barreled toward him. Ronnie whirled and darted for the door.

"Ronnie Purl," Rusty roared, "don't you dare fucking move!"

Chapter Ten

Ronnie's shoulders rose up toward his ears, but he froze in place, allowing Rusty to catch up with him and grip his elbow.

"Suppose you come along with me, Ronnie." Rusty kept his voice low and fierce. "We're going to have a little chat."

"Heh." He gave Rusty a feeble smile. "Fancy meeting you here. Thought you'd be on a job."

"Not today." Rusty jerked his chin toward the table where Jordan was watching them with wide eyes. "Let's go."

He hauled Ronnie across the bar, dodging tables, ignoring the wary glances from the bartender as he polished glasses that were already gleaming. But when he got to the table, he couldn't ignore the curious stares from other patrons. Granted, there weren't that many, but somehow it seemed like they were all focused on Rusty's little group. He glanced down at Ronnie, whose gaze kept darting for the door, and sighed. Ronnie wasn't the most trustworthy guy in the *correct* timeline. Who knew what he'd been up to in this one?

He kept a firm grip on Ronnie's elbow and looked down at Jordan. "You said your deal went down in the storeroom?" Jordan nodded, still looking like a deer shifter in the headlights. "Let's go there. Less of an audience."

Towing Ronnie, Jordan trotting in their wake, Rusty barged through the curtain that hid the stairs to the basement levels and plunged down the first flight into the storeroom. The only sounds were the buzz of the fluorescent lights and the faint sounds of Shivaree's "Goodnight, Moon" filtering down from the upstairs sound system. The door to the fight pens was tightly closed and no noise came from below—the fight pens weren't active all the time and never during the day, so they wouldn't be interrupted unless the bartender made a supply run.

Rusty dragged Ronnie to the corner and boxed him in between a stack of Widmer IPA cases and a metal shelf unit stacked with glassware and paper goods. For a moment, all he could do was glare down at the little shit, breath coming hard through his nose. Even Ronnie, as clever as he was at weaseling out of corners of his own making, couldn't mistake Rusty's barely controlled anger for anything but what it was.

"Rusty, I don't know what you're thinking, but—"

"I'm wondering why I shouldn't wring your neck, Ronnie."

His eyes widened, whites showing around the near-black irises. "Rusty," he croaked, "you'd never. Not to me. Not to anyone. You're not a violent man. Everybody knows that."

"I'll make an exception this time."

"But I didn't *do* anything!" Ronnie wailed.

"You sold me that potion," Jordan piped up.

"So? Gotta make a living somehow, don't I? No laws against that."

"Depends on how you do it," Rusty ground out between clenched teeth. "How did you get that potion, Ronnie?"

Ronnie's gaze shifted to the left. "Guy I know."

"Try again."

Ronnie peered up at Rusty with a sappy grin. "Goblin market?"

"Nope."

"Ah, come on, Rusty. Have a heart. My sources won't work with me anymore if I give them up."

Rusty loomed over Ronnie, who cringed. "I don't for one minute think you got that potion legitimately. You stole it, didn't you?"

"Rusty." Ronnie managed to infuse his voice with real hurt. "I'd never—"

"Stow it, Ronnie. I don't have time for your crap. Did. You. Steal. The potion?"

Ronnie dropped his gaze. "Maybe."

"Do you even know what it does?"

Ronnie gave him an outraged glare. "Of course I do. It's one of those time thingies. You know." He swooped one hand through the air.

"Time-surfing."

"Yeah, that's what they said."

Rusty's eyes narrowed. "Who's *they*? Druids?"

"I'd never pinch anything from a druid!" Ronnie leaned toward Jordan. "They do human sacrifice, you know."

Jordan's eyes widened. "Really?"

Rusty huffed. "Don't listen to him. That's a lot of propaganda that was old in the Middle Ages. Druids are the only people I know with access to this spell. If you didn't get it from them, then where?" Ronnie's gaze cut to the stairs in back of Rusty. "Don't even think about running, Ronnie. I am not in the mood."

Ronnie huffed, his shoulders slumping. "Fine. From a mage, okay? A fire mage. Lives up in the West Hills. Him and his son."

"You stole from a *fire mage*?" Jordan's tone blended disbelief, horror, and admiration. "Seriously?"

"Ronnie, do you have a *death wish*?" Rusty hissed. "You're afraid of druids, but not of mages who can literally *set you on fire*?"

"That's different. Druids, they're connected, you know? To the earth. And ferrets fall under earth, not fire. They'd be onto me before I got ten feet away."

Rusty cocked an eyebrow. "Fire mages would know, too. They can scry in the flames."

Ronnie's eyes threatened to pop out of his head. "They can?"

"They can." Any hope Rusty had of undoing the damage was fading faster than his last glimpse of Cas. "Why'd you pinch the potion, anyway? You go in for soft and cozy things, not sparkly shit, and definitely not potions."

"I heard 'em talking, see? Devin and me, we were there on a job. Rewiring the maid's quarters. Devin had me shift to run the cables through the walls, and I heard 'em in the workroom. The mage, the dad, he was saying this was the only time they could work the spell. Something about rare ingredients and fire not working well with water. I didn't pay attention to that part."

"Then why did you care enough to steal it?"

"Because it was *rare*, okay? If they couldn't make more, stands to reason it was valuable."

"So you sold a one-of-a-kind potion to a random werewolf kid."

"Hey!" Jordan protested. "I'm not random. Well, okay, maybe random, but I'm not a kid."

Ronnie shifted uneasily from foot to foot. "When Devin and I went back to finish the job, I heard the mage's son raging around the place because he couldn't find the potion. I figured it was too hot to hold on to."

"Gaia, Ronnie, you are really a piece of work."

"Well, you said it. That mage guy could set me on fire, but his son is the scary one. No magic, but he'll go off the rails at the drop of a fly."

Rusty's shoulders slumped. "I don't have the money or the clout to talk a mage of Pierce Martinson's stature into making another potion for me."

"You couldn't anyway," Jordan said. "Remember? Ronnie said it was a one-shot deal."

Rusty gazed at Jordan with a weary smile. "And that means we're stuck with things as they are. Without any more potion, we have no chance to fix things." *No chance to save Cas. Save Dr. Kendrick. Save Mal and Bryce and Ted.*

"I said it was a one-time *spell.*" Ronnie unzipped his backpack and pulled out another little crystal vial. "I didn't say it was only one potion."

Chapter Eleven

Rusty held out his hand, gaze locked on Ronnie's eyes until he sighed and set the vial in Rusty's palm. Rusty held it up to the light to check the liquid's level. It was nearly full. "Did they make two doses, or did you split it to increase your profits?"

Ronnie's gaze shifted again. "Well…"

"Ronnie," Rusty growled.

"Okay, I divided it in half, all right? I mean, why not?"

Hope warred with apprehension in Rusty's chest. After his previous experience with the time-surfing potion, he knew that the amount consumed affected the length of the surf. Would there be enough to fix this problem? Furthermore, *how* could he fix the problem? He couldn't very well go back to the moment Jordan encountered David. Meeting two naked guys in an alley would probably make David flail hard enough to break both ankles and an arm.

He narrowed his eyes, gaze cutting from Ronnie to Jordan. "The potion sale went down here in the storeroom?" They both nodded, Jordan enthusiastically and Ronnie warily. "When?"

"How would I know?" Ronnie asked. "I don't keep track of that kind of crap."

"Day before yesterday," Jordan said. "At 9:07. At night."

Rusty blinked. "You remember that precisely?"

Jordan gave him a quizzical glance. "Well, yeah. Doesn't everyone?" Rusty jerked a thumb at Ronnie. "Oh. Right. I guess not. I know it was the day before yesterday because I shopped for my club outfit yesterday morning, and took the potion last night."

Of course he did. "About eleven-thirty?"

Jordan's eyes widened in wonder. "How did you know?"

Because that's when I jerked awake with nausea and disorientation. "Never mind. Let's go back to the potion handoff. How are you so certain of the time?"

"Ronnie told me to meet him here at nine. I got here at 8:00, because I wanted to be *sure*, you know? Then I kept checking the time on my phone." Jordan cut a glance at Ronnie. "He was seven minutes late."

"Traffic," Ronnie muttered.

"I was afraid I'd missed him anyway, because, um…" A flush crept up Jordan's throat. "I'd had a couple of sodas upstairs before I came down, so I had to, you know"—he pointed toward the ceiling—"visit the restroom, and there was a line. I went upstairs at 8:55 and kept checking my phone while I waited. At 9:07, when I ran downstairs again, Ronnie was here."

Rusty scanned the storeroom. "Did this place look the same then?"

"It's a stinkin' storeroom, Rusty," Ronnie groused. "It had stacks of crap around then and it's got stacks of crap around now."

Jordan pointed to three cases of Montinore Pinot Noir. "Those weren't here." He gazed around, biting his lower lip. "There were two more crates of the Widmer IPA. Three less of the Angry Orchard cider." He pointed at the shelves. "And one more box of bar napkins."

Rusty blinked. "You remember all that?"

"I was waiting for over an hour. I didn't have anything else to do except look around."

"That's… That's terrific, Jordan. Well done. You've given me everything I need." *I hope.* "You two go back upstairs and wait for me." He pointed at Ronnie. "And I mean *wait*. Do not pull a runner on me, Ronnie."

"Don't know why it should matter," Ronnie mumbled. "You got what you wanted."

"Because if it works, you won't be here. You'll never have been here. And if it doesn't, if this doesn't..." Rusty took a shaky breath. *It has to work. It must.* "If it doesn't, then we'll all need a drink."

Jordan lifted his chin, his jaw tight. "Don't worry, Mr. Johnson. I won't let him leave."

Rusty gripped his shoulder. "Good lad."

Jordan smiled apologetically. "And I'm really sorry."

"It's okay. But next time? Don't take any potion unless you know it won't have any apocalyptical side effects. Also? Never buy anything from Ronnie again."

"Hey!" Ronnie protested.

"Who, by the way," Rusty said, fixing Ronnie with a glare, "will be giving you a full refund."

Ronnie puffed out his chest and opened his mouth. The look on Rusty's face must have made him rethink his protest, because he snapped his teeth shut with a clack. "You're gonna ruin me, Rusty."

"Somehow, you'll recover. Promise me, Jordan."

He nodded. "I promise."

"Don't forget." Rusty pointed to the stairs. "Go on up. I'll be there shortly."

Ronnie kept his head down as he trudged up the stairs, but Jordan glanced back worriedly once before he disappeared.

Rusty gazed down at the vial in his hand. *One chance. One chance to get it right.* He hoped like all the hells that Ronnie's itch to double his profits hadn't halved Rusty's chance of success. *I'll just have to talk fast.*

At least he'd had immediate experience intimidating Ronnie —and a very strong incentive not to pull any punches.

Chapter Twelve

Rusty stripped, folding his clothes and setting them on top of a stack of bar towels. *Hope the bartender doesn't need to restock the bar mats in the next few minutes or he'll get an eyeful.*

From his earlier experience with time-surfing, Rusty knew the drill. *First, make the trip from a fixed spatial point.* Since Jordan had identified the stack of Widmer as present two nights ago, Rusty picked a clear spot near them. *Second, don't drink the potion until you've created a definitive mind picture of where you want to go.*

There was a third item, one he hadn't mentioned to Jordan or Ronnie: the very real danger that repeated time-surfing could damage his genetic makeup. *I have to risk it. Maybe Cas and I can't be together again if I'm changed enough that my blood is poison to him, but at least he'll be alive.*

Rusty unstoppered the vial, staring down at it for a long moment. He trusted Bryce, his ethics, his competence. Could he really trust a fire mage with Pierce Martinson's reputation? *I don't have a choice. It's this or nothing, and I can't accept that.*

He inhaled, exhaled on a huff, then closed his eyes, envisioning the changes to the room and its contents from Jordan's description, focusing hard on the time—9:00, before Jordan returned from the restroom but in time to catch Ronnie's arrival. When he had a clear mental picture, he raised the vial to his lips and knocked it back.

"Pfaugh!" Bryce's potion had tasted grassy yet tart, with a hint of bitterness. This one was *foul*, worse than duergar holly ale, and it burned all the way down his throat. *Gaia, I hope it behaves the same—*

Rusty screamed, his spine arched, lips pulling back as his jaw locked and his muscles seized. Then he doubled over, grabbing his knees as fire snaked from his belly all the way to his fingers and toes.

Eyes closed, he panted through the pain, so different from the nausea and vertigo of his earlier trips. *Gaia, did it hit Jordan like this too?* The kid must be tougher than he looked.

As the pain receded, Rusty was afraid to open his eyes. If the potion and its effects were so different, would it have worked at all?

Then two sounds penetrated the roaring in his ears: the muffled chorus of Creedence's "Bad Moon Rising" and footsteps clomping down the stairs. His eyes flew open in time to see Ronnie's familiar scuffed boots appear.

"Gaia!" Rusty snatched a bar towel off the shelf where his clothes would be two days from now and held it in front of his groin as Ronnie's chest came into view.

He took a deep breath. Channeling the pain and rage and anguish that had swamped him all day, he let it all out.

It must have showed on his face, because as soon as Ronnie caught sight of him, he froze, then pivoted as though to bolt back up the stairs.

"Ronnie Purl!" Rusty roared. "Get over here right now or your brother will never work for me again."

Ronnie stopped, one foot on the lowest step. He turned slowly, a scowl on his face. "That's not fair, Rusty. You've got no call to threaten my brother."

"Then get over here now."

Ronnie eyed Rusty's chest. "You been in the fight pens? I didn't think you could shift."

"Stop wasting time." *Because I don't have a lot of it.* Sweat prickled along Rusty's hairline. Did that mean the potion was wearing off? "Hand it over."

Ronnie drew himself up in mock outrage. "This is sexual harassment, that's what this is."

"Don't be ridiculous. I don't want you. I want the potion."

His gaze cut to the side. "Don't know what you're talking about."

"Don't be a pain in the ass, Ronnie. The time-surfing potion you stole from the Martinsons which you were about to sell to a were kid without warning him what could happen."

Ronnie put a hand on his chest, a completely fake injured expression settling over his narrow face. "Now, Rusty, you're a businessman too. You know that it's up to the buyer to beware."

Rusty narrowed his eyes. "You were going to hand over a magical item that has the power to alter our whole fucking *reality.* To a kid!"

Ronnie licked his lips, probably stalling while he tried to come up with an exit strategy that kept his skin, his inventory, and his brother's professional career intact. "It wouldn't be that bad, surely? I mean, it's just a potion. It's not like it could hurt anybody."

"No? Anti-freeze is just a potion. Bleach is just a potion. Rat poison is just a potion. Deadly potions."

Ronnie's brows snapped together. "If the mage was gonna let his son take it, it wouldn't poison anybody."

"I'm done arguing. Give me the damn potions. *Now.*" Rusty tossed the towel aside and advanced on Ronnie. "Give them to me now or I'll *take* them. And then I'll blackball you and Devin with the contractor's board. Never mind working for me. You won't work in this *state* again."

To give Ronnie credit, he didn't pay much attention to Rusty's nudity. He unzipped his pack and drew out a vial. "You gonna tell Pierce Martinson I pinched his potion?" He placed the vial in Rusty's outstretched hand.

"Trust me. He already knows." Rusty wiggled his fingers. "The other one too."

"There was only one!" Ronnie protested.

"There was only one when you stole it, but you split it. Come on." Rusty wiggled his fingers. "Hand it over."

Ronnie hugged the pack to his chest. "But if Martinson knows, he'll have my ass if I don't return it."

"Since you can't return the whole thing, he'll have your ass anyway." A faint burn started in Rusty's toes. *No, no. Not yet.* "Ronnie. Now. Before the kid shows up."

"Fine," he grumbled, drew out the other vial.

Rusty snatched it as the heat increased, inching up his legs. He stared down at the vials. *I can't take them with me.* If he vanished, leaving the vials behind, Ronnie could retrieve them. Even if he didn't sell them to Jordan, he could sell them to somebody else, which was a risk Rusty couldn't take.

He dashed the vials to the concrete floor, earning a wordless protest from Ronnie. The glass shattered and the liquid splattered, but that wasn't enough. He stumbled for the Widmer crates, his feet clumsy. He lifted the top one and let it drop onto the remains of the potion, making a mental note to pay the Bullpen for any possible breakage.

As the burn wound through his belly, and Jordan's footsteps pattered on the stairs, Rusty turned to Ronnie. "Thank you, Ronnie. In the future? Stay away from mages. And *don't* steal shit you don't understand."

"That's easy for you to say. If I—"

Rusty howled as the fire reached his heart and his vision went black.

Chapter Thirteen

Sensation returned to Rusty's legs first, a bright, sharp pain in his knees. Hearing returned next. At least he thought it did. His ears didn't feel stuffed with cotton, but it was eerily quiet.

But then he caught snatches of muffled conversation from overhead, accompanied by the clink of glasses and the muted intro to Bryan Ferry's "I Put a Spell on You." He blinked rapidly, and his vision slowly faded back in. He squinted as he scanned the storeroom. He was alone, so either Jordan and Ronnie had followed instructions and stayed upstairs or else they'd never been here in the first place.

He heaved a shaky sigh when he spotted his clothes on the shelf. He pushed himself to his feet and glanced down at his knees. Blood trickled from a half dozen spots. *I must have landed on the broken vials.* He touched one of the wounds gingerly. There didn't seem to be any glass embedded in his skin, so either he hadn't picked it up or else it didn't survive the return trip.

After he got dressed, Rusty crept up the stairs and peered through the curtains into the bar. He didn't see Jordan or Ronnie, thank Gaia, but that didn't mean everything was back to normal.

He retreated to the dim hallway and dug out his cell phone, holding his breath as he called Dr. Kendrick's office.

"Dr. Kendrick's office. This is David. How may I help you?"

Rusty's knees gave way and he ass-planted on the floor, his back against the wall.

"Hello?" David's voice was laced with concern. "Is anybody there? Do you require medical assistance?"

"No. Hi." Rusty cleared his throat because his voice sounded like a broken table saw. "David. Good to hear your voice." *You've no idea how good.* "This is Rusty Johnson."

"Oh, Rusty!" David's tone brightened. "How are you doing?" He chuckled. "All ready to play your part when you stand up with Bryce at the handfasting next week?"

Rusty rested his head on his drawn-up knees, ignoring the twinges from the tiny cuts. *Thank Gaia. Another thing put back the way it should be.* "Yeah. I, um, have what might be a weird question."

"You've come to the right person, then. Shoot."

"Is, um, Kristof Czardos doing okay?"

"Of course. Why wouldn't he be?"

Rusty exhaled shakily. "No reason. Thanks. I've, um, got to go."

"Sure. See you in Faerie!"

Rusty stared at his screen. He should call Cas. Make sure *everything* was right again. But he couldn't. Not yet. Because what if he didn't answer? He levered himself upright, counting it as a victory when his legs actually supported his weight. He tucked the phone away and strode through the curtains and up to the bar. "Close out my tab?"

Rusty held his breath until the bartender slid a leather folio over to him. He checked his receipt. His whiskey, but nothing else. No soft drink. *So Jordan wasn't here.* He laid a twenty in the folio and pushed it across the bar. "Thanks. No change." He tucked two more twenties into the tip jar and sprinted for the door.

His truck was right where he'd left it. He pulled out of the parking spot, but instead of heading for I-5 South toward Eugene—*not yet*—he headed for the Doghouse. When he

knocked on the door, it was opened by a stocky, black-haired
were holding a bag of Doritos.

Rusty smiled at him. "Hector, right?"

Hector wiped his hand on his jeans. "Yeah. You're Mr.
Johnson, right?"

Rusty's smile widened. If Hector remembered him, that
meant the wedding—*his* wedding, *Cas's* wedding—had
happened. "Got it in one. Is Jordan around?"

Hector blinked. "Jordan? Yeah. I think he's out back. Want to
come in?"

"No, thanks. I'll wait here on the porch, if you could ask him
to join me?"

"Sure." Hector glanced over his shoulder. "Just so you know,
I think he's got a little crush on you, so if he acts weird, that's
probably why."

Rusty chuckled. "It's okay."

Hector nodded and walked back into the house, leaving the
door ajar. "Jordan! Somebody's here to see you."

Rusty tucked his hands into his vest pockets, running his
thumb over his wedding band. Jordan bounded into sight a
minute later, a rather tattered Frisbee in one hand.

"Mr. Johnson!" He glanced down at the Frisbee and tossed it
aside before stepping onto the porch. "It's nice to see you. I…
Wait." His brows pinched together. "Was I… Was I supposed to
do something for you?"

Rusty waved his hand in a *never mind* gesture. "Couple of
questions for you, Jordan, and maybe a bit of a warning, too."

His eyes widened. "Did I do something wrong?"

"No, no. Just wanted to give you a heads-up." He leaned
forward. "If Ronnie Purl ever offers to sell you anything—"

"Ronnie Purl? The ferret shifter?"

"The same."

"I, um, *may* have talked to him about buying something, but
he didn't come through."

"Trust me. That's actually a good thing. Let's just say his merchandise can be a bit sketchy. And sometimes dangerous. Besides, there's nothing he can offer you that you can't work out for yourself. So promise me you won't fall for his spiel."

Jordan gulped. "I promise." His eyebrows shot up. "Wow. I just got the weirdest feeling. Like I've said that to you before." He smiled a little shakily. "Déjà vu's a thing, I guess, right?"

"Definitely." Rusty caught sight of a gaggle of other young weres peering at them from the dining room. "Everything okay here? Chase and Tanner still around?"

"You remember them?" Jordan huffed a laugh. "Of course you do. Mud monsters. How could anyone forget?" He gazed up at Rusty in a worshipful way that made Rusty want to beat a hasty retreat. "You and your sledgehammer were *awesome*." He sighed, but then seemed to catch himself. "Did you need to see Chase and Tanner? They're not here right now. They're both out registering for school."

"Think you'd like to do that?"

Jordan wrinkled his nose. "Eww. No. I'm, um, not the best in classroom situations." He brightened. "Dr. MacLeod says I'm a kine...kine..."

"Kinesthetic?"

"Yeah, that! I'm a kinesthetic learner. I have to *do* something before it sticks."

"Think you might be interested in working construction?"

"Well... I'm good at digging. Would I get to use a sledgehammer?"

Rusty chuckled. "We'll see." He dug into his pocket and handed over a business card. "Give me a call and we'll see about setting up an internship for you."

Jordan took the card almost reverently. "Really? Wow. Th-thanks." He blushed. "I really appreciate it."

Rusty began to turn away, but then had another thought. "Jordan. Do you remember anything about trying to go to a club? Maybe running into somebody in an alley?"

His eyes widened. "I had a dream like that! One of those weird ones where you're naked in the worst places." He flushed. "I mean, *you* weren't naked. Or, um, maybe?" His face crumpled. "It ended up being a pretty lousy dream. Everything went wrong."

Rusty was tempted to tell him it hadn't been a dream, but would that make things better or worse? A curious guy like Jordan, one with no filter and no sense of self-preservation, might just try to dig further and end up... well, Rusty didn't want to think about that. But at least he could give the kid a bit of advice. "If those dreams give you more trouble? Talk to Dr. MacLeod about them."

Jordan frowned. "Dr. MacLeod? But he's not *that* kind of doctor."

"No. But he's a druid." Rusty leaned forward and lowered his voice. "They *know* things."

Jordan nodded sagely. "Riiight."

"Take care, Jordan. Give me a call if you'd like to talk about that internship. And remember—"

"Don't buy anything from ferret shifters." He ticked things off on his fingers. "Talk to Dr. MacLeod about scary dreams." He waggled the business card. "And call you about an internship."

"You got it." Rusty raised his arm. "Thank you."

Jordan tilted his head like an inquisitive puppy. "For what?"

Rusty paused with a foot on the porch step, suddenly desperate to get on the road, to find out if the rest of his life had gotten back on track. "For knowing when to ask for help."

He left Jordan goggling at him from the porch, the business card pressed against his chest as though it would grant his greatest wish, and ran for his truck.

Chapter Fourteen

Rusty gripped the steering wheel, eyeing his cell phone on the passenger seat. *Yes. Now. Can't wait.* So far, everything else had been back to normal, so why not the rest of his life?

He snatched up the phone and speed-dialed Cas, holding his breath as it rang once, twice, three times and connected. He pushed down a sob. "Cas? Thank Gaia you're—"

"Hello, you've reached Casimir Moreau, however I cannot take your call at present. Kindly leave a message, preferably one with teeth."

Gah! Voice mail. There could be reasons for that. Ordinarily, Cas slept in the afternoon so he'd be awake when Rusty got home from work. He might be in the shower. He might be... doing something. Rusty refused to believe that he might be gone.

At least I didn't get a 'This number is out of service' message. That had to mean something, right?

He started the engine and connected the phone to the truck's Bluetooth, although he didn't pull out into traffic yet. "Call Bryce."

Bryce answered after a couple of rings. "Hey, Rusty. Got those knots worked out yet?"

Rusty laughed a little shakily. Cas had provided a number of interesting incentives for practicing the complicated handfasting knots, most involving their new headboard. "I won't let you down, Bryce."

"I know. Something else up with the wedding plans? It's only a week away." Bryce couldn't disguise his excitement—his voice fairly vibrated with it.

"Nothing about the wedding. I wanted to give you a heads-up about something else." He swallowed. "It, uh, seems you're not the only one who knows how to make the time-surfing potion." There was silence on the line for so long that Rusty glanced at the phone to make sure it hadn't disconnected. "Bryce?"

"Who?" Bryce croaked.

"An elemental mage cooked one up. Pierce Martinson. You know him?"

"Unfortunately. Are you sure?"

"Absolutely. Although according to the guy who stole the potion—"

Bryce barked a laugh. "Somebody had the balls to steal from a *fire mage*?"

"I'm not sure if it's having the balls or not having the brains. Ronnie Purl. He said the potion was a one-time thing." Rusty's grip tightened on his phone. "But what if it isn't? Bryce, Ronnie sold the potion to Jordan Tate."

"Shit," Bryce muttered. "Of all people."

"Yeah. The thing is, he used it. For a pretty innocuous reason. To go to a club with his friends."

"Naked?"

"Yeah, he didn't know about that part, and Ronnie, as usual, was sketchy on the details, since he had no idea what they were in the first place."

Bryce chuckled. "Considering the world is still spinning and zombies aren't roaming the streets, we can be thankful he didn't cause anything cataclysmic."

"The thing is, he did."

"Did what?"

"Caused something cataclysmic. Bryce, when Jordan surfed, he encountered David."

"David? Mal's brother-in-law?"

"Yes. But before he worked for Alun. And because of that encounter, he *never* worked for Alun. Never married Alun."

"Never..." Bryce was quiet for a moment. "That would mean —"

"Yeah. You didn't know you were a druid. Rodric Luchullain was the de facto Seelie King, and Mal... Well, you never met him and he—"

"Would have been ordered to execute his own brother." Bryce's voice was dull.

"And Cas... Cas was dead."

"Oh, Christ, Rusty. I'm so sorry. Is he—"

"I don't know yet. He didn't answer his phone, but that might not mean anything. At least I hope it doesn't. But I can't — I mean, what if what I did changed something else, something that would keep Cas and me from meeting again?"

"Wait. *You* surfed again?"

"Yeah. I used the second half of the potion Ronnie pinched to go back and keep him from selling it to Jordan. Destroyed it in the Bullpen storeroom."

"Rusty. This isn't good. I mean, it's good that you fixed the timeline, at least where our family and friends are concerned. But the effects on you... Well, the more you surf, the more sensitized you become to changes in the time-stream."

"Those time footprints you told me about. Yeah. Been there. You, too."

"You talked to me in the alternate stream?"

"Yeah. You'd resigned your professorship. You thought you were losing it because you kept seeing—"

"Mal." He sighed. "There might be other side effects too. Druids don't like to monkey with time because it upsets the balance."

"I have a feeling Martinson didn't have the same scruples. I don't think his potion was the same as yours either. The flavor was way different." The back of Rusty's throat still burned, and he still had that nasty taste in his mouth. "The sensations weren't the same either. More severe. Painful."

"Rusty." From Bryce's tone, he was trying to control himself with an effort. "That might not be the potion. It might be because you've surfed too many times."

"Yeah? And just how many times have you tried it?"

A beat of silence. "A few. But my relationship with my partner isn't dependent on my body chemistry. Yours is."

Rusty sighed. "I know. But it was worth the risk, okay?"

"Okay."

"Listen, is there anything you can do to make sure Martinson doesn't try it again?"

"I'll speak to the archdruid." Bryce cursed softly. "Which means I'll have to confess that I've surfed myself. That'll be uncomfortable."

"Whatever you can do."

"I'll take care of it. I promise. The stakes are too high."

"Jordan doesn't remember taking the potion. He only remembers the alternate stream as a dream. I hope it's okay, but I told him that if the dreams bother him, he should talk to you."

"Good move." He chuckled. "Although knowing Jordan, I may hear about *all* his dreams, not just the ones related to his surf."

"Thanks, Bryce."

"No problem. And Rusty? Good luck. If Cas isn't there and I can do anything at all to help, you know where to find me."

"I do. Thanks."

Rusty disconnected. He put the truck in drive. "Fuck this." He didn't head for the highway—the two-hour drive to Eugene was too long. Instead, he drove to the Pearl District and parked in front of the building that formerly housed Supernatural

Selection and now was—or at least should be—home to Quest Investigations.

As he burst through the street door and took the stairs to the lobby two at a time, he chanted, "Please, please, please."

The dark-haired, bespectacled demon behind the reception desk was familiar, but that wasn't a bad thing—Zeke Oz had segued from his job with the matchmaking agency to working for Quest.

His sweet smile dawned. "Mr. Johnson. How nice to see you! How can we help you today?"

"I, um…" *One more test.* "How's Hamish?"

Rose-colored blotches rose up Zeke's throat and across his pale face. "He's wonderful. Hunter's Moon has a concert tonight in New Orleans and Niall and I will be leaving soon to get there before curtain."

And that's *what I wanted to hear.* Not only that Zeke and Hamish, Niall and Gareth were safe and together, but that a shortcut through Faerie was still on the table. "I need a favor."

Zeke folded his hands on the desk and looked up at Rusty attentively. "Of course."

"I need to get back to Eugene right away. Do you think I could…" He spread his hands in entreaty.

"I thought you were going to ask me something hard." Zeke chuckled and opened a drawer to draw out an oak leaf emblazoned with a gold rune. "You can call an FTA driver from our fourth floor translocation door. You know the activation code?" When Rusty nodded, he passed the leaf to Rusty's shaking hand. "Do you need me to escort you up there?"

"No. No, I've got it." He'd been through that door before. "Thanks, Zeke."

"No problem. See you at the handfasting!"

Rusty lifted a hand in farewell and then barreled up the stairs, past the vending machines, to the door that led… elsewhere. He pressed his thumb to the rune. *"Cludo."*

The door swung open to reveal a hulking duergar. "Where to?"

"Eugene. Northwest side of Dawson's Lake."

The duergar grunted. "Beaver shifters. At least it'll be private. Let's go."

Rusty practically sprinted through the door, although he had to let the duergar take the lead. Luckily, duergars weren't chatty, because anticipation and trepidation had paralyzed Rusty's vocal cords. He led Rusty out of Faerie at the head of an unpaved road, marked *Private,* that led down to what Cas persisted in calling Lake of the Beavers.

"Thanks," he croaked.

"Don't mention it," the duergar replied. "Next time you need a driver, ask for me. Frang. I like riders who don't talk my ear off."

As Frang disappeared into Faerie, Rusty took off down the road at a dead run. Would the house—his and Cas's house—be there? Or would there be nothing but empty shore?

When he burst past the tree-line, there it was: the beautiful, sprawling Craftsman with its wide porch, flagstone walk, and the gravel path leading down to the short dock and the little building on the shore that he and Cas used after their midnight swims if they didn't want to walk all the way to the house to make love. His knees wobbled, the butterflies in his belly threatening to lift him right off the ground as he laughed despite breath labored from his dash through the woods.

The sun still gilded the lake, but that wouldn't matter. Thanks to ingesting Rusty's Inactive blood, Cas could be out in daylight now. *As long as the blasted fire mage's spell hasn't fucked that up.*

He bounded up the porch stairs and flung open the front door. "Cas?" he called. When there was no answer, he ran down the hallway. "Cas?" The bedroom was empty, the duvet smooth across the king-sized bed. For a moment, his heart seemed to stop, but then he noted the new headboard and caught the sound of the shower. He scowled as he strode across the room to grip the bathroom door handle. *It better not be Fletcher.*

Pausing for a moment, he rested his head against the smooth wood. *It's Cas. It has to be him.*

Then he eased the door open and peered inside. Steam filled the oversized glass shower stall, but through it, Rusty glimpsed long, pale limbs and caramel-colored hair darkened with water. *"Cas,"* he croaked, and then couldn't wait any longer. He lunged across the room, flung open the shower door and stumbled inside—jeans, boots, down vest and all—and enveloped Cas in his arms.

Cas squawked. "Rusty. What are you doing?"

"I'm so— You can't— I didn't know if—"

"Elmer. Use your words."

A laugh escaped from Rusty's belly, breathless, a little high, more than a little relieved. *He's here. He's okay.* We're *okay.* "I love you."

"I love you, too, but you smell like wet goose."

Rusty stilled, gazing down at him. "Wet goose? Is that all? I don't smell nasty to you?"

"Underneath the stench of sodden feathers, you smell as delicious as always." Cas tilted his chin, but Rusty didn't let him go. *Couldn't* let him go. "However, isn't it customary to remove your clothing"—he glanced down—"not to mention your massive footwear, before your ablutions? Or is this a beaver thing? Because I must say—"

Rusty kissed him, catching all the words in that dear, sharp, French-edged voice. Cas didn't resist. He returned the kiss with interest, twining his arms around Rusty's neck.

Rusty moaned and reared back, baring his throat. "Bite me, Cas. I need to feel you. To know you're here. To know you're okay."

Cas's eyebrows quirked up in those adorable little peaks, and he framed Rusty's face. "You know I relish your taste, my darling, and would never refuse you, but clearly you're operating under severe agitation. Is something wrong?"

Rusty shook his head. "Not anymore. I just… need you."

Cas grinned with that hint of fang that always perked up Rusty's cock. "Then you shall have me. But not, I think, in the shower, because while you are customarily sexy in your manly work clothes, at the moment you resemble a waterlogged wombat." Cas turned off the spray and snatched one of the oversized bath sheets off the hook inside the shower to blot Rusty's face. "Dry off, get undressed, and I'll meet you in the bedroom." His grin widened, his fangs descending further. "As I recall, you have some knots to practice and I volunteer as tribute."

"Yes, Cas." Rusty kissed him again. "Anything you want."

"Excellent." He tickled Rusty's throat with the tip of his tongue. "I have a feeling this is going to be a *very* good day."

Getting the Band Together

About Getting the Band Together

If youknow anything about me, you'll know I love crossover stories, spinoffs, and random cameos, where I pull in characters from one book into another. Sometimes I drop in to fill in some gaps (like with *First Flight*, which occurs between Chapter Thirty-Three and the Epilogue of *Assassin by Accident*) or to extend a story a bit (like *Second First Date*, which is essentially a seven chapter epilogue for *Vampire With Benefits*).

There's also what I call the story seed effect, when I stick some random reference into a story with no intention of it going anywhere else, usually to flesh out something that's happening in one of the main characters' arc.

But then it comes back to bite me on the butt. (Although I suppose you could say it gooses the muse...)

Take this throwaway line from *Cutie and the Beast*, when fae psychologist Dr. Alun Kendrick discovers that David, his irritating--and horrifyingly human—temporary office manager, has brought tabloid newspapers into the office lobby (because, in David's opinion, the clients need something to occupy themselves while they're waiting for Alun to poke around in their psyches):

> The blurry photograph of a shambling, fur-covered figure that accompanied the story was all too familiar—Ted Farnsworth, one of his past clients, a bear shifter with an exhibitionist kink who'd gotten into trouble with his elders for exposing their existence to humans.

I never expected that to go anywhere else. However, when I was brainstorming about a followup series, thinking about who needed their own HEA, this line came back to me. That's how Ted ended up starring in his own story, *Single White Incubus* (although, FYI, he doesn't truly have an exhibitionist kink--he's just a lonely extrovert and wants somebody to talk to).

This story looks backward instead of forward—a fill-in-the-gaps tale, if you will.

In *Cutie and the Beast*, I'd tossed in that Alun's brother Gareth's band, Hunter's Moon, was comprised of shifters: two werewolves, a jaguar, and a kangaroo. I don't recall thinking much about it—I just thought that combination, along with the fae bard frontman, was amusing. Then in *Bad Boy's Bard* (Gareth and Niall's story), I sort of doubled down with this paragraph in Gareth's POV, as he's thinking about his brothers and the band:

> He'd resented it. Resented being forced to emerge from the dark room of his grief. But it had worked eventually. If it weren't for Mal constantly forcing him out of his cave, he'd never have met Josh in New Orleans in the Thirties. Wouldn't have met Spence in Liverpool in '63. The three of them wouldn't have found Hamish and Tiff at Woodstock if Mal hadn't forced them to go.

That paragraph has been kicking around in my head for over six years now, and I'm finally coming around to wondering, "Okay, so what *did* happen in NOLA? In Liverpool? At Woodstock?"

So... presenting *Getting the Band Together*!

This is a backstory story, with a section for each of the band members who doesn't have their own book already (IOW, Josh, Spence, and Tiff, since Hamish is taken care of in *Demon on the Down-Low*).

Are you ready? All righty, then. Let's take this band on the road!

Cheers!
—*E*

Josh

A Coming Storm

The wind whipping down the French Quarter's streets was heavy with the coming storm, and although it was warm, as New Orleans always was in early summer, it chilled Josh's newly bare nape. He clapped a hand to his battered fedora to keep it from blowing away. Let alone that no respectable man went without a hat, he'd made a right pig's ear of his hair when he'd cut it off.

Using a pocketknife in the dark would do that.

He hurried around the corner, glancing up at the clouds that obscured the full moon. What time was it? He'd lost track when he was hiding in the woods behind the compound, waiting for the commotion inside to die down. If he'd missed his audience with the priestess, he—

"Oof!"

Josh staggered backward, his fiddle case nearly slithering out from under his other arm as he stared up at a tall, broad-shouldered man, his tawny curls dancing around his almost impossibly beautiful face in the wind. Josh automatically dropped his gaze, hunching and bracing himself for the blow that was sure to come.

"I'm sorry," he murmured.

"My fault," the man said, his accent marking him as foreign. Maybe British? Not from around here, certainly. "You all right, then?"

Josh nodded. "Yes. Fine. I'm sorry." With his eyes still downcast, he noted that the stranger's trousers were well-made but worn, his boots scuffed but clearly good quality. He was carrying a guitar case nearly as battered as the one that held Josh's fiddle.

"Have a good evening then," the stranger said, and his feet disappeared from Josh's view.

Josh waited for a moment until a shout from a nearby tavern brought him back to the danger of his situation. He glanced around wildly, in case the stranger was biding his time for a different attack, but he was gone.

Josh choked on a strangled laugh. *I'm seeing enemies everywhere.* Of course, enemies *were* everywhere, but a random stranger wasn't as dangerous as the people from Josh's own pack. He took a shaky breath, attempting to settle his nerves. With any luck, nobody had even noticed he was missing yet, and his father's enforcers weren't on the trail. Not with everyone still in an uproar over Maman's death.

His throat thickened, remembering the rattle of her breath as she'd pulled him close, pressing that pocketknife into his hand. "You must leave. Now. After I'm gone, you know what will happen."

He'd nodded, tucking the knife into his skirt pocket. "Maman —"

"Go, my dear." She'd drawn his head down and kissed his forehead, his silver blond hair, still long then, curtaining both their faces. "Don't keep the priestess waiting, not after we've paid so much for you to be graced with her magic. Your clothes and some food are in the shed, along with your fiddle. Now go. Go, *my son.*"

He'd whimpered, from the grief that she'd soon be gone—the only person in the pack who'd ever understood him, who'd ever encouraged him, who'd ever *seen* him—and also because she'd named him for who he was on the *inside.*

My son.

He'd done as she'd asked, binding his chest with the strip of cloth she'd left for the purpose. Changed into the wool trousers and worn linen shirt and shapeless jacket, leaving his skirt and blouse behind.

But he hadn't moved quickly enough, and they'd found her body before he'd left the compound's woods.

And now, he might have missed his only chance.

He hugged his fiddle case to his chest, which was constricted as much on the inside as the outside. His music had been all that had sustained him. His music and his mother. Now she was gone, and he was about to sacrifice his music too, for a chance to walk the world as the man he'd always known himself to be.

"It's worth it," he muttered, trying to convince himself. "It has to be."

But only if he could reach the priestess at the appointed time. He ducked his head against the wind and hurried onward. As he rounded the corner, two men staggered out of another tavern halfway down the block.

No. Not two men. Two *werewolves*. Emmett and Otis, his father's betas. How had they found him? How had they known he was here?

My scent. How stupid could he be? Once they'd found him missing, his father would have ordered them to track him. He and his mother had planned on using a scent blocker, but they hadn't had time.

He pressed his back against the rough bricks of a windowless, hole-in-the-wall business and caught the whispered notes of saxophone and piano from behind its unmarked door. Waiting. Waiting for the inevitable. How had he imagined he could truly escape?

Their gazes didn't immediately snap to where he cowered in the shadows, though. Instead, Emmett retched in the gutter and Otis threw his head back and howled.

Instinctively, Josh scanned the street for witnesses. That howl was *not* a human howl. If anyone heard…

But nobody followed them out of the tavern, where the noise and shouts of men still making up lost drinking time now that the Volstead Act was repealed joined the rush of the win d in masking the noise. The aching notes of blues from the club at his back meant that whoever was inside probably hadn't heard either.

While Josh dithered, Otis stopped howling and glanced furtively behind him, as though realizing he'd exposed his nature. In another second he'd look this way and spot Josh—werewolf eyesight could pierce the darkness without any trouble, and if they recognized him, they'd take him back and he'd be trapped forever. His father would see to that.

If it weren't for Emmett vomiting on his own shoes, they'd have scented Josh by now. His pitiful disguise might fool unobservant humans, but nothing could hide him from a werewolf's heightened sense of smell.

So Josh took the only path available and ducked through the club's door.

First Sanctuary

For an instant, right after he stepped over the threshold, Josh's own werewolf nose detected a vaguely familiar scent. Then the door swung shut behind him, and all his senses were overwhelmed. Despite the heavy curtain that screened the vestibule from the interior of the club, smoke—cigarette, cigar, and pipe from at least three different bowl types—assailed him.

But the music... Gods, the *music*. The soaring notes of the trumpet, the thrum of the bass, the growl of the sax, the bright ripple of the piano—all of it dove right into his soul, calling him to join in, to lift his fiddle and offer up his own soul in return.

It also made him want to weep. Not only from the beauty of it, but because after tonight, he'd never be able to join in again. After tonight, his music would be ripped from him in return for the boon promised by the priestess.

The right to live as his true self.

Can you be your true self without your music?

He shook off the thought. Without the priestess's help, he'd be trapped in the compound for life, just as surely deprived of music, and forced to be something that he wasn't, that he'd never been.

He blinked away the tears that blurred his vision and sucked in a breath. A huge man in shirtsleeves, arms crossed over his broad chest, stood guard in front of the curtain. A finger of light from the single bulb overhead played over his dark skin as he studied Josh, from his disreputable hat to his equally disreputable boots. When his gaze traveled up again, it lingered on Josh's fiddle case.

"Here for the music?" His voice was as deep as the shadows.

Josh licked his lips and nodded.

The big man grunted and drew the curtain aside. "Table in the corner."

"Th-thank you," Josh murmured, and edged past him.

Inside, bright lights illuminated the small stage, although the rest of the room was dim and hazy with smoke. Round wooden tables crowded the floor, most of them occupied, cigars and cigarettes flaring and fading like embers as the audience drew on their smokes. A long bar stretched along the back of the room, and in the corner beyond it, Josh spotted a single empty table.

He crept toward it, careful not to bump into any chairs or jostle anyone standing at the bar. The clientele was... eclectic. Mostly men in the rough clothes of levee workers or in rumpled suits with ties loose around their throats, although a few women were dotted amongst them. Many of the faces raised to the stage lights were dark, but there was enough paler skin among the crowd that Josh didn't feel completely conspicuous.

Josh reached the empty table and took the chair against the wall, its wooden seat hard against his backside. He set the cloth bundle with his meager possessions on the floor by his feet and cuddled his fiddle case in his lap.

His nerves still sang with urgency—the urgency to move, to meet the priestess, to get it *done*. He wouldn't have another chance, couldn't wait until the next full moon, not with his mother gone and no one left in the pack who'd protect him.

He snorted softly. The alphas always imagined they were in charge, but it was the alpha's mate who wielded the true power. That was the only reason Josh had made it to adulthood without being forcibly claimed. His mother wouldn't have allowed it, and with the way the humans were systematically eliminating the gray wolf population here in the south, mating runs were too dangerous, anyway.

That's why there were so few werewolves left. That's why they were retreating more and more into their compounds, reinforcing their gates, patrolling their walls as much to keep the pack in as to keep humans—and other packs—out.

Josh never intended to go back. And once the priestess wove her spell, he'd be no use to the pack anyway, at least not for the use they wanted to put him.

The chair next to him scraped along the wooden floor. Josh startled at the sound and looked up at—

"You!" he said, then clapped his hands over his mouth when his startled cry drew the disgruntled stares of the nearest customers.

"Aye." The man Josh had run into out on the street, the beautiful one with the mass of curly hair, set his guitar case on the floor. "And you too, it would seem."

An Introduction

Josh shrank in his seat, the cloth binding his chest seeming tight enough to crush his ribs yet loose enough to pool around his waist. Did this man *know*? Could he *see*? Would he expect the same thing from Josh as everyone in the pack? "Did you follow me?"

"Just here for the music, same as you, mate." When Josh flinched at the word *mate*, the stranger's tawny brows drew together. "You all right, then?"

Fighting to catch his breath, Josh nodded. *Never show them you're afraid. That only makes them crueler.*

"Mind if I join you?"

"I don't do sex," Josh blurted.

The stranger blinked. "I didn't ask, but fair enough." He sat. "Neither do I, if it comes to that."

Josh released his painful grip on his fiddle. "Oh."

The stranger held out his hand. "Gareth."

Josh's tension ratcheted up again and he couldn't do anything but stare at Gareth's fingers, long and tapered. Even in the smoky dimness, Josh could spot the calluses on the fingertips: a musician's hand, a guitarist's hand, a hand that played over strings, just as Josh's did.

But Josh couldn't offer his own hand in return. Not today. If anybody touched his bare skin today, he might combust.

He swallowed, wondering if the priestess would need to touch him when she took his music. *Combusting might be the better path.* He'd heard that people could do that. Spontaneously combust and burn to ash, especially when the priestess was involved.

Gareth seemed to understand that Josh wasn't going to shake, but he just smiled wryly and dropped his hand to the tabletop, turning to face the stage while one finger kept time with the beat.

When Gareth didn't press for more, Josh was able to rein in his galloping heart. "J-Josh," he murmured, voice all but inaudible even without the music's glorious noise. "My name's Josh."

He didn't expect Gareth to react. He'd only spoken for his own benefit, reminding himself that from tonight, he was Josh, would be Josh forever, even if he'd no longer have the part of his soul that truly defined him.

Gareth surprised him yet again, though. He glanced over and inclined his head. "Nice to meet you, Josh."

And that was it. He turned back to watch the musicians, swaying a little in his chair, and didn't try to force the conversation or dig for more personal details or *overwhelm* Josh with his own life story. That in itself was so peculiar that Josh couldn't drag his gaze away from Gareth's profile.

Even back at the compound, where he'd known everyone from the time he was born, no one in the pack could ever speak to him without boasting of their prowess. After twenty-two years, none of them had anything new to tell, but that didn't stop them from repeating themselves.

His mother had always told him to ignore them. "They're trying to impress you, so you'll pick them when the time comes."

Josh had folded himself into as small a ball as he could manage, knees tucked to his chest under his skirt and shawl over his head. "I won't pick any of them. I don't want the time to come."

His mother had smiled at him, her expression full of love and regret. "I know, my child. But it will happen. Someday I won't be here to shield you from your father." She'd taken both his hands, gripping them almost painfully. "And on that day, if you don't wish to be forced to mate, you must run. Promise me. Promise me you'll run."

"But I don't have anywhere to go," Josh had wailed. "If I shift, the hunters will find me."

"It's not the hunters you need to beware," she'd said grimly. "It's the pack. The hunters will only shoot you. The pack will kill you by degrees, day by day, year by year. Better a quick death than a bottomless pit of despair."

Now, Josh tilted his head, frowning at Gareth's perfect profile, an odd whiff of *other* which was quickly masked again by smoke and the smell of stale liquor. He hadn't had much interaction with human men. Maybe they were different from werewolves, less aggressive, less selfish. He had no yardstick by which to measure. When Josh had been small and his mother had taken him with her when she left the compound to visit the market, she'd only ever spoken to other women.

Although Gareth seemed distantly friendly, Josh couldn't afford to let his guard down. Not now. Not when a different future was so close.

But how close? A frisson slithered down Josh's back. What time was it? Was he too late? Were Otis and Emmett gone? Was it safe to leave yet?

Up on the stage, the band finished their number in a joyous crescendo. The audience erupted into applause and whistles and shouts, making Josh cringe. After the band left the stage, the noise died away to be replaced by the murmur of conversation, the occasional bark of laughter, and the clink of glasses against wood.

Josh took his courage in both hands and leaned forward.

First and Last

"Excuse me?" Josh had to clear his throat and try again when his voice emerged in nothing but a croak. "Excuse me? Gareth?"

Gareth turned his head, one eyebrow quirked. "Yes?"

"Do you happen to have the time?"

"Half nine, give or take." Gareth chuckled, probably because Josh was staring at him as though he were speaking gibberish. "You lot would say half past, I reckon, or nine-thirty?"

"That's not why... You didn't look at a watch. How did you know?"

Gareth's open face shuttered for an instant before his smile was back, although perhaps not as sincere as it had been. "I checked before I sat down."

"Oh. Well. Thank you."

It was far earlier than Josh had feared. He had to reach Congo Square by midnight, which would take some time since he had to stay in the shadows. But with the enforcers roaming the Quarter and with the storm about to break, he was probably safer—not to mention drier—here for a while longer.

A stout man with a white apron around his middle stopped at their table. "What'll it be?"

"Any ale for me," Gareth said.

The man grunted. "Beer it is." He turned to Josh. "You?"

Josh hunched over his fiddle. He didn't have any money. If he couldn't pay for a drink—one that he didn't even want—would they throw him out?

"He'll have the same," Gareth said.

The man grunted again and walked away, and a spark of anger fired in Josh's chest.

"Why did you say that? I don't want beer, and I couldn't pay for it if I did."

Gareth's eyebrows disappeared under the curls that fell over his forehead. "Musicians don't pay for their drinks."

"What?"

He nodded at Josh's fiddle case. "You're here to play, right? Sitting at the musicians' table? They won't pay for your performance, but you'll always have a seat and your drinks come free."

"P-performance?" His heart tried to burst through the bindings. "I didn't... I only came in because... because..." He gulped, staring at the stage. Could he get up there, under those unforgiving lights, where all these people could *look* at him? What would happen if they suspected, if they could tell, if they... if they...?

He pushed the terror down, low in his belly, where he'd learned to bury it since he first knew the truth about himself. He'd only ever played for his mother or alone in the woods, and after tonight, after the priestess, he'd never play for anybody—including himself—ever again.

Wasn't it worth the risk? Wouldn't it be a fitting memorial to his music to have its first performance along with its last?

"I've never... I don't know if I could..."

Gareth smiled, not unkindly. "If you're worried about being accepted by the audience, don't be. They expect to hear new talent. It's why they come here. I've been here plenty of times, and the only thing that winds them up is bad playing or out of tune instruments."

"So you've played here before then?"

He glanced away. "No. I... don't perform in public."

Josh scowled at him, cheek pressed against his fiddle case. "If you can't bring yourself to do it, then it must not be as easy as you say."

"Music should never be *easy*. Not if it comes from your heart."

"And yours doesn't? Is that why you're afraid?"

"It's not that. I—" Gareth blew out a breath through pursed lips. "Goddess, I must be out of my bleeding mind," he muttered. But then he quirked at eyebrow at Josh. "So. You any good?"

Josh straightened his shoulders and lifted his chin. He might be the least of his pack. Small. Weak. Unprepossessing. But nobody—*nobody*—was allowed to question his music. "Yes."

"Well then." Gareth gestured to the stage. "Let's show them."

His momentary bravado deserted him. "You're willing to play with me?" he squeaked. "But you've never... And I've never... And you don't know my tunes."

Gareth stood and picked up his guitar case. "You lead. I'll follow. Trust me." His grin had a feral edge that would make an alpha whimper and bare his throat. "I'll keep up."

The barkeep arrived and set their beers on the table with a thump. He gave them an approving nod. "You'll have half an hour for your set before the band finishes their break. Think you can fill it?"

Gareth shot Josh a conspiratorial glance. "Count on it, mate." He jerked his head toward the stage, his curls bouncing. "Coming?"

Josh grabbed the glass and took a gulp of beer, its hoppy flavor bitter on his tongue. He hated beer, but he needed to wet his dry mouth. *The kick in the pants from the alcohol doesn't hurt either.*

"Yes." He glanced down at his calico-wrapped bundle. "Should I—"

"That'll be fine where it is," the barkeep said. "Nobody who comes in my door bothers a musician or they'll answer to me."

Gareth swung toward the stage with an easy, confident stride that had to be born of experience. Josh crept along behind, keeping his elbows in and trying to look as small as possible. Gareth didn't even bother with the steps at the side of the stage —he just leapt onto it like it wasn't three feet off the floor.

Josh knew his limits. He took the stairs.

Smoke eddied in front of the lights, but they were still bright enough to make him squint. He laid his case on the piano stool and flipped it open. The mellow glow of his fiddle's carefully tended golden-brown wood caught under his heart. It had been his truest companion for most of his life, ever since his mother decided his arms were long enough to play it. He traced a finger along the E string.

He'd never hear it sing again after tonight.

Josh huffed out a breath and lifted it from its worn velvet nest. If it truly was to be the last time, he'd make sure he gave his beloved fiddle the sendoff it deserved.

Duet

Gareth had already slung his guitar strap around his neck by the time Josh joined him in the middle of the stage.

"Do you need to tune up?" Josh asked.

An odd expression flickered over Gareth's face, and for a moment, despite his undeniable beauty, he looked nearly as bleak as Josh felt. "I'm good. You?"

Josh plucked the strings and adjusted the A, because its peg was a little worn. He'd intended to repair it, but...

He pushed the wave of despair away. *One last time.* He'd make it a good one.

As he placed the fiddle under his chin, the familiar *rightness* filled him from his toes all the way to his head. It banished the fear, banished the uncertainty, banished the sorrow, and made him shoot Gareth a challenging grin.

"Try to keep up," he said and launched into the first tune.

Gareth laughed, and to Josh's astonishment, did just that.

No matter how quickly Josh's bow danced over the strings, Gareth's guitar was there, chords blending seamlessly, both supporting Josh's music and pushing it forward.

Then something changed and instead of pushing, Gareth was *luring* Josh, daring him to go further than he'd ever gone before. Josh's heart was so full it was as though it was beating right there on the stage with him, visible to anyone who cared to look.

The glow inside, that glow that music always stoked, grew and grew and grew until Josh couldn't contain it. The audience faded from his consciousness because only the notes flying from his fiddle and Gareth's guitar mattered, glittering in the air, so real he could almost touch them.

If he can do it, so can I.

So Josh met Gareth's gaze and, with a trill, followed by an arpeggio, passed the lead to him.

Gareth grinned, white teeth flashing in the light, and picked up the cue. Now *Josh* was following *him*, and no matter what Gareth had claimed, it was easy, so easy, like breathing. They didn't even pause between one improvisation and the next, just passed the lead back and forth between them for what seemed like forever and also no time at all.

And then Gareth started to sing.

It wasn't any language that Josh recognized, but that didn't matter. Between his voice, his guitar, and Josh's fiddle, the sound was... *oh*. Josh would have stopped to listen except he couldn't bear to stop playing.

But then... it ended, coming to the most natural, the most inevitable end, the final note of Josh's fiddle dying away with Gareth's words and last chord.

In the silence that followed, Josh's breath caught up with his heart as he and Gareth stared at one another, and he let his bow drop because his arm couldn't hold it up any longer.

He smiled tremulously at Gareth. "Thank you," he murmured. *Thank you for a fitting goodbye to my music.*

Then the applause started like a clap of thunder, the cheers and the hoots and the stomping feet rolling over Josh like a wave.

Gareth lifted an eyebrow. "Take a bow, mate."

When Josh just stared at him, blinking, Gareth grasped Josh's wrist, raising both their arms in the air. Since Josh still couldn't make himself move, Gareth shook his head and gently took Josh's fiddle and bow. He replaced them in their case and handed it off to Josh who took it reflexively. Still bemused, Josh followed Gareth offstage, pattering along behind him through the still applauding crowd until they reached their table.

Their abandoned beers had been replaced by fresh glasses that flanked a scatter of coins and a few bills. Josh stumbled to a halt and stared at it all.

"I thought you said they wouldn't pay us."

"The club doesn't pay. But the audience is free to tip the musicians if they like the performance." Gareth smiled crookedly. "I reckon they liked us."

Josh plopped into his chair because his legs couldn't hold him up anymore. "I... That was... I didn't know..."

Gareth sat down next to him and nudged Josh's glass toward him. "Here. You probably need water more, but around here, the beer's probably safer to drink."

Josh eyed the beer, nose wrinkled. *Ugh. Beer.* But his mouth *was* dry, so he took a gulp, grimacing at the taste again. "How did you come up with lyrics on the fly? And what was that language?"

"It was naught but my shopping list." When Josh goggled at him, Gareth shrugged. "Everything sounds impressive in Welsh. All those syllables and consonants, and nobody can tell whether it rhymes or not." He swept the money toward Josh. "You take this."

Josh held up his hands, shaking his head wildly. "No! You should take half. Maybe more. I'd never have gone up there if it weren't for you."

"Nah. It won't do me any good where I'm going next. You take it. Although..." Gareth scooted his chair closer and rested his elbows on the table. "I think we make a good pair." When Josh shrank away, hiding behind another gulp of beer, Gareth held up one palm. "Just for the music, mate. Nothing else. How'd you like to do it again?"

Leaving It Behind

The future crashed back down on Josh. "I can't. I'm… I just can't."

Gareth studied him with a frown. "What's wrong? You in trouble? Can I help?"

"No." For courage, as false as it was, Josh took another gulp of beer. "Do you know what time it is?"

"We were playing for an hour so—"

"An hour? But the barkeep said thirty minutes."

Gareth lifted one shoulder, frown fading into a mischievous smile. "He knows better than to break into an act when the audience is as rapt as they were. He can serve them round after round and they pay without thinking. Besides, the house band would have refused to take the stage. They respect other musicians too much."

Josh scooped the money into his hands and stuffed it in his jacket pockets. He was desperate, not stupid, and he'd need it if he intended to leave the city and then the state, getting as far away from the pack as he could manage. "I've got to go."

Gareth flinched slightly at Josh's abrupt tone. "Already? We could do another set."

"No. I have an… an appointment. I can't miss it."

"Then meet me tomorrow. Anywhere you like." He smiled a little sadly. "I've been on my own for a good while now. It might be nice to be part of a duo for a change."

Josh's throat ached with yearning, but his path was set and he couldn't afford to step off, not now, not when the end was so close. "I can't. Truly. I'm sorry. This has been…" He swallowed and forced a smile. "This has been wonderful. I wouldn't have done it—*couldn't* have done it without you. So thank you. From the bottom of my heart, thank you."

He pushed the chair back and rose to his feet before regret threatened to overwhelm his resolve. What would it be like to play music every day, every night, with someone whose gifts meshed so effortlessly with his own? Someone, moreover, who didn't expect Josh to bring anything *other* than music to the partnership?

He would never know, because after tonight, his music wouldn't belong to him anymore. It would be the property of the priestess and her Loas and out of his reach forever.

Josh gave Gareth a quick nod and made his way toward the door as the house band broke into a blues tune that made Josh's heart clench. At the door, the bouncer gave him a nod of approval.

"Leaving? Wouldn't mind hearing you play again."

"Thank you. Yes. I can't stay."

"Come back any time."

Josh ducked his head, mumbling something that *might* have been agreement if nobody had ever heard a cry of agony before, and slipped through the door.

As soon as he crossed the threshold, the wind slammed into him, snatching his hat off his head and sending it sailing down the street. He was tempted to let it go, but he didn't have the money for another, and it was much easier to hide his face under its brim.

He tucked his fiddle case under his arm and took off after it, his bundle with its makeshift strap bouncing on his back with each step. Josh might not be large, but he was quick. He caught the hat at the corner, snatching it off the pavement before it could skitter into the gutter. None too soon, because as he jammed it back on, thunder boomed overhead and the skies opened up.

In a heartbeat, Josh was drenched, the wind swirling the rain so it seemed to come from all directions at once. The wool of his soaked jacket offered some warmth at least, but his shirt clung clammily, and the bindings lost tightness.

Josh wiped the rain out of his eyes, peering around to reorient himself. He fought against the wind, trudging back the way he'd come. Between the rain pounding on the pavement and the runoff rushing down the gutters, Josh could barely hear anything, despite his werewolf senses.

He passed one corner. A second. Then stopped when he reached a third. Could this be right? He hadn't run so far, had he? He pivoted, squinting through the rain and the dark. Which way? He'd memorized the route to Congo Square, but he didn't know the city at all, and now he'd lost his way.

The club. If I can make my way there, I can find my path again.

Josh stretched his senses, straining to hear a whisper of music, a smatter of applause, anything that would point him in the right direction. Another clap of thunder nearly deafened him, but in its aftermath he *thought* he heard the wail of the trumpet.

He put his head down and turned toward the sound, his sodden shoes slipping on the cobblestones, rain lashing against his face as he held onto his hat with one hand and clutched his fiddle to his chest with the other.

"Jerusha!"

At that shout, at the sound of that hated name, Josh froze. Only for an instant, no longer, but that instant was his downfall. A huge hand grasped his arm and jerked him back against a solid chest.

Confrontation

"Jerusha." Emmett's breath, still reeking of vomit, was hot against Josh's cheek. "Did you really think this outfit would fool us? That we couldn't smell you?" He snatched Josh's fedora off and tossed it aside, to be borne away on the wind. Then he stuck his nose in the crook of Josh's neck and inhaled, growling. "We all know that scent."

"Let me go." Josh struggled against Emmett's hold. "Please."

Otis laughed, low and cruel, as he strutted around to crowd Josh in from the front, sandwiching him between both enforcers. "Not a chance. The alpha'd like a little chat with you."

"I don't have anything to say to my father."

Emmett joined Otis's laughter and then barked, "Nobody can say anything to him anymore. He's dead."

Josh sucked in a breath, as though he'd been punched in the gut. He'd never liked his father, had always been three parts terrified and one part disgusted by him, but dead? "Wh-what?"

"Without his bitch, he was useless to the pack. Beau challenged him and won. That's right. Tore your daddy's throat clean out, fair and square. Now that Beau's in charge, he says it's time you learned your place." Emmett licked a stripe up Josh's neck. "Under him." He laughed again. "Maybe under all of us. Now let's go home."

When he jerked Josh forward roughly, Josh's numb fingers lost his grip on his fiddle case, and it clattered to the cobbles, inches from the water rushing down the gutter. Josh cried out, reaching for it, but Otis grabbed his other arm. They were both so much taller that they lifted him off the ground until his toes barely brushed the street.

"Oi!"

The shout filled the air, drowning the drill of the rain, the rush of the gutters. It ricocheted off the buildings, echoing as though they were in the ravine that bordered the pack lands instead of the middle of the city.

For some reason, both enforcers froze, and since Josh was pinned between them, he could feel the muscles in both men strain.

"What the fuck?" Emmett muttered.

Footsteps approached, sharp against the cobbles, and then Gareth was standing in front of them, his curls plastered to his forehead and a look of absolute fury transforming his ethereal face. An avenging angel.

Then he met Josh's gaze and his expression softened. "You all right, mate?"

"No," Josh whispered.

"That's what I thought." Gareth glared first at Emmett and then at Otis, his eyes practically glowing under another flash of lightning. "Release him."

Thunder crashed after those words, but Josh could swear it was Gareth's voice, low and absolute, yet somehow more primal than an alpha's howl, that made the enforcers release Josh as though he were on fire.

"Who the fuck are you?" Emmett barked.

Gareth ignored him. "Better get your violin, Josh."

Josh scrambled to do just that as Otis scoffed. "Josh? That what she said her name was?"

Gareth's face could have been carved of marble. "I don't like you, and I don't think Josh likes you either. We're leaving." He stepped between them and held out his hand to Josh. "I know you didn't want to touch me before, but if we're to get away now, it's necessary."

Josh's gaze skittered between Gareth and the two enforcers, who seemed rooted to the ground, their arms frozen at peculiar angles as though they still held Josh between them. "What?"

"You don't want to go with them, do you?"

Josh shook his head wildly. "No! Never."

"Then trust me." Gareth smiled—not challenging or mischievous or wry, or any of his moods from the club—but so kind, so *understanding* that Josh's throat thickened. "One musician to another."

Josh nodded and placed his hand in Gareth's.

"Jerusha!" Emmett bellowed. "You can't get away. We'll find you. And you'll be sorry."

Gareth shot them a scornful glance. "I think not." Then he met Josh's gaze again. "I won't be able to hold them in place once we're moving. But when I say jump, jump. Get it?"

Josh nodded again. "Got it."

"Good." Then Gareth grinned. "Let's go."

He took off at a run, heading straight down the middle of the street, Josh pounding along beside him, clutching his fiddle with his other hand for all he was worth.

"Jerusha!" Emmett roared and Josh flinched, because clearly he and Otis weren't frozen anymore, their heavy footsteps getting closer, closer, closer, as Josh and Gareth reached the surging gutter.

"Jump!" Gareth called, and Josh obeyed.

The two of them cleared the gutter, but instead of hitting the sidewalk on its other side, they landed somewhere... else.

Springy grass and soft earth cushioned Josh's landing, and the sky was suddenly cloudless, the air tinged with woodsmoke, not exhaust.

Josh let go of Gareth's hand and looked around wildly. Instead of the gutter, they stood beside a rushing stream. Instead of the brick walls and wrought-iron balconies of the French Quarter, a hill, crowned by trees, rose in front of them.

"Wh-where... What... How?"

Gareth shrugged and glanced around with a grimace of distaste. "Welcome to Faerie, mate."

Rescue

Josh goggled at Gareth. "Faerie? Like, actual Faerie? It's real?"

Gareth cocked an eyebrow. "For a werewolf, I'd think you'd be less surprised about supernatural shite."

Josh blinked. "You... you knew?"

"Well, not at once. Not from anything you did. But those other blokes? They clearly hadn't bathed since their last shift. They stank like wet dog. *Filthy* wet dog." He studied Josh's face, eyebrows bunched with worry. "I got it right, didn't I? You didn't want to go with them?"

Josh laughed shakily. "I've been trying to get away my whole life, so that would be no."

"Thank the goddess." Gareth passed a hand over his head, further disarranging his wet curls. "I've been known to make unfortunate, impulsive decisions. Glad I made the right one this time."

Josh peered at him in the light of a full moon that seemed far larger than it ought to be. "If you don't mind my asking, who *are* you?"

Gareth placed his fist on his chest and bowed slightly. "Gareth Cynwrig, also known as Gareth Kendrick, last true bard of Faerie." He stood again, and that expression of disgust was back. "For my sins."

"Josh Wills," Josh blurted, his southern manners kicking in automatically. Then what Gareth said registered, and, for a moment, Josh couldn't find his voice, but finally he managed, "B-bard?"

"*True* bard, mate. It's a whole... thing." His gaze drifted to the hill, lips flattening into a grim line. "And they never let me forget." He turned back to Josh and smiled, this time genuinely.

"Although in this case, it worked out well, since it let me freeze those arseholes in their tracks."

Josh glanced behind him nervously. The stream chuckled over mossy rocks, and a meadow dotted with wildflowers that glowed in the moonlight stretched away on its opposite bank. New Orleans had disappeared as though it had never been.

"Can they follow us?"

"Nah." He grinned. "*They're* not the last true bard of bloody Faerie. The portal won't open for them."

"Oh. That's... good, I guess." Josh hugged his fiddle case for comfort, to anchor himself in a place without any familiar landmarks. True, he hadn't been *happy* in his old life, but at least he'd known the rules. "But how do *I* get out?"

Gareth set his guitar case at his feet. "Do you want to get out?"

"I... I have an appointment. I can't miss it. It's my only chance to... to..." Josh's voice broke.

"Here now." Gareth stepped closer but didn't breach Josh's personal space. "If you truly want to go back, I'll take you. But do you really think those arseholes will have left? Given up? Since we haven't passed a full day here, the same amount of time will have passed in the Outer World. You'll be right back where you started. And didn't they say they could track you by scent?"

Josh's shoulders slumped and his legs gave out. He plopped onto the ground and hunched over his fiddle. "It was my only chance."

Gareth hunkered down in front of him. "Only chance for what, mate?" His voice was soothing, inviting. "Tell me."

Josh narrowed his eyes. "Are you using that true bard hoodoo on me?"

"I'd never use it on a friend. But I'd like to help." He laughed ruefully. "And trust me when I say that's not something that's happened in over two hundred years."

Josh chewed on his lip, gazing into Gareth's eyes. He was good at reading people—their intentions, their sorrows, their resentments. He'd had to be, to survive in the pack, even with his mother's protection. But he couldn't detect any ulterior motives behind Gareth's words.

Maybe he truly does want to help.

"I'm to meet the voudoun priestess at midnight. She'll... change me. My body. Make me who I am."

"Ah," Gareth said. "What's the price?"

Josh blinked. "How do you know there's a price?"

"There's always a price, mate."

"My music." Josh's voice was barely audible over the burble of the stream. "The price is my music."

Gareth's face hardened. "No."

"You don't understand. I—"

"Oh, I understand, all right. But your music makes you who you are too. You can't sacrifice half of yourself for the other half."

"But—"

"Tell you what." Gareth stood and propped his fists on his hips. "You come along with me now. I don't spend any more time in Faerie than I have to, but my brother has a place we can stay tonight. Tomorrow, we'll talk again."

"The priestess won't give me another chance."

"Good. Because the cost of that chance is too high. We'll find another way." He held out a hand. "Now let's go. It's a bit of a climb and you've had a shock. Think you can manage?"

Josh hesitated for only an instant before taking Gareth's hand and standing. He balanced on shaky legs. Something about Faerie made him... not uneasy. Wary, perhaps, as though many eyes were on him. Measuring him. Evaluating him. Judging him?

He dropped Gareth's hand and straightened his shoulders, unwilling to appear less in front of those hidden watchers. Then he lifted his chin. Watchers be damned, he refused to appear less in front of *Gareth*.

"Do you promise? That we'll find another way?"

Gareth met Josh's gaze steadily. "Trust me. In the morning, things will look very different."

Another World

As Josh followed Gareth up the hill—which he called *the* tor, as though it were the only one—he had a hard time staying on his feet. For one thing, he was in *Faerie*. With an actual *bard*. Who had frozen two hulking werewolf enforcers in place *with his voice*.

That had to be why he felt so... peculiar, with pins and needles prickling under his skin as though his whole body had fallen asleep.

Maybe it had. Maybe this was a dream. Maybe he was still cowering in the woods behind the pack compound.

He blinked up at the sky—was it actually *purple*?—tripped over a rock, and stumbled into Gareth's back.

"Easy, there, mate." Gareth steadied him with a hand on his arm and then immediately let go, as though he *knew* how touch could spike Josh's anxiety. "You all right?"

Josh didn't really mind Gareth's touch, however. For one thing, it was fleeting. For another, there wasn't anything threatening or amorous about it. He was just... helping, and never mind Faerie, and bards, and voice magic. In Josh's experience *that* was the truly unbelievable thing.

"I'm fine. Thank you." Josh tried a smile, and it wasn't even hard to hold on to. "Just wasn't paying attention to my feet."

Gareth cocked an eyebrow, but then simply nodded and turned to resume the climb. And Josh stumbled *again*, because suddenly they'd topped the tor when Josh had been certain there was still at least a quarter of a mile of uneven ground ahead.

Gareth paused and waited for Josh to join him. "Not far now." He gestured at the path ahead that wound through the woods, tree branches dotted with white blossoms laced overhead to form a living archway. "Just down this path, through the ceilidh glade, and we're there."

The path was wide enough that they could walk abreast. Gareth didn't say anything as they cleared the trees and crossed a mossy clearing with a low wooden dais at one end. Josh caught a glimpse of enormous towering stones beyond that, but before he could ask about them, they were under the trees again and then... out.

Josh caught his breath. A broad lake stretched out below them, its water gilded with moonlight. A building that looked like something out of a book of fairy tales—*heh*—stood on its shore, smoke curling out its chimney.

"Looks like my brother's home." Gareth cut a glance at Josh. "Don't let him alarm you."

"Is he so alarming? Is he a bard too?"

Gareth's wide mouth twisted. "No. Not a bard."

They walked down the grassy slope and up to the wooden door framed by a rambling rose. Gareth didn't even knock—just pushed it open and walked inside. Josh glanced over his shoulder once, still unable to catch a glimpse of those unseen watchers that he was *positive* were there, and followed Gareth across the threshold.

A man stood next to the fireplace, his back to the door. He was... tall. Taller than the enforcers, taller than any alpha Josh had ever met. Josh sucked in a breath and ducked behind Gareth, because while the man's shoulders were so broad Josh doubted he could walk through the door without turning sideways, it wasn't his *size* that was alarming. At least not entirely.

It was the enormous *sword* that was strapped to his back, its hilt extending above his head and the scabbard halfway down his thighs.

The man turned, and from his spot peering over Gareth's shoulder, Josh could see that he was just as beautiful as Gareth, although his hair was black and wavy and his eyes a startling darker blue, almost cobalt.

Then he grinned and his beauty increased tenfold. "Gareth!"

Josh grimaced inwardly. While he could recognize their beauty—appreciate it even, as he would a painting or a statue—he still had no desire to *do* anything about it. Like always.

The other man strode across the room, his arms outstretched as though to embrace Gareth, but then his gaze snagged on Josh, cowering in Gareth's shadow. And his grin grew even wider.

"Goddess strike me blind, Gareth, you did it. I never thought you'd get over—"

"Mal." Gareth's voice was sharp, but Josh could detect a thread of despair in it. "Stop."

The man, who apparently was named Mal, didn't. He took Gareth's shoulders in his big hands and gave him a little shake. "When you weren't holed up in that sorry excuse for a house in the Orkneys, I hoped you'd finally started getting out there again. Trust me, music and men. That's the best medicine." He grinned. "Well, not the music so much for me, but definitely for you. Where did you go? Paris? Rome? Vienna?"

"New Orleans," Gareth mumbled, "but that's not—"

"New Orleans? Brilliant!" Then Mal's expression changed, serious and maybe a little hopeful. "Alun's in America now. Did you see him?"

Josh wasn't touching Gareth, but he could sense the tension fairly rolling off him. He stared into Mal's eyes for a full eight-count before he spoke.

"No."

Time Matters

Josh blinked. It was the first time since he'd met Gareth that his rich voice was wooden.

"Gareth. You know he never—"

"Give over, Mal. It'll never happen." Gareth's shoulders rose and fell with an audible breath. "And whatever else you think happened in the Outer World, didn't, and never will." He took a slight step to the side. "This is Josh. Another musician. I met him in a club in the French Quarter."

Mal's eyebrows drew together for a moment as he studied his brother's face, but then turned that dazzling smile on Josh and held out a hand.

"Good to meet you, mate." Josh's lungs froze, both at the word and at Mal's proximity, both arms locking around his fiddle case. Something flickered across Mal's face then, and he dropped his arm. "Ah." Then he cocked his head. "Wait. Werewolf? Don't think we've ever had one in Faerie before. I'm surprised the gateway spells let you in." He smirked and jerked a thumb at Gareth. "Although since you were with this bloke, I suppose it's not a shocker. Faerie'll do just about anything for him.

Gareth shot a glare at Mal. "Josh was having trouble with a couple of his packmates—"

"They're not my packmates," Josh said, low and fierce. "It's not my pack. Not anymore." He glanced away. "I don't think it ever was."

Mal's eyebrows rose nearly to the shock of hair that waved across his forehead. "Lone wolf? That's a tough row to hoe, mate."

Josh lifted his chin. "Better alone than with them."

Gareth shot Josh an encouraging smile, then faced his brother again. "So we took a little detour here to shake them off our trail. I was hoping we could stay with you for a bit until Josh decides what he'd like to do next."

Mal grimaced, running a hand through his thick hair. "Shite. You know you're always welcome. You too, Josh. But I've got an audience with the Queen and Consort."

"You do?" Gareth's voice held breathless hope. "Are you going to ask her about—"

"She already said no. Twice. I can't bring it up. Not again."

"But—"

"Gareth. They don't want to hear it. They're not about to confront the Unseelie King and risk an outright war. Not for one human." Mal glanced at Josh. "No offense."

"Not human," Josh reminded him.

"Right. Anyway, this is a command appearance. They've got a job for me and I'm already late. I don't know how long I'll be, but put the kettle on and make yourselves at home." Mal's gaze cut to Josh and then back to Gareth. "But watch your time, all right? Don't know if werewolves are subject to the same time rules as humans, but you of all people should make sure he knows his options. And their consequences."

"I'll pretend you didn't say that." Gareth gripped Mal's forearm. "And Mal? Don't tell her I'm here."

Mal smiled crookedly. "She's the Queen, mate. She already knows." He nodded to Josh. "Good to meet you, Josh. Welcome to Faerie." And then he was gone, latching the door softly behind him.

Gareth let out a shaky breath. "So. That was my brother."

"I gathered," Josh said dryly. "What did he mean about watching our time?"

"I'll get to that." Gareth gestured to a round wooden table next to a curtained-off doorway. "Have a seat. I'll put the kettle on as ordered and then we'll chat."

Josh settled into a ladder-backed chair with a woven rush seat and set his fiddle case at his feet. Gareth disappeared behind the curtain, and Josh heard the telltale sound of a water pump. He took a moment to look around the cottage. This main room wasn't huge, but it wasn't tiny either. It was… cozy, with two overstuffed chairs drawn up near the fireplace. The wall opposite the front door held two other doorways, one curtained and one with a door made from the same rough boards as the floor.

Gareth emerged with a black kettle in his hand. "I don't know why Mal hasn't modernized his kitchen. He was quick enough to put a toilet and shower in his bathroom."

He hung the kettle on an iron hook mounted next to the fireplace and pushed it over the flames before settling in the chair across from Josh. He folded his hands on the table and studied them for a long moment.

"So. About the time issue." He looked up and met Josh's gaze with an expression that Josh could only describe as shame. "We fae have… an unfortunate history with humans."

"You mean the stories about kidnapping babies and leaving changelings in their place?"

Gareth snorted, but clearly not from amusement. "Babies weren't the only humans we kidnapped. We've been known to spirit away humans who… who catch our fancy. Keep them here in Faerie until we tire of them and then?" He flicked his fingers out. "Discard them. Send them back to the Outer World. The problem with that is that time doesn't run at the same pace here as it does out there. If they've spent much time here, even as little as one full day, they could return to a completely different world than they left. Time will have passed and left them behind."

"How… how much time?"

Gareth shrugged. "It's hard to tell. I've always suspected that Faerie has its own agenda, an agenda that doesn't take anyone's fortunes or true feelings into account." He scowled. "Which is one of the reasons I stay out of here as much as possible." His gaze drifted to the window beside him. "This is the first time I've done anything other than pass through on my way from one place to another in… well, in a very long time."

"How long?" Josh whispered.

Gareth's crooked smile didn't reach his eyes. "Almost two hundred years."

Tea with a Bard

"Two hundred *years*?" Josh gripped the edge of the table. "Why? Is it dangerous?"

"No more than anyplace else, I reckon."

"Should we leave now? If you don't want to be here—"

"No." Gareth heaved a sigh. "It's not that. I mean, I *don't* want to be here and I may not like it, but I can stomach it for as long as we need to stay. If we were to go back now, I'm not sure your situation would be much better than it was when we left. At this point, the time difference is essentially one for one, so your pursuers could still be waiting. But if we stay for longer—a day, two days, three—I'm not sure what we'll find when we return."

"You say *we*..."

Gareth met Josh's eyes, his gaze intent, and Josh felt as though he were pinned in place. "I'll not abandon you, mate." But then his expression softened, and Josh could breathe again. "Not if it means we can play music together again."

Josh smiled for what felt like the first time since his mother died. "I'd like that. And if it means escaping the pack, I don't care how long we stay. Although when we go back, do we have to return to New Orleans? Is that the only place there's a... a portal?"

Gareth shook his head, his damp curls glinting with gold in the firelight. "No. There are many gateways." His smile turned mischievous and perhaps a little evil. "And as a bard, I can open any of them I fancy." Josh shivered and Gareth's smile faded. "Shite. You're still all wet. For that matter, so am I."

Josh shrugged. "It's not so bad. We dried off a little as we walked and it's not like it's really that cold, either here or in New Orleans." Gareth's lips twitched. "What?"

"It's your accent. *Nawlins*."

"*I* don't have an accent." Josh primmed his lips and stuck his nose in the air. "*You* have an accent."

Gareth slapped a hand to his chest. "Me? I'm just your ordinary Welshman. Sound the same as any other bloke in Cardiff or Aberystwyth."

Josh smirked. "Accent. Definitely. And I'm pretty sure nobody anywhere truly sounds like you." He waggled his eyebrows. "Last true bard of Faerie and all that?"

"So sassy now," Gareth said, his tone admiring. He gestured toward the wooden door in the opposite wall. "Mal's got a brownie cleaning service, so I'm sure there are some towels in the loo."

Josh's eyes widened. "Brownies? They're real?"

"They are, and they'd probably ask the same thing about werewolves since, as Mal said, Faerie's not familiar with your sort." Gareth scowled. "Just as well, or I'm sure some entitled arsehole would decide to kidnap one."

"I'd like to see them try," Josh muttered.

Gareth sobered. "No. You don't." He turned away and strode toward the other curtained door. "I'll look out some dry clothes for us. Mal has a boring wardrobe, but there's always a lot of it."

"He's about twice my size. Nothing's going to fit me."

Gareth shot a grin over his shoulder. "This is Faerie, mate. They'll fit." He disappeared into the other room.

Josh bit his lip. He really did want to get out of these wet things. His thighs were chafed from the long hike in rough, damp wool, and his bindings were loose enough to shift uncomfortably too. His armpits felt hot and raw.

He stood, but before he could take a step, he caught a whisper of sound from outside—a soft thump followed by a tiny scratch at the front door. Somebody without a werewolf's acute hearing would have missed it.

His nose twitched and he inhaled deeply, mouth watering. *And someone without werewolf's sensitive nose would have missed the delectable aroma of pastries.*

He listened, straining his ears for more sounds, but there was nothing. He crept to the door and eased it open. There, on the doorstep, was a wooden tray with a plate of round, perfectly browned... what? Not biscuits, at least not the kind Josh was used to, with grits or sausage gravy. Their scent held a hint of sweetness, and they were studded with small, dark fruit whose smell Josh didn't recognize.

He poked his head out the door but couldn't see anybody or detect any movement at all. However, nobody wandered the woods and left plates of fresh-baked goodies on random porches. Clearly this was an intentional delivery meant for the cottage's resident. Granted, the resident was usually Mal, but Mal had told Josh and Gareth to make themselves at home, and it would be a crime to leave something that smelled *that* good outside at the mercy of ants or opossums or— Wait, did Faerie have ants or opossums?

Josh shook his head. It hardly mattered, and in any case, he hadn't had anything to eat since he'd fled the compound, and he wasn't about to look a gift biscuit in the mouth.

He picked up the tray and brought it inside, nudging the door closed with his hip. He set it on the table, biting his lip and glancing from the plate to the curtained doorway. *Should I wait?* According to what he could hear from the other room, Gareth was tossing his brother's bedroom like a burglar. He could be in there for*ever.*

Josh snatched one of the biscuits—*oh, it's still warm*—and scuttled into the bathroom.

Transformation

Gareth had mentioned that Mal had updated his bathroom, and it was certainly more modern than the facilities at the compound, which were still heavily dependent on betas digging out the privy pits regularly. Josh blinked at all the gleaming white porcelain and the black and white checkerboard tiles underfoot.

But then he caught another enticing whiff of perfection and had no attention to spare for anything but the biscuit cradled in his palms.

He closed his eyes and inhaled its aroma slowly, letting it invade his senses. He'd *never* smelled anything this luscious before. It was more than just a scent. It didn't just tease his nose or tantalize his mouth. It felt as though it invaded his very blood, lighting him up from the inside.

He couldn't wait another instant.

When he took the first bite, his eyes nearly rolled back in his head. The *flavor*. Sweet, but not too sweet. Nutty, with the burst of tartness from the unfamiliar fruit. The *texture*. Flaky and flawless, melting on his tongue as though it were made of air. He swore he could *feel* it, dancing along his palate and down his throat to warm his belly and... and... and...

Josh collapsed against the door, the biscuit falling from his suddenly lax fingers. He slid down, the wood rough against his back, rucking his jacket up around his armpits.

What is happening?

The warmth in his middle spread, bloomed, *expanded* until it reached all the way from his toes to the roots of his hair—which stood on end, despite still being wet.

His gaze caught on the biscuit, and he remembered the old tales of people who'd visited Faerie and been changed because they'd been foolish enough to eat or drink while they were there.

How could I have been so stupid, so greedy? I should have waited for Gareth. I should have asked. I feel so... so...

He sucked in a breath and held it until spots danced in his vision. For a moment, everything went dark until he remembered to exhale. Shivers chased along his skin, his nerves firing as though little fireworks burst along his veins. It was... uncomfortable, but never crossed the threshold into pain. It was similar to his shift, but... not, because while his bones didn't reform into his wolf, his *flesh* was a different story.

Panting, eyes clenched, he rode out the waves, alternating heat and cold and electricity, until at last it receded. He cracked his eyelids and blinked until his fuzzy vision cleared.

He let his head drop back against the door, wriggling to adjust his shirt and jacket so it wasn't bunched up. When he yanked on his shirt, though, his bindings fell away as though... as though...

It can't be.

With trembling fingers, Josh unbuttoned his clammy shirt. The bindings were around his waist because there was nothing for them to *bind* anymore. His chest, smooth and hairless, bore the gentle muscle definition of pectorals, nipples small and flat.

Holding his breath, he leaned forward and peered down at his crotch, eyes widening when he realized that while his shirt hid a lot *less*, his trousers clearly hid *more*.

Gingerly, he prodded the bulge behind his fly. "Remus's balls." *No, not Remus's.*

Mine.

Josh let his head thump against the door, a sound escaping his throat that might have been laughter or a sob or a muffled scream. Here in this fairy tale cottage, his dreams had finally come true.

"Josh?" Gareth said from the other side of the door. "You all right in there, mate?"

"Yes." *Gods*, yes.

"I've got some dry clothes for you. I'll just leave them here outside the door. Looks like we've got some scones to go along with our cuppa, so come out whenever you're ready."

Scones. Not biscuits, then. "Gareth?"

"Yeah?"

"Are scones magical?"

His warm chuckle filtered through the door. "Only because they're delicious. If you're lucky, I'll save one for you." Gareth's footsteps retreated across the room.

If the scone wasn't magical, then how... Could this be an illusion? Hallucination? Fever dream? He didn't *feel* sick. In fact, he felt fantastic. *Whole*, for the first time in his life.

I have to look.

Josh scrambled to his feet, fingers fumbling with the buttons on his fly. When he peeked inside his underwear, he uttered a strangled laugh. He had a cock and balls.

True, they weren't enormous, but they were *there* and they were *his*. He patted his flat chest. *My body matches my self.*

He took a deep breath and everything just *settled*. Outside and inside, aligned at last. Joy threatened to fountain out the top of his head, although it was tempered with relief at his lucky escape. If he'd kept the appointment with the priestess, she might have remade his body, but it would have been at the cost of his music, his very *soul*.

He cracked open the door, snagged the dry clothes, and closed the door again. After he stripped off the old, damp clothes, he took a solid minute to gaze down at himself. *I'm finally me.*

He wadded the old clothes up because they'd been a disguise, nothing more, and now he didn't need it anymore.

He snatched the scone off the floor and kissed it. "Thank you." Then he took advantage of Mal's modern toilet to... try out the new equipment.

Oh. It's so much easier to aim *this way!*

When he'd washed himself thoroughly and dried off with the fluffy towel—yikes, those things were *sensitive*—he dressed in the soft linen shirt and underdrawers. He stroked the trousers' soft nap. Sueded leather, a luxury only the alpha was allowed back at the compound. Given Mal's size, Josh had his doubts about the fit, but when he pulled them on, they were perfect, even to the length. And the way they hugged his crotch?

He choked on half-hysterical laughter. *Magic indeed.*

Pushing the laugher down—although it kept rising like bubbles to burst from his lips—he studied his face in the mirror over the sink. Same blue eyes. Same blade of a nose. Same fine blond hair. He traced his jawline. Was it a little squarer? Was his chin a little less pointed? Or did he only *perceive* them that way because this was how he saw himself in his mind? Now, for the first time, he didn't have to imagine, didn't have to wish, didn't have to pray anymore. Now he only had to *be*.

And it was *glorious*.

A New Path

Josh's gaze caught on the scone, and his euphoria bled away to nothing. Were these changes permanent, or was this one of those enchantments that had an expiration? Would he wake up tomorrow in his old body, the one that had never fit?

"Tea's ready whenever you are," Gareth called.

Josh took a shaky breath. The last true bard of Faerie was on the other side of the door. If anybody should know the answers, it ought to be him.

He stooped to retrieve his clothes, which was a different experience now that there were *things* in the middle of his body. With the bundle tucked under one arm and the scone in the other hand, he stepped out of the bathroom.

Gareth glanced up from where he was filling two sturdy white mugs from a squat earthenware teapot. "Ah. I see you spotted the scones." His forehead wrinkled as he squinted at it. "Didn't you like it? Some folks don't like fruit in them, but I've —"

"No. The scone was fine. But it..." Josh paced across the room, and even *that* felt different, as though his center of gravity had changed, no longer centered between his hipbones but higher, up beneath his calon. "It *changed* me."

Gareth's eyebrows rose. "Changed? It's not a spell, mate. It's just a scone. Brownie made, and they're a dab hand at baking, but it's still just a scone."

"Then how do you explain this?" Josh let his clothes drop and patted his flat chest. "Or... or *that*?" He pointed to his groin. "And I didn't even have to *sacrifice* anything for it."

"Ah. That. Well..." Gareth sighed and pointed to the chair. "Have a seat and drink your tea." When Josh didn't move, Gareth gestured to the chair. "Come on. It's just tea, same as that's just a scone, but you'll feel better with something inside you for this conversation."

Josh sank into the chair, the scone still clutched in his hand and starting to crumble until Gareth passed him a blue plate painted with delicate white flowers. Josh set the scone on it, grabbed the mug, and took a gulp, the brew scalding his tongue.

"Hot," he croaked.

"That's because it's tea, not beer."

Josh took a more judicious mouthful. "It's good."

"Not sure I'll take the compliment, considering you've just singed your tastebuds."

"If it wasn't the scone, then what was it? The priestess demanded a price, and from what my mother told me, the transformation wasn't going to be nearly as... as complete."

Gareth sighed and lifted his own mug. "Thank the goddess I ran into you then, because that would have been both a travesty and a tragedy."

"What do you mean?"

"Tragedy? Depriving the world of your music. Travesty? Letting anybody else—whether the priestess or those wankers in the street—make decisions about your body. Let me tell you something about Faerie."

Josh frowned at Gareth over the rim of his mug. *Is this where the other shoe drops? Where I'm proven a fool for trusting a stranger?* "What about it?"

"In Faerie, gender is... optional."

"Optional?"

He nodded. "I've heard that some Unseelie fae don't have any at all, or change things up according to their needs or when they reach a certain age."

Josh glanced down at his lap. Already the differences felt natural. *Ordinary.* "Will I change back? When we leave?"

Gareth frowned at that. "Am I right in thinking that how you are now is your true self?"

Josh nodded. "Yes."

"Then it should hold."

"Why didn't it happen as soon as we arrived then?"

Gareth chuckled. "Faerie might be a magic place, mate, but even magic has to take a bit to scout things out. It probably took this long for it to understand you. As Mal said, you might be the first werewolf to cross our threshold." His frown deepened. "I wonder…"

"What?"

"The thing is, while the transformational magic should stick, once we leave—and sorry, mate, but we will be leaving. Faerie is not my home anymore."

"I understand. And that's perfectly fine."

"Once we leave, if you *overwrite* the transformation…" Gareth spread his hands, palms up, in a gesture of helplessness.

Ah. And there's the other shoe. "You mean if I shift."

"Aye. Chances are that you'd negate the magic then, because Faerie made *this* body because your old one didn't match your… persona, I suppose you could call it. From Faerie's perspective, it was reversing a spell or a curse, some malevolent magic that had turned you into something you were not." He grimaced. "And while I don't want to make this all about me, it might actually be about me, at least a bit."

"How do you figure?"

Gareth made a disgusted sound in the back of his throat. "Faerie wants me to come back, and it's always trying to get on my good side. It probably thought it was doing me a favor by helping my friend."

"If that's what it was doing?" Josh looked up at the ceiling, where bundles of dried herbs hung from the rafters, and shouted, "Thank you." He lowered his chin and met Gareth's eyes. "And thank you. For performing with me. For rescuing me. For *seeing* me. It means more to me than I can possibly say."

"That was no hardship for me, mate. I'd do it again in a heartbeat. But I want you to understand. If you should shift into your wolf form and then back, you'd probably return to the way you were before. And then, even if I brought you back here, the One Tree—"

"The One Tree?"

"The heart of Faerie's magic. If the One Tree senses that you *rejected* what it bestowed on you…"

"Then it might think I was ungrateful and be angry."

"Not angry. More embarrassed." He smiled and picked up his mug. "Faerie doesn't like to be wrong more than anybody else does."

"So what you're saying is… if I want this to stick, I can't shift again? Ever?"

Gareth spread his palms again. "I can't say for certain, but there's a risk that you'd lose this chance. A big one, since there's no guarantee that even if I begged a boon and asked for a do-over, the One Tree would grant it."

Josh inhaled and blew out his breath through pursed lips. He'd been wrong—there *was* a price to pay, and the price was his wolf. That was… a big thing. But there were shifters who were inactive, who weren't able to transform into their animal aspect, and they were still part of the supernatural community.

"I… I understand. Besides, it's not as though I want to belong to a pack anyway, and if giving up my wolf means I can be myself in all other ways, it's not too much to ask." He smiled, a little shakily. "I'm still grateful. To you. To Faerie. To the One Tree, I guess. So thank you. For everything."

Gareth dropped his gaze and set his mug on the table. He turned it in careful quarter turns. One revolution. Two revolutions. As he began the third, Josh's old anxiety began to creep back in.

"If you need me to leave—"

"No!" Gareth flinched, almost knocking over his tea. "Sorry. I mean, no. You don't— That is, I'm the one who should be thanking you."

"What? I've done nothing but hang on your sleeve since we met."

"Maybe that's what I needed. A reason to look outside myself."

Gareth closed his eyes, his shoulders lifted as he took an enormous breath, and it wasn't only his body that shook as he exhaled. It was as if the room, the cottage, *Faerie* itself released an ancient tension.

Josh waited, unmoving and on edge, while Gareth apparently wrestled with some inner demon. His own breath was quick and shallow, as though whatever choice Gareth made next would chart his own destiny as well.

Then Gareth opened his eyes, and though their corners were still pinched with pain, they were clear and blue. Unshadowed. "I've been traveling for years, always on my own, only playing in private with other musicians. Never for an audience. Not until tonight." He swallowed and looked down. "There are... reasons why I haven't. Why I couldn't."

"If I forced you—"

"You didn't. I *wanted* to help, and maybe that's the wildest magic of all. That I *could* want to help. Being up on that stage with you reminded me of what I've lost. What I want to find again."

Gareth's expression when he met Josh's gaze wasn't quite a smile, just a hopeful quirk of his lips. "So how about it, Josh? Think you might like to stick with me for a bit, travel together, see where the music takes us?"

Josh felt as though the sun were rising in his chest. "I'd like that. Very much."

"I'll warn you—the path isn't going to be easy. I'll still have dark moments, dark days, maybe entire dark years."

"For... for reasons?"

Gareth nodded. "Yes. I'll tell you about them. Not tonight, but soon. Because you deserve to know what you're getting into."

"Tell me whenever you're ready. Because now? I've got nowhere else to be. Everything I've ever wished for—freedom, music, my true self—I've already gotten thanks to you. I can grant you a little grace, don't you think?"

"Only a little grace?" Gareth's almost-smile blossomed into a grin. "I want more than that."

Josh lifted an eyebrow. "Is that so? What might that be?"

He nudged Josh's fiddle case with his foot. "Take out that violin, mate. It's time to get to work."

Spence

A Strategic Retreat

"Spencer! Spencer Lloyd! Get your arse back here. We're on in twenty minutes."

Spence didn't bother to answer Nigel, the New Pennies' pissed off guitarist, because if he opened his mouth right now, very, *very* bad things would happen.

However, the band's front man— whose name Spence could never remember because it was pretentious as all hell—was barricaded in the backstage restroom, and finding a public toilet in Liverpool was not something you could do, evidently, not when the overflow crowd from the Cavern Club was practically rioting because they couldn't get in to see the Beatles in what was bound to be their last performance in such a small venue.

So instead Spence raced down the hall with his hand pressed to his mouth, burst out the back door, and beat feet for the nearest alley with Nigel pounding along behind him.

"Spencer!"

Ah, great. Now Nigel had been joined by Derek, the bassist.

Spence braced both hands against the alley wall, the damp brick rough against his palms. Clenching his eyes shut, he fought the nausea roiling in his belly by focusing on something, anything, *everything* other than the empty stage awaiting the New Pennies in that club.

The New Pennies. Stupid name for a band, anyway. Spence had snorted beer out his nose when Derek had told him they changed it from *The Pennies* when there was a typo on a flyer that left out an N—which led inevitably to people calling them *The Penis.*

Nigel poked Spence in the shoulder, which didn't move him an inch. *Or a centimeter, since they're threatening to go all* metric *here.* Nigel was decently fit, but no human could budge a werewolf who didn't want to move. Who didn't *dare* move without puking.

"Listen, you wanker. There's a bloke in there from EMI."

Sure there is. Spence kept his lips clamped shut, but Nigel must have read the skepticism in his expression, because his scowl deepened.

"If you bollux up our big break…" Nigel lifted his hands as though to run them through his hair, but stopped before touching his head.

Yeah, Remus forbid he disarrange his coiffure. Spence inhaled sharply through his nose. Fuck, even his thoughts were approaching terminal sarcasm.

"I'm sure what Nigel means," Derek said with a nervous smile, "is that we need to put our best foot forward. We've made such musical progress since you joined us this month. Now's our chance to debut our new sound."

"Mmmhmm." Spence still didn't dare open his mouth.

"Derek's right. We timed this first gig deliberately." Nigel tapped the side of his nose. "When the mob can't get in to the Cavern Club, what do you think they'll do?" When Spence didn't reply, Nigel answered his own question. "Pop into another club, that's what. Captive. Audience."

Yeah, I'm pretty sure anybody who's looking for the Beatles isn't going to settle for the New Pennies, but dream your little dream, buddy.

Nigel folded his arms, his expression smug. "And it worked."

"Mmmph?" Spence grunted.

Derek nodded enthusiastically. "The place is absolutely *packed.*"

Fuck. All those people. Already ticked off. Staring at him. Daring him. *Judging* him.

Spence finally lost the battle with his insides. His stomach made a break for it, and he only just managed to keep his shoes out of the firing line. Nigel wasn't so lucky.

He stumbled backward, his hands in the air as he stared down at his feet. "Christ, Lloyd. Do you know how much I paid for these boots?"

Spence braced his hands on his knees, wrestling the nausea back down. "No, but I can guarantee it was too much." He glanced up at Nigel through his bangs—and no, he refused to even think of the hair that flopped across his forehead as *fringe*, especially as it was shaggier than the average sheepdog's. *I really should have gotten it cut after my last shift.* "You couldn't judge good value if it bit you on the ass. Look at your guitar."

If Nigel's eyes could have shot fire, Spence would be in flames. "That's *custom*. One of a kind."

"Maybe one of a kind in Liverpool, but back home in Santa Fe, you can grab it at Sears for eighty bucks. Nothing against Sears. They've got some decent stuff. But your guitar ain't one of 'em."

Derek, who'd at least had the sense to keep his distance, said, "Sorry, lads, but we really do need to get back."

Spence closed his eyes again. "I'm not sure I can make it."

"What the fuck?" Nigel started to lunge forward, but apparently thought better of it. "You're *copping out* on us?"

Spence glared up at him. "You really want me to spew all over the stage? Not sure the club's keyboard is up to that, and I'm pretty sure if there *is* a guy from EMI in there, he won't be impressed either."

Nigel's fingers curled into fists. "You—"

"Watch it, pal." Spence bared his teeth, and with how off-balance he was right now, he was pretty sure his canines were a little longer than usual. "If you punch me, you really think you'll be able to manage the guitar break in that 'Johnny B. Goode' cover? You're no Chuck Berry, and you can't hit it half the time when your hands are in good shape."

The way Nigel growled, he could have fit right in with Spence's old pack. "Derek, you talk to him. I've got to clean off my boots." He stalked out of the alley, but Spence's werewolf hearing picked up his muttered, "Useless bloody Yank."

From the way Derek winced, Nigel probably intended it to be overheard.

"Sorry about Nigel, Spence. He gets like this when he's nervous."

"Yeah, well, I get like *this* when I'm nervous." Spence glanced at the puddles of vomit next to the wall. *Not sure who comes out on top in* that *face-off, but I kinda doubt it's me.*

An Unexpected Kindness

"I can dig that you're not feeling, uh…" Derek eyed the puke too, and started to back away. "We've all faced the morning after a time or two. But try to get past it, mate, yeah?"

Spence clamped his lips together and nodded. "Mmmhmm."

"Great!" Derek said, far too heartily, and gave Spence a thumbs-up. "We could go back to the arrangements we used before you joined us, but we sound so much better with you on keys." He lobbed one last grenade before he disappeared around the corner. "Wouldn't want to miss our first performance in front of an audience, would you?"

Aaannnd *hello* again. By this time, Spence didn't have much inside to come back out, but dry heaves and bile were bad enough.

Remus's balls, why did I ever think I could do this? The answer, of course, was that it had never come up. *Ugh, poor choice of words.*

With the restrictions that had werewolves all cowering inside their compound since the Thirties, and the contentious relationship with his father and brothers that kept him locked out of pack activities more often than not, Spence'd had nothing to do but practice, day after day, week after week, month after month, year after fucking year. He'd gotten damn good at the *music*. But playing in front of anybody?

Not once. Ever.

Until the day his brothers and their thuggish friends, bored with panting after girls who were too smart to give them the time of day, had stumbled upon him playing in the barn. At their first shouts of derision, Spence's fingers turned into sausages, fat and floppy and fumbling, which only invited more sneers and catcalls.

After that, it became their new favorite pastime—to ambush him when he tried to sneak away. He'd tried to resist, knowing they'd get bored eventually, but the ache to touch the keyboard was too great, and they'd found him. Over and over and over, until he'd started to *anticipate* it, and the first creak of the door or a glimpse of one of their smirking faces peering over a windowsill had sent him riding the train to Barftown before he ever put his hands on the keys.

He'd thought—he'd *hoped*—that things would be better in England, away from his family and their judgment. After all, he'd made it through the New Pennies' audition a month ago and managed rehearsals just fine. He'd thought he was past his little... problem.

He still wasn't sure why neither of those situations had bothered him. Maybe because they were all musicians too? Because they were playing along with him? Because there'd been nobody else watching? He didn't know. But now that there was an actual *audience*—a packed house, damn it—he was right back on the vomit express.

Spence stood with his hands braced against the wall, head down, sucking in air through his mouth after the last heave. *My problem is alive and well and living in Liverpool.* As Nigel's boots could testify.

"Here."

Spence's head shot up at the soft, unfamiliar voice. A slender blond man stood next to him, holding out a folded handkerchief. Spence just stared, mouth agape, because he'd never seen anybody so... appealing. Not beautiful in the strictest sense—*whatever the fuck that was.* The man's nose was a little too long, his mouth a little too wide, his chin a little too pointed. But put those all together with his soft-looking hair and big blue eyes that held nothing but kindness, and Spence was absolutely speechless.

He held the handkerchief closer. "It's damp. I wetted it down in the WC."

Spence took the offering gratefully and used it to mop his mouth and the rest of his sweaty face. "WC? I'm pretty sure that's not what they call a bathroom where you come from."

The man smiled and a dimple peeped in one cheek. "What makes you think I don't come from here?"

"That drawl is pure American south. I might be from further west—New Mexico—but I know that much."

He tilted his head. "You don't sound drunk."

"Why would you…" Spence glanced down at the mess he'd made and moved away. "Ah. Can't blame you for that conclusion. But no." He grimaced. "Stage fright. Pretty pathetic for somebody who wants to be a professional musician."

"Does this happen every time you're about to go onstage?"

Spence snorted. "This is the first time I'll actually *be* onstage." He winced. "Assuming I can actually get up there. Assuming they haven't already fired me. But yeah. Every time somebody's watching me." He tried a smile. "Judgment, know what I mean? It's a thing with me."

The man nodded. "I know all about that, trust me. I'm a musician too. Josh Wills."

Spence was going to hold out his hand to shake, but despite Josh's very welcome handkerchief, his hands weren't exactly pristine. "Spencer Lloyd. Spence."

Josh's smile was like a benediction. "Nice to meet you, Spence."

"Likewise." He glanced over his shoulder. "Too bad it's not under better—and less smelly—circumstances."

"I'm not sure any circumstances are ever ideal." Josh dug in his jacket pocket and pulled out a pack of gum.

"Wrigley's Spearmint," Spence murmured, a strange constriction in his chest.

Josh held it out. "I've got Juicy Fruit too, but this one's unopened."

"No. This is my favorite."

"You can have the whole pack."

"You sure?"

"Absolutely."

Spence took it, and when his fingers brushed Josh's, he felt a tingle all the way to his toes. Josh gasped and snatched his hand away, so either he felt it too or Spence had just crossed a line. *No surprise there.*

Josh stuffed both hands in his jacket pockets. "I know you'd probably prefer water or maybe a toothbrush, but maybe this'll do until you've got the chance."

"This is great. Thank you. But if you don't mind my asking, why are you doing this?"

"Doing what?"

"Being so nice to me? Helping me? You don't know me."

Although Josh's expression was wistful, there was a decided twinkle in his eyes. "I know enough. Besides, a stranger helped me when I needed it most. It only seems right to do the same whenever I can."

Spence ducked his head and tore open the Wrigley's, unable to meet Josh's eyes. "Not sure I've ever done that."

He'd been too focused on his own problems to consider anybody else's, to the point of leaving the compound in the middle of the night without saying goodbye, regardless of what effect his absence would cause. Briefly, as he unwrapped a stick of gum, he wondered if anyone had even noticed he was gone.

"It's never too late to start."

"I guess." Just the scent of the gum settled his stomach. Spence shoved it in his mouth, and cool spearmint dispelled the sour taste of vomit. "I'll... what do all the politicians say? Take it under advisement?"

Josh chuckled. "Maybe the first thing you should do is show up for your gig."

Showtime

Spence's belly threatened to rebel again, but he kept his eyes fixed on Josh's kind face and chomped determinedly on his gum.

"You're right." He grimaced. "Wish you were gonna be there, though. With the sight of a friendly face, I might actually be able to make it through the set without"—he jerked his thumb over his shoulder—"you know."

"What makes you think I won't be?"

"Because you're probably here to see the Beatles down at the Cavern Club like everybody else in town. Who'd want to see a no-name band at a second-rate club like Bazzard's when they have a chance like that?"

"Do you want me to be there?"

Spence met Josh's eyes, and there was *something*... He could swear there was *something*. If only the alley didn't smell like the insides of Spence's belly. "I think I want that more than just about anything I've ever wanted in my life."

"Then I will be. And don't worry, Spence. You can do this." Josh turned and walked toward the corner.

"Wait!" Spence staggered forward a step. "Nigel said the place was packed. You won't be able to get in."

Josh flashed a mischievous grin. "I said don't worry. Break a leg." Then he vanished onto the street.

Spence glanced down at his hands, which still held the pack of Wrigley's and Josh's balled-up handkerchief. He slid the gum in his shirt pocket and folded the handkerchief neatly to tuck it into the back pocket of his jeans. Yeah, it would probably make his ass damp, but he needed that reminder—the reminder that there were still people in the world who'd help just because they could.

Because he didn't believe for one second that he'd ever see Josh again.

He took a deep breath—*gah! Mistake!*—and hauled ass out of the alley and through the milling crowds to Bazzard's rear entrance. The doorman recognized him from the sound check earlier and let him inside.

Once through the door, he detoured to the bathroom and paused for a moment to stare at the *WC* sign on its door. God*damn*, Josh had been adorable. Adorable and kind and probably as full of shit as everybody else Spence had ever known.

But he washed up, rinsed out his mouth, guzzled about a quart of water from his cupped hands, and popped another stick of gum. He gazed at the packet. Three sticks left. *I'm keeping them.* As a souvenir. A testimonial that everything wasn't all about him and maybe he should get out of his own head once in a while.

Or maybe just get my head out of my ass.

When he slinked into the band's ready room, everybody's reaction was about what he'd expected. Derek smiled in relief, Nigel growled, "It's about fucking time," Mick, the drummer, blinked and said, "Wha...?" and the front man didn't even register, since he was too busy looking at himself in a hand mirror.

Spence had cut it right down to the wire because not a minute later, the club's manager poked his head in the door and said, "You're on."

I will not throw up. I will not throw up.

The front man had made it very clear in what order they were to take the stage. He, of course, would swan on at the end, after everyone else was already in place, so Spence trailed Mick out the door, chomping on his gum for all he was worth.

When they stepped out of the wings, the smoke drifting in the air burned Spence's nose and made his eyes water. He took his place behind the keys, grateful that the harsh light masked all but the people standing closest to the stage.

He blinked, trying to clear his vision, as the front man sashayed onstage and posed behind the mic. Spence's stomach rolled again as Nigel hit his opening chord, but then...

He spotted Josh's face.

Josh was *right there*. In the front row, no less. Not center stage, but stage left, only five feet from Spence. A tall man with a halo of honey-colored curls stood next to him and although Spence vaguely registered that the guy's face was perfect enough to belong in a museum, it was Josh who captured all his attention. And when he smiled at Spence, Spence's fingers weren't clumsy at all. They hit every note, followed every riff, pounded every chord, but Spence couldn't remember anything about the set except Josh's unfaltering smile.

The applause at the end of the set wasn't enthusiastic, but it was respectable. They played one encore, and even though the front man was bouncing backstage in expectation of a second, *that* didn't happen. For Spence, though, it was a triumph, because he'd actually made it through a public performance.

Because of Josh.

He craned his neck, scanning the dispersing crowd from the wings, but couldn't spot Josh's shining hair. He'd have barreled back onstage, jumped down onto the club floor, and barged through the mob to catch Josh before he left, but couldn't ditch Nigel, who held Spence's elbow in a vise grip.

Spence growled low in his throat, his wolf *this close* to the surface. He was stronger than this asshole, stronger than most humans, but he couldn't risk a Secrecy Pact violation, especially here and now, when he was a lone wolf with no pack at his back. So he let himself be herded back to the ready room.

On the Street

Nigel released his death grip on Spence's elbow, but followed it up with a sharp jab at his chest with a stiff finger. "I don't know what your problem was before the show, Lloyd, but at least you held it together for the set. Next time—"

"There won't be a next time." Spence batted Nigel's hand away, careful to pull his strength back enough not to break the guy's hand. Yeah, Nigel was an idiot, but Spence wouldn't do that to a fellow musician, not even an annoying one. He grabbed his duffel from the corner and slung it over his shoulder. "I'm out."

The keys belonged to the club, so he didn't have to worry about packing up any equipment. All he wanted was to get onto the street and see if he could locate Josh before he vanished for good.

As he strode out of the room, Nigel shouted, "Lloyd! You can't do this. You have a contract!"

"No, I don't," Spence shot back. He paused with his hand on the back door's panic bar. "You made sure of that, remember? You told me I was just sitting in. A test phase, you called it. Guess what? You didn't pass my test."

"You're not getting paid!"

Spence snorted and thrust the door open. "Yeah, like you were ever gonna pay me in the first place."

He hurried around to the front of the club. The sidewalk was packed as people exited after the show, milling about aimlessly. Spence was tall enough that he could see over most heads, but he couldn't spot Josh's shining hair in the throng.

Spence growled again. Didn't these people have lives? Somewhere to go? Then he laughed, because who was he to judge? He didn't have anywhere to go, either. Hells, he'd been crashing with Mick, so he'd probably burned that bridge to cinders.

Even if he found Josh, what then? It wasn't as though Spence had anything to offer. The money he'd been hoarding since he'd decided to leave the pack was all but gone. If he made any overture other than friendship—assuming Josh even shared Spence's preferences—he'd expose Josh to danger or arrest. Expose *both* of them to danger or arrest.

In other words, no different from back home.

The weight of his duffel, even though it was nearly empty, threatened to drag him to the pavement. He'd just trashed his life again, shooting himself in the foot on his first chance at a musical career. He snorted. Career? What kind of career could he hope for? He was only able to hold it together this time because Josh was there to ground him, center him, inspire him.

Since Josh wouldn't be there, where did that leave Spence?

He hitched the duffel strap further onto his shoulder. *Get over yourself, Lloyd.* So he'd never be a performer. So what? He could be a session musician. That could be a decent life. If he only had to play for other musicians, maybe he wouldn't board the vomit train.

Scoring the gigs would be a problem, though. For that, you needed connections to even get through the door, and by walking out on the New Pennies, he'd probably just put himself on the top of the blackballed list. So here he was, in a country not his own, staring at a slow slide into poverty. At home, humans had stopped shooting wolves on sight—mostly—so he could have shifted and lived in the woods as long as he stayed hidden. But he didn't even know where the woods *were* in England. They certainly weren't anywhere close to Bazzard's.

He stood in the middle of the sidewalk, not caring when people bumped into him as they passed or swore at him for being in the way. He rubbed at his watering eyes—not that he was crying. Of course not. But literally everybody around him was sucking on cigarettes, and Remus's *balls*, but Spence hated tobacco smoke. All weres did because it dulled their sense of smell. And, seriously, fuck his imagination, because it decided this was the perfect moment to deliver the faint whiff of another werewolf amid the stench. Then it was gone again, along with Spence's last shred of hope.

"Spence?"

Spence's head jerked up. *Josh.* Josh was here, forehead wrinkled in concern, the curly-haired man from the club at his back, and it was as if the sun came out, even though it was long after dark.

"Hey," Spence croaked.

"Are you all right?"

Spence choked out a laugh. "Not even close."

"Is there anything I can do to help?"

"Not sure it's anything that can be fixed with a pack of gum, but thanks for asking."

Josh gnawed on his lower lip before glancing over his shoulder at the other man, who nodded. "Spence, this is my friend Gareth."

Gareth held out his hand. "Nice to meet you, mate. You've got some serious chops. What are you doing with that lot of wankers?"

"I'm not with them anymore. I just quit." Spence shook, and the calluses on Gareth's fingertips told the tale. "Guitarist?"

"Among other things." He jerked his head toward Josh. "Fancy a cuppa with Josh and me?"

"I can't pay. I'm flat broke."

Gareth flashed a model-perfect grin. "No worries, mate. Come around to ours and we'll get you sorted."

Off for a Cuppa

Ours.

Spence's heart dive-bombed his boots because he knew what that meant. Josh and Gareth were together. *Living* together. He wouldn't have had a chance even if he'd had more to his name than the contents of his duffel.

Don't be an idiot, you idiot. He's human. Werewolves and humans weren't allowed to... what did the werewolf council call it? Fraternize? Not only because of the Secrecy Pact, but because weres had a keen survival instinct and *really* knew how to hold a grudge. Who knew how many humans had wolf pelts nailed to their barn walls that had come from *lupus sapiens* rather than *canis lupus*?

Trust. It was hard to build, but easy to shatter.

"Spence?" Josh's soft voice broke Spence out of his dark dive. "Is everything okay?"

Spence nodded, forcing a smile. "Yeah. Sure. Thanks. I'd love a... a..."

"If you've been in England for more than half a mo," Gareth said with a revoltingly handsome smirk, "you must know what *fancy a cuppa* means."

Spence tried not to glare at him, but probably wasn't too successful. "I've been here a month, and since that comes up roughly every five minutes with you Brits, yes, I do."

Gareth's face shuttered, going completely blank, his eyes bleak, but only for a moment. Then his smirk was back, although it held an edge. "Don't call a Welshman a Brit, mate. We've got our standards."

Josh glanced sidelong at Gareth before gracing Spence with his brilliant smile again. "It's not far. Shall we?"

"Why not?"

Spence fell into step beside Josh, Gareth striding along on Josh's other side as though he owned the street.

"You've only been here for a month, then?" Josh asked.

Spence nodded. "Practically fresh off the boat."

Josh *hmmm*ed, but didn't dig deeper, which Spence appreciated. He wasn't exactly proud of stowing away on that freighter, considering it was a cockamamie impulse at best. He'd planned to head for Mexico after he'd bolted from his pack, but the freighter had been *right there* in Corpus Christi, and the music out of Britain held an exciting edge that American and Mexican folk music couldn't match.

"Have you two been, um, living here long?"

"A few years."

Spence goggled at him. "Years?"

Josh slid a glance at Gareth again. "Gareth wasn't happy with our last place, and I wasn't happy with where I was before that, so we decided to give this a try for a bit. The music here has an exciting edge."

"That's exactly what *I* thought!"

Josh grinned at him. "Kismet."

"Kismet? What's that mean?"

"Oh, you know. Fate. Destiny. Luck. Lives are like that, don't you think? Nothing is really random. Coincidence isn't really coincidence. If your life touches someone else's somehow, that connection plants a seed. Ignites a spark that never really goes away. We meet who we're supposed to meet when we're supposed to meet them."

"That's a little fatalistic, don't you think? Predestination? I've met some folks who believe that"—*like every alpha of every pack ever*—"but what about free will?"

Josh shrugged. "I said we meet when we're supposed to. That doesn't mean you can sit around and *wait*. You still have to do the work. Build those connections. Nurture the seed." He grinned. "Fan the spark."

"I suppose that makes sense." Spence snorted. "Although there are some connections I'd rather cut." He returned Josh's grin. "Sparks I'd rather douse. Seeds I'd rather uproot."

Josh gazed at him, expression somber. "Is that why you're so far from home?"

"Part of it." He looked down at the cracked pavement, at the scuffed toes of his boots. "Some seeds are harder to uproot than others. Like dandelions. They're inescapable, like crabgrass. The only choice is to dump weedkiller on 'em and run."

"I know the feeling," Josh said.

"Same," Gareth said as they turned onto a narrow road lined with two-story red-brick row houses. "That's why it's good when you run into somebody else in the same spot." He smirked again, but this time there was a glint in his eye. "Especially when they're a stellar musician."

A tendril of warmth snaked through Spence's chest. "You think I'm good?"

"Mate, you were so far above those wankers, you might as well have been playing on the roof." He flicked a finger at a house about halfway down the block, with bay windows both upstairs and down. "This is us."

Gareth led the way up the short walk and cracked open the green door. He didn't use a key, which… oookay. This seemed like a nice enough neighborhood compared to where Spence had been staying, but it raised Spence's hackles. Gareth was obviously packing some muscles in his broad chest, but Josh was slender. Not quite delicate, but not exactly sturdy either. He should be staying somewhere safer. Definitely behind a locked door. Maybe one with two deadbolts and a chain.

Gareth looked down at Spence from the stoop, his hand on the doorknob. "Those are two of three reasons we're inviting you in."

Spence laughed nervously. "What's the third? Because you're looking for another body to bury in the back garden?"

"No." He pushed the door open and stepped into a narrow hallway with a staircase on one side and an open archway on the other.

Josh followed him in and they both turned and waited, shoulder to shoulder but not quite touching, Josh with a tremulous smile and Gareth with an expression like somebody facing a firing squad.

What the hells.

When Spence climbed the steps and crossed the threshold, both men broke out into grins that held as much relief as joy.

"All right, I'll bite. Lay it on me."

"It's because you're a werewolf," Gareth said.

And the door slammed shut.

You're a What?

Spence froze, mouth agape. "What? I don't know— That isn't — You can't—"

"Relax, mate." Gareth jerked a thumb at Josh. "He is too."

Gareth hummed low in his throat, and suddenly Spence could *smell* it. Smell *Josh*. That tantalizing whiff in the street hadn't been Spence's imagination after all.

"You... You're a were?" Spence croaked, and Josh nodded. "How couldn't I tell? I mean, granted, that alley was rank, and the smoke in the club was thicker than fog on the mountain, but there's no way I should have missed *that*. Missed *you*."

Josh's cheeks flushed an adorable peach. "That's Gareth's doing. He's fae. He used his glamourie to shield me. To shield us both."

Spence tore his gaze away from Josh and looked at Gareth, who... Remus's balls, how could *anyone* mistake somebody that... that *transcendent* for anything other than supernatural? "You can do that?"

Gareth quirked one absolutely perfect eyebrow. "I'm a bard, mate."

"You say that like it's an explanation."

He grinned. "It is." He nodded toward the archway. "Now go on in while I put the kettle on."

Mick—when he wasn't too wasted to speak—had used a word that perfectly described Spence's mental state: gobsmacked. He stumbled through the archway, expecting a parlor or lounge or whatever the Brits called it, but instead—

"Holy *shit*," he breathed. "Is that a Hammond B-2?"

Spence crept across the room where the organ sat against a floral-papered wall to run his fingers over its keys. "Man, I'd *kill* for one of these. Yeah, the B-3 is nice, but this one? It has *personality*." He shook his head. "Classic."

Josh chuckled from behind him. "Gareth appreciates fine craftsmanship. You should see his harp. When he found out they were discontinuing these, he asked his brother to make a special trip to buy one."

Spence paused, frowning. "His brother? Why didn't he go himself?" He lifted his palms. "Sorry. Not my business."

Josh's smile was both wry and wistful. "It's all right. The two of us were staying at his brother Mal's place in Faerie at the time, and Gareth has a... complicated relationship with his brothers, not to mention with Faerie itself. He really doesn't like to spend much time there. He was already getting antsy. He was afraid that if he left, he wouldn't be able to make himself come back, so he asked Mal to take care of it."

Nobody had ever accused Spence of being sensitive, so since Josh was okay with answering questions, Spence figured he'd just keep going until he got shut down. "If he hates it so much, why go to Faerie in the first place?"

Josh shrugged. "For me."

The light dawned. "He was the one. The person who helped you. The reason you helped me."

"Yes to the first, and partly to the second. He rescued me from a bad situation and, well, changed my life when he took me out of New Orleans and into Faerie. But we weren't sure whether those... changes would stick once we left, so we stayed for longer than he would usually. Gareth and I had started writing songs together by then, and when we saw the direction music was taking in the Outer World, we decided to leave Faerie."

Spence lifted an eyebrow. "*We* decided?"

"Fine." Josh sighed. "*I* decided. I saw how staying in Faerie was affecting Gareth, affecting Gareth's *music*, so I told him I was ready to take the risk. Find out if my... transition would stick. And, well, it did." He pushed his hair back and smiled. "I still can't believe it sometimes. I'd been ready to sacrifice literally *everything* else that mattered for that chance, and all it took was meeting Gareth in a club and jumping over the gutter."

Spence chuckled. "I've heard jumping over things can get you in trouble sometimes. Never jump over a broom with a selkie or you'll find yourself married."

Josh blinked. "Good to know."

"So how long were you there before you came back out?"

"By the stars of Faerie, two weeks. Here in the Outer World, it was much longer. Years. And from what I've heard about those years, I can't say I'm sorry to have missed them."

Spence's other eyebrow lifted. "Translate for me. Exactly how many years out here?"

"We stepped into Faerie in 1937 and out in 1961."

Whoops

"Hope you don't mind packaged biscuits." Gareth appeared with a wooden tray laden with an earthenware teapot, three mismatched mugs, and a plate piled with cookies. "Neither Josh nor I are much use in the kitchen." Gareth stopped, his gaze shifting from Spence's undoubtedly stunned expression to Josh's apologetic smile. "What did I miss?"

"Th-thirty years?" Spence croaked.

"I just told him about our time in Faerie," Josh said.

"Thirty *years*?"

Gareth set the tray down on a low table next to the sofa with a sigh. "And here we go."

"Thirty. *Years*?"

"I think you're rounding up, mate. Twenty-four at most."

"Not the point," Spence ground out between clenched teeth.

"You're not helping, Gareth." Josh took Spence's elbow and led him to the sofa. "Why don't you sit?"

Spence plopped down. "You were together in Faerie for thirty"—he shot a glare at Gareth, who snapped his mouth shut, probably because he was about to comment on Spence's math skills—"years?"

Josh sat next to him, not quite close enough to touch. "It was only that long here in the Outer World."

Gareth thrust a mug of tea at Spence. "Here. Drink this."

Spence took the mug in shaking hands. "I'd ask for something stronger, but I don't think it would help." He took a sip of the steaming brew and coughed. "Fuck. This could take the paint off a Buick."

Josh nudged a sugar bowl and cream pitcher closer. "Doctor it a bit. That'll render it drinkable." He shot a smirk at Gareth. "Gareth drinks his straight, but he likes to suffer."

Something flickered across Gareth's face—pain, loss, despair? Josh immediately jumped up and hurried over to him. "I'm sorry. I didn't mean that."

"It's all right. I've got to— I'll just be— Enjoy your tea." He turned around and bolted out of the room, and a moment later, footsteps pounded up the stairs.

Josh watched him go, shoulders drooping. "I really wish I hadn't said that." He heaved a giant sigh and turned to Spence. "Anyway. Haven't you ever heard stories about Faerie before?"

"Nah. Not so's you'd notice, anyway." Spence dropped a sugar cube into his tea, hesitated, then tossed in two more along with a dollop of cream. "I'm from an isolated pack in New Mexico. Nobody's poked their noses outside our compound since I can remember, and I was born two years before you made that jump."

"Well, Faerie has some peculiar rules, but one of 'em's around what belongs there and what doesn't. If it doesn't think you belong, you can't get in. Period. If you *do* get in and you stay for one full day, you're on Faerie time, which, like I said, runs differently."

"Oookaay."

"If Gareth had taken me back out again right away, or even after a few hours, only the same amount of time would have passed. But we stayed for longer." Josh's gaze cut to the stairs visible through the arch. "Even though he hates it there, we stayed." Josh met Spence's eyes again. "My situation in my pack was… bad."

"Wait." Spence took another gulp of tea—which wasn't horrible now that he'd neutralized its sucker punch a bit. "You said 1937. That was the year—"

"The year the last gray wolf was killed in the American South."

Spence gazed at him in wonder. "So you lived before the Lockdown. Before we retreated into our compounds and shut out the Wider World."

Josh smiled wryly. "The council had just declared the Lockdown, but it wouldn't have made much difference in my pack, anyway. We were always insular, never mixing much with humans in the nearby towns. The Lockdown just gave leadership an excuse to make it official… dogma." His voice lifted on the word and his eyes held a decided twinkle.

Spence gave him a flat stare. "Dog jokes? Really?"

That was *definitely* a twinkle. "If I can't make them with another were…"

Spence burst out laughing. "A point. Nobody else can truly get them."

"Or if they did—"

"We'd have to kill them," they both said together.

They sat there, grinning at one another, and Spence couldn't help it. He blurted, "I bet your wolf is fucking gorgeous."

And Josh shut down. That was the only word for it. The twinkle disappeared. The grin vanished. He seemed to… deflate.

"I don't shift," he said so softly that if Spence didn't have werewolf senses, he wouldn't have heard it.

Spence winced. "Shit. I'm sorry. Trust me to put my big paw in it. Are you Inactive?" Spence slapped his forehead. "Fuck. There I go again. It's not my business. You don't have to—"

"No." His hand drifted toward Spence, but he snatched it away before he made contact. "I want you to know. If what we want—what *I* want—is going to happen, then it'll be your business." His smile glimmered just for an instant. "Or at least business adjacent."

The Offer

"Business adjacent?"

Josh nodded. "Gareth and I didn't invite you back here for tea just because an American werewolf in Liverpool—or should I say, *another* American werewolf in Liverpool—was an anomaly. But an American werewolf—or any supe, really—who can play the way you do?"

He cut his gaze to the Hammond and Spence's fingertips tingled. In another were, that would signal imminent claw breakout, but Spence recognized it for what it was.

Keyboard lust.

"You… you want me to join your band?"

Josh chuckled. "So far, there's not a band, really. Just Gareth and me. But yes, we'd like you to join us, and if you decide to do that, you deserve to know the truth about us. We both have…" Josh glanced away. "…issues."

"Issues? Join the club." Spence snorted. "I'm a musician who hurls at the idea of performing in front of an audience. How's that for an issue?"

Josh's forehead wrinkled. "Stage fright is nothing to be ashamed of. You were fine onstage at the club."

Spence took a deep breath and stared down into his tea, which, with all the cream he'd dumped into it, was almost as pale as Josh's hair. "That was because of you."

"Me?" Josh's tone held both surprise and… was that a touch of delight? "Because I helped you in the alley?"

"Partly." Spence looked up and met his gaze. "But if you hadn't been there in the club, right where I could see you, I'd have probably lost it again, all over the stage." He lifted his mug in a mock salute. "Still want me to join your not-a-band-really?"

"That won't be a problem. At least not for now. We don't perform anywhere."

Spence's brows drew together as he tried to parse that out. "So you just... what? Hang out here and play for each other, like an endless practice session?"

"We write music, too. Sometimes find other musicians to play with, but privately. Other than the night Gareth and I first met, though, we've never played for an audience." Josh spread his hands, palms up. "So you see, you'll be safe."

"Wait." Spence's frown deepened. "If you don't perform, where do you get money?"

"You don't need to worry about money."

"How can I not? I'm kinda addicted to eating on the regular, and I'd rather not nap on the street."

Josh chuckled. "Sorry. I should have been clearer. You'd live here, of course. With us."

"Charity? I don't know—"

Josh huffed. "I do not understand why *receiving* charity is such a bad thing, when *granting* charity is not." His eyes narrowed. "You're not an alpha, are you?"

Spence snorted. "Hardly. Not even alpha potential, which my brothers and my father never let me forget."

"Stupid pack hierarchy," Josh muttered. "Any one of us has the potential to be whatever we want, as long as we're willing to put in the work and accept the responsibilities and consequences of our actions."

"Got some feelings about it, do you?"

"Don't you?"

Spence frowned, considering. "Yeah, guess I do."

When it came down to it, Spence had no trouble with living somewhere rent-free. That's what he'd been doing since he left the compound. But watching Josh and Gareth together might be more than he could handle.

But... keyboard lust. Could he really turn down a chance like this?

"If you're still worried about stage fright—" Josh hesitantly reached out again, and this time his hand made it all the way to Spence's forearm and rested there, light but so warm. "—look at it this way. If you do join our not-a-band-really, and we ever *do* get around to performing, I'll always be there, right where you can see me."

Spence blinked and a smile tugged at his lips, banishing his frown. "Yeah. Yeah, you would, wouldn't you? That's an *excellent* point."

"Anyway, to return to our... issues. It's not that I can't shift. I'm able. But I don't."

Spence didn't want to pry—okay, he did, but he was *trying* not to be that guy. "Is that something you want to share because of... business adjacency?"

Josh nodded. "I told you my stay in Faerie changed my life. That's not entirely true. Well, it's true, but it's more the result."

"Uh..." Spence scratched the back of his head. "What?"

Josh's dimple peeped, but his eyes were wary. "Faerie changed my life because Faerie changed *me*. Not who I am inside. I've always known I was male, but Faerie saw that, saw who I was, and changed my outsides to match."

Spence couldn't help it. His gaze flicked down across Josh's flat chest to the fly of his jeans. When he met Josh's eyes again, the wariness had grown, as though Josh was waiting for Spence to throw some kind of asshole tantrum and reject him.

Fat chance.

"You're... incredible. In werewolf culture, your life must have been absolute hell before. You're so brave to have made it through and still find room to be kind to perfect strangers." Spence shook his head. "Alphas might think they're the strongest in the pack, but they've got nothing on you."

Feeding the Spark

Josh's breath caught, his eyes glistening, and he withdrew his hand from Spence's arm to fold his fingers together in his lap. "Oh. Th-thank you."

Spence turned sideways and rested his elbow on the sofa's low back. "Did... did it hurt?"

Josh shook his head. "No. It was a little peculiar, but not painful."

"But it's stopped you from shifting."

"Not exactly. I mean, I think I could if I tried. But if I did, the magic that enables weres to shift might undo what Faerie did for me, one transformation canceling out the other. So chances are high that my wolf would be female, and there's no guarantee that my human body wouldn't be female again when I shifted back." He lifted his chin, his eyes clear once more. "I won't risk it."

"But if Faerie changed you once, couldn't it do it again? Couldn't you just go back and get re-transformed?"

Josh shook his head. "No second chances. That's one thing Gareth was certain about. Faerie would see it as me rejecting their gift." He smiled wryly. "Mal said it hates being wrong. So it would either be too embarrassed or too sulky to do it again."

Spence lifted an eyebrow. "You talk about Faerie like it's a person, not a place."

"It's sort of both, maybe? It definitely has a heart. The One Tree, which is at the center of all fae magic. I was the first werewolf to cross its threshold, though, so Gareth and Mal think it wasn't entirely sure what to do with me. There are other fae shifters, but their transformations are linked to the One Tree. Ours isn't. When it realized my body didn't match who I really was, and because I was in company with Gareth, it thought it was doing him a favor by reversing what it saw as a spell or a curse."

"A curse?"

Josh smiled wryly. "There are precedents. Listen to some of those old British ballads sometime. And I can't really say it was wrong." His gaze shifted to a point beyond Spence's shoulder. "It always felt like a curse to me."

"What if you shifted first and then crossed the threshold? Would it change your wolf to match your... your you?"

"We don't want to take that chance. What if it decided it made the mistake on species and trapped me that way, like a form lock? What if the form lock was not only wolf, but female?" Josh shuddered. "No."

"You said Faerie made the first transformation as a favor to Gareth. Why?"

Josh lifted one pale eyebrow. "Gareth told you he was a bard. That's not the truth. Well, not the entire truth. He's *the* bard. The only one. The last true bard of Faerie."

Spence squinted. "I'm guessing that's a big deal?"

"Huge. And normally Gareth refuses to go to there unless he's forced, so when he does visit, Faerie practically falls over itself to appease him." He winked. "Beatlemaniacs have nothing on Faerie when Gareth makes an appearance."

"If Faerie is such a big fan, can't Gareth just ask it to help you out?"

"He won't."

Spence scowled, and this time when his fingertips tingled, it was definitely a claw intro. "Why the fuck not?"

Josh patted Spence's shoulder. "Calm down. He won't because he doesn't think it will do any good. He's only asked Faerie for one thing in his life."

"I'm guessing he didn't get it."

"No." Josh's gaze drifted to the staircase, his expression both sad and fond. "He's been waiting for two hundred years for Faerie to change its mind."

Spence cleared his throat. "Are you and Gareth…?" He brought his hands together. "You know?"

"What?" Josh shook his head, hair flying. "No. Gods, no. That thing Gareth asked Faerie for? An enemy fae abducted his human lover. Niall is the only person Gareth ever wanted. Still does. He's never looked at anyone else that way since."

"Does that make you unhappy? That he'll never want you that way?"

"It does not." Josh met Spence's gaze. "Because I don't want that either." He dropped his chin and looked up at Spence from under his lashes. "At least, not with him."

Spence's heart stuttered. Could Josh mean… Could Spence be lucky enough to… "But w-with me?" He held his breath, waiting, hoping, praying.

Josh looked down at his clasped hands. "I think so. I mean, yes. I do."

Spence exhaled in a whoosh. "Thank the gods. Because I want you so—"

"Mostly." Josh winced and looked up. "Sorry. I don't mean to be a jerk. But what I want—what I can *handle*—may not be the same as what you want and need." He ran a hand through his hair. "It might not even be what *I* wanted yesterday or what I'll want a week from now. Does that make any sense?"

"Not yet, but I'm still listening. Is it okay…" Spence swallowed past his heart lodged in his throat. "May I touch you now?"

Josh took a shaky breath and rested his hand on Spence's arm again. "For now, yes. But maybe not tomorrow? It's just"—he shuddered—"sometimes touching calls up especially bad memories for me. But if I don't want it at any one moment, it has nothing to do with you. It's me."

"Well, being judged by people is what sends me reeling, and my reaction is both messier and smellier than simply avoiding touch, so I think you're already ahead of me."

"It's not a competition, Spence."

Spence looked at Josh with wonder. "You really feel that way, don't you? You don't buy into the whole pack mentality of fighting your way to the top."

"Since as far as my old pack was concerned, I was destined to be quite literally at the bottom? No. I don't. Whatever we decide to be—you and me, the band, the future—we get to figure that out as we go."

"But together, right? I'll be living here? With you?"

Josh nodded. "With Gareth and me. There's plenty of room. The house is his and the money for its upkeep I *think* comes from Faerie through his brother. Faerie really doesn't want to lose its last true bard, and they're trying to lure him back. They know threats won't work, since from his perspective the worst thing has already happened. So they're willing to give him space, keep him comfortable, keep him connected to music in the hopes he'll come home, eventually."

"Do you think he will? Go home?"

Josh wrinkled his nose. "The thing that the Queen and even his brothers don't realize is that Faerie will never be home to him. Not as long as Niall isn't there. The Queen won't intercede for whatever reason, so unless Niall returns by some miracle, they'll be waiting forever."

"So what you're saying is"—Spence narrowed his eyes— "we're living here and sponging off Faerie out of spite?"

"Pretty much, yeah."

Spence grinned. "Then count me in."

"Oh, thank goodness," Josh murmured.

He caught Spence's gaze, unblinking, and leaned forward slowly, so slowly. Spence didn't dare breathe, just waited, praying that he didn't still smell and taste like puke.

Then Josh's lips were on his, just a soft press, gone between one heartbeat and the next, but inside Spence's head, it lasted *forever*.

Josh bit his lip and peered at Spence through his lashes again. "Was that horrible? I've never done it before."

Spence shook his head wildly. "Not horrible. At all. No, it was fantastic. Happy to do it again, although maybe after I've brushed my teeth and gargled with about a gallon of Listerine."

Josh chuckled softly. "Don't worry about that. You're fine." He laid a gentle palm against Spence's cheek. "More than fine. As for the rest—whatever this will be to both of us—we'll have all the time in the world to discover."

"Assuming you pass the audition," Gareth said from the archway.

Spence froze, waiting for his stomach's usual rebellion, but with Josh's fingers on Spence's cheek and his hand on Spence's arm, it didn't come.

Josh frowned at Gareth. "Gareth. Stop it. He already passed the audition."

Gareth sauntered in, a Stratocaster in one hand, and although his words had been challenging, bordering on arrogant, his eyes were pinched with pain. "We've seen how he can lift up the mediocre. But can he keep up with us?"

Spence patted Josh's hand before standing up. "That's not the question, bard."

Gareth lifted an eyebrow. "No? What is it then?"

"The question is, can *you* keep up with *me*?"

For a moment, Spence thought he'd gone too far, but then Gareth threw back his head and laughed. He slung his guitar strap over his shoulder and grinned.

"All right, wolf boys. Let's jam."

Tiff

On the Edge

Tooth and claw, but Tiff *hated* getting wet, especially when it was for nothing. She growled low in her throat, her fist tight around the handle of her Precision Sunburst's case.

Fucking Bill Graham. This was all his fault. Ever since he'd taken over Santana's management, he'd done everything in his power to shut Tiff out, even though Chepito had vouched for her and Carlos had praised her chops.

Graham had talked Carlos and the band into this hellish gig, too. Was he fucking loco? This was a fucking *cow pasture*. Packed with humans who probably hadn't bathed in weeks even before they were camped out here with no way to wash unless they jumped in a pond.

And men. *Diosa*, they were disgusting. They'd whip out their dicks and pee *anywhere*.

To top it off? Rain. Match rain with a fucking *cow pasture* and the fucking *humans* and that got you mud. Which Tiff hated even more than getting wet, if that was possible.

You've got nobody to blame but yourself. She should have stayed home. She should never have believed Carlos when he'd promised to let her sit in on a couple of songs. She should have known that Carlos would cave under Graham's pressure.

Graham. She growled again. He didn't believe a woman could hold her own as a rock musician. A vocalist, maybe. He'd sure sunk his claws into Janis, not that it was doing her a lot of good right now. The girl had issues that were gonna kill her if she didn't get some help.

But Graham's stable had zero female instrumentalists, and the suggestion that a woman could play bass well enough to match Carlos's guitar licks practically made him speechless with patriarchal outrage.

"You'd think the asshole had never heard of Carol Kaye," she growled as she watched Santana set up after the end of Country Joe McDonald's surprise set—which wouldn't have happened if the band had been ready on time. Which they would have been, if they'd let Tiff play like she was supposed to. Instead, she'd gotten booted out of the performer's pavilion.

Into the fucking *rain*.

"You know, sheila, you can't actually set them on fire with your eyes. Even with eyes like yours."

Tiff whipped her head to the side. A tall man with a bush of dirty blond hair was grinning down at her, bouncing on his toes. The shoulders of his tie-dyed T-shirt were soaked from the drizzle. He had a pair of drumsticks jammed in the pocket of his jeans and a worn rucksack on his back.

She glared at him. "My name's not Sheila. And what are you talking about?"

The guy tapped his temple. "Your eyes. Better scale back the rage a little. Your kitty's about to pounce."

Shit.

Tiff glanced down at her hand. It wasn't aching from her death-grip on the case's handle. Her claws had actually emerged to pierce the heel of her palm. Chances were, most of the humans crammed together nearby were high enough they wouldn't notice, but the sphinxes who monitored Secrecy Pact violations weren't exactly flexible. For them, if someone *could* have seen, even if nobody *did*, it counted.

I dare even those uptight winged killjoys to spot anything in this mess.

Nevertheless, she took a couple of calming breaths, willing her big cat to settle down. When the band struck up their opening number, she had a slight relapse but managed to keep her reaction down to a hiss. As her feline visual acuity faded back to as human-normal as it ever got, she realized she recognized the tall guy.

"You're that drummer, right? The Aussie. Chepito's friend."

He twirled his hand in the air and made a mock bow. "Hamish Mulherne, at your service."

"Uh huh." Tiff sniffed twice. "Why do you smell like curry?"

He winced. "Sorry. Been on the road for a while, so I'm a bit ripe. That's how us kangaroos smell. The blokes, anyway. Getting my hair wet makes it worse."

She eyed him, head tilted to one side. "Kangaroo, huh?"

Hanging with a fellow supe might be a good plan, especially since Tiff had a feeling her ride had gotten canceled when the band turned their backs on her. She was sure Chepito would try to put in a good word, but even Carlos was under Graham's spell.

This guy was good-looking enough, not to mention friendly, enthusiastic, and a musician. Tiff was equal opportunity when it came to sex, so it wouldn't hurt to hang for a bit and see what happened. If nothing else, it would give the sphinxes somebody else to focus on.

"I'm Tiff," she said. "What brings you to this fucking cow pasture?"

He positively beamed. "Are you joking? This is *brilliant*. The *energy*." His long arm swept out at the crowd on the hillside who were grooving to "Waiting," the song Tiff *should* have been sitting in on. "What's better than days full of music? Where else can you see bands like this—Sly, Ravi Shankar, Janis, Joe Cocker, The Who, for fuck's sake—all in one place?" His grin widened, if that was possible. "The performances alone are worth more than gold, but connections mean almost as much."

"Connections, huh?" She glanced sidelong at the stage. She'd *thought* she'd had connections there. More than one. But Graham had cut those like a Wichita lineman. "Tell me more."

A Deal

"Think about it," Hamish said. "Our world, the music world, isn't that big. It makes sense to touch as many people as you can, because you never know where the next gig will come from. I just spent twenty minutes talking to John Sebastian while these blokes"—he jerked his thumb at the stage—"were messing about. That wouldn't have happened if I was moping down in Queensland."

Tiff snorted. "John Sebastian? Not exactly a rocker. Besides, the Spoonful broke up last year."

"Oi, you can't say 'Summer in the City' didn't rock."

"I suppose."

Hamish's gaze drifted to the stage where Santana was getting ready to launch into their second number. "And 'Darling, Be Home Soon' is classic."

"Oh, gods." Tiff rolled her eyes. "You're a romantic."

He grinned down at her, apparently not in the least embarrassed. "Nothing wrong with that."

"Maybe not for you. But I…" Tiff froze as the first notes of "Evil Ways" wailed out of the amps, and all those calming breaths were for nothing. Her fingertips tingled and her vision started to change, a sure sign that she was losing it.

"Hey, hey, hey." Hamish took her arm and towed her away from the stage. He turned her so that she was facing his chest, her back to the crowd. "What's going on? You were fine a minute ago."

"Fucking Bill Graham," Tiff growled. "That fucking song. It's not one Carlos wrote."

"I know. Bloke by the name of Sonny Henry. Willie Bobo recorded it a couple of years ago. You got a problem with covers?"

"Not with covers. With *that fucking song*. Graham convinced the band to record it as a dig at me."

"Look, I know music is powerful and the best songs are universal, but—"

"I'm not on some giant-ass ego trip, if that's what you're thinking. I *know* Graham did it because he told me so." She leaned sideways to glare at the stage, but Hamish repositioned her, which was probably a good thing, because all ten of her claws were out now.

"Okay, setting aside you know Bill Graham well enough for him to talk to you—"

"It wasn't exactly a friendly chat."

"Got it. But why would he push this song in particular as a dig at you?"

"Because he didn't like my *influence* on Carlos." Tiff didn't rein in the disgust in her tone. "Or that I was seeing one of the session musicians and a waitress from the El Sombrero at the same time. A musician named Gene," she said through clenched teeth to keep her fangs from emerging, "and a waitress named Joan. Gene and Joan. Like in the lyrics."

Hamish blinked. "Ah. Right. That seems a bit... pointed."

"You *think*?" Tiff swiped angrily at her eyes, scraping her cheek with the tip of a claw. "Fuck. I suppose I can't blame Carlos. Money and fame. That's what every band wants, right? Money and fame'll leave friendship in the dust every time, especially if the opposite is staring you in the face." She tried for a laugh, but it didn't make it past her collarbone. "This business kills friendships faster than a bite to the throat. Look at John and Paul."

Hamish gazed down at her, his brows drawn together. "That doesn't always happen. Look at Bob and Frankie."

"Who?"

"Oh, come on. Bob Gaudio? Frankie Valli? The Four Seasons? The group changed, *music* changed, but Bob and Frankie are still friends, still partners, all on a handshake deal." He stuck out one enormous paw. "So how about it?"

She frowned at his hand. "What are you talking about?"

"Take a look around. There are probably half a million humans crammed on this hillside, but somehow, two shifters ran into each other. That seems like grounds for a handshake-deal friendship, even if it just gets us through the weekend. No other strings, I swear." He leaned down and murmured, "I've got sandwiches."

Tiff's belly dropped. *Food.* She'd forgotten. Not only had she lost her ride when she'd gotten booted from the pavilion, she'd lost access to the food she'd packed for the band—which was one of the few things Graham thought she was good for, the big patriarchal asshole.

The guys she'd known for two-plus years had turned their backs on her without a thought, but this stranger was offering to share not only companionship but his provisions? Her gaze shifted from his hand to his face, where a hopeful smile crinkled the corners of his gray eyes.

There wasn't really a downside. They could hang out, watch the concert, share his food. Hells, maybe she could cadge a lift from him to get out of this mud pit after Jimi played on Sunday. She wasn't in any danger. She was a jaguar; he was a kangaroo. If worse came to worst, she outgunned him.

Her vision morphed again, so she could tell her pupils looked human once more, and her claws retracted. She shook his hand.

"Deal."

Settling In

Hamish peered up at the sky, which had started to clear a bit. "Let's find a spot to sit."

Tiff snorted. "Good luck with that. Between mud and the sea of humanity, you might just as well wish for a flying carpet."

"I don't need a flying carpet. I've got charm." He patted the strap of his rucksack. "And tarps." He waggled his eyebrows. "*Some* people might not know how to prep for a walkabout like this, but I'm not one of them. Come on."

He marched up the hillside, staying near the fence line, even though the fence itself hadn't fully survived the human incursion, and stopped within a hundred yards of stage left. "This looks proper."

Tiff eyed the cluster of humans, male and female, all of them way too young to be swapping a paper bag-wrapped bottle among them, let alone the doobies. "You're joking, right?"

"Just watch."

He bounded over to the group and flashed that thousand-buck grin. "G'day, mates. Mind budging over a bit?"

One of the women gaped up at him. "Oh, wow."

Another clasped her hands under her chin. "Say it again."

Hamish lifted his sandy brows. "Say what?"

"What you said."

"Mind budging over?"

She shook her head. "No. The other thing."

"Oh. You mean g'day, mates?"

They all giggled at that—males and females alike, which made Tiff roll her eyes. A bare-chested guy offered a joint clamped in a roach clip to Hamish, who shook his head.

"Nah, thanks, mate, I'm good. Just need a bit of real estate for me and the sheila."

They all skootched over, and Hamish produced a tarp out of his pack like a magician conjuring a rabbit out of a hat.

As he spread it, Tiff muttered, "My name's not Sheila."

He winked at her. "Don't spoil it for them." He tossed her a hand towel that had appeared as magically as the tarp. "For your case."

Nonplussed, Tiff caught it. "Thanks." The case was watertight, so she wasn't worried about water seeping in and harming her bass. On the other hand, while the leather was oiled, so water beaded up on its surface, it wasn't impervious. At Hamish's extravagant gesture, she sat down on the tarp and blotted the case dry.

He plopped down next to her. "You expecting to play that sometime this weekend?"

She glowered at him, although she dialed it back when he handed her a hefty sandwich wrapped in wax paper. When she peeked inside, her mouth watered. Hoagie roll, cold cuts, pepperoncinis, and was that cojita?

"That ship has sailed," she said before she took a bite and moaned. "*Diosa*, that's good."

"Thanks. Made it myself." He pulled another sandwich out of the pack and held it out. "This one's turkey and gouda, if you'd rather trade."

She snatched her sandwich out of his reach. "No chance." Then she sighed. "Although if you'd prefer this one, you can have it. I mean, it's your sandwich."

He beamed at her. "Nope. Now it's yours." He took a bite of his own. "If you're not gonna play, you should protect your case."

"How exactly?" She took another bite. "Gonna offer to put it in your pouch?"

"I'm a bloke. We don't have pouches. We have ball sacks."

Tiff rolled her eyes. "That's really something I didn't need to know."

"But seriously. I've seen the weather reports. It's gonna rain on and off all weekend. I've got more tarps. I can rig something up."

Tiff glanced down at her case. The kangaroo had a point. The leather was spotted from the earlier shower, despite Hamish's towel. "Yeah. All right. Show me what you've got."

He started to put his sandwich down, but she stopped him with a hand on his arm. He looked down at it, and then up at her, and she knew. Right then, she knew.

She was never gonna fuck this guy.

Because if she fucked him, it would *fuck* him, and he didn't deserve that. She snatched her hand away.

"Eat first. The case can wait."

He nodded, still looking a little dazed. She turned away as Santana rolled into "Soul Sacrifice," and took a vicious bite of her sandwich, imagining it was Bill Graham's head. Except this was an excellent sandwich. It didn't deserve the comparison.

"I've, uh, got a couple of thermoses in here. Tea or water, if you're thirsty."

Tiff frowned at the rucksack. "What else have you got in there? A VW?"

He chuckled at that. "Nah. Just the basics. How about it?"

"Water, please." For once, it didn't chap Tiff's hide to be what her abuela called *un poco gracioso*. In fact, she added, "And thank you. For everything."

Inroads

"No worries." Hamish passed a green thermos with a chrome topper to Tiff. "A do like this... Well, it's better with friends, yeah?" He gazed out at the crowd. "Sometimes you just get a feeling, you know? This is might never happen again, or at least not for years. It's a watershed."

Tiff snorted. "I can only hope I'll shed water if what you say about the weather is true."

He grinned. "I've heard that cats don't like getting wet. Guess rumors don't lie."

She gave him a narrow-eyed look. "Shut it, kangaroo."

His grin didn't fade as he pulled out a bag of potato chips. "I've got crisps, too."

"*Diosa*, what *don't* you have?" But she took a handful of the offered chips, and she had to confess, having something to munch on meant she didn't actively grind her teeth when Santana left the stage to thundering applause and deafening cheers.

"They're gonna be huge." Hamish's low tone somehow cut through the crowd's noise.

Tiff sighed. "Yeah, I know."

He held out an Oreo. "Biscuit?"

Eyes prickling, Tiff took the cookie and bit down savagely, waiting for the followup questions, the probing, the *sympathy*. But it didn't come. Instead, Hamish rummaged in his rucksack again and pulled out yet another tarp.

"What say we use the time before the next band to rig up something for your case?"

Tiff tossed the last bit of Oreo into her mouth and considered. "I may not like getting wet, but I'll survive. If we get a downpour, though, the leather might never be the same. I guess wrapping it in a tarp would be a good idea."

Hamish made a weird sound, almost a raspberry but not quite. "We can do better than that. A carryall. So you can sling it on your back and keep your hands free if we decide to go walkabout."

She lifted an eyebrow. "You're good, kangaroo, but how are you gonna make a backpack out of a big square of plastic? Got a sewing machine in that rucksack, too?"

"No, but I've got a pocket knife, and you've got, you know" —he jerked his chin at her fingers—"your own brand of hole punchers. You gonna tell me you don't have a spare strap or two? Because if you do, I won't believe it."

Tiff huffed, but opened the case and took out two of her spare straps, one leather and one of her abuela's inkle-woven numbers. "Here. Show me your magic."

And he did, which shouldn't have surprised her anymore. By the time the stage was set for the next act, he'd managed to contrive something that would let her carry her case on her back like a turtle shell.

She set the protected case on the tarp next to her and gave it a pat, not able to meet his gaze. "Thanks. This is… This is great. I hate carrying things in my hands."

"Who doesn't?" His attention shifted to the stage, where a shaggy-haired man in a tie-dyed shirt walked on carrying an acoustic guitar. "Oi. It's John Sebastian. He told me he was just here to watch the show. Why do you reckon he's performing?"

Tiff shrugged. "Probably more trouble with bands not being ready." She snorted. "Country Joe McDonald had to do an unscheduled set because Santana didn't get their shit together in time."

A guy in a jeans jacket who was staggering by with a nearly empty bottle of Jack Daniels clutched in one hand leaned over, swaying so much that Tiff was surprised he didn't fall face first into Hamish's sandwich. "Egg-zactly. I heard that Incredible

String Band refused to go on 'cause the stage was too wet." He chuckled. "Afraid of 'lectrocution. Bet Sebastian's doin' them a favor." He leaned forward even more, and Hamish whipped one of his drumsticks out of his pocket and planted it on the guy's sternum so he'd stay upright. "That's why he's only using an acoustic."

The guy smiled down at them vacantly, arms limp. Hamish must be packing some strength in his lanky frame because his biceps weren't even straining, even though he was clearly supporting the guy's weight.

Hamish shot a glance at Tiff that momentarily robbed her of breath—not because it was hot or suggestive, but because it *wasn't*. With his mouth echoing the lift of his eyebrow, he both invited Tiff to share his gentle exasperation and acknowledged that he knew she already did.

"Thanks for the tip, mate." Hamish stood and turned the guy around to give him a gentle push and send him on his way.

Hamish sat again, shaking his head. "Do you think there's anybody in the whole bloody place who isn't high?"

"Probably not." Tiff finished off her sandwich. "And that includes the musicians."

He studied her, brow furrowed. "Does that include you?"

"Are you kidding? Even if that shit worked on… you know, *us*, it's too risky. We always have to watch our backs around humans."

He smiled a little crookedly. "Unless you've got someone to watch it for you."

She blinked at that. When was the last time she'd had someone at her back? Not since she'd left Nicaragua in defiance of her abuelo's orders to settle down and find a mate. She'd been on high alert ever since, following Abuela's advice when she'd snuck Tiff out of the village.

"You are strong, mija," Abuela had said. "You do not need the pitiful sops they offer in exchange for your surrender. Make your own way. Follow your own path. Stand on your own."

She'd kissed Tiff's forehead. "Now go. Do me proud." She'd smiled sadly. "Do what I never could."

Tiff had taken those words to heart, but maybe she'd taken them too literally? Maybe she didn't *need* anybody—although given her situation when the band turned their back on her in this godsforsaken middle of nowhere, she might need to rethink that.

But this was different. This was *situational*, not *foundational*. And in situations like this, it might not be a bad thing to have someone she could trust beside her.

She glanced at Hamish, who'd offered help and companionship—and a really terrific sandwich—only because he'd noticed that she was on the verge of losing it, big time. He was… genuine, something she couldn't say about many of her acquaintances.

Acquaintances.

Yeah, that was the problem, wasn't it? Tiff had *acquaintances.* She didn't have *friends*. But maybe it was time to find one or two of those. It wouldn't make her weak, not if the benefits were mutual.

Right?

Is that...?

Tiff glanced sidelong at Hamish, who was smiling beatifically, humming along with Sebastian as he sang "Darling Be Home Soon," drumsticks tapping the rhythm on the tarp. Musicianship had always been her ultimate yardstick when she decided whether any relationship was worth her time. Even Joan, the waitress from El Sombrero who'd put her in Graham's crosshairs, had caught Tiff's attention because she had perfect pitch and a glorious alto voice, even when she'd only been singing as she'd bused tables.

Chepito had declared that the Aussie had chops, and although the tarp wasn't the best drumming surface, Tiff could tell it was true. She'd reserve final judgment until she heard him on his kit, then—

No. What had *judgment* ever gotten her? Abandoned in the middle of a fucking *cow pasture*, that's what. She grabbed the thermos and took a swig of water, fingers tight around the cool metal. Maybe it was time for her to stop being so damn judgy all the time. She glared at the performers' pavilion. Not about fucking *Bill Graham*, but about other people.

They still had to pass the decent person test, of course, but Hamish had passed that one with flying colors. It wouldn't hurt her to see if friendship might just shore her up instead of tearing her down.

The sun peeked out during Sebastian's set, although by the time the Incredible String Band got over themselves and took the stage, it was clouding up again and had resumed raining before they finished.

"They played for barely half an hour," Hamish said, beating out a nine-stroke roll on his jeans-clad thigh. "Do you suppose they were always intending to do such a short set?"

"Could be," Tiff replied. "Although the rain might've scared them off early." She peered up at the sky. Sunset was at least an hour away, but the clouds made it seem like twilight had come early.

Suddenly, Hamish scrambled to his feet. "I don't believe it."

"What?"

He bounced on his toes and beckoned to her. "Come on." He grabbed his rucksack. "Get a shift on, sheila."

"Why? I thought you wanted to sit," Tiff grumbled, but she stood up. "And my name's not—"

"Sheila. I know. But that seems to be the only thing that'll get you moving and we don't want to lose out."

"Lose out on what?"

He grinned. "Connections."

"What about your tarp?"

"My mates there can have it. I've got more." He bounded down the slope, the crowd somehow not slowing his headlong rush.

"Thanks, man," the shirtless guy called.

"Unbelievable," Tiff mumbled as she rose and slipped the straps of her case carryall over her shoulders.

She'd figured out by now that Hamish was impulsive at best, reckless at worst. Look at how he'd adopted a borderline homicidal jaguar shifter in the middle of a sea of muddy humans. On any other day, with any other random person, Tiff would be content to let them reap the consequences of their actions and let the chips fall.

But here? Today? She couldn't do it. Not with Hamish.

He'd talked her off the ledge during Santana's set. He'd kept her case dry. He'd given her a *sandwich*, dammit. And *Oreos*. The least she could do was stand by him and share the fallout.

She caught up with him when his momentum was stopped by a clot of people surging for the stage. He hopped in the air, apparently trying to see over their heads.

"Roger! Oi! Roger!" Hamish called.

"What are you doing?" she hollered over the buzz of the crowd.

"It's Roger Daltrey." He pointed over the heads of the people in front of him. "See the hair? It's absolutely Daltrey. The Who must have gotten here early."

Stupid tall people. "All I can see is a wall of backs."

She jostled sideways until she could peer between two shorter—although still soggy—bodies. A tall man with a shoulder-length mop of golden curls was striding in the direction of the performer's pavilion. She couldn't see his face, but, yeah, okay. That hair was unmistakable.

"He's not gonna stop to talk to us."

Hamish grinned down at her. "Why not?" He grabbed her hand. "If he doesn't, he can tell us to bugger off, but if we don't at least try, we'll never know." He towed her toward Daltrey, who had stopped to speak with two guys who were certainly not Pete Townshend or John Entwhistle, and *definitely* not Keith Moon. A slight blond man stood shoulder to shoulder with a sturdier guy who was dark-haired like Townshend, but—

The wind shifted and Tiff caught the scent.

Werewolf. Her nose crinkled. *Wet* werewolf.

"Hold on, Hamish. I don't think that's—"

But she was too late. Hamish had already closed the gap.

"Roger, I wanted to tell you that I…" Hamish trailed off when the man turned and, as Tiff had begun to suspect, was *so* not Roger Daltrey.

Now, Tiff was the first to admit that Roger Daltrey was a fine-looking man, especially since he'd stopped straightening his hair and let it grow out. But this guy was on a whole other level. The eyes, the cheekbones, the jaw, the nose, the mouth—they were so perfect and harmonious that he almost didn't look human.

Then she blinked and he looked almost plain. Except for the hair. That didn't change, although the wet-dog werewolf odor vanished like it had never been. Which could only mean one thing.

Fae.

Fateful Encounter

Tiff had never had direct contact with the fae because she wasn't an idiot. You didn't mess with those *maníacas* unless you had a death wish. Even the beautiful ones could creep into your thoughts until you'd agree to follow them anywhere, never to return. And as for the others, the ones who weren't so beautiful? Well, if you saw one of those *bastardos*, you ran. Fast.

She didn't know what those two werewolves were doing with the fae—he'd probably hit them with glamourie and turned them into puppets, because werewolves were hardwired to follow commands. Unless they were alphas, in which case they were all about *giving* commands. Throwing their weight around, just like fucking *Bill Graham*.

Either way, she refused to let any of them sink their claws into Hamish. Hamish was *nice*. Hamish was her *friend*. And friends looked out for each other.

She strode forward and stood next to Hamish, glaring at the werewolves and letting her eyes do their jaguar thing. The taller werewolf growled and moved in front of the blond one.

Hamish raised both palms. "Oh, hey. Sorry, mate. My mistake. I thought you were—"

"Roger Daltrey," the blond guy said. "I told you the hair would be a problem, Gareth." He edged in front of the taller were so gracefully that it *almost* didn't seem like an intentional protective move. *Smooth.* Although his voice held a soft Southern drawl, Tiff suspected it hid a spine of steel.

He held out his hand. "I'm Josh." He jerked his head toward the other were. "This is Spence. And the fellow who shares Daltrey's hair stylist is Gareth."

Interesting dynamic. Tiff would have bet good money that Josh was the weakest member of the trio—he was certainly the smallest by a wide margin, no taller than she was herself and probably about three quarters of her weight—but the other two let him take the lead.

"G'day, mate." Hamish shook Josh's hand enthusiastically, bouncing on his toes. "Hamish. And the sheila here is Tiff."

From the sidelong glance Hamish slid her, Tiff knew he was baiting her on purpose, but by now it was almost their schtick. "My name's not Sheila."

He widened his eyes at her. "Did I say it was?"

Josh chuckled. "I couldn't place your scent, but with that accent, I'm guessing... kangaroo?"

"Too right." Hamish glanced at the stage where Canned Heat had just broken into "Going Up the Country" as the rain pattered down. "Looks like we're in for a wet night, eh? But no worries. I've got—"

"Tarps," he said at the same time as Josh, who patted the pack on Spence's back.

Hamish grinned widely. "Yeah? Did you bring sandwiches, too?"

"Of course. And fried chicken. My mama's recipe. I been practicing and think I've finally got it down."

Tiff studied the other two men, who seemed to be content to let Josh take the lead. Gareth was gazing at the stage, an expression on his face that Tiff had seen on her own when she looked in the mirror after another day of getting shut out by music business assholes.

Loss.

Spence, on the other hand, was staring at the audience, clearly on the verge of bolting. He was quivering as though Josh's arm pressed against his was the only thing keeping him in place.

"You blokes been here long?" Hamish asked.

"No." Josh cut a glance between Gareth and Spence. "We were... delayed a bit."

"Yeah, traffic was completely mad. Half the bands had trouble too, and some had problems with the rain. Did you see John Sebastian before? He was just here to watch, but they pulled him onstage for an acoustic set because the stage was too wet for electric instruments." Hamish snorted. "Or so they said."

Spence's eyes got even wider, if that was possible. He clutched Josh's hand like a lifeline. Tiff blinked and then checked to see whether anybody had spotted the touch. Two months ago, Stonewall had lit a fuse, changing the landscape for gays, but acceptance wouldn't happen overnight, even in the cities, and this was a fucking *cow pasture*.

"They can do that?" Spence asked. "Just ask people to sit in? P-p-play?"

"Not just any people," Tiff said. "It's not like talent night at the roadhouse. The promoters'll reach out to people they know." *Unless they've been blackballed by fucking* Bill Graham.

Gareth still hadn't spoken, but Josh patted Spence's hand. "Don't worry. Nobody knows who we are. You're safe. We can —"

"Gareth? Gareth Kendrick?"

A man in a yellow rain slicker bulled toward them through the crowd. Tiff recognized him—he was one of the minions from the performers' pavilion who'd evicted her after Santana turned their backs on her. She growled under her breath, earning a startled glance from Josh.

"Steady, there, sheila." Hamish's murmur, a warning infused with his signature irreverence, brought her back from the edge.

"My name's not Sheila," she repeated. It was almost like a mantra now, grounding her by breaking the cycle of her anger, redirecting it at Hamish's poke and turning it from rage to annoyance.

As he'd no doubt intended.

Gareth slowly turned to face the man. "Yes?"

"Oh, thank god. The Who hasn't arrived yet, but once I spotted the Daltrey hair, I knew it had to be you."

Josh snickered, but Gareth didn't so much as glance at him. "Is there something you need?"

"Yes!" He squinted down at Gareth's empty hands. "You don't have your axe?" He glanced at Josh. "Or your violin?"

"We're not here to perform," Josh said mildly. "Just to watch the show."

The man flapped one hand as though he were waving away a mosquito. "That's no problem. We can find instruments for you, and keys for Spence, too."

"I'm sorry," Josh said. "Why would you think we would need instruments? We're not a band."

The man scoffed. "Yeah, right. Robbie Robertson said he jammed with you when he was on the UK tour with Dylan, and he told me you guys were the tightest group he'd ever heard. So you don't have a record deal yet. So nobody's heard of you. So what?" He gestured to the crowd. "Half a million people will have heard of you by the time you finish your set."

A Refusal

Tiff frowned at the minion and then peered at the three supes. Gareth had gone pale, Spence looked positively green, and Josh... Well, Tiff wouldn't have believed such a soft-spoken, friendly guy could look so murderous.

"I'm sorry." Nobody but a fool could mistake Josh's bared teeth for a smile. "We're just here to watch the show."

This guy apparently *was* a fool, however, because he barreled right on. "Sure, sure. But—"

"I said"—Josh's words held an edge now, a danger that his drawl didn't mask—"we're just here to watch the show."

Whoa. *Respect for the rip-your-throat-out subtext, wolf boy.*

The minion, who obviously had never heard of subtext or learned to recognize it when it was staring him in the face, barely glanced at Josh—*big mistake*—before clearly dismissing him as unimportant and focusing on Gareth.

"*Bill Graham* himself booked some of his clients for this event. You do him a solid and you've got an in to the business that people would *kill* for."

Gareth could have been a statue by this time, as white and unmoving as marble, staring fixedly at the trees beyond the pavilion, and Spence was greener than the sodden grass. For an instant Josh's blue eyes glinted gold, and Tiff wasn't the only one growling low in her throat.

Fucking Bill Graham.

"All right." Josh's faux-affable tone made Hamish suck in a sharp breath. Yeah, the kangaroo got it too—the minion was playing with fire. "We'll go on."

"Fantastic," the minion crowed.

"Josh," Spence croaked, a clear protest.

Josh folded his fingers around Spence's wrist and gave him a small smile. "But only if all five of us can perform."

The minion blinked and glanced around, as though a guitarist or two might burst out of the ground like nuclear dandelions. "What? Five? Robbie said there were three—"

"Our band. Gareth, Spence, myself"—Josh gestured with the hand that wasn't grounding Spence—"and of course Hamish and Tiff. We couldn't possibly play without them."

The minion's jaw dropped—which meant he matched Tiff and Hamish. Tiff snapped her mouth shut and elbowed Hamish in the ribs hard enough that he *oof*ed.

"That's right." Tiff folded her arms. "All of us or none of us."

The minion finally looked at Tiff and his eyes narrowed. She could practically see him donning his male superiority hat. "You."

"Yep. Me."

He turned away, dismissing her as though she didn't matter —because to men like him, she didn't. "I can work it for the tall guy, but not the chick."

"Oi!" Hamish pointed a drumstick at the minion. "Show some respect for the sheila." He turned his head so the minion couldn't see him wink at Tiff.

"Sorry, but she's not allowed onstage. Graham's orders."

"I guess you've got your answer then," Josh said. "You'll have to find somebody else to sit in."

"I don't—" The minion grimaced, clutching his wet hair. "Look, it's as much as my job's worth to go against Graham's orders. I can't let her anywhere near the stage or he'll can my ass."

Josh shrugged. "Not our problem. If you'll excuse us, we have an appointment with some fried chicken."

He turned and walked away, still gripping Spence's wrist, and the crowd parted to let him through, because unlike the minion, they instinctively stood clear of that palpable werewolf killing intent, even if they didn't know exactly what made them move. Gareth strode after them, staring straight ahead.

Hamish shared a glance with Tiff and then saluted the minion. "G'day, mate. Good luck finding a ringer." Then he bounded after the three men.

Tiff only took a moment to grin, flip the guy off, and say, "Give Graham my regards," before she followed.

They didn't stop until they reached the fence line, not far from where she and Hamish had sat earlier, although their tarp was now doubling as an impromptu tent for the people who'd been sitting next to them. When Tiff caught up with them, Josh was murmuring something to Spence, Gareth was still rocking the thousand-yard stare, and Hamish—as usual—was bouncing on his toes.

Tiff waited until Josh had finished speaking and Spence had taken a shuddery breath, before she said, "Not that I mind sticking it to Bill Graham, but how did you know I'd been banned from the stage?"

Josh studied her, his face somber. "I didn't."

That made Tiff bristle. "So you just assumed he'd refuse because I'm a female bass player."

"Is that why Graham blackballed you?" Josh snorted, a tiny, almost kittenish sound. "You'd think he'd never heard of Carol Kaye."

Despite the rage that had been brewing in her middle all day, Tiff had to grin. "I think I like you. But that still doesn't tell me why you took the chance. What if he'd taken you up on your bluff?"

Josh shrugged. "Then I guess we'd have performed." He smiled, flashing his pronounced canines. "And we'd have killed it."

An Invitation

Spence whimpered and Gareth grunted at Josh's matter-of-fact pronouncement.

"How d'you know that, mate?" Hamish flipped a drumstick. "For all you know, we might not even be musicians."

Josh lifted one pale eyebrow. "You nearly impaled that guy with your stick, and she's got a bass case strapped to her back. It wasn't hard to figure out."

Hamish looked at the stick in his hand. "Fair cop. But we might be shit. What then?"

He tilted his head. "I don't think you are. You both wear your music on your skin. But even if I were wrong—"

"Which he isn't." Spence's tone was almost challenging, as if daring anyone to disagree. "Not ever."

Josh patted his arm. "You're biased, dear heart." He turned back to Hamish. "Even if you weren't as good as I think you are, nobody would have noticed. Not once Gareth started to sing."

Tiff narrowed her eyes at the fae. "Upstage everybody, do you?"

Gareth didn't respond, but Josh stepped in again. "No, but this isn't the best place to talk." He edged closer to Gareth. "Do you want to leave? I know you wanted to hear Robbie play, not to mention Jimi, Sly, and The Who."

Gareth closed his eyes, a visible shudder passing through his body. "Yes. Let's go. I'll apologize to Robbie and we can catch everyone else some other time."

Now that he'd said more than one word, Tiff caught his accent. *A Brit, then.* "We're on one side of a cow pasture packed with humans, most of 'em in an altered state of consciousness, and the roads are all on the other side. It'll be tomorrow before we can get out of here."

The corner of Gareth's mouth lifted and he turned, walking straight for the pavilion. Josh towed Spence along in his wake, but stopped to look over his shoulder after taking half a dozen steps.

"Coming?"

Tiff frowned. "Coming where? Even if they'd still let me into the pavilion—which they won't—now that you've kicked the minion in the balls, they're not about to let you in there either."

"We're not going to the pavilion." Josh pointed to the stand of trees that rose beyond it. "We're going there."

"The woods?" Hamish asked. "What, you've got a flying carpet in there?"

Josh smiled. "Something like that." He turned to Spence and placed a hand on his chest in a way that was shockingly intimate. "Go with Gareth, dear heart. We'll catch you up."

Spence shot a narrow-eyed glance at Tiff and Hamish. Tiff suspected that if he weren't obviously fighting the urge to hurl, he'd have insisted on staying. Instead, he nodded. "Don't be long."

"We won't."

Josh watched Spence's retreating back until he'd joined Gareth and both of them were swallowed by the crowd, and then turned to Tiff and Hamish.

Hamish, a wrinkle between his brows, gestured between Josh where Spence had gone. "Are you two..."

Josh huffed out a breath. "It's complicated, but if we were, would that matter?"

"What? Bloody hells, no." Hamish grinned. "I'm just a nosey parker."

Josh met Tiff's gaze. "You?"

She spread her hands. "Hey, I'm an equal opportunity dater, sometimes multiple opportunities at once, so I've got no room to judge."

His smile bloomed, and Tiff could understand why Spence was so whipped. "Good. I thought it was you, but I wasn't sure."

"You thought what was me?"

"I was using the plural you. I meant both of you." Josh chewed on his lower lip, studying first Tiff, then Hamish. "This may sound unbelievable…"

"More unbelievable than four shifters and a fae running into each other in the middle of half a million humans?" Tiff asked. "I mean, I've heard of coincidences, but this stretches my willing disbelief to the limits."

"That's just it," Josh said eagerly. "It's not a coincidence at all. It's fate."

"Fate," Tiff said flatly. "Seriously? You believe in that shit?"

"I believe that some people's… I don't know… life streams, I suppose, can flow in the same direction. Mingle. Converge. It was only a dream really, a fancy of mine, until I met Gareth at precisely the right time to change my life completely. Then I met this person—"

"Spence?" Hamish asked.

Josh shook his head. "No. Not then. Not yet. Gareth and I had settled in Liverpool. He was out one day and this person showed up at our door."

"A person." Hamish flipped a drumstick. "Like a traveling salesperson? They want you to buy a vacuum? Maybe some brushes or a set of encyclopedias?"

"Not a salesperson." Josh's eyes glinted and he leaned forward, dropping his voice. "An *oracle*."

Tiff groaned. "Not an oracle. Those fucking know-it-alls. They think they're so superior."

"Not this one. Del's different. They're just coming into their prophecy heritage, so their insights are spotty. But they've been right so far. They're the one who sent Gareth and me to the club where we met Spence." He met their gazes somberly. "And they sent us here. To meet you."

Fate?

"To meet us?" Hamish's eyebrows climbed all the way up his forehead. "What, they just said, 'Oi, trot on across the pond so Hamish Mulherne can mistake your mate for Roger Daltrey and make a right charley of himself in front of Tiff Rodriguez?'"

Tiff stared at him, astonished. "You actually remember my name? I figured you'd forgotten, which is why you always call me sheila."

He smiled down at her crookedly. "I remember everything about you."

She rolled her eyes. "Stow it, kangaroo. We've known each other for four hours. There's not that much to forget." She turned to Josh. "But he's got a valid question. Care to answer it?"

Josh gnawed on his lip again. "Del didn't name you specifically. Their visions don't usually work like that. Even when they told me about Spence, they didn't go into details. Just told me that we needed to be at that club at that time because we'd meet someone important, someone…" He trailed off and dropped his gaze.

"Someone what? Don't leave us hanging, mate."

Josh lifted his chin. "Someone necessary."

"Necessary?" Tiff scowled at him. "Is that what they told you this time? That you'd meet more necessary people?"

"Not exactly." His smile glimmered. "They said if we came here and followed our noses, we'd finally be complete."

"Complete?" Hamish asked. "Complete how?"

Josh spread his hands, palms up. "We've got Gareth on lead guitar and vocals, Spence on keys, me on violin and rhythm guitar. But we were missing drums and bass." He extended his hands. "And here you are."

Tiff's scowl deepened. "That's another thing. How'd you know I'm carrying a bass? The case is the same size as an electric guitar."

He grinned at her. "Fate."

"*Diosa*," Tiff muttered.

"I dunno." Hamish tapped his drumsticks against his thighs in a double paradiddle. "He might have a point. You've gotta admit, it's pretty long odds that you and I ran into each other and then into them, considering how many other people are here to be run into. Wouldn't hurt to scope out their scene." He grinned at Josh. "See if *they're* any good and worthy of our valuable talents. Besides." He waggled a stick under Tiff's nose. "It's coming on to rain again. You want to hang about and get wetter?"

Tiff pushed the stick away, but had to admit Hamish had a point. "Fine." She jabbed a finger at Josh. "But we need assurances."

"What kind of assurances?" Josh asked.

"Well, that you won't murder us, for one."

Hamish scoffed. "Like you couldn't take them all down."

Josh was obviously trying to bury a smile. "Maybe I should be asking for your assurances on that point. Let's say no murders of any kind. What else?"

"That you don't leave us stranded," Tiff said. "If things don't work out, you'll make sure we both get home safely."

"I'm on a bit of a walkabout now. No home to speak of."

Tiff blinked at Hamish. *He doesn't have anywhere to go?* Tiff at least had her shitty apartment in Encino, assuming she could make it back across the country with no money or transportation. Maybe Josh and his *oracle* could be useful after all. Who knows? Maybe they had a tour bus or a Piper Cub in their back pockets. "Taken to a place of our choosing, then."

"No problem with that. You're free to leave whenever and to wherever you like." Josh's expression turned serious, almost pleading. "But I really hope you'll give us a chance. I've got a really good feeling about this."

"Good feeling, huh?" Tiff jerked her chin in the direction Gareth and Spence had gone. "Didn't look like either of them was feeling all that good, especially after the minion tried to get you up onstage. What was that about?"

Once again, Josh worried his lower lip with his teeth. "That's a longer story, and one that I don't feel comfortable sharing with you until you've decided to stay with us. Let's just say that both of them had… feelings about coming here, and they only agreed out of deference to me. Because I said it was important."

Tiff raised her eyebrows. "And that's all it took?"

Josh shrugged. "Gareth's brother nagging him to get out of the house might have helped. But we trust each other." He grinned a little impishly. "Plus, I promised they wouldn't have to perform."

"Wotcher, mate? You said if the minion hadn't backed down, we'd have all piled on stage. So much for trust, eh?"

"There was no danger," Josh said placidly. "I knew he'd refuse."

"How?" Tiff asked.

Josh's impish grin widened. "Because the oracle told me so."

"Welp." Hamish jammed his stick in his back pocket. "That's good enough for me."

Tiff jabbed him in the ribs. "Are you loco?"

Hamish looked down at her, and for the first time since they'd met, his expression was entirely serious, without even a hint of his irreverent exuberance. "Tell me something, sheila. Why did you come here?"

"I—" Tiff scowled, because she couldn't really justify her decision. She'd *known* the band would cave to Graham and refuse to let her perform. Hells, Chepito had told her what would go down, but she'd tagged along anyway because *something* had told her she should, that she'd regret it if she didn't, that it would be worth it in the end. Tiff had chalked it up to another mysterious *feeling*, the kind her abuela told her never to ignore. She'd assumed that was just jaguar instinct.

Could it be something else? Could it be… fate?

A Shortcut

Nope. Uh uh. No way. Tiff wasn't ready to admit that anything as chaotic as *fate* could have her in its jaws, so she just growled, "My name's not Sheila."

"Know why I came?"

"For the *watershed* moment," she said.

Hamish huffed a laugh. "Yeah, but maybe the watershed wasn't so much a musical watershed as a personal one. I was in Boston. Planned to head to San Francisco. But something told me to take a detour up here. I hadn't even heard of the festival until I got to Hartford." He nudged her shoulder with his own. "And a little something else told me I should make sandwiches enough for two."

"You wanna tell me the little *something else* was fate?"

Hamish shrugged. "Why not? Come on. What have we got to lose?"

Tiff glanced over at the stage where Canned Heat had just finished their set. That hard lump of resentment in her middle would just fester and grow with every act that took the stage if she had to watch.

"If you'd really rather not," Hamish said, his voice soft, "that's cool. I'll stay here with you."

That pulled her up short. "Why? You don't owe me anything."

He shrugged. "That's where you're wrong. Yeah, this sounds like an adventure, and who wouldn't want a chance to make music? But we're mates now." He shot a flustered glance at Josh. "I mean, not *mates* like *mates* mates, but friends. Fellow travelers. I'd never want to be like those wankers who turned their backs on you."

Tiff's throat tightened and the corners of her eyes prickled. *No. I will not cry. I never cry.* So instead, she covered up with a scowl. "You'd do that?"

"In a hot minute."

"Even though you want to go with them?"

"Well, yeah. It sounds like a laugh. A chance." He grinned, waggling his eyebrows. "Maybe even fate. But I met you first." He rocked back on his heels. "So if you'd rather hang out here…"

Tiff glanced at the field of soggy humans and the lowering clouds overhead, which showed zero signs of dispersing. She turned to Josh. Sure, he seemed harmless, but he was a werewolf. Tiff had no intention of dropping her guard.

"Let's go." She pointed at Josh's chest and let a claw extend. "But I'm warning you. First sign of fuckery, and you'll be sorry."

"No fuckery, I promise."

"Oh, yeah? Where exactly are we heading then?"

His smile bloomed, bright and ingenuous. "Laurel Canyon. This way."

"Laurel Canyon? Wha—"

But he was already trotting off in the direction Gareth and Spence had gone.

Hamish grinned down at her. "Roll with it, sheila. If it looks dodgy, we can always turn around and go back. I'm not out of tarps yet."

"Fine," she grumbled, and lengthened her stride to catch up because she refused to do something as undignified as *trot*. Although she and Josh were about the same height, his legs were longer. Hamish, of course, who topped her by a head, had no trouble strolling along next to them.

They walked past the pavilion—Tiff gave it one last, nasty glare—and into the small copse near the pond.

"How exactly are we getting to your place in Laurel Canyon?" She cut a glance at Hamish. "Magic carpet?"

"Nope." Josh grinned. "I've got something better." He rounded a spindly maple and stopped where the runoff from the rain cut a furrow in the mud as it chuckled toward the pond. "A shortcut."

On the other side of the instant creek, the air between a birch and a sycamore shimmered, and suddenly there was somewhere else beyond them—somewhere with a wider, more boisterous brook, a broad meadow, and a looming hill that was definitely *not* part of an upstate New York cow pasture.

She whirled on Josh. "I don't know what you're trying to pull, but I've been to Laurel Canyon, and I can tell you that's not it."

Josh's smile didn't dim. "You're right. This is the shortcut I told you about. Through Faerie."

"Faerie? That's brilliant!" Hamish bounded forward.

"Hamish!" She grabbed for him but missed, and he leaped over the runoff, darting between the trees and into the *other* place.

He spread his arms and gazed upward, turning in a circle. "You've got to see this. The sky is *purple*."

Josh met Tiff's already morphing eyes, his expression turning serious. "I promise on my *calon* that nothing will hurt him." He cocked his head like an inquisitive puppy. "That's what matters most to you, doesn't it, more even than the chance to play?"

She cut her gaze away and growled, "He's too trusting."

"Ever think you might be too suspicious?" When she bristled, Josh held up his palms. "No judgment intended. I know you've got reason."

"How could you possibly know what I— what all women have to put up with in this industry? In this *world*?"

His smile was wry. "Because until I met Gareth and stepped into Faerie for the first time and its magic *aligned* me, I was one. At least on the outside."

A New Start

Tiff's jaw sagged. "You were... Oh." She stood numbly in place as Josh joined Hamish beyond the... the portal.

Because that's what it was, wasn't it? A gateway to another place, maybe another life, an *authentic* life. Josh had found it. Tiff's goals and ambitions weren't as monumental as Josh's had been. She didn't need to scale a mountain *that* high. She just wanted a level playing field. Recognition without compromise.

Love on my own terms.

But that was definitely below music on her list. It could wait. And in the meantime, maybe friendship would do.

"What the hell," she muttered, and stepped across the threshold.

Once her feet touched the lush grass of Faerie, she whirled and looked behind her. The sparse trees were gone and the mutter and rumble of the crowd was replaced by the sound of water over stones. She gazed up at the sky. Hamish was right— it was purple, but more to the point, it was clear.

When she turned back, Spence had joined Josh and Hamish, and his fingers were laced with Josh's.

"Gareth's waiting downriver. We can cross over there, right to our backyard."

"Do we have to go right now?" Hamish raced in a circle around them, skipping every third step. "Can't we look around? What's up that hill? Those trees look huge. Will we see any other fae?"

Josh's smile was apologetic. "Sorry. Gareth doesn't really like to spend much time here. He's got... reasons. But it's the quickest way to travel. You can literally get from anywhere to anywhere through Faerie, as long as your take-off and landing don't expose us to humans." He gestured to the brook, which widened into something that Tiff would definitely call a river, complete with rapids. "Crossing over water is standard, but Gareth's got more options."

"Why's that?" Hamish asked.

Josh grinned. "Because Faerie answers to true bards, and Gareth's the only one of those around."

He took off along the riverbank, hand still clasped with Spence's, Tiff and Hamish bringing up the rear. They approached a figure whose back was to them, although with the moonlight gilding those Daltrey curls, it was obviously Gareth. Tiff could practically see the tension rolling off him in waves.

He glanced at them and a smile curved his lips. "Glad you decided to join us."

"Yeah, well, we're not *committing* to anything," Tiff said. "But we're..."

"Open to possibilities," Hamish said.

Gareth pointed to the river, which was... suddenly very narrow and shallow, with three flat stones placed conveniently —suspiciously so—for crossing to the opposite bank. "Follow me. Step on the stones and nowhere else. Look at your feet. Do not look up, forward or back, not until you're across. Understand?"

Tiff narrowed her eyes. "Why?"

Gareth lifted an eyebrow. "Because that's the way out. The only way out."

"It really is," Josh says. "Just keep stepping on the stones, no matter how long it takes."

"How long could it be?" Hamish said. "There's three of them, and I could probably jump across this little stream without them, anyway." He crouched, obviously ready to prove his point.

Josh put a hand on Hamish's elbow. "Don't." He cut a glance at Gareth. "Please."

Tiff remembered. *Gareth doesn't like to spend time here.* Tiff could relate. There were places—and people—she never wanted to see again, either.

"Settle down, kangaroo," she said. "Nobody doubts your ability to hop, yeah? But I, for one, would like to sit down somewhere that isn't full of mud and humans and maybe have a beer. You got any at your place?"

Gareth quirked an eyebrow. "Happens that we do."

"Then lead on."

Tiff had expected the crossing to take seconds—after all, Hamish was right. There were only three stones. But as she kept her eyes on her feet, stepping from one stone to the next, there were somehow more, and then more, and then *more*, although they were never so far from one another that she had to jump between them. When she finally reached the opposite bank, she was as out of breath as though she'd been running for a mile.

Hamish joined her, followed by Josh and Spence, and she looked around, slack-jawed. A gibbous moon floated overhead, and the scent of sage and mint drifted on the warm breeze. Backed by the hills, the two-story house that rose before them looked as though it had sprung up from the earth organically. Or perhaps like it was some fae creature, sprawled in the moonlight, watching them lazily.

They were clearly in the backyard, because a wide flagstoned patio thrust forward into the grass from a pair of sliding glass doors.

Josh spread his arms. "This is home."

"You all live here?" Hamish asked, and Josh nodded. "Brilliant!"

"As you can see, there's plenty of room, so you're welcome to stay too."

"I've got a place in Encino," Tiff said absently. A shithole of a place. Nothing like this house with its many, *many* gleaming windows, but it was hers. Was she ready to give up that independence and hitch her wagon to this particular circus?

She'd thought she'd found belonging before and look how that had turned out.

"Well, keep it in mind," Gareth said. "The invitation's open." He pointed to another building at the bottom of the sloping yard, set against a tall fence backed by eucalyptus trees. "There's the studio."

Tiff blinked. "You've got your own studio?"

Gareth shrugged. "Why not? Doesn't mean we can't play in the house, or even out here, but the acoustics are better."

Hamish faced Gareth, his eyes gleaming. "Have you got a drum kit in there? Please tell me you've got a drum kit in there."

"We've got a drum kit in there."

Hamish whooped and leaped in the air, thrusting both drumsticks toward the moon. He landed in a crouch and then rushed over to Tiff.

"What do you say, sheila? Let's give it a go, all right?"

She gazed up at him, the look in his eyes hitting her like a falling amp.

Oh shit. A lovelorn kangaroo. Now what do I do?

Tiff knew her own heart, and by now she had a good notion of Hamish's, too. There was no way she'd jeopardize their friendship—and yes, she could admit to the friendship—by being stupid enough to fuck him, because for her it would be fun, but not *enough*.

For him? He'd never understand when she wanted to date someone else—not *instead of*, but *in addition to*. He'd be hurt, and though she may not be sure of much right now, one thing was certain.

She'd savage anybody who hurt Hamish. Including herself.

But at least she could give him this.

Tiff turned to Gareth. "All right, bard. Show me that studio and show me what you got. I want to find out if your chops are up to my— to *our* exacting standards." She shrugged the straps of Hamish's tarp carryall off her shoulders and set her bass at her feet. "But first—how about that beer?"

Gareth

Rehearsing

Gareth let his voice fade along with the last note from Josh's violin. After only three hours of rehearsal, the new song was perfect.

"Damn," Spence said, shaking out his hands. "You guys outdid yourselves with this tune. It's killer."

Josh smiled at Spence. "You always say that, love. I think you might be a touch biased."

"Spence is right." Tiff fingered the last bass chord. "But aren't the lyrics a little... well..."

Hamish pinged his high hat with a fingernail. "Depressing?"

"Hamish." Josh's voice held a gentle warning.

"What?" Hamish spread his arms, his truly impressive wingspan wider than his equally impressive drum kit. "You can't say it's not true."

"I think—"

Gareth stopped Josh's rebuttal with a lift of his hand. "He's right." Because the song was about Niall. All Gareth's songs were about Niall, and since Niall was gone, that meant all Gareth's songs were melancholy at best and downright doleful at worst.

He suspected Josh had told Spence at least a part of the story, since Gareth had given him permission when they were recruiting Spence in Liverpool. Truthfully, he wouldn't have allowed even that much if he hadn't detected the spark between the two of them. He wasn't so twisted in his own grief that he could deny others the chance at the kind of happiness he'd found with Niall, and Josh had needed the leverage to convince Spence to stay.

He'd never told Tiff and Hamish, though. Maybe it was time.

Hamish perked up. "I am? Yeah, I am. We've gotten tight from all the practice, but if we lighten up our set list, we'll be ready for the next step."

"I hate to give it to the kangaroo, but he's on the right track," Tiff said. "We're better than good enough to try for a record deal."

Gareth frowned, running his fingers along the Strat's neck. "Do you trust anybody in the industry to do right by us? We have to be careful. Becoming public figures could potentially violate the Secrecy Pact."

"I don't trust anyone in the industry any farther than I can dropkick them, but they're the gatekeepers, so we've got to deal with them one way or another." Tiff snorted. "As for the Secrecy Pact, it's not like we're gonna shift onstage."

"That's not what I mean."

"I get it," Josh said, defusing the situation with his soft drawl, like he always did. "It might not be a problem today, or even in ten years. But in twenty? Thirty? We'll look pretty much the same as we do now and all the bands who stay in the spotlight will look like—"

"Raisins?" Hamish said, flipping a drumstick.

Josh touched one finger to his nose and pointed at Hamish with the other hand. "Bingo. We have to be strategic about this if we want a lasting career. Del told us as much when they sent us to find you and Tiff at Woodstock." His pale brows drew together and he glanced at Gareth. "Have you heard from Del lately?"

Gareth shook his head. "They only communicate with me if they've got something that affects me, or in this case, us. Their oracle abilities are still developing, so their insights are infrequent and need a trigger of some kind. They can't predict things on demand."

"What good are they, then?" Spence groused.

"Cut Del a break," Tiff said. "So they haven't had a vision lately. We've been playing together for three years and we don't even have a name for the band yet."

"Good point," Hamish said. "Hard to drum up excitement for a group called To Be Announced."

Spence smirked as he powered down the Hammond. "Then let's pick a name. How about… Kendrick?"

"Like Santana?" Tiff snorted. "Fuck no." She glanced sidelong at Gareth. "Unless that's what you—"

"Fuck no," Gareth echoed. "I'm not the only person in this band."

"I still like Four Blokes and a Shiela," Hamish said, adding a rim shot.

Tiff scowled at him, although her lips twitched. "Don't make me hurt you, kangaroo."

"How about Rocket Shift?" Spence said.

"I'm sorry," Tiff said. "What now?"

"You know. Because we're rockers. And also shifters."

Tiff pointed at Gareth. "He's not a shifter. Plus, that's just begging for the Secrecy police to come down on our asses. Anyway, it's a terrible name."

"No worse than The Band. I mean, how generic can you get? It's almost as bad as To Be Announced. Or Jefferson Airplane? What does that even mean?"

"Probably that they're always high," Josh said.

"I dunno." Hamish beat a soft tattoo on his tom. "Maybe they just picked the name of a dead president out of one hat and a vehicle out of another. We could do that too. We could be… Washington Unicycle. Lincoln Skateboard. Madison Vee Dub."

Tiff narrowed her eyes in her patented only-for-Hamish glare. "Why would that even be a thing for us? You're not from this stupid country. Neither am I. He"—she jabbed a finger in Gareth's direction—"isn't even from this planet."

Gareth hung the Strat in its spot on the wall. "Technically, I am from this planet. Just a different dimension."

"Details," Tiff grumbled as she set her bass in its stand. "Whatever. I don't know about you jokers, but I'm ready for a beer."

"Too right." Hamish hopped off his stool and shoved his sticks in the back pocket of his jeans. "Lead the way."

Josh opened the studio door and a gust of unseasonably warm air swirled inside, riffling the sheet music on the stands and tossing his fine blond hair. "Whoo! What did you call these winds again?"

"Santa Anas," Gareth said.

"They're so peculiar."

Spence joined Josh and dropped a kiss on top of his head. "Says the guy from hurricane country."

Hamish and Tiff exited, still bickering, but Josh didn't follow Spence immediately.

"Gareth? You coming?"

"As soon as I shut everything down. Don't let me keep you from the beer."

"It'll wait." His blue eyes were far too knowing, seeming to pierce right through Gareth's carefully constructed social shields. "You know I'm perfectly happy with our music, don't you? We don't need to take it in another direction until you're ready."

"I know. And I appreciate it." Gareth forced a smile. "But it's not fair for me to expect Hamish and Tiff to take everything on faith. Even Spence doesn't know my whole story." He paused. "At least, I don't think he does."

"No!" Josh shook his head. "I told him only what you gave me leave to share."

"I wouldn't have blamed you if you'd gone farther, you know."

"I would never betray your trust that way, Gareth. Not after what you've done for me. Not ever."

Gareth wasn't sure if today was a day that Josh didn't mind touches, so he kept his hands to himself and simply inclined his head. "I've never doubted that, my friend. But I also trust your judgment, if you'd thought it was necessary." He sighed. "It won't be an issue in the future. I'm telling them everything tonight."

"Are you sure?"

"I am." He chuckled and made shooing motions with his hands. "Now go. I'll join you shortly."

A Name and a Path

Gareth stood at the studio door as Josh walked up the sloped lawn to Spence, waiting for him at the patio's edge with a beer in each hand. He handed one of them to Josh, who took it with a smile and kissed Spence's cheek. The two of them turned and joined Hamish and Tiff, who were already seated next to the firepit with their own brews.

The warm wind stirred Gareth's curls as he watched his bandmates—his *friends*—and marveled at how his life had changed.

From the moment Niall had been taken by that Unseelie swine, Gareth had been on the move. From one town to another, one house to another, one brief encounter to another. Not *those* kinds of encounters, never *those*, but playing harp or lute or guitar with others he met on the road, letting the music keep the gods-bedamned Voices at bay. Always in private, though, never with anyone else watching, because whenever he faced an audience, he couldn't help searching the faces for the one who would never be there.

Niall.

Until he stepped onto that stage with Josh in New Orleans, he hadn't played for an audience in almost two centuries. He hadn't intended to do it then, but something about Josh had caught his attention, and, for a wonder, the Voices were silenced.

They'd remained subdued during the years he and Josh had traveled together, played together, lived together. Then they'd met Spence. Gareth still didn't want to perform, but with the three of them playing, he could mute the Voices even better, so much so that they only haunted him at night, when he was alone.

Alone.

But was he still alone? Yes, his bed was still empty and always would be, but Tiff, Hamish, Josh and Spence all lived here in the house with him. Hamish hadn't left after they'd gotten back from Woodstock. It had taken Tiff another six months or so, but she'd finally let go of her apartment and joined them, especially since they spent so much of their time in the studio at the back of the property.

And as day followed day, month followed month, and year followed year, Gareth had been content to stay put. To stop running. To rest. And maybe to heal?

Nobody could replace Niall in Gareth's heart, but perhaps he could make room for others. Not lovers, but friends to fill the vast space that had first yawned, threatening to swallow him whole, when Niall followed that Unseelie bastard without a backward glance.

It hit him then. *This. This* was what he'd been hunting for all along and had never realized it until he'd found it with these people. Connection. Camaraderie. Synergy.

Music.

He walked out of the studio, shutting the door behind him, and walked up the hill to the patio. A full moon floated bright and serene above the hills in the October sky—the Hunter's moon. Gareth gazed at it and started to smile.

"Hunter's Moon," he said.

Josh stopped laughing with Spence and glanced over at him. "What?"

He smiled at them all. "Hunter's Moon. That us."

Tiff tilted her head, tapping the rim of her beer bottle against her lips. "Hunter's Moon, huh?" Her grin, always just this side of feral, dawned. "I like it."

"What she said," Hamish said, raising his own bottle in a toast.

"I'm not sure about a record deal or performing in public yet, but I'll think about it. And I promise Josh and I will work on some more up-tempo tunes." He glanced around the firepit. "Hey, where's *my* beer?"

"Sorry," Spence said. "I didn't know how long you'd be and didn't want to bring it out too soon. I'll get it now."

"Never mind. I can get it myself." He walked across the patio and paused with his hand on the handle of the sliding glass door. "Anyone else need anything?"

"Nachos?" Hamish said hopefully.

Gareth chuckled, shaking his head. "Don't press your luck."

He stepped inside, the dining room dim except where a slash of light from the kitchen door cut a butter yellow swath across the table, and slid the door closed. Before he made it across the dining room, though, the doorbell rang.

Gareth frowned as he strode through the arch into the darkened living room and then the vestibule. He wasn't expecting anybody, and none of the others had mentioned visitors either. Their neighbors here in Laurel Canyon were far enough away that the sounds of their rehearsals wouldn't reach them, and even if they did, they were all musicians anyway and didn't mind—although Cass Elliott was still a little disgruntled that Gareth hadn't ever attended one of her parties.

He opened the door to find Del standing on the front porch. Gareth lifted an eyebrow. "Why not just walk in?"

Del shrugged. "I thought I'd give you a chance to ignore me if you didn't want visitors. That way, I could avoid your surly comments."

"Am I really that bad?"

"You're getting better. May I come in?"

"Please." Gareth stood aside so Del could enter. "Everyone else is out back. Want to join us for a beer?"

Del stopped while Gareth closed the door, apparently staring at nothing, and then said, "Yes."

Gareth headed into the kitchen, blinking as his eyes adjusted to the light. He opened the refrigerator and bent down to peer into its depths. "What's your poison? Hamish hasn't drunk everything in sight yet, so I've got—"

"It's time."

He popped his head above the door to peer at Del. "What?"

Del was gazing at the patio through the big window over the sink. "Time to go back."

Gareth shut the refrigerator with exaggerated care. "Go back where?"

Del shifted his gaze and met Gareth's, their opalescent eyes swirling as they always did when Del was *seeing*. "You know where."

"Del, you know how I feel about Faerie. Until the Queen changes her stance—"

"This isn't about you, Gareth. Not you alone, anyway." They tilted their head toward the window. "It's about them. About the band. About Hunter's Moon."

Gareth squinted at Del. "How did you know that's the band's name? We only decided about three minutes ago."

Del tapped their temple. "Oracle, remember? Talk about ripples in the firmament, that decision launched a veritable tsunami. So here I am."

"So you showed up because of that? Within three minutes?"

"More like five, but yes." Del shook their head, a mock mournful expression on their narrow face. "Gareth, you're Faerie's last true bard. Did you seriously imagine Her Majesty wouldn't park a gateway practically on top of your house?"

Gareth scowled, crossing his arms. "And this is exactly why I won't go back. The Queen wants all the control and obeisance, yet offers none of the noblesse oblige."

"Again, this is not about you and your feud with Faerie. The band is ready, but the Outer World is not. Not yet. Not until the new century is at least a decade old." Del smiled wryly. "That means a couple of weeks in Faerie, doesn't it? A month at most?"

Gareth looked away from that penetrating gaze. "It's hard to tell."

"Regardless, a short amount of relative time. You can handle it for that long, can't you?" Del gestured to the patio where Josh and Spence were sitting in side-by-side Adirondack chairs, only the tips of their fingers touching. Hamish, his face bright with laughter, was gesturing to Tiff with his beer. Tiff wasn't looking at him—her trademark scowl was aimed at the firepit, but her lips were quirked in that buried smile that was rarely absent when she was around Hamish. "For them?"

Oak and bloody thorn. Gareth threaded both hands through his curls and gripped them. Hard. As much as Gareth hated Faerie and the rigid rules that had cost him nearly everything, he cared more about the band. They couldn't replace Niall, of course. Nothing could do that. But they at least made life… bearable, and although it surprised him to admit it, even joyful at times. It was hard to stay despondent in the face of Hamish's breezy ebullience, Tiff's acerbic wit, Josh's gentle strength, and Spence's steadfast loyalty.

Not to mention the music. Which was brilliant.

"Trust me, Gareth. It's the best path. For all of you."

Gareth exhaled and let his arms fall to his sides. "All right."

"Good." The tension almost visibly bled from Del's shoulders. "I'll send Mal to get you when the time is right. All you need to do is—"

"On one condition."

The tension was back. "What?"

Gareth grinned and leaned forward. "That you sign on as our manager."

Del's gleaming eyes widened and then clenched shut. "Fuck," they said. "I never saw *that* coming."

And for the first time in what felt like forever, Gareth laughed until he cried. Then he walked outside and joined his band.

First Flight

About First Flight

First Flight is another "sidecar" or companion story. It's not intended to stand alone. Instead, it assumes the reader's familiarity with other books. In this case, it's an extra peek inside some off-page antics for Nevan and Seb between Chapter 33 and the Epilogue of *Assassin by Accident*.

So if you haven't already read *Assassin by Accident*, you'll probably want to put this story aside until you do. Otherwise, you know, spoilers!

Cheers!
—E

Chapter One

The mural on Seb's living room wall was like Nevan's own Faerie lake rendered as an illustration for one of the many, many children's books on Seb's bookshelves. The resemblance was uncanny, as though the artist had sat, unseen, in the trees along the shoreline, and captured the scene with whimsical, exuberant brushstrokes.

Nevan stared at it in the morning light streaming through the wide front window. He kept intending to ask Seb who had painted it for him, but in the two days since he and Lulu had moved in, what with getting Lulu settled in her new room, arranging their Outer World identities with the help of Quest Investigations' tech specialist, and Seb starting his job as Noah Tate's nanny, he hadn't found the time.

"Nevan?" Seb's voice drifted down the stairs, followed by his footsteps. "Do you think I should take these to Quest with us this morning?"

Nevan realized he was kneading his left palm. He inhaled sharply and quickly shifted his grip to his knees, scaring up a smile for Seb. Despite the ghost of pain that continued to haunt him, it wasn't hard to do. Seb invited smiles from even the most taciturn.

Like me.

But Nevan's *calon* always glowed extra brightly whenever Seb was near.

Zână. Did Seb's folk have *calons*? Is that why Nevan had been so drawn to him, even when he'd believed the worst of him? Some supes didn't have calons. Vampires, for instance, although the reasons for that had never been clear. Perhaps nobody knew. However, Seb had been accepted as a supe by the council, and that was all that mattered.

For once, Seb wasn't smiling at Nevan as he crossed the living room. Instead, his brow was puckered as he studied the folded cloth in his arms. A pair of soft brown boots dangled from his fingers by their laces. He looked up and met Nevan's gaze, and *there* it was.

Seb's smile.

"Are those the clothes you found by the river, *cariad*?"

"Mmmhmm. From what Jordan said, they belong to somebody he knows, but he never told us who. And he's been so busy with his Quest case that I haven't had a chance to ask him. When I pick up Noah in the morning, Tahmina's the only one at the Doghouse. Do you think Zeke might know? He seems to know most things, so he might be able to get them to the right person." Seb grinned. "Although Quest *is* a supernatural PI firm, so even if they don't know, they could figure it out, right?"

Nevan scowled, and once again he had to stop himself from massaging the spot where Yvo's geas brand... wasn't. "I don't see why we have to take her there."

"Lulu?"

"Yes. Hasn't she been through enough?"

Seb set the clothing on the coffee table and sat next to Nevan on the sofa, lacing the fingers of his right hand with Nevan's left. *I doubt that's an accident.* Seb's smooth, warm skin against his always banished the pain ghost.

"Mage Evil won't be there, remember? The druids..." Seb's face assumed what Nevan thought of as his *wonder* expression: brows lifted, eyes wide and sparkling behind his glasses, lips slightly parted. "I can't believe there are *druids*." He waved his other hand dismissively. "Not relevant. Anyway, they've reconstituted him, but they've got him safely locked away in some supernatural containment unit. From what Zeke told me, he's been spewing his usual brand of bullshit. They need Lulu's testimony for their case against him."

"I don't care." Nevan's gaze drifted to the mural again. "They could have come here to meet with her. It's only been three days since she was freed. They should have consideration for her... her trauma."

Seb glanced toward the hallway, where Lulu's voice was audible from her room, raised in the same sprightly—and loud—song she'd been singing almost nonstop since they'd returned from their tour of the supe school yesterday. Then he gazed at Nevan, head cocked, a soft smile curving his lips.

"If you don't mind my saying so, sweetheart, I think Lulu's managing the incident better than you. She was alarmed, yes, lonely, sure, and bored, definitely. But don't forget, she still believes she scared Yvo away with her sword. In a way, it was an empowering encounter for her. You, though?" He glanced down at their clasped hands. "You still have a lot to work through. Mal told me that his brother is a psychologist. Do you think it might be a good idea for you to talk to him?"

Nevan avoided Seb's too-perceptive gaze. "I'm fine. I'm an adult. I entered the bargain with my eyes open."

"I think you're wrong about that." Seb bumped Nevan's shoulder with his own and squeezed his hand. "Yvo concealed a number of pertinent facts from you, tortured you, threatened you, and tried to enslave you. That's a lot to unpack."

Nevan sighed. "I suppose you're right." He smiled crookedly. "You usually are." He pressed a soft kiss to Seb's lips.

Seb's cheeks pinked as they always did when Nevan showed him affection. *So beautiful. So good.*

"Sebbie?" Lulu appeared in the dining room doors, her arms so full of books that several threatened to slide down her front onto the floor.

Seb rose and hurried over to catch them before they escaped and fell on her feet. "What's all this?"

Lulu gave him her *adults are so clueless* look. "Books. For when Noah and me go to school tomorrow."

Seb studied the pile in her arms solemnly. "Don't you think Teacher Tholo might have books in the classroom already?"

She firmed her lips. "He might not have *enough*. When I learn to read, I'll need lots and *lots*."

"I'm happy to hear that. But if we take all these without checking first, don't you think Teacher Tholo's feelings might be hurt? He seems to love his classroom and is probably just as proud of it as you are of your sword."

Lulu's round face bunched in thought. "You really think it might make him feel bad?"

"I don't know for sure, but it might, and it's always best to be kind whenever we can. Why don't we wait until your first day? When we take you to school, we can check the bookshelves in your classroom, and I'll offer to let Teacher Tholo borrow any books he might not have."

She sighed and glanced down at the books in her arms. "Okay. I guess we can do that. I suppose I won't have time to read everything on the first day, anyway." Her eyes widened. "Teacher Tholo said we'd learn about *numbers*, too."

"Exactly," Seb said heartily. "Besides, you told Teacher Tholo that you wouldn't start school until Noah could come back. Tahmina said he hasn't been cleared to return yet."

"He will be," she said decisively.

"How do you know?"

She gazed up at him and said matter-of-factly, "Because I'll be there." Then she turned and trotted back to her room.

Seb shared a bemused glance with Nevan. "She seems... confident."

Nevan shrugged. "She's an ora, and as she told us herself, she's looking after Noah now. We'd best trust her." He curled his fingers so he wouldn't be tempted to rub his palm again.

"But I still think they could have conducted their interview here."

"Sweetheart." Seb returned to stand between Nevan's knees and look down at him. "If she *is* suffering from trauma—and trust me, I'd like her to meet with Dr. Kendrick, too, and have him evaluate her—don't you think it would be better if she didn't associate that trauma with our home? Quest is already linked to her rescue in her mind, so it has context for her in relation to Yvo, but I'd just as soon keep him far away from here, if it's all the same to you." He stroked Nevan's cheek. "He already has too much of a foothold in your mind."

A rhythmic thumping from the hallway had them both turning to see Lulu hopping toward them on both feet, singing again. Seb arched a brow as if to say, *not traumatized in the least.*

"Who the blazes is Bunny Foo Foo," Nevan muttered to Seb, "and why is there a song about him?"

Seb chuckled. "She learned it from some of the kids at the school when we visited yesterday. They're apparently"— wonder suffused Seb's face again—"*jackrabbit* shifters. I mean, seriously? The conservation of mass alone..." He squeezed his eyes shut. "Not relevant."

Lulu stopped before she careered into the coffee table. "I put the books back on my shelf, Sebbie." She held out her arms and twirled twice in place. "I'm ready to go!"

She was wearing purple leggings patterned with stars, and rainbow-striped socks with her Little Mermaid sneakers. She'd belted an oversized Hunter's Moon T-shirt—it hit her just above her knees—with a gold lame sash, her sword tucked through it at her hip, and topped the whole ensemble with a tricorn hat.

Love for her—and what Seb called her distinctive personal style—welled up under Nevan's heart. "Where did you get the T-shirt, *eniad*?"

She tucked her chin as she looked down at her chest. "Zeke gave it to me. His boyfriend is in the band, same as Mal's brother." She looked up and bounced a little on her toes. "He said we could go to a concert sometime, if it was all right with you and Sebbie."

Nevan blinked. Lulu at a rock concert? When he hadn't been able to keep her safe at a tiny children's boutique? "We'll see."

She grinned up at Seb. "That means yes. Can we go now? We don't want to be late to pick up Noah."

"We're not seeing Noah today, remember?" Seb said gently. "He's visiting his old pack."

"Ugh." She wrinkled her nose. "He *hates* it there. He likes it much better with Jordan and Doop and Tahmina." She tugged the hem of Seb's polo. "Can we get him a present today, Sebbie? He'll feel bad when he comes back from there."

Seb crouched down, putting him at eye level with her, and took her hands. "I think that's an excellent idea. Why don't you think of something that would make him feel better and we'll pick it up on our way home?"

She nodded eagerly, curls bobbing. "Oh, that's easy. A Frisbee."

Seb laughed. "All right. A Frisbee it is."

She flung her arms around his neck. "I love you, Sebbie!"

He glanced at Nevan over her head, and even though one corner of her hat was perilously close to his eye, his face positively glowed. "I love you too, Lulubelle."

This time, his heart threatened to overflow. Maybe everything would be all right—maybe *he'd* be all right—as long as he had these two by his side.

And love.

"You know, though," Seb said as he drew back, "I think we should leave the sword at home today." He leaned forward and whispered, "It might make Mal jealous, because he can't carry his sword in the office."

She gripped the sword's rubber hilt, but then heaved a huge sigh. "Okay." She pulled it free and handed it to Seb. "You'll keep it safe?"

"I promise. I'll put it back in your pirate chest."

She smacked a kiss on his cheek. "*Thank* you, Sebbie."

Then, as Seb strode off down the hallway, Lulu launched herself at Nevan and snuggled into his chest. "I love it here, Nevvie, don't you?"

"Yes. I do." He repositioned her hat so he could stroke her curls. "Are you worried about this meeting, Lulu *fach*?"

"Oh, no," she said, toying with his waistcoat buttons. "Zeke promised me it wouldn't be bad, and he *never* lies. Demons don't, not his sort anyway."

The same can't be said for elemental mages, more's the pity. "Well, if you want to leave at any time, you just let Seb or me know."

She patted his chest as Seb reappeared, his car fob in his hand. "Don't worry, Nevvie. You'll be fine."

She scrambled off his lap and ran to the door, obediently waiting for them since they'd let her know she wasn't to open it herself.

Nevan stood and joined Seb. "*I'll* be fine? What's that supposed to mean?"

Seb linked their elbows with a chuckle. "I think it means she knows you better than you know yourself. Let's go."

All the way to the Quest offices, with Lulu in her booster seat in the back, caroling a Bunny Foo Foo duet with Seb, Nevan stared out the window. The city, the roads, the traffic—all of it was so different from what he was used to. He'd told Lulu he loved it here, but really it was Lulu and Seb he loved. Seb had his house, and now a steady job. Lulu had friends and was about to start school.

Nevan had the two of them. But what else? He didn't have a place in the Outer World. He had no skills to speak of—when you lived most of your life underwater, coursing through rivers and lakes and streams, there was no call to develop any. What could he do here? How could he contribute, not just to their family, but to the community?

Maybe Seb was right, and he just needed time to recover. But what then? Nevan sincerely hoped something would occur to him before he became another burden for Seb to bear.

When they entered the Quest lobby, Lulu immediately skipped over to the desk and propped her chin on it. However, she wasn't looking at Zeke, who rose from his chair with a smile. Instead, she was gazing raptly at a spot in the air over the manual typewriter that sat next to Zeke's more modern office equipment.

"Good morning," Zeke said. "Mal, Bryce, and Elder Bowen are waiting for you up in the conference room."

"Elder Bowen?" Seb asked rather faintly.

"She's the senior member of the region's druid circle," Zeke said, "sits on the supe council, and will be presiding over the, um…" He glanced over at Lulu, who was grinning up at that spot in the air. "The *proceedings* involving the *incidents*."

Nevan deduced, therefore, that this Elder Bowen would be the arbiter of Yvo's fate. Since druids were fanatical about maintaining balance, he suspected she'd take a very dim view of Yvo's attempt to tip the scales entirely in his own direction.

"I have tea and scones waiting. Hot chocolate for Miss Luljeta. If you'd like to come with me?"

Zeke gestured for them to accompany him, but stopped at the foot of the stairs because Lulu wasn't following.

"Lulu?" Nevan said. "Zeke has pastries upstairs for us."

Surprisingly, Lulu, who had quite the sweet tooth, didn't immediately join them. Instead, she rounded the desk to stand next to the ladderback chair behind the typewriter. She raised up on her tiptoes, and smacked a kiss into the seemingly empty air, although it sounded exactly like the kiss she'd bestowed on Seb's cheek not half an hour ago.

Then she scampered across the room and took Seb and Nevan each by the hand. "I'm ready now."

"What was that you did, *eniad*?"

"Oh, I just gave Miss Pennybaker a kiss. She looked like she needed one this morning." She looked up at Zeke. "You should make sure she gets more."

Zeke's eyes widened behind his glasses, and he glanced from Lulu to the desk and back again. "I'll... Hmmm. Yes. Well. I'll see what I can do. Shall we?"

Chapter Two

Elder Bowen—the *druid*—was a tiny, energetic woman wearing a sunshine yellow headscarf and carrying a cane, its head carved in the shape of an acorn. Her air of experience and authority lived up to her title, although she didn't appear any older than Madame Persephone from the carnival and never leaned on her cane even once.

She'd smiled kindly at Lulu, asked her to call her Auntie Cassie, and proceeded to conduct Lulu's interview with a bright-eyed intelligence and gentleness that Seb appreciated. She hadn't talked down to the little girl, which Seb also approved. She'd listened gravely to Lulu's very succinct tale of her encounter with Yvo.

"Not *one single toy*, Auntie," Lulu had said, wide-eyed with outrage. "Can you *imagine*?"

"Indeed, I cannot."

Elder Bowen had smiled and sent Lulu off with Zeke and a plate of blueberry scones. Then she'd turned to Nevan and things had gotten real. By the time they were done, Nevan had been sweating and shaking—which Seb definitely did *not* approve.

Once the interrogation completed—and that's what it was, even if they called it a *deposition*—Elder Bowen had been ceremoniously escorted out of the room by Mal and his husband

Bryce. *Another* druid, and OMG, would Seb *ever* get used to this?

Now, at least twenty minutes later, Nevan still sat, staring at the wall, his hands gripping the arms of the chair, and if Nevan didn't need him, Seb would have tracked the three of them down and... and... Well, he wasn't entirely sure what he could do to a fae and two *druids*. He could hardly put them in time-out, but he'd definitely hit them with his best no-nonsense nanny lecture on kindness and consideration.

"Nevan?" Seb laid his hand on Nevan's arm, which was so rigid it might as well be made of marble. "Are you all right, sweetheart?"

"He lied," Nevan croaked. "That wanker *lied*. How dare he claim that I approached him? That I proposed a... a *partnership*? I would never ally myself with him willingly. But he'd taken Lulu. I had no choice. They must see I had no choice."

"They do. I'm sure they do. Lulu's story backs yours up. So does mine." Seb scooted his chair closer so he could press his shoulder against Nevan's. "And since Yvo didn't have any idea that I was with you almost the whole time—which, by the way, can be corroborated by others, including the Quest staff—he's dug himself a hole he'll never crawl out of." Seb frowned. "Although, considering he's an earth mage, he probably *likes* holes. But—"

"Cheers, mate," Mal said as he strolled in with Bryce at his side, smiling as though he hadn't been on Team Intimidate Nevan for the last hour and a half. But he winced when Bryce jabbed him in the ribs with an elbow. "Eh, sorry about the third degree, but the tribunal was scrying the whole interview with mages breathing down their necks, so we had to address all their bloody points, even if they were total shite." He peered down at Nevan. "You doing all right there?"

Nevan nodded, throat working. "I... I will be."

Seb's ire simmered down. A little. "Could he have some water, please?"

"Zeke'll be along with another of his tea trays shortly. That'll set you to rights." Mal grinned. "Although this news might set you up even better. Zeke was able to work his magic with the assassin's guild—"

"I *still* can't believe there's a guild for *assassins*," Seb muttered.

"I know, right?" Bryce said. "It's *a lot*."

Seb blinked. "You think so too?"

"I'm fairly new to the supe community—raised as human, like you—so some of this shit still boggles my mind." He shot Mal a fond glance. "But the benefits are worth the occasional head explosion. Plus, you know"—he waggled his eyebrows—"*magic*."

"Done taking the mickey yet?" The smile Mal turned on Bryce belied his tart words. Bryce just grinned at him, and although Mal was the epitome of masculine perfection and Bryce had the whole rumpled, bespectacled, professor vibe going on, they clearly fit together perfectly.

Seb glanced sidelong at Nevan. *Kind of like us.*

"As I was saying, Zeke got through to the guild. They've given their testimony, but they're digging in their heels at the council's order to suspend operations while their spells are evaluated." Mal shrugged. "They'll cooperate, eventually. If word gets out that their safeguards are shite, it'll be bad for business."

"What about the carnival witnesses?" Seb asked. "Madame Persephone and Samson were *right there* when Renata threw that dagger."

Mal spread his hands, lips quirked in an apologetic smile. "Carnival's moved on."

"Can't you go after it? I mean, with the FTA, you could get there with no trouble." Because shortcuts through Faerie were now a thing in Seb's life.

"It's not that kind of carnival." Mal slid a glance at Bryce. "Magic."

Seb goggled at him. "The *carnival* was magic?"

Nevan stirred and placed a hand on Seb's knee. "Think about it, cariad. No ordinary fun house could have an exit into an alternate dimension."

Seb slapped his forehead. "D'oh! *Obviously*. And Madame Persephone knew what I was." He let his hand drop to his lap and drummed his fingers on his thigh. "I wonder who else in the carnival was magical?" He shuddered. "I hope it wasn't the clowns. *Ugh*. Can you imagine? Ordinary clowns are bad enough, but *magical* clowns? I may never sleep again."

"Don't worry, cariad." Nevan kissed Seb's temple. "I'll take care that you sleep soundly."

Mal cleared his throat. "Yes. Well. Let's not get into whatever sleep aids you have in mind. You're free to go now."

Nevan glanced between Mal and Bryce. "You won't release Yvo, will you? You said the magicians were protesting his arrest."

Bryce shook his head. "At first, yes. But after they heard about his plans, they did a total one-eighty. They didn't lodge a single protest when the tribunal sentenced him to Govannon's forge."

"Govannon?" Seb asked. "As in the *god*?"

"The very same," Mal said.

"Ah." Nevan's shoulders relaxed for what seemed like the first time since they'd gotten the summons. "That's all right then."

"Wait. What?" Seb frowned at Mal and Bryce. "The trial's happened in the last twenty minutes?"

Bryce smiled at Seb kindly. "It's been going on since the gnomes turned Yvo's bucket over to the council. Time runs at different rates depending on the realm, remember?" His smile turned wicked. "And may I just say that the reconstitution ritual I developed for Yvo was one of the most satisfying exercises I've undertaken since my druid powers awakened."

"What did you, er, do?" Seb asked.

"Weeelll," Bryce drawled, "*traditionally* druid potions have a reputation for tasting extremely nasty and often come with painful side effects. Since Yvo was a bucket of mud, he got the full immersion treatment."

Mal raised his eyebrows. "But your trademark is making your potions less unpleasant. Some are even downright tasty."

Bryce sniffed, although there was a decided twinkle in the dark eyes behind spectacles even nerdier than Seb's own. "Time was of the essence," he said piously. "I didn't have the leisure."

Mal smirked at Nevan and Seb. "Nor the inclination, I'll wager. Anyway, you lot have nothing to fear from Yvo Offerman. If he ever gets out of the forge, he'll have so many magical compulsions hanging about him he won't be able to so much as conjure a hankie without alerting the council." He executed a little bow. "Case closed."

"Th-thank you," Seb said.

Bryce offered Seb a business card. "Come by to see me sometime, either at the house or my office at Northwest College of Arts and Sciences. I'm spearheading a project to document our community, and we've never had a zână to interview before."

"Well, I'm not sure you've got one now," Seb said. "I mean, yeah, I *am* a zână, but I don't really know what that means."

Bryce's smile was warm and reassuring. "All of us who were raised outside the community—and there are more of us than you'd expect—are just trying to find our way. No expectations or judgment, but your input would be invaluable."

"All right then." Seb tucked the card in his back pocket. "Thanks."

Lulu appeared in the doorway, apparently holding hands with… the air. "Miss Pennybaker says you're finished and that I deserve a treat."

Lulu's pleading look broke Nevan out of his post-interrogation funk. He smiled as he grasped Seb's hand and stood.

"Indeed you do, Lulu *fach*."

"Yay!" She clapped and jumped up and down, setting her curls bouncing and sending her hat cockeyed. She looked into the air next to her. "I told you Nevvie would say yes."

Nevan chuckled. "Have you something in mind already? A new outfit? A special toy? Ice cream, or perhaps a cupcake?"

"*Things*." Her tone dripped with six-year-old scorn. "*Things* aren't the most 'portant."

"They're not?" Seb asked. "But you want to get a Frisbee for Noah."

"It's not the *Frisbee* that's 'portant, Sebbie. It's how Noah *feels* when he *plays* with it. And all the other Frisbees at the Doghouse are in the ground." She wrinkled her nose. "And they were all chewed up even before that. He needs a new one."

Seb couldn't fault that sentiment. Experiences and the *feelings* they engendered were what stuck with kids the longest. True, sometimes they had an associated memento of some kind, but that was because it was linked in their minds and conjured up those same feelings, not because the object itself was valuable.

"So you want to go on an adventure, Lulubelle? Is that it?"

She nodded so vigorously that Seb was surprised her hat didn't fly all the way off. "Yes."

"Would you like a playdate with the children you met at school?" Seb pulled out his cell phone. "I have their mother's number, so I can give her a call if you want." He glanced up at Nevan. "She's expecting and has two still in diapers, so I imagine she'd be grateful to have the elder two otherwise occupied for a bit."

"I'm guessing you met Molly Cotton," Mal said. He shook his head. "Jackrabbit shifters. They dearly love a full house."

Lulu shook her head—and, really, *how* was that hat staying on? "I want to play with Cecy and Jay Jay, but not today." She raised her melting gaze to Nevan. "I want you to take me to our lake, Nevvie."

Nevan smiled down at her. "Of course, *eniad*. We can—"

"And then to take me flying."

Nevan jerked, gaze darting from Lulu to Seb to Mal and Bryce. "That's... that's not the safest, Lulu *fach*."

Her lower lip trembled. "You promised, Nevvie. You promised that when I was bigger, you would take me up. I'm big now." She puffed out her chest and stood on her tiptoes. "I'm going to *school*. That's big enough to take a ride." Her eyes glistened with unshed tears. "And you said I deserved a treat today. This is what I really, really, *really* want."

Seb bit the inside of his cheek. Lulu's act wasn't fooling him for a second, but it was definitely working on Nevan. Judging from Bryce's smirk, he recognized a master manipulator when he saw one, too.

"Ah, shite," Nevan muttered, running a hand through his hair.

Mal took Bryce's hand. "I don't think you need us for these negotiations, mate. But if you're bound for Faerie, you can use the translocation door on the fourth floor." They edged past Lulu and disappeared into the hallway.

Seb stared after them. "There's a *translocation door*? In this *building*?" He scrubbed his hands over his face. "I've got to stop being surprised by this stuff."

"Please, Nevvie? I haven't been back to our lake, and Sebbie hasn't ever seen it." She turned *that look* on Seb, and though he knew exactly what she was doing, it still did the job. "*You* want to see our lake, don't you, Sebbie?"

"As a matter of fact, I do." He took Nevan's hand. "I didn't have a chance to sightsee the only other time I was in Faerie." He stroked Nevan's cheek. "The lake is your home."

"*Was* our home," Nevan said, turning his head to press a kiss on Seb's palm. "Our home is with you now."

Seb's chest warmed, but the feeling didn't erase the pinch of worry—that Nevan was giving up part of what he was to stay with Seb.

"You will *always* have a home with me," he said fiercely, "but you love your lake. I mean, lots of people have second homes. You told me we could live in Faerie if we wanted." He nudged Nevan's shoulder. "How can I make that decision without a tour?"

Nevan shook his head. "Between the two of you, I'll never win an argument, will I?"

"Don't think of them as arguments, Nevan," Seb said, nose in the air. "Think of them as thorough explorations of our options before we choose the best one."

Nevan lifted a brow. "Which will be yours?"

"Naturally." He turned to the empty doorway. Since Lulu was looking up at a spot that was approximately head height on a person an inch or two above five feet, Seb assumed Miss Pennybaker hadn't returned to her desk. "Miss Pennybaker, could we trouble you to show us the translocation door?"

There was no answer, of course—Hector must not have upgraded Miss Pennybaker's voice synthesizer yet—but Lulu's hand was once more suspended in the air. She turned and trotted down the corridor. They followed her up a flight of stairs, and down another curved hallway, past a couple of very ordinary vending machines, to an equally ordinary door with a security keypad next to it. The pad beeped several times and then its indicator light flashed green.

"You can open the door now, Nevvie." Lulu looked up. "Thank you, Miss Pennybaker." She stood on her tiptoes and kissed the air again, presumably where Miss Pennybaker had leaned down to present her cheek.

Following Lulu's imperious instructions with a wry smile, Nevan opened the door. According to the laws of physics and the little Seb knew about building construction, there *ought* to be a wall or, at most, a storage closet on the other side. Instead, a forested vista lay beyond, stretching as far as Seb could see. Not fifty yards away—and really, fifty yards should have put them right on the streetcar tracks in the Pearl—an azure lake lapped at its shore. A waterfall cascaded down a mossy hillside at its far edge, kicking up spray that sparkled in the sunlight.

Nevan sucked in a breath. "My lake. I thought we would have to travel through the land to get to it, as it's in what used to be the Unseelie sphere, far from the ceilidh glade."

"I probably can figure out the answer to that by now." Seb pointed at the keypad. "Magic, along with a little tech assistance. Ready?"

"Yes, Sebbie." Lulu took Seb's other hand. "Now Nevvie can take us flying."

Seb blinked, his belly tumbling. "'Us?'"

"Yes, silly." She raised that look to him. "It's a 'sperience for *all* of us. You're flying too."

Seb closed his eyes. "Oh, god."

Chapter Three

"Are you sure, cariad?" Standing atop the hill over his lake, Nevan gazed down at Seb, his hands gentle on Seb's shoulders, his words muffled by the sound of the waterfall. "Lulu doesn't need to always have her way."

Seb was trembling under Nevan's grip. "I know. But in this case, I think it's important. *This* is what she wants to erase the kidnapping, to erase Yvo, to erase her fear." His smile was a little wobbly. "Let's be honest, too, shall we? It's what *you* need for the same reason."

Nevan couldn't deny that. True, he'd been able to shift next to the riverside, but that flight had been short and hindered by his physical weakness and fear for Lulu. He needed this—to fly free over the lake that had been his home for two thousand years.

He caught a glimpse of Lulu dancing through the trees, probably with a lesser fae who was too shy to show themself to Nevan and Seb. *I have a different home now. One that's defined by this man and that little girl.*

Sharing a cleansing flight with both of them was exactly what his soul needed to purge itself from Yvo's taint.

But not at the expense of Seb's anxiety.

"Wait here a moment."

Seb nodded and sat on a flattish rock next to where the river tumbled over the ledge to plummet into the lake below. Nevan kissed the top of his head and then hurried to the cave that had been his only shelter before he'd found Lulu and built her a cottage.

The cave was deep, wide, and high enough that he could stand without colliding with its rough walls, even in his horse form. He'd kept a pallet here, although he hadn't often slept on land before Lulu.

As for what else the cave contained...

He reached into a head-high crevice, his belly clenching as his fist closed around the jumble of iron and leather hidden inside. He'd never thought to touch it voluntarily. In truth, he'd only kept it because he didn't want anyone else to get their hands on it. Just the thought of what it meant made his palms sweat and his lungs seize.

But if it helped Seb feel safe, he would overcome his dread.

He strode out of the cave to where Seb waited, his gaze fixed not on Faerie spread out below them, which Nevan had expected, nor even on the color spectrum sky, orange now with mid-morning, but on Lulu and her antics.

Of course. Seb's first instinct would always be to care for others, not to pursue his own enjoyment. Which was exactly why Nevan was going to do this.

He held out his hand to Seb. "Here."

Seb frowned and touched the tangle of leather. "What's this?"

"A... a bridle." At Seb's shocked expression, Nevan hurried on. "I know this won't be easy on you, that it's not something you would choose, given your fear of heights and your unfortunate history with horses. So if this makes you feel safer, more secure, then I'll endure it." He set the bridle in Seb's hands and closed his fingers around it. "I trust you not to abuse the power."

"What? No!" Seb tossed the bridle on the ground as though it had burned him. He stood and cradled Nevan's face between his palms. "I never want anything between us that smacks of coercion or that even *hints* at binding your will. I refuse to do that to you, Nevan. Not after Yvo."

"Are you sure?"

Seb nodded. "Positive. Just as you trust me, I trust you." His tone was firm, although the way his tongue darted out to moisten his lips betrayed his nervousness. "You won't let us fall?"

"Never." Nevan nodded to the ledge. "That's why we'll be taking off from up here." He smiled a little slyly and leaned down to murmur in Seb's ear in an effort to distract him. "While I know you can take me so sweetly between your legs, my back in horse form is much wider than my—"

"Nevan!" Seb's eyes widened in shock and he glanced toward where Lulu was singing her Bunny Foo Foo song, The crashing in the underbrush probably meant her companions were getting into the act as well and hopping through the Faerie forest in her wake. "Not where Lulu can hear."

Nevan chuckled and smoothed Seb's hair off his forehead. "I was going to say human hips, but if your thoughts went immediately to—"

"Never mind," he grumbled.

"Without a saddle, inexperienced riders can't be expected to stay on horseback in a trot or canter or gallop, which I would have to do in order to launch from flat ground. As well, when I beat my wings to gain height, the movement can be... unsettling. If we drop from the cliff, however, I can catch a thermal and glide. We'll circle for a bit and then land. A short flight only. Long enough to keep my promise to Lulu, but smooth enough to keep you both safe."

"A-all right." He swallowed, his Adam's apple sliding in the column of his throat.

"Cariad." Nevan cupped Seb's cheek. "If you are truly afraid of this, I'll not force you. Lulu will be disappointed, but she will recover."

"You'd take her up on her own?"

"No. She's still too small for that. She'll need to wait a bit longer."

Seb's jaw firmed. "No. I don't want to do that to her. I don't want our first family outing to be linked with disappointment in her mind." He nodded decisively. "I like your plan. Let's do that."

Our first family outing. Our first, but not our last.

"Very well." He kissed Seb softly. "I'll shift in yon cave. Call Lulu from her playmates and wait for me here."

Nevan scooped up the discarded bridle and retreated to the cave to shove it back in its crevice. Then he shed his clothes, and let his magic take him. The transition from human to winged horse was as smooth and effortless as normal, much easier than at the riverside because, thanks to Seb, he was once again hydrated and well-nourished.

He paced out of the cave, his hooves *thunk*ing on the mossy ground, and joined Lulu and Seb where they waited atop the rock, Lulu almost dancing with anticipation. Keeping his wings tightly furled, Nevan knelt down as close to them as he dared.

Seb lifted Lulu into his arms. "Up you get, Lulubelle." He set her gently on Nevan's back. "Grab on to Nevan's mane, all right?"

"I *know*, Sebbie." Nevan couldn't see Lulu where she perched astride him, but her imperious tone drew an amused whicker from him. "Now you get on behind me."

"Here goes nothing," Seb muttered. But he swung his leg over and settled behind Lulu.

When Nevan felt two sets of hands gripping his mane, he unfurled his wings slowly.

"Man." Seb's tone was almost reverent. "Your wings are so awesome. I—*eep!*"

The grip on his mane tightened when Nevan stood, which Nevan could understand. No matter how carefully he rose, getting to his feet meant that his back shifted and tilted. Not as much as the floor in that thrice damned fun house, but enough to make Seb feel unsteady. He made sure to keep his gait reassuringly slow and even as he paced to the edge of the cliff.

"Oh, god," Seb croaked. "We're *really* high up."

A tiny hand pounded Nevan's withers. "Now, Nevvie!"

Nevan had never launched so smoothly, nor found the thermal so quickly, catching the air without the need for a powerful downstroke. He canted his wings ever so slightly, taking them into a long, flat glide out over the water.

Lulu's laugher was balm to Nevan's soul as they passed close enough to the waterfall for droplets to patter his flanks.

Seb wasn't laughing. Was he afraid? Worried? Terrified? Judging by how tightly his legs clamped to Nevan's sides, and the death grip on his mane, the answer to all three was *yes*.

In this form, Nevan couldn't check, couldn't reassure him, couldn't ask what would make things easier. But then, as they soared over the trees, their tops brushing Nevan's hooves as their glide took them lower, Seb's voice rose in a familiar tune.

"Oh, they fly through the air with the greatest of ease. The daring—*ack!*—young folk on the flying—*eeep!*—hoooorse."

Seb's note seemed to fall away behind them as Nevan angled down to land on the lake shore. Lulu and Seb both bounced a bit on Nevan's back in the few steps it took him to slow to a stop. He knelt again to let them dismount.

Lulu clapped her hands. "Again, Nevvie!"

Seb slid off Nevan's back, and his hand on Nevan's shoulder was trembling. "Maybe not today, Lulubelle. But if Nevan is willing to carry us another time, I'm totally on board."

Nevan turned his head to peer at Seb from one eye. He was?

Seb smiled as he lifted Lulu off Nevan's back and held her on his hip.

"The experience was... surprisingly not terrible. The only chancy bits were when you made an unexpected jog. Air currents, maybe? I think I could get used to it, though, provided you work on your landing." He rubbed his arse. "I think I'll have bruises, and your back is really slippery. Maybe I can get some Velcro pants so I don't slide off."

Lulu patted Seb's cheek. "Silly Sebbie. Nevvie would never let us fall."

"I know." He tilted his head, eyebrows pinched together in his *thinking* expression. "Somehow, I didn't worry about that a bit when we were in the air."

When he set Lulu on her feet, she looked up at him. "That's 'cause I made sure you didn't."

She turned and hopped toward the trees, once again singing about Bunny Foo Foo.

"Uh..." Seb turned his wide-eyed gaze on Nevan, before retrieving the pack he'd left on the doorstep of Lulu's cabin when they'd first arrived at the lake. "Did she just say what I think she said?" He held up a hand. "Never mind. Not relevant."

But when Nevan had shifted back, and donned the clothes Seb had brought for him, Nevan said, "It is indeed relevant, cariad. Lulu is like you. Born to care for and protect others." Nevan remembered Lulu exhorting Zeke to make sure Miss Pennybaker got sufficient kisses. "Even when they are no longer alive."

"We don't say no longer alive," Seb said primly. "We say *untethered souls.*"

Nevan barked a laugh. "Just so. Do you know, I think with you protecting Lulu and Lulu protecting you right back, the two of you might be well nigh invulnerable."

"You think?" Seb brightened. "I'm good with that."

"But tell me truly." Nevan searched Seb's face. "Did you really not mind the flight?"

Seb caught Nevan around the waist. "Really and truly. It was... an adventure. But not just for me and Lulu. For you, too. You've made a new association—carrying someone on your back and bringing them safely to earth again. From now on, when you think of taking someone on a ride, you won't only remember those other times, the bad times. You'll remember this. Flying through the air, perhaps not with the greatest of ease, but definitely with the greatest of joy."

If Nevan thought his heart was full before, he'd been seriously mistaken. Because this, *this* was a perfect contentment, a perfect satisfaction. A perfect love.

He kissed Seb again, and would have continued to do so, had not Lulu called from the trees, "Can we go get Noah's Frisbee now?"

This is a perfect life.

Purgatory
Postscript

About **Purgatory** *Postscript*

I engineered a collision between my Mythmatched world and *Purgatory Playhouse*—the book I wrote as part of the multi-author Magic Emporium series—with *At Odds with the Gods*. But when I had the opportunity to participate in a Valentine's Day event for Ream authors and our Followers, I decided these two worlds deserved another mashup!

Besides, I wondered exactly why Hermes was behaving so badly prior to the last Playhouse production. The answer was obvious—clearly he was suffering from unrequited love, right? If he behaves himself this time, he might get another chance…

Cheers!
—E

Chapter One

Wilson dodged yet another bike messenger and checked the address on the paper in his hand. "This oughta be the place," he muttered.

But there was a big moving van parked in the driveway and a couple of guys even bigger than Wilson were maneuvering a leather sofa out of the door.

Maybe he should have called first? Echo, their mutual agent, had given Wilson Lonnie's contact information and assured him that Lonnie and TD would be thrilled to see him, but maybe springing this visit on them wasn't the best plan. True, Lonnie had only spent half as much time at the Playhouse as Wilson, and TD had only been there for one show, but in Purgatory, surprises were *never* a good thing.

The thing was, *Wilson* hadn't even known the visit would be on the table until he'd gotten the call about the casting change yesterday. He only had twenty-four hours before his first performance, and eight of those had already been taken up with travel. Since he was in the same city now, at least for a couple of weeks, he'd wanted to check in with Lonnie. Thank TD again for what he'd done to make this new life possible.

But yeah. Maybe a heads-up would have been a good idea.

Wilson sighed and tucked the paper back in his jeans pocket. As he was about to turn away, though, Lonnie himself appeared on the porch, and his face lit with his brilliant grin.

"Wilson! Oh my word, is it really you?" He leaped off the steps and raced across the lawn to fling his arms around Wilson and hug him fiercely. "You look *fantastic*."

"Thanks, man." Wilson stepped back so he could study Lonnie properly. "So do you. Happy."

Lonnie laughed, something Wilson had seen far too little when they'd been inmates of Purgatory. "The happiest." His smile faded as he cocked his head to peer up into Wilson's face. "Although I can't say you look especially chipper. Is something wrong?"

Wilson forced his smile into something more genuine. He was an actor, damn it. He could play *happy* when called for, even when *lonely* was still the biggest emotion in his bag of theatrical tricks.

"Nah. It's all good." He jerked his head at the movers. "Although it looks like I've come at a bad time?"

Lonnie scoffed. "It's never a bad time to see a friend." He grabbed Wilson's hand. "Come on. There's somebody inside who's gonna be thrilled to see you."

"TD?" Wilson let Lonnie pull him across the grass, even though the other man was inches shorter and about fifty pounds lighter.

Lonnie scrunched his nose. "No. Unfortunately not. TD's already on location."

"Location?"

"Yeah. My new TV series is being shot in Toronto and TD's on the tech crew so we're leasing this house and moving up there. I'm joining him the day after tomorrow."

"Congrats on the new gig, man." Wilson grimaced, rubbing the back of his head. "Guess my timing sucks. I was hoping to spend some time with you while the tour's in town."

Lonnie stopped on the porch step, putting him eye level with Wilson. "Tour?"

Wilson's grin returned for real. "The *Hamilton* tour. You're looking at the new Lafayette/Thomas Jefferson."

Lonnie's jaw sagged, but then was immediately overtaken by his wide smile again. "Shut *up*. That is *brilliant*!" He launched himself at Wilson for another hug. "You'll be amazing." He pulled back. "Is the tour stopping in Toronto anytime soon?"

Wilson shrugged. "To be honest, I don't even know. Yesterday I was the alternate for the Broadway show. I only know we're in Portland for another two weeks."

"Well, never mind. I'll find out. TD and I will absolutely catch the show at one of the stops." He tapped Wilson in the biceps with his fist. "Probably more than once. Because you are gonna kill it."

"Thanks. I mean, at the Playhouse, I never advanced beyond pit singer until the last production, but—"

"That was only because Dionysus was a short-sighted imbecile who didn't know talent when it was staring him in the ass."

Wilson blinked, because that wasn't Lonnie's voice. "Is that…"

Lonnie stepped aside to reveal a pocket-sized stunner with black curls, big dark eyes, and a wicked smirk. "Ganymede?"

The vision rolled his eyes. "It's *Gary*. Or Gany. *Anything* but Ganymede." Then *he* was hugging the stuffing out of Wilson, a feat considering he was about half Wilson's size, but that compact little body packed some strength.

"Great to see you, man," Wilson said, patting Gany's back.

"Likewise." Gany smacked a kiss on Wilson's cheek. "But I've got to run. Busy day at the bakery. Will you be around for a while?"

"Couple of weeks."

"You have to come to dinner and meet my fiancé."

Wilson's eyebrows rose. "Fiancé?"

Gany grinned. "I've got *so* much to tell you. But later. We'll hang. Ciao!" And he trotted off across the lawn, nearly colliding with another bike messenger as he sprinted across the road.

"He's walking?"

"His bakery is only a few blocks away. Come inside and meet Finn, Gany's guy."

But after waiting for the movers to cart a massive dresser out the door, the first thing Wilson saw when he stepped inside wasn't a man—it was three enormous dogs, their ears pricked and their square-muzzled heads tilted at precisely the same angle.

They didn't *seem* to be aggressive, but...

"Lonnie? Should I be worried?"

"Nope." He chuckled. "Wilson, meet Sir, Bear, and Ozzie."

"Sir. Bear. Oz— Are you telling me those dogs used to be Cerberus?"

A tall, well-muscled man with shaggy brown hair and a confident swagger emerged from the hallway. "Even hellhounds deserve a second chance, am I right?" He held out a hand. "Finn Lassiter. And you are?"

"A friend from Purgatory Playhouse. Wilson."

"That's all? Just Wilson?"

Wilson shrugged. "When I was first earthside, folks like me weren't always granted a name, let alone two."

Finn grimaced. "Ugh. I get it. Sorry."

Wilson shrugged. "No big. My first name's Virgil." He held up both palms. "Awful, I know, but I had to trot it out to join Actor's Equity and they have to put *something* in the program, so—"

"Lonnie? Does this box go or stay?" The shout from down the hallway lifted the hair on Wilson's neck. And then one of *them* walked into the room. He spotted Wilson and smiled. "Oh, hey, Wilson."

"Eros," Wilson hissed, not certain whether to back up or throw a punch.

Lonnie patted his arm. "It's okay," he murmured. "He's harmless."

"But—"

"I'll fill you in later." To Eros, he said, "That goes. Just pass it to the movers."

Eros nodded happily and trotted out the door.

"What the hell, Lonnie? One of the gods? Here?" His belly tried to escape through his spine. "Are there others? Zeus? Is Gany safe?"

Finn crossed his arms and seemed to expand, the three dogs alert around his feet. "Trust me. Nobody is getting to Gany."

"But Eros is just... here? Running tame in your house? I thought all the gods were supposed to be doing time."

"They are, but it's more community service than incarceration."

Wilson licked his lips. "You mean they're not all"—he pointed to the floor—"down there?"

"No. The Fates decided they could give rehabilitation a shot, but extreme punishment is still on the table if they don't behave."

Wilson's heart lurched, but he refused to think about why. "Ah. Got it."

"Eros has been making good progress, but we asked him to help with the move because"—Lonnie spread his palms—"Valentine's Day. It's a little triggering for him."

Finn nodded. "We don't want him to backslide."

Wilson glanced out the open door in time to see a van with *Nectar & Ambrosia* stenciled on its door pull up at the curb and cause another bike messenger to veer around it. When the driver approached the door with a giant pink and white striped box in his hands, Lonnie chuckled.

"Looks like Gany's sent you *another* Valentine's gift."

Finn shook his head, his smile crooked. "He warned me. Every hour on the hour. Hope you like baked goods, Wilson, because by the end of the day, we'll be stockpiled."

"If Gany baked it, I'm sure it's—"

"Divine?" Lonnie said with a smirk as Finn accepted the box from the driver. But then his expression turned stony, his gaze fixed on something in the street. "Wait here."

He strode out the door, shouldering past Eros on the porch and beating the driver back to the curb in time to step directly in the path of yet *another* bike messenger.

Finn peered after him. "What's wrong?"

"Uh oh," Eros muttered.

Finn whirled to face him, a scowl darkening his face. "What?"

Eros grimaced. "That's, um, Hermes."

Wilson sucked in a breath. *He's here.*

"Remus's balls," Finn muttered. "When will these guys *learn*?" He made a quick hand gesture and then he was sprinting across the lawn with the three dogs at his heels.

Wilson crept toward the door. "They won't... hurt him, will they?"

Eros shrugged. "Not if he can convince Finn that he's not a threat. But Finn doesn't take shit from any of the Olympians, so he's gonna have to be *really* convincing." Eros pulled out a cell phone, fingers flying in a way that Wilson's hadn't managed after over a year. "That's weird. He hasn't moved the boulder an inch."

Wilson frowned at the busy, colorful screen in Eros's hand. "What is that?"

"It's an app." Eros's eyebrows rose. "OMG, don't you have a cell phone?"

"Of course I have a cell phone," Wilson grumbled. "Everybody has a cell phone. But that doesn't mean I spend all my time staring at it."

"Oh, honey." He rolled his eyes. "You have seriously got to get with the twenty-first. Here." He held the device on his palm and pointed to a tiny white-columned temple atop a craggy mountain. "This is Olympus. And this"—he swiped one finger sideways, and the display changed to a chart with multiple columns. "And this is us. We have to work our way home.

Prove we've learned our lesson. Atoned for past behavior. See?" He tapped the center column. "Zeus keeps creeping up and then dropping back down, but I'm almost halfway there. And you know what?" He leaned closer and dropped his voice to a conspiratorial whisper. "I didn't even have to *do* anything."

"Noninterference?" Wilson said dryly. "That's what you had to learn?"

Eros shrugged. "Whatever. Hestia made it all the way after about a month, but she still comes earthside to work in that soup kitchen of hers. But Hermes has zero app history. It looks like he hasn't even tried."

Wilson gazed out the door, where Lonnie, Finn, and the dogs were surrounding Hermes on his bicycle. "Maybe that's what *he* had to learn."

Chapter Two

Hermes clutched his messenger bag to his chest, cringing away from the scowl on the unfamiliar man's face. That guy was *scary*. Lonnie wasn't much better, but he had reasons. Hermes hadn't been the most stand-up god back in the day.

He dropped his gaze to the three dogs, who were staring up at him with their heads cocked. Hermes blinked. "Oh, hey. Hi, guys. Remember me? I used to visit you on the regular." All three of them lifted their lips to expose a fang. "Yeah, I guess you do."

"You've got ten seconds," the strange guy said, "to explain why you're here before I give them the signal."

Hermes held up his palms. "I don't mean any harm. I swear on the caduceus. I'm just"—his gaze cut to the open door where *he* was just visible—"taking a ride. You know." He brandished the messenger bag, although the red roses peeking out the top were considerably worse for wear. "Making deliveries. You get I'm part of that flower company, right? I'm their freaking logo."

"Yeah?" Lonnie said. "Then what's the name of the service?"

"Hold on. I know this." Hermes grimaced. "It's three letters. AOL? IRS? BMW?"

"Try FTD." Lonnie's tone could have parched Poseidon.

"You can't blame me for not remembering. I learned to read with the Greek alphabet."

"Maybe you should limit your deliveries to frat houses and sororities then," the scary guy said. "You'd fit right in."

"Wow." Hermes widened his eyes. "And I thought TD was a sarcastic asshole."

"Setting aside the fact that you just insulted my husband," Lonnie said, "I know exactly what you're doing. You're stalking Wilson."

"I'm not!" Hermes tugged at the collar of his stupid monogrammed shirt. Chitons were so much more comfortable. "Not *stalking*."

"No? You were *obsessed* with him when we were still in Purgatory, and you've been riding up and down this street ever since he got here."

Shame curdled Hermes's insides, and his shoulders drooped nearly as much as the roses. "I know I didn't behave well back then."

"Hermes, you *never* behaved well. You and your trickster god buddies nearly got us all *poof*ed out of existence when you set fire to the *Midsummer Night's Dream* scenery."

"But that worked out well, right? I mean, you met TD as a result, and then you all got released. If I hadn't done that, then —"

"Don't. Just don't." Lonnie heaved a sigh. "What do you want?"

Hermes's gaze flicked to Wilson again. Hades, but the man was just so *beautiful*. Hermes had been absolutely *gone* the first time he'd set eyes on him. "To talk to him. Just talk. There are things he needs to know before... before..."

"Before what?" Scary Guy barked. Really, he could almost be one of the dogs.

Hermes gritted his teeth in a parody of a grin. "Before he shows up for the performance tomorrow and finds out I'm part of the orchestra?"

"What?" Lonnie's shout could probably have been heard on Olympus. But then, the guy had great projection.

"Want me to loose the pups, Lonnie?" Scary Guy asked.

"He'll be *traveling*. I need to keep him *safe*," Hermes said desperately. "I didn't do anything *nefarious* for the gig. The second violinist got called back to New York for a spot in the Broadway show. I *auditioned*. They hired me, fair and square."

"I find that hard to believe," Scary Guy growled.

Hermes glared at him. "Listen, whoever you are—"

"He's Finn," Lonnie said, "Gany's fiancé."

Hermes was surprised into a real smile. "Gany's engaged? That's awesome. Is he here? I—"

Lonnie pinched the bridge of his nose. "Let's not get sidetracked, okay?"

"Right, right." He focused on Finn again. "Look, I invented the lyre *on the day I was born*. I've been playing stringed instruments for millennia. Apollo *wishes* he were as good." A movement at the door caught Hermes's eye. Wilson had moved forward, out of the shadows, so the sunlight gleamed on his gorgeous dark skin. "But I didn't want it to be a shock for him. Not when he just landed this part."

"That's…" Lonnie heaved a sigh. "Okay, that's commendable. But why are you still stalking—"

"Not stalking!"

"Fine. Why are you still not-stalking him?"

Hermes dropped his gaze. "Because I love him. He's the only person I've ever loved."

"Dude," Finn said. "Didn't you hook up with, like, dozens of different people and have a whole passel of kids?"

"I never claimed to be a saint, okay? But those were different times, and I wasn't like Zeus or Apollo. I never *pursued* anyone if they didn't want it. They all *liked* me. I'm a likable guy."

"So you say," Finn growled. "Is Wilson one of the side quests in that stupid app? Are you using him to get back to Olympus?"

"I swear I'm not." He turned to Lonnie. "Could you just ask him if he'll speak to me? If he says no, I promise I'll leave. I'll keep out of his way at performances, stick with the musicians. Please?"

Lonnie hummed under his breath. "Fine. Wait here."

He strode across the lawn. Hermes's heart was in his throat as Lonnie spoke quietly to Wilson. If Wilson refused, Hermes would have to accept it and somehow learn to live without him. He was a god, after all. He could do it.

That didn't mean he'd like it.

Wilson's gaze locked on Hermes for a moment, and Hermes could *swear* time stopped. His breath certainly did. When Wilson nodded, and Lonnie beckoned, Hermes sucked in a lungful of air and sprinted across the lawn, letting his bicycle clatter to the ground behind him.

He stopped at the base of the steps, gazing up into Wilson's bottomless brown eyes and everything slotted into place, because Wilson was smiling.

At him.

Hermes smiled back, and even though a tear tracked down his cheek, he didn't bother to wipe it away. "Hi."

Then someone else appeared behind Wilson—someone completely unwelcome.

"Hey, Hermes," Eros said. "How's it hanging?"

Hermes scowled at him. "What are you doing here? You're not trying to"—he made a jabbing motion—"Wilson, are you?"

"What? No. I've given up that whole arrow thing. It wasn't getting me anywhere." He smirked at Hermes. "Speaking of not getting anywhere, you're doing worse than Zeus."

Hermes rolled his eyes. "Nobody's worse than Zeus. Trust me. I know. I had to carry the can for him forever."

"That's not what I meant. The app—"

Lonnie cleared his throat. "Wilson, if you'd like some privacy for your chat, you can take Hermes into the backyard."

Sir, Bear, and Ozzie appeared at his side with Finn behind them. "The pups will keep you company." Finn slid a glance at Hermes. "Just in case."

Wilson glanced between Finn and Hermes. "That's not really necessary. I'm sure we'll be fine."

"Uh uh." Finn laid a hand on one dog's back. "Gany would kill me if I let any of the gods pull something when I could have stopped it."

"And TD would murder me if I let anything happen to you, Wilson," Lonnie said. "This is non-negotiable."

Wilson frowned. "I don't think—"

"It's fine." Hermes didn't care if they all tagged along, not if it meant he could talk to Wilson again. "Besides, it's been a while since I last saw Cerberus." He looked at the dogs. "Come on, buddies. Let's go."

Chapter Three

Wilson followed Hermes, Finn, and the dogs to the rear of the house, where Finn opened a sliding glass door and gestured outside. "The yard's big. Lots of privacy options." He glared at Hermes. "But the pups can reach any point in the yard in a blink, so don't get any ideas."

Hermes held up one hand, palm out. "No ideas. I promise. Mind completely blank." He stepped outside, accompanied by the dogs.

Wilson hesitated before joining him. Hermes was just as perfectly beautiful as he'd always been, standing there in the sun, holding a bag full of wilted roses. But there was something different about him. Wilson bit his lip, trying to figure it out.

Oh.

For a change, he didn't look wasted.

Hermes *seemed* to be sincere, but Wilson had always found him enigmatic at best and incomprehensible at worst. It was as though he'd never really committed to his part, his words and actions always contradicting his true feelings.

As much of an asshole as Hermes could be—and he could be an enormous blazing asshole—he could also be oddly sweet, even if he was tipsy all the time. Wilson was pretty sure that Hermes had been the one who'd left Wilson's favorite throat-soothing tea and high-protein snacks in his dressing room during *Midsummer Night's Dream* rehearsals, and who had left flowers outside the door on opening night. While Hermes had never claimed credit, nobody else had either.

He was such an odd combination of arrogance and humility, of grace and awkwardness. His clumsy pursuit of Wilson had been almost laughable—Wilson *had* laughed—but it also seemed like *Hermes* was laughing too, as though they were both in on the joke.

Wilson gave Finn a reassuring nod and stepped outside, sliding the door closed behind him. A cool breeze carried the promise of herbs and flowers, and just the movement of air, let alone the scents... Well, after nearly a century of limbo, it still hadn't gotten old. He heard the trickle of water from somewhere beyond a stand of birch trees.

Wilson lifted his eyebrows. "That way?"

Hermes nodded, and they struck out across the flagstone patio, one of the dogs bounding ahead while the other two flanked them. Wilson glanced sidelong at the god. Hermes had always had the most alluring pout, as though he were perpetually brooding, like Hamlet. Or James Dean, who'd logged his own time in Purgatory. While he still had that same vibe, there was an unfamiliar edge to it, as though Hermes was... nervous? What did an actual god have to fear?

Wilson stepped out from under the last tree to find a charming little pool with a quirky stone statue crouched at its lip. He turned to face Hermes.

"This is as good a place as any. What did you want to talk about?"

Hermes snatched the ball cap off his head, revealing a riot of black curls—leave it to a god not to suffer from hat hair—and twisted it in his hands, much to the interest of the dogs.

"There are a few things, actually. I—" He winced. "Sorry. I'm not very good at this."

"At what?"

"At, well, *talking* to people. People I..." His voice caught and he swallowed. "People I, you know, *like*."

Wilson had to bite the inside of his cheek to keep from laughing. "Aren't you the god of language? The messenger of the gods?"

"That's different!" Hermes said hotly.

"Why?"

"Because none of those messages *mattered*. Not to me."

"And this one does?" Wilson asked gently.

Hermes blinked those big dark eyes, and seriously, were *anybody's* eyelashes that long? "You have no idea."

"All right." Wilson spread his arms. "I'm listening."

"Here goes." Hermes took a deep breath, expanding his wide chest even further. "I don't want you to be shocked when you get to the theater tomorrow, but I'm…" He screwed up his face until he was squinting at Wilson out of one eye. "I'm kind of in the orchestra?"

Wilson took a step backward. "You're what?"

"Second violin in the string quartet."

"What happened to Asuka? You didn't break her fingers or something, did you?"

"What? No." He scowled, and even *that* was gorgeous. "Why does everybody assume I had to trick my way into this?"

"Because you're the literal trickster god?"

"Okay, fair. But I was never *violent*. I'm not like Apollo or Dionysus or, Furies forbid, Hera."

"You didn't do some hand-wavy thing to make them hire you?"

"No. I auditioned, same as anybody else."

"Why?"

"I *had* to! You were going on tour. *Anything* could have happened to you. I needed to keep you safe."

Wilson narrowed his eyes. "How do you know I was going on tour?"

Hermes's gaze cut to a spot over Wilson's right shoulder. "Because, um, I heard it in the lobby?"

"The lobby. Of the Richard Rodgers? In New York?"

"Yeah. I've, um, been working as an usher there since you got cast as the alternate." He smiled crookedly. "I've never missed one of your performances."

Wilson's belly dropped. "Wait. You didn't do some hand-wavy thing to get *me* the part, did you?"

Hermes's eyes widened for an instant before he guffawed. "Are you kidding? It's *Hamilton*. Nobody can weasel their way into the cast unless they've got the talent, even with divine intervention. You earned your place, just like you earned your role in the touring show." Hermes's face softened. "I was so proud."

For some reason, Hermes's approval sent a zing from the base of Wilson's skull to his heels. His breath caught. He *never* had that reaction to anybody or anything, not even when he'd gotten the call from Echo that he'd landed the *Hamilton* gig.

"Thank you."

"You're welcome." Hermes bit his lip, strong white teeth denting the plush flesh, sending *another* zing down Wilson's spine. "There's more."

"More?" Wilson croaked.

"I wanted to apologize to you."

Wilson lifted an eyebrow. "For stalking me?"

"It wasn't stalking!" Hermes flushed. "Okay, I suppose it was a little bit like stalking."

"Or a lot."

Hermes clenched his eyes shut and took another breath. "Okay." He opened his eyes again, his chin set at a determined angle. "I apologize for that too, even though I'm not really sorry. If I hadn't been there, that taxi would have mowed you down in the street when it skidded on the ice last year."

"Wait. You're the one who pulled me back to the curb?" Hermes nodded. "But I didn't see you. By the time I'd caught my balance, there was nobody in sight."

"Yeah." Hermes widened his eyes comically. "Because I didn't want you to think I was *stalking* you."

Wilson laughed shakily. "All right. Thank you. Please go on."

Hermes glanced down at his feet, where he was scuffing the grass with the toe of one... Wait. Were those vintage PF Flyers? Wilson hadn't seen a pair of those since 1937. "It was my fault."

"Could you be more specific?"

Hermes peered up at him from under his lashes. "That you weren't ever cast in a major role at the Playhouse. I bribed Dionysis with a lifetime supply of Beaujolais nouveau to keep you as a pit singer."

Wilson blinked. "So it wasn't because—"

"Not because you weren't talented. Hades, Wilson. You and Lonnie were the most talented people ever to hit Purgatory Playhouse. I knew that if either of you got onstage before... well, *before*, then you'd win and then everything would have gone to Tartarus in a handbasket."

"You purposely kept me, kept *us* out of the cast?"

"I didn't *want* to. But I *had* to."

Wilson tried to keep his temper in check. After all, the past couldn't be changed. "Why, exactly?"

Hermes hung his head, and one of the dogs nosed his hand until Hermes stroked the square head and flattened ears. "After my son Autolycus was born, Tiresias told me there was no point pursuing any mortals because nobody would ever truly satisfy me, not until I met my soulmate." A second dog leaned up against Hermes's other side, also angling for pets.

"Did he tell you who this alleged soulmate was?"

Hermes raised his head, and his gaze, when it locked with Wilson's, was both somber and intense. "Yes."

Wilson's breath stalled. "Me? But... but how?"

"He was a seer, Wilson. He *saw* things. But Cassandra told me more."

"I thought nobody listened to Cassandra, thanks to Apollo."

"Please." Hermes rolled his eyes. "Nobody's better acquainted with that asswipe's tricks than me. *I* listened, because I'm not a fool. That's why..." He dropped his gaze again, and one dog licked his hand. "The fire. At the Playhouse. The one that destroyed the sets and costumes? It wasn't an accident."

"What?"

Hermes looked up again, his expression bleak. "I set it on purpose. She told me that if I didn't, you would all have been doomed for eternity, worse than Tantalus, worse than Sisyphus, worse even than Prometheus. That the fire would be hard on you at the time, that you'd blame me, maybe hate me, but it was the only way to finally release you."

As Wilson tried to realign his thoughts, the third dog approached with a tattered Frisbee in his mouth, nudging Hermes's hip with it until he relented and tossed it across the yard in a perfect arc—which, Wilson supposed, was fitting since Hermes was also the patron god of athletics. All three of the dogs tore off after it, leaving them alone.

"So let me get this straight. You kept Lonnie and me offstage, coming back to Purgatory year after year, and then practically burned down the place because Cassandra told you to?"

Hermes nodded miserably. "She said it was the only way to stop the cycle, but what if she was wrong? What if I'd ruined your chances, ruined Lonnie's chances, to ascend, made everybody's unlives miserable, and it didn't work? I stayed wasted all the time to fight off the guilt and got *super* wasted to work up the courage to take the last step."

Something fizzed in Wilson's chest. *Vindication.* He'd known Hermes wasn't as bad as the rest of them. He'd *known.*

The dogs raced back and dropped the Frisbee at Hermes's feet, and he obligingly tossed it again. He peered at Wilson, almost fearfully.

"So. Do you hate me?"

Wilson stepped closer and took Hermes's face between his palms. "How could I hate my soulmate?" He pressed a soft kiss to Hermes's lips. They tasted like honey and fire. They tasted like home.

Except...

Wilson gasped and stumbled back.

Hermes reached for him, steadying him before he could fall into the ornamental pool. "What is it? What's wrong? Am I a bad kisser?"

"No, that's not it. You're an amazing kisser. But Eros told me about the app. About the atonement. Working your way back to Olympus. Is this—"

"I'm not going." His smile could have lit the Rodgers' entire stage.

"But..." Wilson let Hermes draw him back into his arms. "Why not?"

"Because you're not there, of course." Hermes smiled and traced Wilson's cheek with one finger. "Now, let's head back to the hotel. We've got a show tomorrow and after my evening's plans, we'll need our rest."

Wilson wrapped his arms around Hermes's waist. "Valentine's Day plans? You know Eros will take credit for this, right?"

Hermes kissed Wilson again. "He can gloat about it for the next eon, I don't care. I've been waiting for you, to *be* with you, for millennia. I don't want to wait another day. Do you?"

"Nope. And *this*"—Wilson returned the kiss with a grin—"is our cue to exit, stage left."

A VERY
QUEST
SOLSTICE

ABOUT A VERY QUEST SOLSTICE

A Very Quest Solstice is a 12K-word holiday coda which builds on characters and situations from the first four Quest Investigations books. It takes place the month following *Death on Denial* and is not intended to stand alone.

It's our first holiday together, and I'm determined to make it special for Lachlan. Only problem? I know zip about how selkies celebrate, so I don't even know *which* winter holiday to pick.

With Lachlan out on a fishing charter, I try to tease some suggestions from my friends, but they're surprisingly unhelpful. And when we get a tip about a Disappeared sighting, my opportunity for more research evaporates.

I guess I'll just have to improvise. Again.

Dammit.

CHAPTER ONE

"Hey, Eleri?" I set my camera bag on the credenza in the Quest staff room and sank onto the loveseat next to my self-proclaimed BFF, my notebook in hand. "What kind of traditions do you fae have around the holidays?"

Eleri didn't even glance up from her phone, where, judging by the goofy—dare I say besotted?—smile on her face, she was text-flirting with Sierra, her human crush. "What holidays?"

"Hello? It's the middle of December, so what holidays do you think? *Winter* holidays."

She glanced up at me. "Perhaps I should have said *whose* rather than *what*. We fae, as you so charmingly put it, *Hugh Mann*, are not homogenous."

"Are you being intentionally unhelpful?"

"Are you being intentionally nonspecific?"

I sighed and leaned forward, propping my elbows on my knees. "Sorry. I don't mean to be—"

"A wanker?"

"Insensitive. And sorry for interrupting." I gestured to her phone. "Tell Sierra hi. Oh! Does she have more photos of her latte art? That squirrel the other day was really cool." I leaned sideways to peer at Eleri's screen.

She snatched the phone against her chest and then shoved it under the sofa cushions on the side opposite from me, something like panic flickering over her face. "Do you *mind*?"

I held up both hands. "Sorry. I didn't mean to, you know, be Jordan."

"What about me?" Jordan trotted through the door with Doop at his heels.

"Nothing," I said. "Not really. I just inadvertently breached Eleri's privacy boundaries."

"Oh. Got it," he said, apparently not the least insulted.

"I'm trying to get her to dish on fae holiday traditions." I studied Jordan as he plopped into the wingback chair across from us and started rooting around in his backpack—aka, the Dooper bag—for something. "What holidays do werewolves celebrate?"

Jordan pulled one of Doop's dog cookies out of the pack and held it on his flattened palm. "All of them."

I blinked. "All of them?"

"Hold."

I froze at his unexpectedly authoritative tone until I realized he was talking to Doop, not me.

"Hold. Hold." Doop's gaze flicked from the cookie to Jordan's face, nose quivering. "Hooollld... *Take it.*"

After Doop took the cookie almost delicately and retreated under the table with it, Jordan dusted off his palms and looked up at me.

"We're not like fae or demons, you know. We've never had a separate realm like they do, and since we've always lived among humans, it made sense to learn all their customs." He wrinkled his nose. "Although some of them were more fun than others, so we might have..." He waggled his palm.

"Customized the customs?" I asked dryly.

He beamed. "Exactly. So now I suppose they might not be recognizable as what they started out. In fact, you guys should totally come over to the Doghouse this evening. It's wassail pong and karaoke night."

"I'm sorry," I said. "What holiday includes karaoke?"

"Well, they used to call it *caroling*, but it's a lot more fun with the karaoke machine and a wider song choice. Hector even got the twinkle lights to blink in time with the music."

"You, uh, don't go door to door and serenade your neighbors, do you?"

Jordan scoffed. "Of course not. We don't have any way to carry the disco ball."

"Go on." Eleri snagged a scone off the platter on the coffee table and took a bite. "Tell him the *real* reason you don't go door to door."

He squinted one eye. "Weeelll, the thing is, not all werewolves can, um, carry a tune."

She smirked around another bite of scone. "He means that they can forget themselves and start to howl in the middle of an especially rousing chorus."

"We don't—"

"'All the Single Ladies,'" Eleri fake coughed.

Jordan winced. "Oh. Right. But it's not like all supes can sing, anyway. I mean, have you heard Frang and his duergar buddies' drinking song?"

We all shuddered.

"Point taken," I said. "So other than the twinkle lights and the disco ball, do you have other decorations?"

"Lots! Although we, uh, might have had a little trouble with Noah and the Yule yew. He got caught short while he was shifted and... *Anyway*, the good news is that the cleanser Dr. MacLeod made me to clean up after Doop? Totally works on werewolf pee, too." He sighed. "We had to get another tree, though."

"Jordan Tate," I said severely, "you did *not* cut down a tree, discard it, and cut down another one."

"Of course not! We're not *monsters*. They're live trees. In pots." He smiled up at Eleri. "Thanks for swapping it out for us."

"Don't mention it," she said and turned to me with her smirk still in place. "What's the sudden interest?"

"It's not exactly *sudden*. I'm always interested in supe details. You know that." I tapped my notebook's battered leather cover. "This is the third journal I've filled with notes."

She eyed it. "I'm aware. The day you don't make a note— Well, let's say we might actually have found the Disappeared by then."

Jordan slid onto the floor next to Eleri and looped one arm around Doop's neck. "You think we're getting close?"

"I don't know." She traced the trumpet vine pattern on her green leggings, not meeting his gaze. "I mean, we haven't had a new lead in a while now."

"Face it, Eleri," I said. "We've *never* had a new lead. And who knows? Maybe one of my notes will at least lead to a lead. Someday."

All three of us sighed and then murmured, "Someday."

It was kind of our mantra, both a wish for the return of all the Celtic fae who'd vanished without a trace over the years, as well as a prayer that we'd be able to keep our jobs. Quest Investigations was founded explicitly to locate the Disappeared and bring them home—or at least let them know they'd be welcomed in Faerie after the Seelie/Unseelie convergence. None of us wanted to fail at that, and not just because of job security.

Now that I was a sort of adjunct supe, thanks to my rather unconventional marriage to a selkie—

Aaaand pardon me while I take a moment to moon over my spouse.

Okay, *whew*. Moving on.

Because of my relationship with Lachlan, my interest in the well-being of the supe community wasn't strictly intellectual anymore.

Now, the stakes were *personal*.

But every time I went to the coffee shop or the grocery store, or hell, listened to the radio for more than five minutes, I was bombarded by the fact that it was the holiday season and I had no idea what that meant to my husband.

And yes, I could still call him my husband, even though the IRS and other human governmental agencies might not recognize the validity of our rather peculiar nuptials. But Lachlan and I had only jumped the besom about a month ago, thanks to a pod of interfering selkies, so I was still trying to figure out how to meld my honorary supe citizenship with my human life.

There wasn't exactly a manual—I'd checked.

Supe/human pairings weren't recognized in the community except in very rare cases, selkies being the one race that got a blanket pass. But selkie history was all oral—it's not easy to keep hardcopy records when you spent most of your time in the ocean.

With flippers instead of hands and feet.

Bryce MacLeod, the same druid who'd concocted Jordan's highly effective cleanser, and Tanner Araya, one of Jordan's werewolf friends, were working on a project to record as much of the oral history across the community as they could. It wasn't a speedy process, though, especially since Tanner was still the de facto supreme alpha, not just of all werewolves everywhere, but of all supes, too.

Long story, involving a curse, a necromancer—ugh, hate those guys, they can cause trouble even when they're dead— and a power grab that went spectacularly wrong.

"Hugh," Eleri said. "*Hugh.*"

I looked up from stroking my notebook. "Huh?"

"I don't know where you went to just then, but I've asked you three times—why do you want to know about fae holiday traditions specifically?"

"Oh." I set the notebook aside—it was way too easy to get distracted by a random fact and fall down the research rabbit hole until I couldn't see daylight. "It's Lachlan's and my first holiday season together, and I want to do something special for him."

Both Eleri and Jordan got that *awww* expression, as though I were doing something *cute*, for Pete's sake. As though I were no older than Jordan's little brother.

I squeezed my eyes shut. "Please don't make that face."

"But it's lovely that you're thinking of him that way." Eleri patted my arm. "It's nothing to be ashamed of. Why not just ask Lachlan?"

"Because I want it to be a surprise." I slumped against the loveseat cushions. "Bryce has been working on stuff for the druids' solstice ceremonies for weeks, and he's of Scottish descent, so I thought he might have some ideas. But all his preparations are druid-centric, not explicitly Scottish and nothing to do with selkies." I rolled my head to the side to peer up at her. "He gave me a mistletoe ball, but when I hung it up at home, Lachlan ended up in St. Stupid's overnight. Turns out he's allergic." I winced, remembering his labored breathing and the hives that covered his body. His *entire* body. And I mean *everywhere.* "*Highly* allergic."

"Good thing he recovered all the way," Jordan said.

I squinted at him. "He did, but how did you know?"

Jordan's big brown eyes got even bigger. "Uh…"

"*Obviously*, if he spent an entire night at St. Stupid's, he's better," Eleri said tartly. "The medimagical staff wouldn't have released him otherwise, and you wouldn't be here now if he was still in hospital. Besides, that was three da—" She cleared her throat. "When did that happen again?"

"On Friday," I said glumly. "And yeah, he was fine when they released him, but he had to ship out with a fishing charter Saturday afternoon and he won't be back until tomorrow."

Jordan's eyebrows bunched, as did Doop's, making them look remarkably similar. "But—"

"*Jordan*," Eleri said loudly, "could you check in with Miss Pennybaker, please? She said she had an assignment for Hugh."

Jordan paused in the act of reaching for a scone, confusion clouding his face. "She did?" He jerked, wincing slightly. "Oh. Yes. She did. I remember. I'll be, um, right back."

He scrambled to his feet and hurried out of the room, Doop shadowing him as usual.

I gave Eleri the stink-eye. "Okay, what's going on?"

CHAPTER TWO

Eleri's attempt at an innocent expression wouldn't have fooled Noah. "I don't know what you mean."

"Don't pretend you didn't just kick Jordan to send him on some bogus errand. And making him talk to Miss Pennybaker? That's just mean. You know how much she freaks Doop out, and that makes Jordan skittish."

Regret flickered across her face for an instant before she banished it under a glower. "He's a barely senior werewolf. He's always skittish. And it's not bogus." She glowered at me, but her fingers didn't sprout thorns, so I figured I was okay. "Miss Pennybaker really does have an assignment for you."

"Really?" The thrill that always swept through me when I got to investigate the actual *supernatural* warred with regret. "Our case load has been so light lately that I was kinda hoping we'd be able to take time off over the holidays, *whatever* those holidays happen to be." I narrowed my eyes and jabbed a finger in her direction. "And don't think I haven't noticed you *still* haven't answered my question about those, by the way."

"Maybe I haven't answered because I don't know. Have you thought of that, you great numpty?"

"You're bound to know more than I do."

"Oh really? I'm not the one with a trunk full of journals."

"It's not a trunk full," I muttered.

"Hugh. Did you never think that as a dryad, a *landbound* fae and Welsh at that, I might not have the same customs as Scots selkies? Who, I might just mention, aren't fae because they live in the ocean, not Faerie?"

"Yeah, yeah, okay." I sighed. Lachlan wasn't exactly on great terms with his selkie clan anyway, given that they wanted him to be king and he was determined not to take the job. For that matter, they weren't all that happy with me at the moment either, seeing as I managed to derail their plan to force him onto the throne with a technicality.

A really big, really red, really *sparkly* technicality in the form of a ruby the size of my fist.

"Maybe it would make more sense to invent our own celebration." I leafed through my journal until I got to a fresh page and pulled a pen out of my shirt pocket. "I could follow the Doghouse pack's lead and pick bits of everyone's customs. A la carte traditions. Pick one from each column and glom them together to make something new."

"I'd steer clear of karaoke caroling, though. Lachlan doesn't strike me as the kind of bloke who'd enjoy belting out 'I Will Survive' to a room full of half-drunk supes."

"Augh!" I clapped both hands over my eyes. "Why did you put that image in my head?"

"You're right. He'd go more for 'My Way.' Or maybe 'Bohemian Rhapsody.'"

I choked on a laugh. "No. 'Holding Out for a Hero.' In a kilt." I peeked at her through my fingers to find her smirking at me. "Do you suppose Lachlan has a kilt?"

"You're the one who shares a closet with the man, not me."

"I don't *snoop* amongst his clothes."

"Don't think of it as snooping, Hugh. You're an investigator. *Investigate.*"

I scooted up so I wasn't sliding half off the loveseat like one of Dali's melting clocks. "We've only been together for a little while, Eleri. He's already made compromises for me. The last thing I want to do is invade his privacy. But…" I doodled a Celtic knot on the corner of the page. "Do you think he has a kilt?"

She shrugged. "He's Clan Brodie, and they've got their own tartans. It's possible, although I don't know how the human clan and the selkie clan intersect."

I sighed again. "It would be so great if he had a kilt."

I reached for a scone absently while I imagined what Lachlan would look like on the deck of *Cridhe na Mara*, gray clouds massed dramatically behind him, the wind ruffling his sun-streaked brown hair and flattening his kilt against his long, muscular legs. The wind off the Pacific could be pretty brisk. What if it *lifted* the kilt?

I shivered and tore off a vicious bite of scone. These fantasies weren't doing me a damn bit of good right now because A) for all I knew, Lachlan didn't own a kilt and B) he wouldn't be back from his charter until tomorrow.

Beside me, Eleri was once more typing furiously on her phone. Since she was clearly not about to reveal any special holiday secrets to me, I'd just have to figure out something on my own. And she was right about one thing—I was an investigator, dammit. I could do this.

Selkie culture predated Christianity, so it was likely that their celebrations centered more around the solstice, which was the day after tomorrow. Since Lachlan wasn't due to dock until late tomorrow, that gave me approximately two days to get my act together.

Hmmm. Mistletoe was obviously out. But holly was a thing, right? I finished off the scone and stood up.

"What are you doing?"

At Eleri's almost panicked tone, I glanced at her as I tucked my notebook into my camera bag. "I'm heading upstairs to the portal to call Frang."

She surged to her feet—and her hair kept surging, leaves and vines whipping around her head. "You can't leave. What about

Miss Pennybaker's assignment?" She looked around wildly. "Damn it, where's that blasted werewolf?"

I chuckled a little nervously. When dryads started sprouting, things didn't always end well.

Ask me how I know.

"Chill, BFF. I just wanted to ask him if he could source some holly for me. Since it's a main ingredient for the duergars' signature cocktail—" Ugh, and seriously? Dragon piss muddled with holly berries? Those guys *really* needed a better mixologist. "—he'll probably have some on hand or at least know where I can get it."

The vines settled down, although a few tendrils still twitched. "Holly grows all over Portland. It's an invasive species, so I can find you a bush within a mile of here and be thanked for removing it."

"Oh." I glanced at the door. "But wouldn't holly from Faerie be more… festive?"

"It's holly, Hugh. Not magic beans."

My shoulders sagged. "I guess." I brightened. "What about a Yule log? Not the fancy dessert kind, but the actual wood, the kind that's supposed to burn for twelve days? Bryce could probably spare one for me. He was stockpiling them when I got the mistletoe from him."

"And where would you burn it?" Eleri planted her fists on her hips. "Your cottage doesn't have a fireplace, and you can't very well fire it up on Lachlan's boat."

"A point."

My house—*our* house—in Dewton didn't have a fireplace or even so much as a hibachi, and we hadn't fully… integrated our lives yet. A man of Lachlan's size took up a lot of real estate just by standing in the middle of the room, and we were in the process of consolidating. At the moment, my ratty furniture was nearly buried under boxes while we got everything sorted. Not exactly a festive atmosphere.

I snapped my fingers. "That's it! I'll book us a getaway." I wrestled my phone out of my back pocket, which was more difficult than it should be. I'd started wearing *much* tighter jeans lately because Lachlan liked how they cupped my ass, and I liked the way Lachlan's eyes flared when he watched them cupping my ass. Although why I bothered to wear them when he wasn't around to see was a mystery. I hit speed dial seven.

Eleri squinted at me. "Who are you calling?"

"Herne."

"What?" she squawked. "What do you need Herne for?"

"He can get Lachlan and me to that place under Loch Ness." My face heated as the call rang. "It's special to us. It's where Lachlan actually asked me to be his mate."

Eleri practically leaped over the coffee table to snatch the phone out of my hand.

"Hey!" I protested.

She jammed her finger against the screen, cutting off the call. "You can't just *call* Herne the Hunter."

"Yes, I can. I have *permission*. He said I could call him any time." I grabbed for my phone, but she held it out of my reach—with an arm that got longer and sprouted a few thorny twigs as I watched. "Gimme that."

"Not until you promise to behave like a sensible person."

I counted to ten. Slowly. "Look. I know Herne has a pretty big footprint in your culture—"

"You *think*?"

"—but he and I have a different relationship." I wouldn't go so far as to say we were friends, exactly, but after I more or less rescued him from certain death, we had a bond. "He takes his obligations very seriously. He'd be upset if I *didn't* call him."

"Oh, really? The solstice is one of the days the Hunt could be called out. Show some consideration, Hugh. You know he's not fond of answering to the horn."

She had a point. One of the things that always galled me was how many supes were subject to magical coercions. If somebody blew that blasted horn—as it were—Herne would have to answer. Not only that, but on the Celtic quartern and cross-quartern days, of which the solstice was one, the veil was thin enough between realms that others could call down the Hunt with nothing more than a few herbs, a determined chant, and a libation or two.

"Okay, fine. I won't call Herne. May I *please* have my phone back?" I pointed at her nose. "And don't you dare block his number. He gave that to me by his own choice."

Her arm resumed its normal proportions, although it retained a few angry-looking twigs. She studied me through narrowed eyes. "How do I know I can trust you?"

"Seriously? Are we BFFs or not? I *told* you I wouldn't. And I'm the last person who'd want to pile any more stress on Herne's shoulders. Or antlers."

I held out my hand, and she set my phone on my palm, although from the look on her face, I expected her to snatch it back at the last minute.

I peered at the screen, calling up Herne's contact, just to make sure she hadn't deleted it.

"Seriously?" She echoed my inflection precisely. "Are we BFFs or not?"

I gave her my best snooty look. "How do *I* know I can trust *you*?"

For a moment, I expected another thorn eruption, but then she laughed. "Fair. I know you'll keep your word and you know I'll keep mine."

"In that case," I said, attempting to keep my tone as innocent as possible, "I believe you promised me some holly."

"What? Now?"

I made a production number out of surveying the very empty room. "Why not? You can't pretend you were doing anything except texting Sierra—which, by the way, I very pointedly *haven't* mentioned to our bosses as a possible Secrecy Pact violation, seeing as human/dryad pairings aren't exactly sanctioned— so you might as well. Who knows? If we do catch a case, you won't have time to get it later and I'd like to have at least *one* festive accouterment on hand when Lachlan gets home."

She glanced furtively at her own phone, abandoned on the loveseat cushion, and then nodded. "Very well." She collected it and tucked it into the pocket of her denim skirt. "I won't be more than ten minutes. Promise you'll wait here?"

"Unless that assignment of Miss Pennybaker's is urgent." I flapped my hands at her. "Go. Shoo. Before the good stuff is all gone."

She quirked one decidedly sarcastic eyebrow. "It's holly, Hugh, not Taylor Swift tickets."

I kept my grin in place until she sauntered out of the room—tough to do, since I was literally holding my breath. I let it out with a whoosh once she'd cleared the door.

Because I'd promised I wouldn't call *Herne*, but I hadn't promised I wouldn't call *anybody*.

My stomach felt like it was auditioning for Cirque du Soleil as I edged toward the windows on the street side of the room, as far from the door as I could get.

This was a call I never thought I'd make. I mean, sure, I was so deep in love with Lachlan that I couldn't see straight, and knew he felt the same about me. But the warmth and comfort of those feelings couldn't completely block the *remembered* ache of past rejection and unrequited affection. I took a deep breath.

And called Ted Farnsworth.

CHAPTER
THREE

Ted answered on the second ring. "Matt! Hey! How you doing?"

My stomach made another barrel roll. Other than Lachlan, who called me *Matthew*, Ted was the only person who always called me by my given name, my *human* name, and not my nom de Quest, Hugh Mann.

"H-hi, Ted. I'm good. Great. Um, fantastic, even. How are things with you?"

"Oh, you know. Can't complain." Ted's warm chuckle, while familiar, didn't send the shiver down my spine that it once had. "Still not used to being this *awake* right at the edge of hibernation season."

"Heh. Yeah. I imagine."

Before I discovered that the supe community was real and that Ted was a grizzly shifter, I assumed that he'd been avoiding me all winter. Now I knew that he'd simply been napping a lot from winter solstice to vernal equinox. Of course, I'd discovered that at the same time that Ted had gotten married to his incubus husband, so it hadn't done me a lot of good in the lovelorn department.

But the thing was... that didn't sting so much anymore. In fact, it didn't sting at all.

So there was no reason this conversation had to be awkward, right? Ted and I were friends before I, er, hit on him and nearly got my lungs ripped out by a jealous incubus. We could be friends again. Ted wasn't the kind of guy to hold a grudge, although said jealous incubus might be another matter.

"So..." Speaking of jealous incubi. "How's Quentin?"

"He's good." I heard the rumble of another voice in the background. "Sorry, babe." Ted's voice was muffled, as though he'd lowered his phone away from his face. "I meant you're perfect."

Oookay, clearly Ted wasn't alone. I did a quick check of my emotional temperature—nope, nary a spike. Well, nothing but the warm fuzzies from knowing that a good friend was happy.

"Tell Quentin hello."

"Matt says hi." Another rumble followed by Ted's chuckle. "Hey, we heard about the selkies."

I groaned. "Jeez. You know about that?"

"Matt, *everybody* knows about that."

I don't know why I was surprised. "You supes are worse gossips than a bunch of teenagers. Who told you?"

"Let's see. I think maybe it was that ferret shifter?"

"Ronnie Purl? He wasn't even there!" Although it had seemed like everybody else had been.

"He heard it from somebody else. Maybe a dryad?" Another background rumble. "No, that's right. Quentin said Paimon put it on his blog." Ted hummed appreciatively. "He was really complimentary about your photoshoot, Matt. You'll probably get a lot of business from his five-star review.

"Wonderful." I pinched the bridge of my nose. Just what I needed. A demon overlord pimping my photography services to the community, with bonus embarrassing details about my introduction to Lachlan's selkie clan: shivering, naked, and dripping wet.

"Congratulations, by the way. We're both really happy for you. Lachlan's a lucky guy."

Warmth infused my chest. "Thanks, Ted. I appreciate that." I cleared my throat. "That's, uh, actually why I called. Well, sort of. I want to surprise Lachlan with a getaway for the holiday. You know, starting our own tradition? I realize it's pretty last minute, but do you think I could book a suite at Wildwood for a couple of days?"

Ted made an odd sound, halfway between a yelp and a groan. "Uhhh… Sorry. We're full. I mean. Closed. Yeah. We're closed. For the week. Two weeks. We're going away. To, um, Boston. Yeah. Boston."

I frowned, holding the phone away from my ear to peer at the screen. Ted's voice had gone surprisingly high. If I didn't know better, I'd think he was lying to me. Or—

Heat rushed up my throat. Dammit, Quentin was there. What were the odds that Ted's husband, a literal *sex demon*, was… distracting him? Probably dead even, considering I hadn't mentioned a reservation date.

"Okay. No problem," I said. "Maybe we can get together for breakfast at Wanda's sometime soon."

"Yeah," he croaked. "That'd be great. Bye, Matt."

The call cut off. Yep, Ted was definitely getting some right now. And you know what? Good for Ted. The only feeling left swirling in my own middle was the regret that I wasn't likely to get any of my own until Lachlan's boat docked on tomorrow.

"Will this do?"

I whirled at the sound of Eleri's voice to find the doorway full of what appeared to be an ambulatory holly bush wearing trumpet vine leggings and forest green Doc Martens below its dangling roots.

"Are you kidding me?" I couldn't even see her head. "I wanted a few sprigs, not an entire hedge."

The bush-in-boots advanced on me, and if you'd ever been targeted by dryads with an agenda, you'd have backed up too. Have you *seen* holly leaves? Those things are *sharp*.

"I'm a dryad, Hugh. I'm not about to amputate the poor thing's limbs, not at this season. They're already stressed enough."

"What am I supposed to do with that?"

"Well, first, you can take it out of my hands."

I peered through the glossy green leaves and the clusters of scarlet berries. I could just make out a more or less central... branch? Trunk? Stalk? I had a dryad BFF. I clearly needed to brush up on my botany.

I reached into the bush. "Ow! Son of a— Those leaves are lethal."

"Don't be a baby. They don't bother me."

"Probably because you asked them not to. Could you extend the favor to me?"

She sighed. "I suppose it wouldn't do for your skin to be marred when— There. Is that better?"

Oddly enough, it was. I was able to grasp the stalk right below Eleri's hand without being stabbed by dozens of murder leaves. She let go and circled the bush to stand next to me.

I looked down at her, nonplussed. "Okay, now what?"

"There's a spell on its roots. All you need to do is set it on bare earth and it'll plant itself."

"Where? There's not exactly a lot of bare earth in the office."

"At your house, of course. Won't it be much more festive to have a live bush thriving outside your door than severed appendages that'll shrivel and crumble all over your house?"

"I suppose." I eyed the bush. "I guess I'll head up to the portal and have Frang take me through Faerie to—"

"No!"

I lifted my eyebrows. "Excuse me? I can't exactly hike all the way to Dewton with this thing. Should I call a different FTA driver?"

"I only meant that you didn't need to call the FTA at all. Jordan and Doop can take you straight to your living room."

I considered that. It was true, Doop could open a portal almost anywhere, but there had to be enough space on the other side for a hound the size of a MINI Cooper to land, along with his attendant werewolf and—at least in this instance—a hapless human with a holly bush sidecar.

My cottage in Dewton wasn't large to begin with, and considering most of the available floor space, not to mention much of the furniture, was presently covered in half-packed cardboard boxes, we couldn't make the hop directly.

"He'll have to take us to Ted's cave. I can probably hike down the hill to my place without putting an eye out."

"Don't be insulting." Eleri stuck her nose in the air and sniffed. "She'd never maim her new host."

I lifted a brow. "I take it that would be me?"

"Provisionally. Once you plant her beside your front door, it'll be official."

"You realize the house doesn't belong to me?"

She waved one hand airily. "If you move, I'll help you relocate her." She pointed at my nose. "But no lopping off branches. If you need a spray for decoration, simply ask and she'll drop one for you."

I eyed the bush warily. "Seriously?"

"Try it." When I hesitated, she said, "Hugh."

When Eleri used that tone of voice, thorns were in the offing, so I cleared my throat.

"Excuse me…" I glanced down at Eleri. "Does she have a name?"

She rolled her eyes. "What do you think? Holly. Of course."

"Right. Sure. Excuse me, Holly. Do you suppose you could spare a sprig, please? For, um, decorative purposes?"

"Goddess bless, Hugh, you don't have to sound so abject."

"Sorry! I've never communed with a plant before."

Eleri sniffed again. "Your loss."

And a bunch of holly, its glossy green leaves complemented by a cluster of bright berries, dropped neatly next to my trainers.

"Okay, I'm ready!" Jordan called from the doorway. He was tall enough now—taller than me, actually, and way taller than

Eleri—that I could see him over the top of the bush. "Uh, why is there a tree in the staffro— Doop! No!"

I closed my eyes. "Please tell me he's not peeing on my shoes."

"Not your *shoes*." Jordan's gritted teeth didn't quite qualify as a smile. "I'll get the cleanser." He grabbed the Dooper bag and unzipped the main pocket.

"Thank the Goddess Zeke replaced the carpet in here with tile," Eleri murmured behind the unmistakable sound of Doop snuffling around my, er, roots.

"What's the assignment?" I asked.

"Assignment?" Jordan, his hands encased in nitrile gloves, lifted the holly spray, and a fat drop of Doop's doggy attentions gathered on one spiky leaf and plopped onto the floor. He looked up at me. "I'm not sure the cleanser will work on this. Do you want to keep it?"

"As long as it won't offend Holly," I said, "I think we can safely say no."

"Holly won't mind," Eleri said. "She's already said goodbye to it."

"Cool." Jordan trotted over to the trash bin, one hand held under the bough to catch additional drips. He pressed its pedal with one sneakered toe and the lid raised. "We need to get one of these at the Doghouse. Our trash doesn't have a lid."

"Does Doop get into it?"

"Not Doop." Jordan dropped the holly into the bin. "Noah."

Eleri chuckled indulgently. "Is your little brother still having trouble with his shifts?"

"I'm pretty sure he could maintain if he wanted to," Jordan said with a shrug, not meeting our eyes. "But I don't want to push it."

Eleri and I exchanged a glance as Jordan returned to his cleanup. If Jordan wanted to pretend that Noah was the one suffering from residual trauma after our last Quest case, neither one of us was going to call him on it. The dark circles under his eyes were evidence that he was still struggling with the aftermath despite regular therapy sessions with Dr. Kendrick.

Eleri cleared her throat. "So. The assignment?"

Jordan looked up from a last swipe of the tiles. "Assignment?"

"Yes. The *assignment*. That Miss Pennybaker has for you and Hugh."

He blinked, brow knotted, until Eleri nudged him with the toe of her boot and his eyes widened. "*Ooohhh*. The *assignment*. Right." He stood and made another trip to the trash to dispose of gloves and cleanup cloths. "There's a rumor."

"A rumor?" My arm was getting really tired of holding Holly out of Doop's reach. "That hardly seems critical. Is it something that can wait until after the holiday?"

"Which holiday?" Jordan asked. "It's Turco Tuesday tomorrow."

"Turco Tuesday?"

He shrugged. "Well, a lot of traditions involve food, especially turkey, for some reason, so we decided to combine it with Taco Tuesday. So Turco Tuesday. But, you know, *festive* Turco Tuesday. There's twinkle lights. And an inflatable snowman in a chef's hat." He washed his hands at the sink in the corner. "Don't worry, though. It's not turkey tacos, because that would be weird. It's roast turkey *and* tacos."

"Jordan," Eleri said between gritted teeth. "Maybe you should tell Hugh about the *rumor*."

"Right! The rumor." He dried his hands on the pristine towel hanging from the rack on the wall. "Someone phoned in a sighting to the Disappeared hotline."

I glanced at Eleri. "We have a Disappeared hotline?"

"Apparently it's been around for a while, but it's more a cold line."

"Yeah!" Jordan said brightly. "It's never even had a single call."

"Until now," Eleri said darkly. And sure enough. Thorns.

Jordan gulped and retreated a step until his hips hit Doop's flank. "Right. Until now."

"In other words, it's time-sensitive. So you'd best get on with it." She made a shooing motion with both (thorny) hands. "Off you go, then."

I frowned at her. "Aren't you coming?"

She turned away to retrieve her denim jacket from the coatrack. "No. I've got a book club meeting."

I shifted Holly from one hand to the other, and to give the bush credit, it didn't draw blood. "If this is such a critical assignment, why are you bailing on it for a book club meeting? Surely chatting about *Silver on the Tree* or *Hexwood* or *The Secret Life of Plants* isn't as important as investigating a lead on Quest's *literal* mandate."

She didn't look at me as she shrugged into her jacket. "Need I remind you that my book club isn't an actual book club? It's the progressive dryad caucus, and we're still lobbying for less root-bound leadership."

"But we're a team." I didn't mean to sound quite so needy, but today was not going the way I'd hoped.

"Yes. But you and Jordan can handle the initial legwork. I'll join you as soon as the meeting is over."

"So will you take, er, Holly with you?"

"What? No. You're her host, now."

"But if this assignment is so urgent, do I really have time to detour for bush planting? It's the winter solstice, not Arbor Day."

Eleri stomped toward the door without looking at me. "Stop dithering about, Hugh. You're responsible for Holly now, and if you have a problem with that… Well, do I need to remind you about what happened the last time you ticked off a dryad grove?"

"Don't worry, Hugh." Jordan shouldered his pack again. "We've got plenty of time."

"As long as you don't *dither*," Eleri said fiercely. "Now go." She strode into the hallway, trailing thorny vines.

I sighed. "Guess we've got our marching orders. First stop, Ted's cave above Dewton."

"Can't we go directly to your living room? Doop's been there before, so he won't have a problem opening the portal."

"No room. The place is full of boxes. The cave is the best we can do." I gestured toward the door with Holly. "So if you could please hand me my camera bag, we'll be on our way. Sans dithering."

Because Eleri had a point: I definitely did *not* want to piss off any more dryads, *especially* not my BFF.

CHAPTER
FOUR

Doop opened a portal from Quest's fourth floor translocation door, and we emerged directly in front of the cave that Ted had used as his shifting bolt-hole before he married Quentin. Jordan immediately darted for the trail that led down into Dewton.

"Hey!" I stumbled after him, which was difficult since I couldn't see the ground in front of my feet through Holly's foliage. "Slow down."

"Sorry," he called, not slowing down. "No time."

"We'll have considerably less time if I fall down the damn hill and break my neck," I muttered. Holly's leaves rattled, but I don't know whether it was in solidarity—her limbs could snap just as easily as mine—or because my gait wasn't exactly smooth.

When I rounded the final sharp dogleg in the path, Jordan was already disappearing down the last slope. Before he vanished completely, though, his cell phone rang—the chorus of "Werewolves of London"—and he stopped to pull it out of his pocket.

"Hector?" he said just as I caught up with him, wheezing, my arm muscles burning like crazy.

Have you ever tried to carry a bush at arms-length for twenty minutes? I really needed to spend more time at the gym.

"Jordan?" Even through the chilly breeze soughing through the firs around us and rustling Holly's leaves, I could hear the panic in Hector's voice on speaker. "Can you get back here?"

Jordan locked his gaze with mine. "I'm kind of on a Quest thingie. Can it wait?"

"Not really. Noah's still wolfy, and he got spooked when we inflated the snowman. When he bolted, he got tangled in the twinkle lights and knocked over the Festivus pole, and when he was trying to shake it off, he popped the snowman."

Jordan winced. "A loud pop?"

"*So* loud. Like fireworks inside the house."

"Noah hates fireworks," Jordan whispered to me. "For that matter, so do the rest of us."

"Now he's trying to hide under the bed," Hector continued, "but he can't quite fit because of the lights and the pole and the deflated snowman, which is also tangled in the lights. He won't come out for us." Through the phone, we could hear pitiful whining and yelping. "You and Doop are the only ones who can talk him down."

Jordan's jaw firmed, his shoulders squared, and suddenly, the dorky frat house werewolf was gone and an alpha stood in his place. "I'll be there in five minutes." He disconnected the call and looked at me, his brown eyes steely. "I'm sorry, Hugh, but —"

"It's fine. Go." I switched Holly to my other arm. "I'll plant the bush. Give me a call when you're ready to go again and I'll meet you back at the cave."

"Thanks, Hugh." He turned to Doop. "Doop, the Doghouse."

The air across the path shimmered and steadied, revealing the Doghouse backyard. An instant later, they were both through it and I was alone on the path.

"Well, Holly. I guess it's you and me now. Allow me to show you to your new home."

Holly didn't protest either, so I took that as agreement and minced my way down the last steep part of the path. My cottage was close enough to the foot of the hill that I didn't encounter anyone on the street who'd wonder why a holly bush had suddenly gone walkabout in town.

And you know what? Eleri was right. As soon as Holly's roots touched the bare earth next to my doorstep, they burrowed right in.

Of course, getting to bare earth was a production number, because Holly insisted on *completely* bare earth not only for her roots, but for any spot under her branches.

Ask me how I know.

With her propped against the fir tree in the front yard, I pulled up clumps of dandelions and a couple of thistles (ow!) and cleared away all—and I mean *all*—of the needles said fir tree had dropped. And there were a lot, both from the tree's natural cycles and the *un*natural additions from dryad attacks last September during the case where I'd first met Lachlan and Eleri.

"At least I don't have to water," I muttered, brushing ineffectually at the mud caking the knees of my jeans.

Yeah, this was Oregon in December, so "dirt" was most definitely "mud." I circled the cottage to the back door that led directly into the laundry room, because *ugh*. I had to wipe my hands off on the seat of my jeans before I could even get enough purchase on the doorknob to turn it and step inside.

I toed off my trainers—also mud-caked—and shucked off the jeans. I thought better of tossing them into the washer, though. Better wait until the mud dried and I could shake most of it off, otherwise I'd just be creating a mud bath inside the machine, which wasn't great for the plumbing.

Again, ask me how I know.

My socks were damp, so I left them with the jeans and padded barefoot into the bathroom. I eyed the clawfoot tub longingly, but since I didn't know when Jordan would be back —and, like all werewolves, he had boundary issues—I didn't want to risk being naked when he showed up. While shifters as a rule had no trouble with nudity, as a mostly human, I preferred to keep my privates private, thank you very much.

I settled for a thorough hand washing. As I was scrubbing the mud from under my fingernails, I couldn't help the flare of excitement in my middle. A lead on the Disappeared! We'd been hoping for a break like this since Mal and Niall founded Quest. Finding the Disappeared and bringing them home was literally the reason Quest existed. If we could trace even one of the long-missing fae, we could justify the King and Queen's confidence in us.

I paused as I was drying my hands and met my own gaze in the mirror above the sink. If we *did* solve the riddle of the Disappeared, would that make Quest obsolete?

Nah. They'd still need us. The supe community had no official police force. They had the Queen's Champion, who doled out punishment decreed by the council or special tribunals, but Quest was the only investigative arm they had. We'd been busy constantly since I'd joined, so we'd still be around if we succeeded.

I hoped.

If we *didn't* succeed, though… Would Their Majesties lose patience and appoint someone else, some other group they decided could get the job done where we'd failed?

I shuffled into the bedroom, dodging both sealed and half-full boxes, and grabbed clean socks and jeans from the dresser. But as I was buckling my belt, I spotted it, peeking out between an open box and the closet door.

Lachlan's go-bag.

Well, shit.

He *always* took it with him on charters. It wasn't strictly necessary—*Cridhe na Mara* was fully outfitted for the passengers' safety and comfort. But the bag held special emergency items that *Lachlan* might need.

There was no point in me driving to the marina with it—the boat had been at sea for two days already. But maybe... FTA drivers could open a portal right onto *Cridhe na Mara*'s deck.

And again—ask me how I know.

In fact, I'd wanted to find a way to prevent that, just so Lachlan and I could depend on privacy when we were at sea. One of the perks of the human-selkie mate bond was that we shared Lachlan's calon, but to maintain that connection, I had to swim in the freaking ocean with him—naked—while he was in his seal form. Being interrupted mid-swim once was one time too many.

However, I hadn't gotten around to asking—okay, begging—Niall to ask his brother the King for that yet. So I could use the FTA to get to the boat, take Lachlan his bag—maybe steal a kiss or two—and be back to meet Jordan in under ten minutes.

I stuffed my feet into my hiking boots and slipped into a heavier jacket, because winter wind on the Pacific could cut to the bone. But as I pulled out the oak leaf that acted as an FTA token, I hesitated.

The spells had been altered to allow riders to request specific drivers, but I couldn't call for Frang, my usual guy. For one thing, he wouldn't be able to fit amongst all the clutter any more than Doop could. For another, he got violently seasick, and I couldn't do that to him.

Jordan had told me that the not-quite-sanctioned app that tech-savvy Hector had developed allowed riders to request drivers by size and nature. Had I warned Jordan and Hector against using the sort-of-illicit app?

Yes. Yes, I had.

Did I also install the app on my own phone?

Why, yes. Yes, I did.

Hey, what can I say? I'm a terrible role model.

I hurried into the kitchen, which had the largest expanse of free floor space, and opened the app.

"*Cludo,* salt water, subcompact." Don't look at me like that. *I* didn't make up the terminology.

Almost immediately, a shimmering portal appeared next to the stove, and a diminutive person with blue scales, wide black eyes, and hair like feathery purple seaweed stepped through it onto the checkerboard tiles, water puddling around their webbed feet.

"Where to?" they fluted.

"Uh…" Man, I *really* wanted my notebook. I'd never seen this type of fae before, and I itched to ask questions. What was their species? Did they live in fresh or salt water? Where had they gotten the tutu and the Hawaiian shirt? But I didn't have the time. "Your name?"

"You couldn't pronounce it. Where to?"

All righty then. "*Cridhe na Mara,* please."

They nodded and beckoned for me to follow. So I stepped out of my kitchen and into another dimension.

And let me tell you, that *never* gets old.

CHAPTER FIVE

I did my usual rubbernecking as I followed my driver. The sky was shading from yellow to green, so we'd passed midday and were heading into afternoon. Before I'd had a chance to do more than gawk at the standing stones just visible atop the tor, they stopped on the bank of the stream that circled its foot.

"That was quick. I— Shit!" I smacked my forehead. How had I forgotten? The FTA spells prevented entry or exit anywhere within sight of humans. If Lachlan's charter was a human party, the portal wouldn't open. I looked down at my driver. "I'm sorry. I should have realized that this wouldn't work if—"

They gestured and the portal opened to reveal *Cridhe na Mara*'s pilot house.

"Oh. Well. Okay. Thanks. Could you wait? I'll need the return trip, too."

They shrugged. "It's your gold."

I crouched and edged forward, mentally bracing myself for the transition from solid ground to rolling waves. It wasn't stormy today—the sun had actually broken out from behind the clouds now and then—but the Pacific off the Oregon coast in December was never, well, pacific.

But when I stepped onto the deck... Nothing. Nothing but a gentle bob and sway, the faint slap of rope against wood, the cry of gulls, and the rev of a nearby engine.

A car engine.

"What the…"

I stood and walked away from the portal to look down at the deck. It was empty. Furthermore, the boat wasn't at sea—it was docked at its usual slip at the marina.

I set the go-bag down, frowning. Had the charter been canceled? That would devastate Lachlan. He was really trying to make this business pay his way without having to fall back on the selkies' many-strings-attached treasury.

I ducked through the hatch. "Lachlan? Are you down there? Are you okay?"

No answer. But he might be behind the door in the berth and not have heard me. So I climbed down into the salon. It was as pristine as it usually was—Lachlan always kept the boat ready to sail and never left after a booking until he'd cleaned up. Were there nautical terms for that? Battening down the hatches? Swabbing the deck? Furling the sails? Not that *Cridhe na Mara* had sails—it was a cabin cruiser after all. But as the mate of a man who made his living with his boat, I should probably brush up on my terminology.

I made my way to the berth, but it was empty too, the blankets so smooth and tight across the mattress you could bounce a quarter off them. I propped my fists on my hips and stared down the length of the boat. Clearly there was nobody here.

Oh.

If something *had* happened to upset Lachlan, he'd probably put on his skin and slipped overboard, the way he always did when he was stressed.

Just to be sure, I strode aft and laid my palm against a specific spot on the bulkhead. It looked like a part of the paneling, but it was actually the bespelled cubby where Lachlan kept his skin.

To be clear, I mean his *seal* skin, not anything *Silence of the Lambs* or *Texas Chainsaw Massacre*-ish. Lachlan had asked the witches' collective who maintained the security spells on *Cridhe na Mara* to add me to them, and apparently since I shared his calon, that was a thing that could happen.

The latch on the hidden door popped, and I opened the cubby enough to peek inside. Then I opened it wider, staring, and touched a tentative finger to the folds of smooth, dark fur inside.

Slowly, I closed the compartment and leaned my head against its panels.

What was going on?

Before you ask, I know damn well Lachlan would never cheat on me. Hell, we never even kissed until he'd severed the knot with his ex. When he gave his word, he kept it. End of story.

But Lachlan had been threatened before, not only by that asshole who'd tried to kill him in the case where we'd met, but by his jerkface selkie clan, who still harbored hopes of tricking Lachlan onto the throne that he didn't want to take.

I pulled out my phone. I never called Lachlan while he was at sea, but, well, it's not like he was *at* sea, now, was he? Cell service could be sketchy at the marina, too. I really needed to get that spell Bryce had created for Dr. Kendrick, the one that used the magic grid for calls, because I had no service.

"Crap."

I climbed up onto the deck and managed one anemic bar, then speed-dialed Lachlan.

"Please pick up, please pick up, please pick up," I murmured, earning a quizzical glance from my FTA driver, who was sitting cross-legged in the pilot's chair.

The call connected and I exhaled in a whoosh, the knot in my belly loosening. But then it cut off without even a voicemail prompt.

I stared at the screen for a good ten seconds as that belly knot tightened again. There could be good reasons for the call to fail. There didn't *have* to be anything seriously wrong.

But then I remembered Eleri's squirrely behavior. Jordan's too, but then Jordan was squirrely on the best of days. Did they *know* something? Were they trying to shield me from bad news?

Well, screw that.

If something was wrong, if Lachlan was in danger, I wanted to know, and I wanted to know *now*.

I turned to my driver. "I'm ready for the return trip. Can you open the portal directly in my kitchen where you picked me up?"

They tilted their head, clearly considering, and then nodded. "It's on the approved list. But custom shortcuts are an extra charge."

"Yes, yes. Fine. Just please, can we hurry?"

They jumped down—the seat was level with their shoulders —waved a hand, and my kitchen shimmered into view.

"Thanks." I grabbed the go-bag and almost sprinted through.

"Be sure to leave a review," they called as the portal began to close. "Your business is important to us. Rider satisfaction is of prime importance to our FTA service. Also driver bonuses."

"Yeah, yeah. Fine. Five stars. Whatever."

I tossed the go-bag aside as the portal faded and pulled my phone out again. I tried Lachlan's number once more with the same result, even though the reception in the house was perfect. But when I called Eleri and *that* call disconnected too, I had to brace my hands on my knees so I wouldn't butt-plant next to the refrigerator.

Even at her "book club" meetings, Eleri always left her phone on and screened her calls. She had to. Everyone at Quest did because we never knew when we might be called in on an emergency. If she wasn't answering, then something, somewhere, was wrong, and if she hadn't clued me in on the problem?

It had to involve Lachlan. And if it involved Lachlan, then it involved me, too, dammit. I refused to be *protected*, shielded, just because I was human.

I locked the door behind me and headed back to the cave. There was no point in calling Jordan—he'd be there soon enough. But once he arrived, I was getting some answers. Or else.

I was halfway up the hill before I realized I'd left my camera bag behind, but frankly? I didn't have time, and I was too steamed to go back and grab it, anyway.

I'd managed to catch my breath from my headlong rush up the hill and had only been pacing in front of the cave for nine minutes and thirty-seven seconds—I checked—when Doop leaped out of nowhere with Jordan trotting behind him.

"Hey, Hugh. Sorry it took so long, but—"

"What's going on?"

Jordan blinked. "Um… What?"

"Exactly. *What*. Lachlan's not on the boat. He's not answering his phone. Neither is Eleri, and she was way too anxious to get me out of the office. So I'll ask again. What's going on?"

Jordan pawed the air until his hand landed on Doop's back. "Nothing." His voice was at least an octave higher than normal.

"Like I believe that. Please, Jordan." My own voice wobbled. "Is something wrong? Lachlan in trouble? I—"

"The rumor! The Disappeared. We have to—" His hand fisted in Doop's ruff, causing the hound to whuff in protest. "Doop, the bog."

Doop's eyebrows quirked in the equivalent of a doggy WTF, but he never disobeyed when Jordan used his alpha authority. He galloped forward.

"Wait!" I called, but the hound was already bunching his hind legs, and then he was airborne.

"Come on, Hugh. We don't have much time."

"Jordan, can we please—"

But he bolted after Doop. I huffed an exasperated breath and followed into…

Wow.

CHAPTER SIX

And when I say *wow*, I'm not talking about a good *wow*.

We were in a dark, dank... forest? Woods? Swamp? The trees surrounding the rough patch of sparse brown grass where we'd landed were gnarled and knobbly, with some kind of moss trailing from branches bare of leaves. The only sound was the whine of insects and an occasional *blurp*.

I peered through the gloom. The ground under our feet seemed solid enough, but the bilious green carpet beyond its edges quivered like unset custard. As I watched, the surface three yards away expanded with a fat bubble as big around as my head. It burst with another *blurp* and released a sulfurous stench.

Jordan had ordered Doop to the bog, and as usual, the hound had hit the mark. This place was as boggish as you could get, however, I had sincere doubts whether anybody else was around, Disappeared or not. In fact, if this had been my only refuge option, I'd have disappeared too.

Doop was peering around dubiously, clearly also wondering why we were here, and I was done.

I crossed my arms. "All right. Out with it. There was no rumor, was there?"

Jordan's gaze slid away, and he became very interested in the knothole in a nearby tree that looked like a special effect from *The Wizard of Oz*. "There, um, might have been."

"Really? When?"

He attempted to smile. He failed. "Sometime?"

"Come on, Jordan. We're teammates. Friends. Could you please tell me the truth?"

"Um... No?"

"Brother," I muttered. "At least tell me this. Is Lachlan in danger?"

He scrunched up his face. "It depends."

My belly roiled and I couldn't have told you whether it was because of anger or fear. "On what? It's not the selkies again, is it? Or a mage? Or the council? Do they have an objection to our mating? Do you know where he is?"

Jordan's face crumpled even more, which I hadn't believed was possible. "That's a lot of questions, Hugh. Which one should I answer first?"

I took a deep breath, because throttling one's co-workers is frowned upon, even among supes. "Do. You. Know. Where. He. Is."

"Oh!" He brightened. "Yes!"

I waited, but he didn't elaborate. "For Pete's sake, Jordan, will you just tell—"

Doop uttered a sharp bark, his gaze fixed on something beyond my shoulder.

I glanced back to see a ball of yellow light drifting through the trees, casting a sullen reflection in the patches of water visible between mats of moss and algae.

The hair on my nape lifted. "What's that? Could that be our contact for the rumor?"

"No. It's only a marsh light. There's no—"

Doop launched himself out from under Jordan's hand.

"Doop! No!" Jordan grabbed for Doop, but missed.

I lunged for him, but he dodged me and I stumbled sideways, staggering into the bog up to my shins and windmilling my arms to keep my balance so I didn't faceplant in the scummy green water.

I teetered for a moment and heard an all too familiar giant splash from behind me: the sound of an enormous hellhound cannonballing into a lake, or in this case, a bog. I turned just in time to get a face full of noxious water and unspeakable green goo.

I spluttered, wiping my eyes clear to see Doop thrashing through the water toward the meandering marsh light. Just as he was about to reach it, it vanished. His bewildered expression as he looked about would have made me laugh if I didn't have swamp water soaking the front of my clothes from my jacket collar on down.

"Doop! Hold on. I'm coming." Jordan, who for some reason was completely dry, hurried past.

"Stop," I said with a sigh. "I'm already wet. I'll get him."

"But—"

"Jordan." I pointed at his nose. "Stay."

For a wonder, he actually obeyed.

By the time I'd wrestled Doop back onto dryish land, his white coat was streaked green and brown and dotted with dead and rotting leaves, and I wasn't much better.

"Thank goodness I forgot my camera bag," I muttered just as Doop shook himself briskly and splattered me with more swamp detritus.

Jordan sidled nearer, still dry. "I'm really sorry, Hugh."

"It's fine." I wiped a glob of moss off my cheek. "But no way am I contaminating my house or the Quest offices with all this" —I shook off my fingers—"muck. It'd take forever to clean up after the cleanup."

"We could go to the Doghouse," he said uncertainly.

"No. The same argument applies there." I shifted from foot to foot, water squelching in my boots. "There's an outdoor shower at Wildwood, and I know Ted keeps towels and spare clothes in the mudroom. We'll can sluice off there before we head anywhere else."

Jordan bit his lip. "I don't think—"

"It'll be all right. Ted and Quentin are away and the resort's closed, but I know where Ted keeps the mudroom key. Come on."

"But—"

"Doop," I said, "Wildwood back deck."

If I wasn't so swamp-logged, I'd have been a little smug that Doop obeyed immediately, launching himself with only a final twitch of his hackles. As far as I knew, I was the only person other than Jordan that he obeyed.

Of course, he was probably just as anxious to get out of the damn bog as I was.

On the other side of the portal, the lake glimmered beyond Wildwood's deck as Doop trotted across the grass and sat beneath the shower head. I whistled, because I would never stop being in awe of Doop's precision.

When he wasn't bounding into bogs in pursuit of phantom lights, that is.

"Hugh—"

"Let's go, Jordan. This stuff stinks and I really want out of these clothes."

I squelched through the portal, shedding my jacket, with Jordan scampering along at my heels.

"Hugh, I really don't think—"

"Don't worry, Jordan." I tossed my jacket on the grass and stripped off my shirt. "I know it wasn't your fault."

"I know, but—"

"Is it okay if I take off my pants?" I asked, as I toed off my boots, my hands on my belt. "I know you werewolves aren't bugged by nudity, but it might be weird because we're co-workers?"

"No, I don't mind, but—"

"Cool. You can turn around if you want." I shucked my jeans down my legs along with my briefs. Gooseflesh rose on my bare skin, but weirdly enough, the breeze off the lake didn't feel as cold now as it had when I'd been encased in swamp-infused clothing.

I held one hand under the shower head as I turned on the water, breathing a sigh of relief when it heated up almost immediately. Thank goodness for tankless water heaters. Before I ducked under the spray, though, I grabbed Doop's ruff.

"Come on, big guy. Let's get you cleaned off first or I'll probably end up covered in bog crap again." But Doop balked, bracing his feet and resisting my grip. "Seriously? What is it about dogs that lets them plunge headfirst into large, nasty bodies of water but freak out about baths? Jordan, could you—"

"Hey, everybody," called an unfortunately recognizable voice from overhead, sending a true chill across my skin, "they're here!"

CHAPTER SEVEN

"What the hell is Eleri doing here?" I glanced over my shoulder at Jordan, who was peering at the deck above our heads. Heart tumbling to my toes—my very bare toes—I looked up.

Eleri was leaning over the railing, grinning, in a bedazzled green satin jacket and tulle skirt, an enormous maple leaf fascinator in her hair. As I watched in horror, she was joined by Mal, Niall, and Zeke. And then by Hamish, Bryce, Gareth, Ted, Quentin, Rusty Johnson, Dr. Kendrick, David, Frang, Blair, Herne, Wyn, and—

"Is that the *King*?" I hissed at Jordan.

He nodded. "And the Queen." He laughed a little anemically. "Surprise?"

Hamish slung an arm across Zeke's shoulders. "I know you humans do things differently, mate, but seems to me that attire's a bit casual for a wedding."

"Wedding?" I clutched Doop's fur, keeping him mostly blocking me from the audience. "Whose wedding?"

The gawkers parted, and suddenly Lachlan was there between Blair and Eleri.

In a kilt.

"Ours, *mo cridhe*. I wanted to do better by you than jumping the besom on the boat with naught but selkies in attendance."

I looked at Jordan. "Did you know about this?"

"Yeah?"

"There was never a Disappeared rumor?"

"Well, there *might* have been, but—"

"Jordan," I said and my tone made Doop whimper.

"Not really," he said, hanging his head.

Doop pulled out of my grip and leaped for Jordan, cuddling close and licking his hand, leaving me with all my parts flapping in the wind.

I clenched my eyes shut. "Why am I always naked at my weddings?"

Oh, well. Might as well own it. I stepped under the showerhead, raising my face to the warm water with a resigned sigh.

"Master?"

I cracked an eye at the high, soft voice. Heilyn, the bauchan who worked at the Keep, was standing next to me, holding out a huge, fluffy towel. I took it gratefully.

"Thanks, Heilyn."

"If you please, I have a bath waiting inside along with fresh clothing as befits your handfasting."

I cast one more glance up at the deck, but everyone had disappeared. "You've no idea how much I appreciate that."

When I came downstairs after bathing and being assisted into a tux by Heilyn, dusk had fallen and the person awaiting me in the vestibule wasn't Lachlan.

It was Ted.

He smiled at me a bit sheepishly. "Hey, Matt. Sorry about our call before. I shouldn't have told you the resort would be empty. But Lachlan had already reserved a suite for you for the week and there was the whole secret wedding thing and I kind of panicked."

I peered into Ted's open, bearded face with its kind brown eyes, and while I'd always feel affection for him, it was the affection of a friend. "It's okay, Ted. I understand."

"Anyway, I'm glad you're having your handfasting here. With the King and Queen officiating—"

"The King and Queen are officiating?" I croaked. "At my wedding?" How was this my life?

"Yeah. Usually, they only conduct ceremonies in Faerie, but Lachlan insisted on holding it here. Eleri said he was, um, quite fierce about it."

I raised my eyebrows. "He was? Weird."

"Anyway, I just wanted to say how happy I am for you. Me and Quentin both are."

"Thanks, Ted." My eyes prickled. And when he enveloped me in a hug, a stupid tear spilled over.

"Matthew."

Lachlan. Over Ted's shoulder, I took in the whole package: the blinding white shirt, the Prince Charlie jacket, the sporran, the hose, the brogues, and of course, the green plaid kilt in what Heilyn had told me was Clan Brodie's ancient hunting tartan— blue and green and black, hightlighted with red and yellow.

Ted released me and grinned sunnily. "Hey, Lachlan. I was just telling Matt how happy we are for you guys."

"Thank you." He inclined his head. "If you could tell Their Majesties we'll be along presently?"

"Sure." Ted trotted toward the big double doors that led to Wildwood's ballroom. "Casimir just got here, so all the guests have arrived. That demon, too. The one with his hair on fire."

I blinked. "Paimon?"

"Yeah. He said he's the official photographer. Something about quid pro quo?" Ted shrugged. "Nobody wanted to argue with him, though, and since you can't take the pictures if you're in them, I figured it would be okay. See you inside." With a last grin and a wave of one big hand, he slipped through the doors and closed them behind him.

Lachlan gazed at me, his eyes soft and his lips curved in a fond smile. "You look grand, *mo cridhe.*"

"Thanks." I swiped a finger under my eye. "I think I deserve to be mad at you right now for springing this on me and keeping secrets and making me *worry*. But with this"—I gestured at his whole *presence*—"all I really want to do is jump your bones."

He chuckled and stalked toward me. "Then my plans are working."

"What plans?"

"I asked Eleri how to honor the winter holidays as humans do so I could make this day memorable for you."

"You wanted to make a holiday celebration for me?"

"Aye. I'd never want you to feel you had to sacrifice aught to be with me."

I carded my fingers through his hair, so soft, and let it fall around his shoulders. "Believe me, I don't feel as though I've given up a thing." I kissed him. "Although I'm curious. Why did you want to have the wedding here? Why not in Faerie?"

An expression, intent and determined, yet almost furtive, settled over his broad face. "Because this is Ted's place."

"Yeah. So?" The shoe dropped. "Wait. You wanted to get married here to, what? Stake your claim in front of Ted?"

His brown cheeks took on a ruddy cast. "Aye."

"Sweetheart, you don't need to worry about Ted and me. There was never anything between us."

"Perhaps." He rolled the R like he always did when he was in a mood. "But I want there to be no mistake."

I shook my head. "I can't believe you were looking for holiday traditions for me at the same time I was doing the same for you. I feel like I'm in an O. Henry story."

"What?"

"Nothing. But just for future reference? I really, really hate irony."

"Noted." He dropped a kiss on my forehead.

I leaned back a little so I could meet his gaze. "Tell me something, though. How *do* you celebrate the winter holidays?"

"I've been known to pour a libation or two, but mostly I don't mark it. That'll change now, though."

"It will? Why?"

He pulled me close and kissed me. "Because now the solstice means something truly special, something more than the turning of the year and the return of the sun."

"What?"

"Now it marks the day we stand before our friends and family and promise in our own words to love and cherish one another forever."

"Lachlan." Dammit, I was going to cry for real this time.

"So in future when you spy a mistletoe bough or a spray of holly or the flame of a yule log, you'll know everyone is marking the best winter holiday of all: our handfasting."

I laughed a little weakly. "I don't think that's what will be on most people's minds."

"It should. But even if it isn't? It'll be on ours." He kissed me again. "And that's all that matters."

He crooked his elbow, and I curled my hand around it and we walked through the door to the cheers of all our friends.

And *this* was something to celebrate. Today. Tomorrow. Next year, the year after, the year after that. Hell, *forever*.

With Lachlan by my side—in a *kilt*—I was more than ready for it.

a message from

ej

Dear Reader,

Thank you so much for reading *Mythmatchedlets*, my collection of Mythmatched "sidecar" stories. I'm so happy you've taken this journey with me! I'd be immensely grateful if you'd take a moment to leave a review at the retailer and any other site you use for reviews. Believe me, reviews make an *enormous* difference to the health and well-being of books (and not incidentally, to their associated authors!).

Pop on over to my website, https://ejrussell.com, for all the deets on my books—my paranormal rom-coms and mysteries, my contemporary romances, and my one lone historical. If you're an audio fan, you can find the audio scoop there too. The Supernatural Selection trilogy (including *Vampire with Benefits*) and the Quest Investigations series, for instance, are narrated by the wonderful Greg Boudreaux. (The QR code on the next page will get you there with your smartphone camera or other code reader.)

Would you like exclusive content and ARC giveaways, not to mention gratuitous dance videos? Then I'd love for you to join me in E.J. Russell's Reality Optional, my Facebook fan group (https://facebook.com/groups/reality.optional). My newsletter is the place to get the latest dish on new releases, sales, and more. (And by the way, the ebook versions of the *Mythmatchlets* stories are available free to my subscribers.) I promise I only send one out when I've got...well...news. You can subscribe here: https://ejrussell.com/newsletter.

All my best,

—E

Paranormal Romance
Mythmatched Universe
Fae Out of Water Trilogy
Cutie and the Beast
The Druid Next Door
Bad Boy's Bard

Supernatural Selection Trilogy
Single White Incubus
Vampire With Benefits
Demon on the Down-Low

Other Mythmatched Romances
Howling on Hold
Possession in Session
Witch Under Wraps
Cursed is the Worst
The Skinny on Djinni
Assassin by Accident (part of Carnival of Mysteries)

Quest Investigations Mysteries
Five Dead Herrings
The Hound of the Burgervilles
The Lady Under the Lake
Death on Denial

At Odds with the Gods (A Mythmatched/Purgatory Playhouse crossover)

Mythmatchedlets (Mythmatched companion stories, free to newsletter subscribers in ebook form, collected in one paperback volume: *Second First Date, Rusty's Really Bad Day, First Flight, Getting the Band Together, Purgatory Postscript, A Very Quest Solstice*)

Magic Emporium Series (shared world)
Purgatory Playhouse

Enchanted Occasions Series
Best Beast
Nudging Fate
Devouring Flame

Ghost Townies Series
Ghostridden

Legend Tripping Series
Stumptown Spirits
Wolf's Clothing

Art Medium Series
The Artist's Touch
Tested in Fire
Art Medium: The Complete Collection (omnibus edition)

Royal Powers Series (shared world)
Duking It Out
Duke the Hall
King's Ex

Science Fiction

Sun, Moon, and Stars Series
Partnership
Principles

Interdimensional Time Bureau
Monster Till Midnight

Historical Romance
Silent Sin

Contemporary Romance
Camera Shy
Summer Kitchen
The Thomas Flair
Mystic Man
For a Good Time, Call... (A Bluewater Bay novel, with Anne
Tenino)

Christmas Kisses (holiday shorts)
The Probability of Mistletoe
An Everyday Hero
A Swants Soiree

Geeklandia Series
The Boyfriend Algorithm (M/F)
Clickbait

Writing as Nelle Heran
(traditional cozy mystery)

Crafty Sleuth Series (with C.K. Eastland)
Die Cut
Mixed Media
Found Objects (*coming soon*)

About the
Author

E.J. Russell (she/her), author of the award-winning Mythmatched paranormal romance series, writes LGBTQ+ romance and mystery in a rainbow of flavors. Count on high snark, low angst, and happy endings.

Reality? Eh, not so much.

She's married to Curmudgeonly Husband, a man who cares even less about sports than she does. Luckily, C.H. also loves to cook, or all three of their children (Lovely Daughter and Darling Sons A and B) would have survived on nothing but Cheerios, beef jerky, and Satsuma mandarins (the extent of E.J.'s culinary skill set).

E.J. also writes traditional cozy mystery as Nelle Heran. She lives in rural Oregon, enjoys visits from her wonderful adult children, and indulges in good books, red wine, and the occasional hyperbole.

News & Social Media:
Website: https://ejrussell.com
Newsletter: https://ejrussell.com/newsletter

www.ingramcontent.com/pod-product-compliance
Lightning Source LLC
Chambersburg PA
CBHW021845010726
47493CB00005B/1556